A DEAL WITH THE BOSSY DEVIL

BAD BILLIONAIRE BOSSES
BOOK 1

KYRA PARSI

CONTENT NOTE

Please note that some of the material in this book will not be suitable for all audiences. This book contains explicit language, drinking, on-page steam, mentions of stalking behavior, mentions of parental death, and light elements of BDSM.

For a full list of content notes for all my books, please visit my website.

1

IT WAS EVERYWHERE.

All over social media, the TV, my group chats. The video of Waldo whacking Adrien Cloutier in the family jewels with a walking cane had—somewhat unsurprisingly—made national news faster than the results of our last federal election.

And people were *here for it.*

I scrolled through the comments of the latest post Jamie had sent me, feeling rather generous with my upvotes.

FaceSittersClub: This is the type of content I pay my internet bills for

FindingHimbo: Who is she?

imtheNPC: Anyone have irl Where's Waldo on their 2020s bingo card? Cuz me neither

UnlawfulMotherGoose: Deranged Waldo running rampant around Toronto and hitting entitled billionaires in the balls with random costume props is my new kink.

And then there were the concerned citizens...

LickMyBallsack69: She's gonna regret this real quick. I can smell Cloutier lawyering up from here. He's gonna rip her life to shreds. RIP

MooMooMilkRoute39: Y'all if you know this girl you better be keeping your traps shut. We don't know where Waldo is. Never even heard of her

The last user had just uploaded a new, shortened version of the clip and linked it to their comment. It was a three-second edit of the cane making hard contact with its target, the shocked gasp-cackle of the person recording, and Adrien's low grunt as he folded onto his knees in front of me, face crumpled in pain.

Except the three-second clip was edited into a ten-hour loop, and the video had appropriately been titled, "ASMR | Soothing Meditation Sounds for Sleeping and Insomnia."

I chortled and forwarded the link to Jamie just as the train started to slow to a stop. This had been the most entertaining commute to work I'd had in ages. Potentially ever.

And you're probably going to pay for it in about ten minutes.

I brushed off the voice, refusing to let it drag me down. There was no point in stressing about something that hadn't happened yet.

People didn't know it was me in the video. The footage only showed the back of my head, and I'd been wearing a wig, a hat, and a pair of glasses. My disguise was solid, and the internet had a short attention span. Chances were good this whole thing would blow over and everyone would forget about it by the end of the week, tops.

I fished my keycard out of my bag and scanned my way up to the fifth floor of our office building, unable to keep the small, wicked smirk off my lips. Every time I so much as blinked, the image of Adrien's scrunched-up face flashed in my mind, sending another shot of bubbly oxytocin straight through me.

LickMyBallsack69 was wrong. The only thing I regretted was running out of the lobby as fast as I had without taking an extra second to really appreciate the justice I'd just served. Adrien deserved it for what he'd—

I jolted as a hand flew out of a door to my left, wrapped around my arm, and yanked me into a small meeting room just down the hall from my cubicle.

"Oh my god," Alba hissed, nails digging into my arm as the door shut behind me. "*Oh my god.*"

I grinned. "I know, right?"

"No. Absolutely none of that," she snapped back, her newly threaded brows drawing together. "This isn't a joke, Ria. He's on a fucking warpath. What the hell were you thinking?"

"He deserved it," I argued smoothly as I wiggled my arm out of my sister's death grip. "Guy's an absolute prick. You know that better than anyone."

"That's your justification?" she hissed. The tip of her nose was starting to burn a telling red. "You smashed

Adrien Cloutier's dick in with a cane because you think he's a prick?"

"No. I did it because he's a gross trash goblin who smacked my butt without consent. The fact that he's also a prick was an added bonus."

She blinked back at me. "What?"

"Yeah. Bet you feel real dumb now, Alba. Yelling at me before you had all the facts."

Her eyes narrowed slowly. "Hold on—start over. You're saying he smacked your butt... in the middle of our flagship hotel lobby?"

Well, sure, when she said it like *that* it sounded ridiculous.

"Basically," I confirmed. "Kind of."

I could practically hear the gears spinning in her massive, overly analytical brain. "The CEO of the biggest hotel group in North America *kind of* sexually assaulted you in public?"

"Yes," I said. "Maybe."

She crossed her arms.

I shifted on my feet, bracing myself. "I mean, I guess there's a small chance it wasn't him."

Her eyes thinned into sharp danger-slits. "What does that mean?"

This conversation wasn't going to go well for me. "In my defense, I was very drunk."

"*Ria.*"

"I was!" I took a step back. She looked like she was getting ready to implode—and not just because she was seven months pregnant with twins. "It was Halloween! We were all wasted."

My excuse didn't seem to help, judging by her expression.

"Explain what happened," she demanded. "From start to finish."

"Okay, but can we just, like, take a few deep, calming breaths first?" I tried, lowering my voice to a more soothing pitch. "I think the rest of this conversation might benefit from a little bit of Zen."

She didn't agree, judging by the prim way her lips clamped together. But I went ahead and took in a long, slow breath anyway, holding it until she reluctantly followed suit. And then we let it out.

Her exhale was short, forceful, and accompanied by an impatient tap of her foot. It was as good as it was going to get.

"All right, *fine*. Let's just do this." I glanced outside the meeting room window to make sure none of the office gossips were watching or listening in, then I lowered my voice again and said, "Okay, so, Arman, Jamie, and I went to the Halloween parade on Friday night—which was less of an actual parade, to be honest with you, and more of a massive street party with a ton of drinking and sloppy Dwight Schrutes making out with sloppier Harley Quinns. It was really gross, but also kind of awesome. I highly recommend it for next year."

She did not look convinced.

"Anyways," I went on, leaning a shoulder against the wall. "At one point, we passed by the hotel, and I needed to use the bathroom, so I ran in."

Except it hadn't exactly been easy. There'd been a whole bunch of security guards lined along the entrance, preventing random partygoers from entering the building —which made sense. I didn't think any of the guests paying four figures a night for a hotel room were all that keen on sharing their space with a pack of drunk, rowdy idiots dressed in ridiculous costumes.

"They let you go in and use the washroom?" she asked skeptically. "Wasn't building access restricted?"

"Um, yeah, I mean... I may have used your all-access employee pass to get in." My voice trailed off into a cowardly whisper by the end of my confession as I watched my sister's glare twist into something lethal.

"*What*." I didn't think it was possible for a word to come out so sharp.

"I know, I know! I screwed up," I said, showing her my palms. "But I really had to go, Alba! It was an emergency!"

"So you used my all-access pass—the one that's supposed to be restricted to me and me only—to get into the building, then hit my boss in the dick with your costume prop? Do you have any idea how badly this could end for both of us?"

"Okay, two things. One, I didn't actually know it was him. And two, *he* definitely doesn't know it was *me*."

The skin under Alba's left eye feathered. "Explain."

"I thought it was just some jackass in a really convincing costume at first," I admitted. "He wasn't the first Adrien Cloutier I ran into that night, he just happened to be the only real one. And, again, I was really drunk. Like... drunk enough that it was a straight-up miracle my aim even met its target."

"Is that supposed to make me feel better?"

"I mean... yeah, kind of."

"Ria." She said my name in that slow, drawn-out way that meant I needed to listen very carefully to every single word that followed it. "I've worked for the guy for four years and have *never* seen him this pissed. He's going to murder you, and then he's going to make me bury your idiot body."

"That's very dark, Alba. Very off-brand."

"You know what else is dark? Coffins."

"You know what's even darker? You ignoring the fact that he assaulted me first."

That shut her up for a solid five seconds.

"Sorry," she eventually muttered, her voice softening with a touch of guilt. "Just... tell me what happened so we can figure out what to do."

I let out a heavy breath. "Okay, so, long story short, when I came out of the washroom, some guy behind me squeezed my butt, smacked it really hard, then said something about a 'tight, fuckable ass' before walking away. It happened out in the hall and... honestly, I kind of froze from shock."

Alba's eyebrows had drawn together again. This time, though, her anger wasn't directed at me.

"The problem is, because I froze for so long, I only saw the back of his head before he turned the corner and disappeared into the lobby. I knew he was tall with dark hair and was wearing a blue suit."

I also remembered the invading, overpowering stench of his cologne. It smelled like he'd dipped his entire body in the musky stuff—clothes and all. It was revolting.

"Then what happened?" Alba pushed, her hands moving to her round stomach as she shifted on her feet.

I pulled out a chair from the small conference table and twisted it around, gesturing for her to sit. "Then the anger happened. I stormed out into the lobby and spotted him right away talking to a bunch of other guys—at least I *thought* it was him. Tall, dark hair, blue suit. And I remember thinking how much he resembled Adrien

Cloutier... but the alcohol in my brain thought it was just some dickhead dressed up like him."

If douchebags had their own magazine, "The Cloutier Look" would have been unironically voted as the costume most likely to get your date to spread her legs. Or something equally gag-inducing.

You could spot his fanboys from a mile away on Halloween. They were all suited up, their sleek hair perfectly swept to one side, and every single one of them was sporting a replica of those stupidly overpriced wrist-watches he always wore.

People were weirdly obsessed with that dude. I really didn't get it.

"So, when I stomped up to where he was standing, I didn't really think twice. I just called him a braindead trash goblin and went for the jewels. I realized, like, two seconds after he went down that he was the real deal."

Yes, Adrien Cloutier had a reputation for being an overly privileged, ruthless dick. Yes, he made Alba's life a living hell. But he was also terrifyingly wealthy and influential, and no amount of alcohol would have prevented me from immediately realizing that attacking him had been a terrible mistake with potentially life-ruining consequences.

Which was why I'd run.

"How the hell did security not follow you?" Alba asked, continuing to rub her stomach. I wasn't sure whether she was doing it to soothe the babies or herself.

"They did follow me. But I disappeared into the parade right away and they must have lost track." Mostly because Arman had been smart and sober enough to get me to remove my hat, wig, and glasses before giving me his jacket. We left quickly after that.

The whole thing was a lot funnier this morning, especially since the video had gone so viral. Because as luck would have it, someone had been taking a video of the famous Cloutier fountain and the grand chandelier that crowned it when everything went down.

It had been an elegant, luxurious scene, enhanced by the soft piano music playing in the background... until Waldo stomped right through the frame with a "highly deranged energy," per the internet, and started screaming nonsensical insults at Adrien Cloutier himself. Next thing you know, *bam*! Man down, fugitive fictional character on the run.

It was awesome.

"Stop smiling!" Alba snapped at me, lightly kicking my shin. "It's not funny, Ria! How many times do I have to repeat myself? Adrien's lost his fucking mind over this whole thing. He's been here since four in the morning in like a rage-fueled productivity episode. I had forty-three emails in my inbox from him before the sun was up."

Honestly, that only made it funnier.

"Stop." *Kick.* "Laughing." *Kick.*

"Ow!" I hissed, rubbing at my shin. "Relax! Nobody knows it was me!"

"*Yet!*" she retorted. "They don't know it's you *yet*. A pair of round glasses and a wig isn't the convincing disguise you seem to think it is."

"Well, that's just not true. The glasses alone would have been enough according to every movie ever made," I argued. "Ever heard of Clark Kent? Now, I'm not saying I'm a *hero* to the people like Superman per se—*ouch*! Stop kicking me!"

"This isn't a joke!"

"Well, it was going to be once I got to the punchline

about Adrien Cloutier being Lex Luther, but you ruined it," I said, tempted to kick her back. "And I am being serious. He wouldn't have recognized me *without* the costume. That dude has no idea who I am, period."

"You can't know that for sure," she argued, though I could see her shoulders relax just a touch.

"Alba, I've been working here for two years and have run into him exactly once. That's it." We'd shared an elevator with two other people last year and he hadn't so much as glanced in my general direction.

"Yes, but you're also my sister."

I gave her a skeptical look. "Does he even know you have a sister? Has he ever asked?"

She rolled her lips and looked away from me, which was answer enough. Of course he'd never asked. Why would he need to know whether his overworked assistant of four years had any siblings? Why would he need to know anything about her at all? Why would he care about anyone but himself?

Worst boss on the fucking planet.

"Okay, well then we don't really have anything to worry about, do we?" I said.

Alba opened her mouth—presumably to argue with me again—but was interrupted by a string of light *ding*s fluttering out of her phone in rapid succession.

"Oh god," she groaned down at her screen. "I'm being summoned again."

I gave her hand a comforting squeeze as I helped her up. "Stop stressing so much," I said, gently poking her swollen belly. "It's not good for the baking process."

"I'll stop stressing if you start taking life a little more seriously," she said, keeping a hold of my fingers. Her features were scrunched with less irritation now, more worry. "This is... Ria, he could press charges. Do you understand how—"

The door burst open before she could finish the thought, making us both jump.

"Oh my god, there you are!" Hassan exclaimed. He was clutching his phone so tight his knuckles were white. "Why aren't you answering your phone? Adrien's got people looking for you."

The guy had zero fucking patience. It hadn't even been thirty seconds since he'd texted her.

"Sorry. I'll go back up now." Alba dropped my hand with a deep sigh, but not before shooting me a look that said she wasn't done lecturing me about this.

"Not you," Hassan said, nudging a chin in my direction. "He wants Ria. His security guys are looking everywhere for her."

I swear I could see my sister's soul drift right out of her stiffening body when his words registered.

Well... shit.

2

You know you're probably in a tiny bit of trouble when one of the wealthiest men in the country has his entire personal security team looking for you.

That's right. According to Hassan, Adrien Cloutier was utilizing *his entire personal security team* to try and find me, which, on top of being excessive, was a little weird. Because I wasn't hiding.

"There she is!" Peter Gladwell yelled the second we stepped out of the room. Like I was some sort of fugitive on the run, and he'd finally caught me. "She was hiding in a meeting room!"

First of all, inaccurate. Second of all, wow. That dude really didn't take rejection well, did he?

"You're Ria Sanchez?" A bald, beefy man in a black suit trudged up to where we stood, his eyes darting over me like he was trying to determine the exact level of physical threat my five-foot-six frame posed against his seven feet of chunky muscle.

They were bulging out of his too-tight suit. It did not look comfortable.

"Guilty as charged," I responded cheekily.

Alba pinched my arm so hard I physically jerked back. "*Ow!*"

She ignored me. "Hey, Frankie. What's this about?"

Frankie shook his head. "Can't talk about it. Sorry, Albs. We've been instructed to escort her up to Cloutier's office as soon as possible. That's all I can say."

"I could have escorted myself," I told him, continuing to rub at my arm. "But all right, let's go."

Alba and I followed him down the hall and out to the elevators, ignoring the stares and whispers of our colleagues as three more security personnel seamlessly fell into step around us, boxing us in. Just in case I was stupid enough to try and run, I guess.

Also, one of them kept mumbling into his own shoulder, and I'd seen enough action movies in my life (two) to know there was probably a microphone tucked in there somewhere.

The whole thing was really dramatic and excessive. Total overkill. Especially for something that could have been communicated in a single email.

"*Come up to my office.*" That's it. That's all I'd needed. One email, one sentence.

I made a mental note to tell him that.

Alba turned to me when we stepped into the elevator. "Promise me you'll behave when you go in there. No thinly veiled insults, no smart-mouthing, and absolutely no sarcasm whatsoever."

"Why? Does he, like, not *get* sarcasm?" My voice was pitched low and appropriately concerned as I pressed a hand to my chest. "Oh my god, poor thing."

The blonde guy to my right let out what sounded like

a short huff of a laugh, then tried to cover it up with a cough.

"What did I *just* say?" Alba snapped exasperatedly.

I had to make a conscious effort to stop my eyes from rolling to the very back of my head. "I promise I'll try to behave."

She let out a heavy breath as she pinched the bridge of her nose. "He's going to eat you alive," she whispered.

Two of the men nodded.

The elevator dinged before I could say anything else, and the six of us stepped out into the hall.

~

Talk about an anticlimactic letdown.

All that fuss with the security guys and Alba's doomsday warnings, and the office was empty when we got there. No fuming Adrien, no HR rep, no threatening lawyers, and no police officers wanting to take statements.

I was instructed to take a seat on the brown leather couch and wait. "He'll be here soon," Frankie said before shutting the door behind him.

And then I had to pretend like I didn't hear him lock it.

That was over an hour ago.

The first forty minutes were fine... but then my phone died, and it was just me and my thoughts, alone in Adrien's massive, lavishly decorated office.

I lasted three minutes.

"Hey, Frankie?" I called after confirming that the door was, in fact, locked. "Any idea how much longer he'll be?"

No answer.

"Okay... do you at least have a phone charger I could borrow?"

No answer.

"Alba?" I tried. Her desk was less than ten feet away from the door. If she was there, she should've been able to hear me. "You there?"

Still no answer.

Technically, this could be considered false imprisonment. Which meant that if Adrien threatened me with a lawsuit, I could potentially counter with this.

Maybe.

I wasn't a lawyer, but it had to be better than nothing.

"Just so we're all on the same page, I'm officially being held here against my will," I shouted at the door.

It occurred to me that having picture and video evidence would probably strengthen my case, and I started to regret wasting the last ten percent of my battery watching cats knock things off shelves while maintaining unwavering eye contact with their exasperated humans.

Sort of. Some of them had been really, *really* funny.

I bet Adrien keeps a few chargers in here somewhere...

My eyes darted around the space, looking for white wires either snaking out of outlets or coiled neatly on wooden surfaces.

It wasn't the easiest task. The large office was crowded with a shocking number of plants. There were so many of them that it made the air smell different in here. Less stale than the rest of the office.

I wandered around, checking each outlet individually, but they were all empty. So, I decided to check his desk.

The mahogany surface was kept impressively neat, free of all dust, clutter, and signs of human life, save for the glaringly out-of-place black box that sat right beside the wireless keyboard.

I ignored it and tried opening the top desk drawer, but it was locked. So was the second and the third and... all of them. They were all locked.

I sighed and dropped into his chair, immediately resentful of how much more comfortable it was than the one I had downstairs. I bet *he* wasn't plagued by a stiff lower back if he sat in this thing for too long. It felt ergonomic as fuck.

I whirled around on it a few times, tapped my foot, my fingers, checked the ends of my hair for split ends, and tried holding my breath to see if it would alleviate some of the boredom. (It did not.)

Another ten minutes passed. Then fifteen. Twenty.

I was so bored by this point that I was tempted to start counting the leaves on the nearest fern as I watched them grow. But then my eyes fell back on the black box.

What if there's a charger in there?

I knew there wasn't. It didn't look like the type of box that would house random office accessories. It was too sleek and expensive-looking for that.

What was in it, then? A gift? Cold hard cash? Virgin souls?

Open me, the box whispered seductively. *I'm filled with so many phone chargers, you don't even know. I'm bursting with them. I swear it on Pandora herself.*

Two things were for absolute certain. One, the box was a liar. And two, my mind was folding in on itself because of boredom. It was bending and twisting and making up increasingly farfetched theories about the contents of the package, just so it would have something to do.

Like, for example, what if this was one of those psychology experiments? Like when you put a kid in a room with a button and tell them not to press it, so all they want to do is press it. What if there was a camera set up in here and Adrien was watching the whole thing, waiting to see how many hours it would take for me to break?

Because it was weird, right? It was weird that this entire office was *American Psycho* levels of organized and clean, and then there was this one random, ominously black box sitting right in the middle of Adrien's desk, completely out of place and begging—*pleading*—to be opened.

Or maybe it was a genie-in-a-lamp type of situation. Adrien Cloutier was trapped inside the box and that was what was taking him so fucking long. Opening it would release him, and he'd be so grateful that he'd forget about the whole cane-to-the-balls thing and grant me three wishes.

Or maybe—and more reasonably—it was a box full of evidence he'd gathered to prove I was Waldo. Close-up snapshots of my face taken with security cameras and stuff.

But also, it could just be a decorative, diamond-encrusted butt plug. (Rich people were, er, an *eccentric* lot. You never really knew with them.)

Or, again, it might be a charger. So maybe a small peek wouldn't hurt, just to be sure...

My hand was moving before I could think better of it, reaching for the smooth corner of the dark lid so I could—

BOOM!

I jumped as everything erupted. The second my finger

nudged the lid open, it triggered a loud explosion of gold confetti and red glitter.

So. Much. Fucking. *Glitter*.

It was everywhere. Floating in the air, dusting the desk, the chair, the floor, the plants, the keyboard. And a shit ton of it had gotten inside my gaping mouth.

I stood there, shocked, holding my trembling hands in the air like I had a gun pointed at me. Because that was exactly what the explosion had sounded like. A gunshot. And it had scared the living shit out of me, holy fuck.

My pulse was thundering, pumping adrenaline through my veins. I could barely breathe as my brain slowly registered the words that had burst out of the box. I was so—

"What the fuck."

I started, my heart jumping straight into my throat. The explosion had been so loud and distracting that I hadn't heard the door open.

There was a man standing there, blinking at my glitter-covered self and the three large words that had popped out of the box in bold, golden letters:

FUCK YOU ADRIEN.

3

ADRIEN CLOUTIER WAS STANDING in the doorway of his office, his dark eyes fixed on my bedazzled crime scene. He'd caught me red-handed. (Literally. My hands were literally covered in bright red glitter.)

And because I was still frozen in place, I had the pleasure of watching his expression morph from confusion to irritation, and then to pure, unadulterated fury.

The man was fucking livid.

This was probably not going to be fun. I was ninety-nine percent sure of it.

"What. The *fuck*," he repeated, stepping inside. The words came out short and sort of... growly. Like he had a bunch of loose gravel churning in his throat.

He jerked his wrist and the door banged shut behind him.

"Is this your idea of a fucking joke?" Adrien barked, taking a whole bunch of angry stomps forward. He halted before he got to the glitter-covered portion of the floor, the rage rolling off him in such palpable waves that I swear I would have been able to taste it if my tongue wasn't coated in shimmering flecks of regret.

He looks different in person.

I wasn't sure why that was the first thought that sprinted through my head when Adrien's sharp gaze clashed with mine, but it was.

To be fair, I'd never actually seen him up close before. Not in real life at least. I'd seen a bunch of pictures of the guy online (and entirely against my will) and had caught quick glimpses of him around the building and at random work parties, but never up close. And on Friday, I'd been too drunk and too concentrated on exacting my revenge on the pervy creep that had slapped my bum to pay attention to his face.

So, yeah, all that to say: I didn't realize his eyes were green.

Stupid, right? I was covered head to toe in crimson glitter, I'd ruined the guy's office just two days after hitting him in the dick with a cane for a crime he may or may not have committed, and all I could think about was how dark and ominously green his eyes were.

They made me think of the rainforest at night. Same color and petrifying vibe. It was the only reason my brain stalled the way it did.

"Miss Sanchez." He said my name like it rhymed with every expletive in the English language. "I asked you a question."

Right. Yes. He'd asked me if this was my idea of a joke.

"Um, no," I said. It wasn't until my tongue moved that I realized just how much glitter had actually gotten into my mouth. It was grainy and dry and... really unpleasant. "I mean, someone clearly thought it would be funny. But it wasn't me."

I started to dust my hands and shirt off while Adrien eyed me. He didn't seem to believe me but that was fair. I probably wouldn't have either.

"I'm Ria, by the way," I said, holding out a shimmering hand.

My attempts at dusting off the sticky little flecks had been futile. Whoever had planned this really hated him. He was going to be finding random specks of red glitter in his office for the next decade. It was going to be sticking to his expensive suits and people were going to be pointing it out to him in the middle of important meetings, making stupid jokes about strippers and stuff.

I was trying my best not to laugh. Because maybe I'd lied—maybe this was a teeny, tiny bit hilarious.

"I know who you are," he ground out, ignoring my outstretched hand.

"Excellent." I nodded, spreading my lips into a small, polite smile. "And you are…"

I know I'd promised Alba I'd try to behave, but holy mother of overinflated egos, was his reaction worth it. I'd never seen someone's entire face twitch before.

I deserved an Oscar for managing to maintain eye contact *and* a straight face.

"You have exactly ten seconds to explain yourself."

Or what?

The itty-bitty voice of self-preservation in the rarely visited, cobwebbed corner of my head managed to stop me from asking that out loud, though.

"I was looking for a charger," I said instead. "My phone died."

Silence.

Seriously, his eyes were an absurdly intimidating

shade of dark green. I was half convinced they were contacts. Or he'd surgically altered their color somehow.

"*And*?" he pushed, his dark brows reaching for one another.

"And I couldn't find one sticking out of any outlets, and all your drawers were closed, so I tried the box," I said, pointing at the torn remnants of the black box on his desk. I was careful to make sure my finger was pointing at the actual box and not the words that had popped out of it. "But then everything exploded just as you walked in."

"You went through my drawers?"

"No. They were locked." Was he not listening?

"You tried to go through my drawers." He said the words slowly like he needed to make sure I understood what I'd just confessed to. "And you're admitting to it. Out loud."

"Yes. I needed a charger for my phone. Like I said, it died."

He eyed me for a few seconds, trying to gauge my exact level of crazy. He landed on "batshit" pretty quickly from the looks of it. "You're aware that's a fireable offense. Not to mention illegal."

His voice had taken on a new, slightly more baffled edge. As if my blatant stupidity was a curveball he hadn't seen coming.

The man thought I was a straight-up imbecile with, like, two fully functioning brain cells max. I could see it in his face, in the slight shift of his features as skeptical confusion started to dampen his rage.

It lasted all of three seconds. Just until I opened my mouth again. "I know, right? It's almost as bad as locking an employee in your office without their consent. I'm no lawyer but I'm pretty sure that's also illegal. It might even be *more* illegal than rummaging through someone's stuff. False imprisonment and all that."

I tried to wipe the sticky glitter off my skin again, but it really wasn't going anywhere. Kind of a bummer. I hated the feeling of sand or chalk or anything grainy and dry between my fingers. It felt like how nails on a chalkboard sounded, and it made me want to scrunch my shoulders to my ears and dip my hands in water.

"You weren't forcibly detained, Miss Sanchez," Adrien claimed in that molten voice of his.

What was up with the whole *Miss Sanchez* thing? What century were we in?

"You could have fooled me," I retorted, crossing my shiny arms. "The door was locked and no one was answering me from the other end. Which, by the way, is a pretty reckless thing to do. What if there'd been a fire?"

"I had security outside. You'd have been let out the second the alarm went off."

"How would I have known that?"

He took another two steps forward, apparently no longer concerned about stepping on the red unicorn vomit. "You think that excuses you going through my things and wreaking havoc on my office? Do you have any idea how long it's going to take to get all this cleaned up?"

Not my fucking problem. "How the hell was I supposed to know the box on your desk contained a glitter bomb of all things? What did you do, piss off a Care Bear?"

I didn't actually know if Care Bears blasted glitter out of their chests, but it was the best I could come up with. My brain still felt a little fuzzy after the whole explosion thing.

Adrien took another three steps forward, and—

Wait, why was I keeping track of how many steps he was taking? That wasn't something I normally did, was it?

"That's none of your business," he said. "You shouldn't have been touching it in the first place. You were given perfectly clear instructions to sit on the couch and wait."

"Yeah, and I was told you'd be here *shortly*," I retorted. My voice came out a little snappier than I'd intended, and I realized my fists were clenched against my ribs. "That was two hours ago, *Mr. Cloutier*."

I didn't know why I said his name like that, with so much sarcastic venom. Or why I was suddenly so irritated. It wasn't going to help my case.

"I had other matters to attend to first." *Step.*

Four more of those and we'd be nose-to-nose. Not that I was still counting.

"And how was I supposed to know you'd actually show up? Or *when*? How much longer did you expect me to sit around and wait?"

A little muscle in his cheek ticked unhappily. "Watch your tone with me, Miss Sanchez. I've spent the last two days cleaning up the mess you made for me on Halloween, and now *this*. I don't know what your fucking problem is, but I'm in no fucking mood to put up with any more of your bullshit."

And I spent last Tuesday comforting my six-year-old niece because you wouldn't give her mom one *lousy evening off to celebrate her birthday! That's my fucking problem, you selfish prick!*

My eyes thinned into a glare, my shoulders coiling.

Okay, so maybe I did know why I was so irritated. Maybe it wasn't all that sudden or out of the blue. Because maybe I was sick of sitting back and allowing him to treat my sister like shit. And having to comfort her while she vented, overwhelmed by her workload and Adrien's ridiculous expectations.

Maybe I resented watching the strain all the extra hours had put on Alba's marriage. Of how many holidays and birthdays she'd been late to—or missed entirely— because "Adrien needs me to stay just one more hour, two tops," or "a meeting's come up last minute and Adrien needs me to attend. I can't make it to dinner. I'm so, so sorry. Give Olive a kiss for me and tell Ben I'll make it up to him. I promise."

I wasn't sorry. Not about Halloween or the stupid glitter or my disrespectful tone.

I'd spent four years listening to Alba's stories about this man, starting from when he was still on the operations team, before his daddy handed him the position of CEO on a silver fucking platter. I knew who he was, and I wasn't sorry about any of it.

"It was you, right?" Adrien said, taking yet another step toward me. He was close enough now that I had to lift my chin to maintain eye contact. "On Halloween. It was you."

I shrugged. "I don't know what you're talking about."

A part of me knew there was no point in denying it, but a bigger, much more stubborn part wanted to make this as difficult as possible for him.

He plucked his phone out of his pocket, unlocked it, and practically shoved it into my face.

Unsurprisingly, it was a picture of me dressed as Waldo. The angle was up higher than anything I'd seen floating around the internet—like it had maybe been taken by a security camera—and was zoomed into my screaming face, right before I'd swung my cane.

I had to bite the inside of my bottom lip to stop the laugh from escaping. I failed.

"You think this is funny?" Adrien growled, the tips of his cheeks tinting a bruised pink. He chucked his phone onto his desk and took one final step forward, right into my personal space. "Do you have any idea what you did? What your little cry for attention fucking cost me?"

My what? "Excuse me?"

"Seven hundred million."

That wiped the smirk right off my face. I blinked. "Wait... what?"

"Seven. Hundred. Million. Dollars." He said it slowly, stretching each individual word out into its very own sentence so that I'd have an easier time understanding. "You know those men I'd been talking to before you marched into the lobby and hit me? Investors. From Japan."

Oh.

Oh, yeah, that I didn't know.

"You know what happened after your little stunt? They fucking pulled out. I'd spent *months* working on this deal. They were there to sign the papers. It was fucking done!"

I thought Adrien had looked angry before, but it was nothing compared to the fury rolling off him now. His eyes were entire forests lit on scorching fire.

A part of me wanted to point out that correlation wasn't necessarily causation and ask if he was sure they hadn't pulled out because of something else. But this was probably a good time to keep my mouth shut, so that's exactly what I did.

"I've spent the entire fucking weekend dealing with the

repercussions of losing the investment, trying to keep the media coverage somewhat under control, and putting out all the other fires you started. And you have the nerve to go through my shit, make a mess of my office, and give me lip instead of an apology? To *laugh* like any of this is even remotely fucking funny? What the fuck is your *problem*?"

I gulped. To be honest, it was slightly less funny when he put it all like that.

He cocked his head. "What's all this about? What do you want?" I could smell a subtle hint of a warm, spicy cologne on him as he moved closer. It was nothing like the violating stench of the guy from Halloween. "Money? Attention? Was this whole thing just an elaborate scheme to get yourself in the same room as me?"

Wait... wait, what?

"Is that why you were going through my shit? Trying to find something to blackmail me with? Or are you one of the stalkery ones who thinks they're in love with me?"

My jaw fell open.

Because *what*?! "No, what? What type of mental gymnastics do you have to—"

"Don't fucking lie to me, Sanchez."

Okay, so we were done with the "Miss" thing then, I guess.

"Dude, I was looking for a charger. I swear I'm not... in love with you."

Holy shit. I couldn't believe I even had to say that out loud.

Was he, like, *okay*?

I took a step back, trying to put a little distance between us, but he followed me.

"What the fuck is it then?" he snapped, matching

every step I took until my back hit the wall. Then he was just towering over me, all heated rage and taut muscles.

Maybe Alba hadn't been exaggerating when she said he was going to kill me and make her bury my idiot body, because he was glaring at me like he wanted nothing more than to strangle me right then and there.

"Okay, listen," I said, trying to keep my voice as calm as possible as my shiny palms came up in a surrendering gesture. "I swear that none of this was done in an attempt to... get you to notice me or whatever. Halloween was just a misunderstanding, I think."

At this point, I was pretty sure he hadn't been the one to smack my ass that night.

His voice was a lot deeper, he smelled a hell of a lot better, and he looked... broader than the other dude. I know I only saw the guy's back and everything, but I definitely didn't remember his shoulders being so wide.

Adrien's frame was almost as intimidating as his eyes.

"The picture you have on your phone is from a security camera, right?" I asked. "So I'm assuming you saw where I was before I came into the lobby. You saw what happened."

A muscle in his cheek jolted, but he didn't say anything. I went ahead and took that as a "yes."

"Was it you?" I asked. "Because I thought it was, and—"

"No." The word sniped out of his mouth, short and firm.

"Okay, well, he was dressed exactly like you... from what I remember. He had dark hair and everything, and I only saw him from the back. So... if it wasn't you, then it was just a misunderstanding."

Adrien remained silent like he was waiting for something else. An apology, maybe.

"And I really was looking for a charger," I said instead, fishing my phone out of my back pocket. "It's dead. See? I'm not lying."

"And what? You couldn't go five fucking minutes without your phone?"

Two hours. You made me wait for two hours, not five minutes, you goon!

But I bit my tongue because he had crazy-eyes and I'd promised Olive I'd take her to Six Flags if she got an A on her math test next month. So, at the very least, I had to stay alive for that.

"Anything else?" he pushed. "Any other bullshit excuses you want to get out of your system or are you all out of ideas?"

I blinked to keep my eyes from rolling to the back of my head. "No other excuses," I assured him. "Just those two."

Then I braced myself. Because this was the part where he was going to tell me that he was pressing charges. And that his lawyers were waiting just outside the door, wanting to talk to me.

This was the part where Adrien Cloutier was going to specify exactly how he planned to ruin my life. And then he'd demand an apology before serving me the papers.

"You're fired. Get out."

It took me a second to register that he wasn't going to add anything else.

"Wait... that's it?" I said stupidly.

Because that couldn't have been it. Surely there were more repercussions lined up.

A muscle wormed through his jaw before he replied, almost like it was protesting his answer. "That's it."

Wait. I'd assaulted the guy, lost him seven hundred million investment dollars, snooped through his stuff, ruined his office, created a mess for him in the media, refused to apologize for it, and... that was it? I was fired?

Something didn't add up.

Adrien Cloutier was a cutthroat, ruthless shark who ruined lives for a hobby (I assumed), and two plus two didn't equal pie.

"Wh—"

"Get. *Out.*"

I bit back the million questions itching at the tip of my tongue and slipped past him, half expecting a swarm of lawyers to be waiting for me outside his office, lawsuits in hand.

There wasn't. It was just Frankie holding an empty cardboard box.

Huh.

4

IT TOOK me all of eight seconds to clean out my desk.

A pair of noise-canceling headphones, a stale pack of strawberry gum I'd completely forgotten about, and a sample-sized tube of hand lotion. That was what went into the giant box Frankie had pushed into my arms when I'd walked out of Adrien's office.

He'd been instructed to escort me through the process of packing and leaving. Just in case I decided to swipe a stapler or something, I guess.

"Done," I announced, picking the box up. "We can go."

Frankie ticked a brow. "Were you just hired?"

"Nope. Been here two years."

"And that's all you've got?"

I shrugged. "Never been huge on collecting junk. Hey, anyone ever tell you that you look like a double-jacked-up Mr. Clean?" He had the earring and the silver eyebrows and everything.

"Yes."

"Cool. You're better looking, though."

"I know," he responded without hesitation.

I laughed and fell into step beside him as we made our way back out to the elevators, ignoring the not-so-quiet whispers and not-so-subtle stares of my former coworkers, two of whom were not so secretly filming my awesome, sparkling departure.

None of them came over to say goodbye, and that was okay.

I'd never made any friends here. Didn't really see the point. This was always meant to be a temporary gig, just until I could find something that wasn't... I don't know. Something that didn't suck on my soul and slowly turn my brain into stale oatmeal, I guess. That would be a good place to start.

Frankie accompanied me all the way out the door and took my keycard, emphasizing that I wasn't allowed back in the building and yada, yada, yada. A rep from HR would be in touch with me within the next few hours. That was all I needed to know.

Though I doubted I'd get any sort of severance. They had more than enough cause to justify my termination according to their corporate code of conduct.

I knew because I'd been bored enough on my second day of employment to read the whole thing.

"Hey, you're home early, wh—" Jamie stopped short when I pushed my way into our apartment, her mouth falling slack as she took in my glitter-covered everything. "Whoa, what the hell?"

"Hey," I said, dropping the massive, mostly empty box onto the floor.

I'd have given it back to Frankie and stuffed the gum and lotion into my purse (or thrown them out), but I wouldn't be able to afford the rent here if I couldn't find another job soon, and moving boxes were expensive.

"What happened?" Jamie asked, eyes wide.

"Well, let's see... Adrien figured out I was Waldo, locked me in his office, and then I accidentally set off a glitter bomb, and got fired. How's *your* day going?"

"You're not coming in here like that," she said. "Go outside and take your clothes off."

"I'm not stripping out in the hall."

"Ria, that stuff is gonna get everywhere. I don't fuck with glitter. How did you even get home?"

"I walked." It had taken forty-five minutes and there'd been a lot of questioning stares. But there was no way I'd have been able to get on a train like this, so I'd just put in my headphones and forged ahead.

Jamie sighed, her eyes bouncing up to the ceiling like she was asking it to grant her patience. "Wait here a sec."

When she came back, it was with a plastic bag and the vacuum cleaner.

"Uh, no," I said, knowing exactly what she had in mind.

"Uh, *yes*. Open the door and step outside."

"What will the neighbors think!" I threw my arms up dramatically as Jamie plugged in her weapon.

Then she held the steel tube up with both arms and pointed it right at my head, her evil eyes thinning.

"Whoa, easy there," I said, bringing my palms up.

"I said open the door and step outside," she muttered through clenched teeth.

I swallowed thickly, taking a step back. "Listen," I said, my voice and hands trembling. "You don't wanna do this I — My name is Ria, I'm a wife and a mom and b-babies. I've got babies. Seventy-eight of them. There's Jolly the Walrus and Bubbles the Fish and Princess the Bear, and

they're going to be worth a fortune in a few years, I promise! We can split the profits!"

But my generous, multi-billion-dollar Beanie Baby
bribe fell on deaf ears.

"You stole him from me!" Jamie screamed. "He was
mine and you just... you took him away!"

"He initiated it!" I insisted as my back hit the door. "I s-
swear it. Toebeans came to my bed willingly!"

I'd known it was wrong. I'd told him to get out—to go
back to her. He was *her* cat. She was the one he needed to
be spending his nights with.

But he never listened.

"Don't do this," I whisper-begged, my shoulders
hunching with fear. "Please don't do this. Think of my
babies."

She cocked her weapon.

Oh god.

As if on cue, Toebeans Maguire trotted out of my
bedroom, chirping like the adorable little cuddle slut
he was.

"Hi, cutie," I cooed as he nuzzled my legs. "Have you
been the bestest, most handsomest boy all morning?"

"All right, seriously get out before you get that shit all
over him. I'm gonna vacuum you."

I let my hands fall. "Fine but stay away from my face.
We'll use coconut oil for that. Oh, and I get to do a Sailor
Mars transformation sequence first. With the sparkly spin
and everything."

She barely agreed.

~

Alba was officially giving me the silent treatment.

I hadn't heard from her in over four days, and it hadn't been for a lack of trying. Even Ben was ignoring my messages. She'd gotten her husband to shun me. That was how pissed she was.

By Friday night I'd had enough. She had every right to be mad at me, but we were going to handle it like grownups, damn it! The least she could do was ignore me to my face, though I much preferred it if she yelled. Around fifteen or twenty minutes of that usually calmed her back down.

I showed up at their front door with a box of Alba's favorite donuts (crème brûlée from this tiny shop on the other side of the city), and a few treats for Olive.

"She's not home," Ben lied as soon as he opened the door.

"I could hear her talking before I knocked, dork. Tell her I need to talk to her."

He hesitated for a few seconds, then threw a glance over his shoulder and stepped outside. The door shut behind him. "Listen. Now's really not a good time," he said quietly, pushing a hand through his brown curls. "You should probably come back in... I don't know. Just give us some space."

Us. He said *us.*

He hadn't been ignoring me just because of Alba. He was pissed. And it wasn't until he shifted under the porch lights that I noticed the dark rings circling his eyes, and the way his hair was sticking out on all sides like he'd been running a frustrated hand through it all day.

"You, uh... you okay?" I asked. Had they been fighting again?

"Not really, no." He shoved his fists into his pockets,

tension squirming through his jaw. And then he said it. "She got fired, Ria. Because of what you did."

At first, I thought I'd misheard him. Because there was no way he meant that *Alba* had lost her job.

Alba, who'd devoted the last four years of her everything and more to Adrien Cloutier.

Alba, who constantly prioritized her work over her own health and sanity and wellbeing. Over her family. Over me.

Alba, who was supposed to go on maternity leave in seven weeks. *Paid* maternity leave. For a year.

"What?" I said.

"He fired her," Ben repeated, his entire body coiled with stress. "With cause. So no package, no severance, no... nothing. She got nothing."

What the fuck?

The air in my lungs went stale as the reality of what he was saying set in.

"She was supposed to go on maternity leave in less than two months. Does she... is she still..."

"Nothing."

I blinked, my mind reeling.

It hadn't been her fault. She hadn't done anything. It had all been me. I'd been the one who'd hit him. I'd made the mess in his office.

"What do you mean he fired her with *cause*?" I asked, my voice unsteady with panic and anger and... shame. This was all my fault. "Alba didn't do anything. She wasn't even there. She didn't even know about it until the video and—"

I cut myself off when the front door opened again, revealing my very pregnant, very tired-looking big sister.

She was a mess.

Her hair was half crumpled into a bun, her makeup-free face weighed down by stress, and her eyes... she must have been crying nonstop for days.

"Hey," I said, swallowing back the ball of barbed wire scratching at my throat. "Ben told me what happened. I don't understand. How or why or... you didn't do anything."

Maybe she had a case. For wrongful termination or retaliatory dismissal or something.

I didn't know.

I wasn't a lawyer.

And whose fault is that?

"Just come in," Alba said, stepping aside to make room. "It's cold out here."

I hesitated, shifting on my feet until she tugged at my sleeve. "Come on. My feet are getting tired."

I walked in and slipped the box of donuts and treats onto the coffee table. "Where's Olive?"

"My parents took her for the weekend," Ben said. "We needed time to... we have some things to figure out."

My fault.

Alba lowered herself onto the couch with a deep sigh and leaned her head back, her throat working like she was trying not to cry.

I stood in the corner awkwardly, waiting for the tongue lashing to start.

Except it never did.

"Albs—"

"The pass," she answered before I could even ask. "You used my pass to get into the hotel and they traced it back to me. Adrien pulled me into a meeting as soon as I got to my desk. I was fired before he even saw you. It's a security thing. I'd signed a document when I first started agreeing it would only be used by me apparently."

My stomach sank. *That* was the business he'd needed to take care of? He'd been late because he was firing Alba?

"Why didn't you tell him I stole the card or something?" I was going to be in trouble either way. It wouldn't have mattered.

I was the one who'd begged her for the pass. "*You're not using the gym anymore anyway!*" I'd argued when she said no. "*I'm paying a hundred and fifty dollars a month for equipment that's basically held together by duct tape.*"

The one at the flagship hotel, though? It was a gym rat's award-winning wet dream, complete with a free smoothie bar, complimentary massages, a pool, and private sauna pods.

After two months of begging and pleading, Alba had finally caved and given me the card for my birthday. All of this was my fault.

"You could still do it. You could still tell him I took it," I said, grasping at the thinnest straw of hope that maybe it wasn't too late. Maybe we could somehow salvage the situation and she'd get her job back. "You could tell him you didn't know, and, and…"

"Why don't you tell her the rest?" Ben interjected bitterly, talking to his wife.

"Ben—"

"She should know, Alba."

I looked between them, my heart crawling up to the base of my throat. "What? What aren't you telling me?"

"He was going to press charges," Ben said. "He was pissed as all hell and was going to press charges and sue for damages. Alba spent two hours begging him to let it go instead of asking to keep her job and keep us afloat—"

"*Ben!*"

He shut up. He wasn't happy about it, but he shut up. Right before he stormed off. "I'll be downstairs if you need me."

"What the hell?" I said.

"He's just stressed," Alba responded. "It wasn't a good time for us to lose my income with... well, you know." She gestured to her stomach. "And it's not like I can get another job right away, so things are going to be tight for a little while. He's worried about the mortgage."

I was having a bit of a hard time catching hold of my breath. "No, Alba, *what the hell*?"

"It's not a big deal," she said. I didn't know which one of us she was trying to convince, me or herself. "Adrien owed me a favor and I cashed it in."

Wait a minute. "He *owed you a favor* and you didn't use it to keep your job? Or have him write you like a billion-dollar check?"

She turned her head to glare at me. "Are you hearing yourself? What part of 'he was going to press charges' do you not understand?"

My heart was galloping inside my chest, my fists tight at my sides. "It doesn't matter! I—"

"It matters to me!" she snapped, cutting me off. "It matters to *me*, Ria! *I* care if he presses charges. *I* care if he goes after you with his lawyers. *I* care if your life gets ruined. *I* do! What the hell's the matter with you?"

I had to remind myself to keep breathing. That a screaming match wasn't a good idea when she was seven months pregnant. She was stressed enough as it was, so I kept my mouth shut.

"Look at you! Look at your life," Alba said, pushing herself upright. Her eyes were wet with frustration, and it made me feel like absolute shit. "You've been on this prolonged self-destructive streak for years and I can't sit back and watch you do this to yourself anymore. It's fucking torture."

She brought a protective hand to her stomach and swallowed a few times, trying to blink back her tears. "I don't recognize you anymore, Ree... and it's... scary. I don't know what to do or how to fix it. I don't know how to help."

Alba paused, waiting for me to say something, but the only thing I could do was stare back at her, unmoving.

"I care," she said again. "*I* care about you." Her lower lip wobbled and she wiped her leaking eyes with a shaky hand. "I know what happened with Josh was unfair. I know how... demoralizing it must have been for you. But it's been ten years, and I just... you've let him win. You *keep* letting him win. You don't care about work, you don't care about meeting new people or making new friends. You don't date. You don't have any goals or ambitions anymore. You laugh and make jokes and pretend like nothing ever bothers you, but you've given up. You've numbed yourself to the point where you just... you don't live. You exist and that's all."

Her voice softened near the end of her speech as she watched for my reaction.

I didn't have a mirror in front of me but judging by the way her eyebrows pulled together, my expression was as blank and empty as I suddenly felt.

"Ree?"

"I didn't ask you to fall on your sword for me."

Her shoulders sagged with a deep sigh. "You didn't have to, that's the point. You're my little sister. Not to mention you would have done the same thing for me."

She wasn't wrong.

"Okay. Anything else?" I asked.

It took her a second to respond. "Huh?"

"Anything else I need to know or that you need to get off your chest?"

"Uh... no."

"Cool. I'll call you tomorrow."

"Wait, what—you're leaving? *Now*?"

I glanced down at my phone. 5:56. Adrien almost always worked late so if I took an Uber, I'd still be able to catch him before he left the office. Maybe. If security didn't stop me.

"Yeah, I've got something to do," I said as I ordered the car. Black Nissan sedan; less than a minute away. "We can finish this conversation later."

She sighed again. "You're mad at me."

"You're mad at *me*," I pointed out.

"Is it because I brought up Goldman?"

I slipped my phone back into my pocket. "Yes. He's on my off-limits list of topics for a reason. We'll chat tomorrow morning." After I'd fixed my mess.

I was out the door before she could argue.

5

THE PLAN WAS SIMPLE: intercept Adrien on his way out of the office and convince him to give Alba her job back. I was going to be polite and ask him nicely and everything.

It seemed foolproof until I got to the underground garage and realized I had no idea what car he drove. And I couldn't just linger around the swanky sports cars like a weirdo, hoping I'd run into him. Not with that one pesky security guard doing constant rounds down here. Thus began Mission Sneak Into The Building And Up to Adrien's Office Without Getting Caught.

My other option was to find out where he lived and wait for him there, but that was stalker-type behavior and he'd already made it clear he wasn't into that, so trespassing it was.

I recognized that this was one of the stupidest ideas I'd ever had, but it was also brilliant and... surprisingly easy.

The majority of the office workers had already cleared out by the time I made it into the lobby, and the guys at the concierge desk were too busy discussing their weekend plans to notice me slipping past them. And then

I just used Alba's all-access pass to scan my way up to the twentieth floor, because no one had bothered to take it back (or deactivate it, apparently).

All in all, I usually had a harder time getting my Sims to stop playing computer games when their surroundings were on literal fire. The security here was *lax.* If I actually was a stalker, Adrien wouldn't have stood a chance.

I made a mental note to tell him that.

The elevator doors opened with a *ding* that immediately jumpstarted my nerves. I wiped my palms against my jeans before stepping out, trying to convince myself that everything was going to be okay. I could do this.

There was a good chance Adrien was going to call security (or the cops) before I could make my argument, but that was okay. I just needed to squeeze my main points in before I was cuffed and dragged out of his office.

It was almost 7 p.m. on a Friday, so the floor was empty except for one room.

I sucked in a deep, somewhat unsteady breath, and started to make my way to Adrien's office. The door was halfway open, and he was sitting at his desk, concentrated gaze glued to his monitor. I chewed the inside of my cheek as I began to internally rehearse my speech again. I only had one real shot at this before being dragged out of the building kicking and screaming, so—

"Are you just going to stand there and stare, or are you going to come in?"

I started, taking a full step back like I hadn't already been caught.

"Um, I wasn't staring," I lied, feeling a tinge of heat creep up to my nose and cheeks. He hadn't so much as glanced away from his computer, and probably didn't actually know it was me. It explained why he wasn't already yelling or calling the cops.

I took a few tentative steps inside, rubbing my palms against my jeans again. "Do you maybe have a few minutes? To talk."

Adrien finally turned in his chair, dark gaze pinning me to a halt midstep. And then he... smiled? He was *smiling* at me.

It was a cold, harsh thing that didn't touch his eyes, but it was there.

"It's... Ria Sanchez," I reminded him awkwardly, just in case he didn't recognize me without the glitter or something.

He gestured to one of the chairs facing his desk. "Sit down, Miss Sanchez."

A feeling of unease spider-crawled up my spine as I slowly lowered myself onto the leather seat. If Adrien was at all surprised by my impromptu visit, he didn't show it. Instead, he studied me for a few moments with a mixture of amusement and distaste, then held out a broad hand. "You can give the pass back to me now."

That's when the penny dropped. This was a setup. The card had been left active and in my possession on purpose. He'd been expecting me to show up.

I fished the card out of my pocket and placed it in his open palm, trying not to show how much more nervous I suddenly was.

Adrien tossed the pass into his drawer and leaned back in his chair, his head tilting slightly to one side. He didn't say anything. Didn't ask why I was here or what I wanted. He just sat there and watched me with those vicious green eyes, waiting expectantly.

Run.

That was what the voice in the back of my head was saying. It was telling me to bolt the fuck out of his office and never, ever look back.

I stupidly didn't listen.

"I'm here to ask you to give Alba her job back," I said. "Please."

He didn't even pretend to think about it. "No."

I shifted in my chair, my fingers fiddling on my lap. "She didn't know about the pass. I took it out of her purse without telling her."

"She already confessed to it."

"She lied to protect me," I said simply.

I swear he was looking at me like he'd predicted this entire thing, down to what shoes I'd be wearing for the occasion.

I felt weirdly exposed, like I'd walked in here expecting to play tennis and had been tricked into a rigged game of poker instead. He knew exactly how shitty my dealt hand was, and somehow, I needed to get him to fold anyway.

"That's worse," Adrien said.

It was? "Why?"

"According to the security footage, you've been using that card to get into the hotel gym for well over two months. If she didn't realize the card had been missing for that long... Well, that's rather irresponsible and negligent, wouldn't you say?" He ticked his brows. "Not necessarily qualities I want in my PA. I almost rather she gave it to you willingly. At least then she'd have known where it was."

The one corner of his mouth twitched in response to whatever expression had just flitted across my face, and before I could shove my big foot any further into my idiot mouth, he said, "Fortunately I worked with Alba long enough to know that she was neither of those things. So, you wanna try again?"

Not really, no. I'd never felt so underprepared for anything in my life.

I shifted in my seat and cleared my throat, but Adrien interjected again. "Oh, and if you try to lie to me one more time, this conversation will be over, and you'll be escorted out of the building."

I shut my mouth and ground my teeth. It earned me another amused smirk.

At least one of us was having a good time.

"You know, I have to say I'm a little disappointed," Adrien mused when I stayed silent for a few beats too long. "I thought you'd march in here a hell of a lot more prepared than this. I expected more from someone with your... record."

I narrowed my eyes at him. "What's that supposed to mean?"

Adrien leaned forward and interlocked his fingers on his desk. "It means that a 178 on the LSAT is incredibly impressive, Miss Sanchez. Especially for someone who didn't pursue a postsecondary education. That score could grant you admission to any law school in North America."

I swear I could feel the blood drain right out of my veins.

"Those scores aren't publicly available." No one even knew I'd taken the test.

He flashed me a perfectly straight, dimpled grin, his green eyes glittering with amusement. "No. They're not."

I licked my rapidly drying lips and tried to calm the fuck back down. My heart was beating inside my throat now, filling my ribcage with dread. "What do you want?"

His head tilted again, mocking. "Whatever do you mean?"

I couldn't believe I'd been stupid enough to barge in here without a better plan. And I *really* couldn't believe how much I'd underestimated him.

"That card wasn't left active or in my possession by accident. Not when you're worried about stalkers." How hadn't that occurred to me right away? Why hadn't I taken him seriously from the get-go?

"Correct," he said. "Keep going."

"You wanted me to show up here because of the deal you struck with Alba. You won't press charges or get your lawyers involved, but that doesn't mean you can't make me pay in other ways." I knew it had been too easy. There was no way he was going to let me just walk away. That would be extremely off-brand for him. "You fired her *after* she cashed in her favor, right? Because you needed something to reel me in with and keep me hooked."

She probably wouldn't have lost her job if she'd just kept quiet. He didn't care about the stupid pass.

"And?" he pushed. Because this was also part of his game.

"And by now you've had five days to think about your revenge, which means you probably know exactly what you want." And it wasn't going to be pretty or easy. Not for me at least. "It doesn't matter what I say or do, this conversation will lead to whatever punishment you already have in mind. Hence my question, what do you want?"

Adrien leaned back again and flashed me another patronizing smile. "Very good, Miss Sanchez. You're not nearly as daft as you like to pretend to be, are you?"

Fuck you.

It took everything I had in me not to hurl the insult right at him.

"Are you going to tell me what you want or not?" I asked.

Adrien *tsk*ed at me like I was a naughty cat pawing at a shiny Christmas ornament I knew I shouldn't be touching. "I'm not sure you want to be taking that tone with me."

Fuck.

You.

"I think the real question is, what are you willing to do?" he mused.

"We both know the answer to that."

He'd known exactly what he was doing firing Alba before she went on maternity leave. How much pressure that would put on her and her family. What corner he was forcing me into. How much leverage it gave him.

Evil prick.

Real, genuine hatred sparked in my chest. I couldn't remember the last time I'd let someone blindside me like this. Or make me feel so... *stupid.*

Adrien tapped a finger against his armrest. "I'd like to hear you say it."

I swallowed back the resistance blocking my throat. My pride went right down with it. "Anything. I'd be willing to do pretty much anything."

"*Pretty much,*" he repeated, the end of the words curling into a semi-question.

"Nothing illegal," I clarified. "Or sexual, obviously."

His grin widened, the lopsided dimples on either side deepening. "Don't flatter yourself, Sanchez. I wouldn't touch you with a level A hazmat suit on."

"Likewise," I bit back without hesitation.

He ignored my jab. "I assure you everything will be

kept perfectly legal. I'm not the one with the criminal record."

I was pretty sure the anger made my nostrils flare because his gaze flickered right down to them, his mouth quivering.

Chill the fuck out. You're giving him way too much of what he wants.

"Is running a background check on someone without their consent legal?" I pushed through my teeth.

He waved a hand. "There are ways around it."

"Great," I managed to grind out. "Can you tell me what you want now?"

He considered me briefly, almost like he was savoring the moment. Then he said, "Beg."

I blinked, my brain stammering. "Excuse me?"

"Beg, Miss Sanchez," he repeated, the right side of his mouth curving into an extremely punchable little smirk. "Ask me nicely."

He was trying to humiliate me because I'd humiliated him. That was all this was. And the more I reacted, the more enjoyment he'd get out of the experience.

Exactly. So just swallow back your pride and get it over with.

I rolled my lips and clasped my clammy hands in front of me, ignoring the flash of glee that sparked in Adrien's eyes at the sight. He looked infuriatingly pleased with himself, but that was okay, because I wasn't here anymore.

I was in the hotel lobby, cane in hand, with Adrien curled on the floor in front of me. There was soft piano music playing in the background, complemented by the sweet sounds of Adrien's misery and seven hundred million dollars disappearing into thin air. My new happy place.

With that image in mind, I cleared my throat, and said, "Adrien Cloutier, please, please, *please* give my sister her job back."

He laughed.

The fucker *cackled* like I'd just told a joke. "No, Miss Sanchez. You're going to be asking for the opportunity to earn Alba her job back."

This was it, wasn't it? The tenth circle of hell.

I almost got up and grabbed one of the potted plants on his desk so I could throw it at his stupid face. The temptation made my fingers tremble, begging to reach for the closest cactus.

"I don't know what that means," I said. "How do you expect me to *earn* her job back?"

He shrugged. "Only one way to find out."

Alba was never allowed to tell me I didn't care about anything ever again. I wouldn't have done this for anyone else. Myself included.

"Okay, fine. Then please, please, *please* give me the opportunity to earn Alba her job back," I said quickly, my tone flat.

"You're really bad at this."

"Bad at what?"

"Asking nicely."

"I said 'please' three times. What else am I supposed to do?"

I could feel the heat trickle to my cheeks as Adrien watched me with a mix of arrogant amusement and... something I couldn't exactly decipher. And it really pissed me off. So, I gave him my sweetest smile and said, "You know, you could always just show me how you'd like it done. I've always been more of a visual learner anyway."

He cocked his head with a dimpled smirk, almost like I amused him.

"Tell you what," he said. "Since you're so terrible at this, I'll let you make it up with something else."

That didn't sound suspicious at all. "Like what?"

"Be here at seven on Monday morning. I'll tell you then."

I pressed my lips together. This whole thing was so unbelievably frustrating. "Could you tell me what it is now?"

"No."

Of course not. He wanted me to agonize over it the whole weekend.

"Fine, whatever," I said. At this point, I just wanted to get out of here and drink this whole experience away. "I'll see you then."

Or maybe I wouldn't. Maybe I'd walk out of here, buy a bunch of lottery tickets and win. Just one—I just needed to win *one* so I could replace Alba's annual salary.

What if I go and buy thirty of them? Or fifty? Or even—

"Oh, and Sanchez?" Adrien called just as I stepped out of his office. "I expect you to bring your own tweezers on Monday."

Okay. But, like, what the fuck did *that* mean?

6

Adrien Cloutier was a depraved sadist. That was what the tweezer thing meant.

I'd spent the entire weekend trying (and failing) not to think about what he was going to make me do with the stupid things, which was exactly what he'd wanted. The mental torment and anguish had been part of his malicious plan.

"He's probably going to force you to pluck out all the hairs on your body, one by one," Jamie theorized on Sunday night once we'd cracked open the second bottle of Shiraz. "Seven hundred million hairs for seven hundred million dollars."

I'd been tempted to throw the stained cork at her head. "First of all, rude of you to assume I have more hair on my body than Chewbacca. Second of all, there is no way it's going to be that easy. Or painless."

Unfortunately, I'd been correct.

Because you know what was a lot more difficult and painful than plucking my entire body bare? Using a tiny pair of stiff tweezers to pick glitter out of dirt.

Apparently, when the hate bomb of doom had gone off, a shit ton of glitter had landed on a bunch of the plants surrounding Adrien's desk. Thirteen of them to be exact.

"You have twenty-four hours to get it done," Adrien had said, barely bothering to glance up from his paperwork when I'd walked into his office this morning. "If you finish, then we can talk."

So, like I said, Adrien Cloutier was a depraved sadist. But he was a depraved sadist who'd underestimated me.

I started with the smallest pot and decided to work my way up. But only after I'd sent out a request for much-needed reinforcements.

"You got the goods?" I asked Jamie in the underground garage an hour later.

She'd gone all out for the occasion—black trenchcoat, heels, gloves, large sunglasses, crimson lipstick, and a dark leather briefcase. She was also entirely "in character" and kept glancing around the lot, trying to hide behind pillars and cars as she snuck to where I was standing out in the open. And I swear I saw her try to dive into a full summersault at one point, before she remembered she was in heels.

My best friend was a freak. I fucking loved her so much.

When Jamie finally reached me, her chin dipped in a curt, professional nod and she handed me the black briefcase. "Good luck, comrade," she said, saluting me. "See you on the other side."

"You're so fucking weird, dude," I told her. "But also, I kind of love this look on you. Very femme fatale."

She beamed. "I know. I look amazing. Like, to the

point where I'm full-on considering a career change to sexy spy. Or real-life Bond villain."

That sounded about right.

Adrien was on a call when I stomped back into his office, and his eyebrows did a surprised little twitch when he saw me. He'd probably assumed I'd given up and left because he thought the task was impossible to complete within the given timeframe... which was why he'd assigned it to me in the first place.

I ignored his dark, sticky gaze and made my way back to the couch. Then I dug the gardening gloves, headlamp, extra pair of tweezers, and magnifying glass out of the black briefcase, and got to work.

And exactly twenty-two hours and eight minutes later, I was done. Every single one of the thirteen pots had been de-bedazzled, double-checked, then triple-checked for stubborn strays. Until I was willing to bet what little remained of my sanity that none of them contained anything other than dirt.

I should have asked Jamie to also bring eyedrops, I thought, rubbing at my strained, dry eyes as the sun began to peak out from behind the city skyline. But at least I had a killer view. Adrien's office was located high enough that—

"You slept here?"

Think of the devil and he doth appear, I guess.

I reluctantly dragged my eyes away from the bruised pink sky and soft, buttery warmth of the sunrise, to where Adrien was standing just outside his open office door, fresh coffee in hand.

And my brain stalled.

It was the exhaustion and the lack of sleep that did it, combined with the fact that I'd been staring at nothing but literal dirt for the last twenty-plus hours. That was what made my brain cells freeze for five agonizingly long heartbeats, *not* the sight of him in the crisp, midnight-green suit that looked like it had been sewn straight onto his body.

It was *not* because the suit was the exact same color as his eyes, and it was *not* because those eyes were currently boring into mine from across the room, pinning my thoughts in place.

It was the lack of sleep. Not him.

"You're staring again."

I cleared my throat and blinked my way out of whatever overly tired trance I'd been trapped in and said, "I wasn't staring."

The right side of Adrien's mouth curved ever so arrogantly. "I think you might not know what that word means."

I crossed my arms and leaned back with a glare as Adrien stepped into his office, his gaze gliding over the thirteen potted plants lined up in front of me.

"I'm done," I informed him, in case it wasn't obvious.

Adrien reached for one of the plants and gently nudged a leaf to the side so he could examine my flawless work.

"Here." I held out the magnifying glass to him with smug pride. He could put these guys under a microscope if he wanted, and he still wouldn't find a damn—

"Found one."

My smirk went stale, dread snaking around my heart, dragging it to the pit of my stomach. "What?"

Adrien clucked his tongue with sarcastic disappointment, then lifted the large leaf he'd been inspecting. "There."

I blinked at the sparkling spec hidden underneath the stem, my mouth parting as a scream built in my throat. Was he fucking joking? "You said my job was to remove the glitter from the soil. The leaves and stems were supposed to have been cleaned already."

He'd said the janitorial staff had cleaned the majority of the mess, but he wasn't going to make them dig through dirt. Which was why I'd been tasked with it. That was what he'd said.

"Did I?" Adrien mocked. "Are you sure?"

And holy shit, he wasn't going to do this to me. I was going to *kill him* if he even thought about doing this to me.

"Yes," I managed to grind out, even though it felt like my teeth had been sewn shut.

Adrien clocked my anger and smirked, entirely too pleased with how quickly he'd been able to rile me up. And then he fucking did it. The bastard tapped the leaf with his index finger until the little sparkle lost its grip and fell... right onto the soil I'd spent all night clearing.

And oh my god, I was going to be arrested for the murder of Adrien Cloutier. I was going to wrap an entire fucking fern around his stupid neck and strangle the life right out of his freaky eyes. The trial was going to be broadcasted live, and I was going to proudly plead guilty and brand myself as a hero to the people.

"Are you fucking kidding me right now?" I asked, rising to my feet. The edges of my vision were tinting red, and I swear if Alba's entire livelihood wasn't on the line, I'd have started kicking and smashing pots and plants.

I was so. Insanely.

Frustrated.

And then he laughed—*he fucking laughed*—at me. Chuckled. Like I was a stupid toddler throwing a stupid tantrum over a stupid toy, and not a full-grown adult running through murder weapons in my head.

The sound of his chuckle grated against my nerves, and I had to physically stop myself from lunging across the table and tackling him to the ground.

I hated him. I *hated* him.

I glared, my molars threatening to crack and crumble as Adrien walked to his desk, waving a dismissive hand in my general direction. "You can leave now."

No. *Fuck* no. "I'm not going anywhere. We had a deal."

"Yes. And you failed the task," he said coolly, sitting down.

Fire. I was going to set his stupid plants—this entire stupid office—on fucking fire. "Do you have any idea what it actually took for me to get this all done on time?"

My fingers, my eyes, my legs, my neck—*everything* hurt. Everything was stiff and tired and sore. Everything was depleted and I felt... so exhausted. I hadn't pulled an all-nighter in almost a decade. I was tired, sore, on the brink of tears, and he couldn't fucking do this to me.

I wasn't going to let him do this to me.

"We had a deal," I repeated, a hint of desperation sneaking into my voice. "You said—you promised—that you'd give Alba her job back if I did this."

"No," Adrien purred, shoulders widening as he leaned back in his chair. "I said I'd consider allowing you to earn your sister's job back if you completed the task on time. Which you failed to do."

I opened my mouth to bite back but stopped myself just in time. Because I saw where it would lead. I saw the rage and venom in Adrien's eyes, poorly masked by his cocky smirk.

He hated me.

And I wasn't talking about a mild, overexaggerated sense of dislike. The man absolutely despised me because of what I'd done and wanted nothing more than to get his revenge. That was what all this was about.

I let out a heavy breath and forced my fists to relax, because as much as I wanted to tell Adrien to go fuck himself with a cactus, what I *needed* was to make things right for Alba.

So, I dragged a hand through my hair and stalked across the large office, until I reached his desk.

"You're taking this out on the wrong person," I said, failing to keep my voice steady. "Alba doesn't deserve to be punished like this for what I did, and you know it. You *know* how much she cares about this job, how hard she's worked for you."

Adrien didn't say anything, but I thought I saw his shoulders stiffen just slightly.

I shifted on my feet. "Don't do this to her," I said quietly. "Please. She's the one that got me this job, and I can't... None of this was her fault. I swear she... Alba had nothing to do with what happened on Halloween. That was all me."

My thoughts felt incomplete and fragmented as I stood there, struggling to form full sentences. My throat had started to burn as helpless desperation bloomed in my stomach. Everything ached, from my stiff muscles to the emotion twisting in my chest. I felt like shit.

I felt like a piece of shit.

"You're angry at me so take it out on me," I pleaded. "Do whatever you want. Cops, lawyers, whatever. Just leave her out of this because she really, *really* doesn't deserve to be punished for a crime I committed."

Nothing. He gave me absolutely nothing. Just sat there and stared at me with bland distaste.

"Do you want me to beg again?" My voice and lips trembled with that one. I couldn't remember the last time I'd been this... anything. Tired, frustrated, desperate, sad, angry.

I couldn't remember the last time I'd felt like crying.

"What do you want?" I asked again. "Seriously, there's got to be something I could do—"

"Time," Adrien said.

"What?"

"Time," he said again. "I'll allow you to earn your sister's job back with your time."

I let out an unsteady breath and tried to blink away the fog of mental exhaustion. "Okay. All right. Sure. What... what does that entail, exactly?"

Adrien leaned forward, intertwining his fingers on his desk. "I spent months working on securing the deal you managed to ruin in under twenty seconds with your unwarranted physical assault. Six months of schmoozing, presentations, redeye flights to the other side of the world, and late-night meetings to make up for time differences— all of which your sister helped with, by the way. It wasn't just my efforts that went up in flames after your little stunt." He paused, tapping an index finger on the back of his fist. "You've set me back six months of hard work, seven hundred million investment dollars, and a shit ton of contacts and resources that would have come with that partnership. Not to mention the damage-control hell I'm still being dragged through with the media.

"Your selfish carelessness has cost me time, money, my sleep, and my sanity. You've gone through my things without permission, wreaked absolute havoc on my office, and I have yet to hear anything even remotely close to an apology come out of your mouth." The muscles in his jaw had tensed during the recap as if just thinking about it pissed him off.

A heavy and expectant silence followed, and I knew what he was waiting for. The apology was at the very tip of my tongue, urging to be let out. But I just... couldn't do it. I physically couldn't bring myself to say it out loud.

So, I dropped my gaze instead.

"One month," Adrien eventually said. The words were tight and strained like he'd barely been able to shove them out from between his clenched teeth. "I want one month of your undivided time, starting next week. You'll be at my beck and call twenty-four hours a day, seven days a week. If you make it to the end of the thirty days, I'll reinstate your sister's position and she'll be compensated for the full duration of her maternity leave."

I chewed the inside of my cheek. "What about... what about the next thirty days? Will she be compensated for that too?"

"Yes."

"And I'd need to be available for the full twenty-four hours every single day?"

"Without exception." Firm. Nonnegotiable.

"Okay. Can you... give me an example of what you might need from me at two in the morning?"

Adrien shrugged. "You'll find out."

He was insufferable.

"The reason I ask is because I live kind of far from here. I don't have a car and I don't think the buses run in the middle of the night, so I'm not entirely sure I can—"

I cut myself off as Adrien reached into his pocket, took out a set of keys, and tossed them to me. "Keys to a two-bedroom apartment in my building, where you'll be living for the next four weeks. Any other concerns?"

My mouth flapped like a freshly caught fish. Surely, he was joking. "You want... you're expecting me to move into your building? The one you live in?"

"I'm expecting you to be available to me at all times."

I looked down at the keys, then up at him, then back down again. And then I pinched my forearm as hard as I could.

"Not a nightmare, I'm afraid," Adrien said.

Could he blame me for checking?

"Okay," I muttered after a long, dense pause. It wasn't like I had much of a choice. "I'll agree, but only if I can get it in writing." I needed to make sure he'd hold up his end of the bargain this time.

Adrien nodded, a dangerous glint lighting up his dark eyes.

And I knew, right then and there, that he was going to do everything he could to make me regret this.

7

"A SLAVE. You're going to be Adrien Cloutier's slave for a month, then."

Jamie was standing at the foot of my bed, arms crossed unhappily as I stuffed my suitcase with clothes.

"He prefers the term 'personal assistant.'"

"That's like slapping a floppy dildo onto a donkey's forehead and calling it a unicorn," she deadpanned.

"Fine," I conceded, ripping my laptop charger out of its socket. "I'm his slave for a month. Happy?"

"No."

"Great. Neither am I." I twisted the charger around my wrist with a lot more aggression than was necessary. "But it's not like I have a whole lot of other options, Jamie. He's not giving me any."

She tapped her foot impatiently. "Does Alba know?"

"I haven't had a chance to talk to her yet." And before Jamie could say anything else, I pulled an envelope out of my bag and held it out to her. "Here. Next month's rent."

I had exactly ten weeks' worth of living expenses put aside for emergencies, which gave me around six weeks to find a new job after this whole nightmare with Adrien was over. The timeline was a little tight, but it could have been worse.

"Take it," I insisted when she hesitated. I could tell she didn't want to, but I also knew she couldn't afford not to.

"Thanks," she muttered. Though it sounded more like a sullen apology than anything else, so I squeezed her forearm gently to let her know it was fine.

An uncharacteristically long silence followed as I went back to packing, and Jamie kept shifting on her heels like she was trying to decide something important.

"All right, *fine!*" she suddenly blurted, making me jump. Toebeans glared at her from atop the pile of folded clothes on my bed. Shouting wasn't tolerated in his home. "We'll move with you."

My hands froze midfold. "What?"

"Stop begging. I already said we'd do it!"

"I didn't—"

She pressed a hard finger to my lips. "Shhh, it's okay. Toebeans and I are willing to make this sacrifice for your sake."

Toebeans yowled his disagreement, tail tapping against my clothes irritably. He wasn't going anywhere.

"He'll get over it," Jamie claimed, knowing full well he wouldn't.

I grabbed her wrist and pulled her hand away from my face. "I'm not making you move with me."

She lifted a shoulder. "I'm insisting."

"You're being ridiculous."

"Yes," she agreed, "but I love you and I'm not gonna let you do this alone. Sorry."

Sometimes I really didn't think I deserved to have Jamie in my life. She was loyal and supportive to a fault.

I opened my mouth to argue with her again, but she held a palm up to stop me.

"If it makes you feel better, I've also got my own selfish reasons for wanting to come," she lied, right to my face. "Firstly, I looked up the address you gave me, and that building is a lot nicer than this one. Secondly, I'll miss you too much. I'm far too obsessed with you, and our relationship is way too codependent for me to survive a full month without you."

"It's not like I won't see you—"

"It's not the same."

I had to bite back my grin. "I think a little space might actually be healthy—"

"Nope!" She whipped around dramatically, shooting a hand into the air. "Pack your Spidey blanky Toebeans Maguire, we're moving!"

I'd never heard a more devastated meow in my life.

～

"Holy shit," Jamie breathed.

"Holy shit," I agreed.

"I thought the whole purpose of making you do this was to punish you."

I dropped my bags and surveyed the living room again, my mouth hanging open. Because *holy shit*, was this a nice apartment. It looked like it had been ripped straight out of an interior designer's bohemian wet dream.

"Do you think it's a trap?" I whispered to Jamie as she brushed her fingers across a particularly luxurious-looking throw pillow. "Like a Hansel and Gretel type thing but with really nice furniture instead of candy?"

She sunk onto the cream-colored couch, her spine melting right into its cushions. "Probably."

Even Toebeans wasn't nearly as displeased with his new surroundings as we'd expected. He was cautious at first, yowling his complaints at us every time we walked past, but it only lasted for a few hours, just until he discovered how comfortable Egyptian cotton was.

"Get off my pillow," I chided for the millionth time. But—*once again*—my request fell on deaf ears. He probably couldn't hear me over the sound of his own purring.

I left him alone and continued to unpack, having promised myself that once I managed to get it all done and organized, I'd treat myself to a glass of wine and a bubble bath.

Not only did I get my own bathroom (a luxury I'd experienced exactly zero times in my life), but the tub was *huge*. I was pretty sure I could swim laps in it, and I fully planned on testing my theory as soon as possible.

"Hey." Jamie popped into my room, holding a hairdryer. "Do you think maybe you should have checked with Adrien to make sure he was cool with us staying here, too?"

I blinked, my mouth parting a bit. There was a slight chance it hadn't occurred to me to let him know until that very second. "Technically he didn't say I couldn't have a roommate. Or a cat. So... this one's on him."

Plus, Adrien hadn't given me any way to contact him. So I wouldn't have been able to let him know in advance anyway.

"Okay, but he technically also didn't say you *could*."

I popped my empty suitcase into the (massive) walk-in closet and shut the door. "You were the one who insisted on moving with me."

She pointed an accusatory finger right at my chest. "You were the one who didn't stop me!"

"I tried."

She snorted. "Barely."

"Um... what the hell happened to being way too obsessed with me to let me go?"

She sniffed theatrically. "You told me I was your one and only."

I sighed. "Don't do this, baby. Don't cry. You know I didn't mean it."

"Don't!" Jamie exclaimed dramatically, trying her best to summon a bout of elephant tears. "Don't you dare tell me you love me! That's what you said last time!"

"It wasn't my fault! It wasn't even my car!" I yelled back, sliding to my knees in front of her. "Jamie, baby, please. Talk to me. Let's talk."

Her lower lip wobbled. "I know about the scarves."

Fuck. "I was drunk," I said, stumbling over my words. "I was drunk and it was May the 4th and you know how I like to celebrate Groundhog Day privately with Michael."

Our nonsensical theatrics were interrupted by a loud, firm knock on the door. Jamie and I looked at each other, both our eyes flaring.

"Were you expecting him?" she mouthed silently.

I shook my head. Our agreement wasn't supposed to start until tomorrow.

Another knock and Jamie fled with a quiet "good luck," sneaking back into her room.

Flustered and unprepared for whatever interaction was about to take place, I quickly ran to the mirror to check the state of my hair and—

Wait a minute, who cares?

Another knock and, oh my god, I'd never met anyone with such little patience.

I rolled my eyes as I made my way to the front door, taking my sweet time. It was petty as hell, but it felt good to make him wait just a few extra seconds, knowing how much it probably annoyed him.

By the time I pulled the door open, he was scowling. Adrien Cloutier was standing in front of my—his—apartment door, dressed in yet another one of his expensive suits (because why give it a rest on a Sunday), looking wholly unhappy to see me. Like just seeing my face was enough to ruin his day.

It felt really, really good to sour his mood. It fulfilled me. Fed my soul on a spiritual level.

I grinned and jerked my chin at him. "Sup."

He blinked slowly, kind of like an unimpressed lizard. "I could hear you dragging your feet. You made me wait on purpose."

"That doesn't sound like me."

The scowl deepened. "Might I remind you, Miss Sanchez, that *you're* the one who asked for the opportunity to—" Adrien cut off, his gaze slicing down to something on the floor behind me.

I twisted my neck to find Toebeans sneaking up to us, his attention locked cautiously on the potential new threat.

Adrien's dark eyes narrowed as they slid back to my face. "You have a cat?"

I let my head slant to the side. "Do I?"

"He's very fat."

Excuse me? "And you blink like a lizard. What's your point?"

Adrien ignored my devastating burn, his attention

slipping back down to my perfect little Toebeans (who was beautiful just the way he was, by the way).

"May I?" he suddenly asked.

It took me a second to understand what he meant. "Uh... you can try," I said carefully. "He's usually not that great with strangers, though. Especially men."

Adrien ignored my warnings and stepped right past me.

I shut the door and leaned against it with my arms crossed, a smirk playing at the corners of my mouth.

This should be interesting.

Toebeans was going to get so many treats when he inevitably scratched the hell out of Adrien's stupid face. We liked to encourage good behavior.

And, in my defense, I'd warned Adrien. It wasn't my fault he chose not to listen.

Adrien sunk down into a squat and held out an inviting hand. "Hello," he cooed. His voice was so gentle and soft that I reeled a bit, watching as Toebeans slowly approached him and sniffed his fingers.

I held my breath, waiting for the incoming hiss and swipe of an angry grey paw.

Except... it didn't come. Instead, Toebeans leaned a satisfied cheek right into Adrien's open palm and happily accepted the pets and scratches that followed.

My mouth popped open.

"You're so soft," Adrien praised, fingers continuing to scritch and scratch. "And such a good boy."

The only thing I could do was stand there and stare as Toebeans started to purr, moving closer and closer to Adrien until he was practically puddled on his lap.

And then Adrien *picked him up*. And *cuddled him*. Right to his chest.

And Toebeans let him! The stupid cat melted right into his embrace!

What the hell?

My jaw was hanging all the way open now. Not that either of them noticed.

"You're going to get cat hair all over your suit," I pointed out to Adrien because he clearly hadn't thought that part through. "He sheds like crazy."

But instead of putting the cat down, Adrien nuzzled him closer. "What's his name?"

I could honestly say that I'd never been more shocked in my life. Ever.

"Um..." I swallowed, giving my head a quick shake. "Toe—uh, his name is Toebeans Maguire."

I didn't know why I stuttered. My brain felt a little fuzzy, and something had started whirling in my chest, sending color to my cheeks.

Adrien rasped an entirely too-soft chuckle, his warm gaze glued to the loud purring machine attached to his broad chest.

Chest—just chest. Not broad.

Sorry.

Who are you apologizing to?

"Clever," he said. "I'm assuming you didn't come up with it?"

Fucking rude.

The whirling grew, shooting more heat through my body. Jamie had come up with the name, so he was right, but I wasn't going to admit it out loud.

Plus, Toebeans was purring so loudly now that Adrien wouldn't have been able to hear me anyway.

I glared at the two of them, my fingers curling into fists as Adrien nuzzled, scratched, and murmured the sweetest little praises to the shameless traitor in his arms.

"I have a roommate!" I blurted. Because watching their interaction was doing things to me that I didn't understand, and I really needed it to stop now.

Adrien finally—*finally*—managed to peel his eyes away from Toebeans and look at me.

The gentle and warm affection coating his features burned to a hard crisp the second his gaze met mine. "What?"

"I have a roommate," I said again. "That I brought with me. Here. Without telling you. Toebeans is her cat."

Was it just in my head or was my voice all puffy?

"Jamie, you can come out now!" I called loudly, sounding a bit too manic even to my own ears.

Adrien kept his hard glare pinned to my face as Jamie reluctantly stepped into the living room. His fingers never stopped moving, though, and Toebeans never stopped purring.

I hated it so much I didn't know what to do with myself.

"Hey," Jamie said awkwardly, slipping her hands into her back pockets. She shot me a questioning look, likely having heard the whole conversation from her room.

I nudged my head toward her cat. It was all the explanation she'd need.

Sure enough, her eyes flared when the realization hit her, her jaw falling completely slack as she watched Toebeans—or should I say *Hoebeans*—rub his stupid, fat, adorable head against Adrien's jaw. He and I were officially in a fight. I'd never felt so thoroughly betrayed in my life.

"Hello," Adrien said to Jamie, offering her a friendly smile.

I didn't know he could do that. The friendly smile thing.

"Hey," she said again, her brows pulling and pushing and twitching with a mixture of confusion and panic. "I'm, um, sorry if this is an intrusion. I was just... a little concerned about Ria's safety and..."

But Adrien was already shrugging. "It's all right. There's no need for you to apologize. It wasn't your job to let me know."

The heat in my cheeks spread, crawling down to my neck, my chest.

Jamie offered him a warm smile of her own before gesturing at her cat. "He really likes you. He's never like this with strangers."

"He's yours?" Adrien asked, his broad form turning to fully face her. She nodded, which seemed to please him. "And the name was your idea, then?"

Another nod and he shot her a charming, dimpled grin. "It suits him."

I couldn't tell if she actually was blushing or if I was just seeing red all around. "Yeah. He used to climb everything when he was a kitten, including walls and stuff, so it seemed appropriate."

He held out his hand. "I'm Adrien, by the way."

She took it. "Jamie."

Dimples. "It's lovely to meet you, Jamie."

Another smile. "Likewise. And you're welcome to come play with Toebeans anytime you want," she offered, which *nope*. "I'm honestly shocked... I've never seen him like this with anyone but me and Ria. He really loves you."

Nope.

Nope nope nope.

"I might actually take you up on that. He's very sweet," Adrien murmured before placing a few quick kisses right behind the cat's stupid, fat, adorable left ear.

Jamie melted, her eyes turning all googly.

The whirling in my chest exploded as the next two years of my life flashed before my eyes, twisting in my stomach like a corkscrew. Jamie and Adrien's first date. Their second. Their one-year anniversary. The surprise proposal in the Bahamas.

Nope nope nope nope nope nope nope.

This wasn't happening. I wasn't going to be the maid of honor at their wedding and watch Toebeans trot down the aisle in a bowtie, wedding rings attached to his stupid, fat, adorable tail.

Nope.

"What do you want?" The words practically hurled out of my mouth, way too quick and *way* too loud. I had to physically stop myself from shoving my body right between them.

Adrien shot me another glare. "Pardon?" he snapped, challenging my tone.

Jamie bit down on her cheek, trying not to laugh. Though I didn't know which part of this she found funny.

"Adrien, would you like something to drink?" she asked him sweetly. "We haven't had a chance to go out for groceries yet, but I can make tea if you'd like."

The tension in Adrien's whole body softened as his attention turned back to her. It was like an On and Off switch with him. "No, thank you. I just came by to give Ria her schedule."

"You couldn't have emailed it to me?" I didn't have his contact information yet, but he had mine.

"We start our day early tomorrow," he said.

"You could have put that in your email, too."

Adrien cocked his head. "Yes, I *could* have. But I'm not entirely convinced that NewMod@AdrienCloutierHate-Club.biz is your real email address so I decided to stop by and confirm it."

Jamie had to suck her lips into her mouth to stop from laughing.

I lifted a shoulder. "I needed a new work email. It's not like I was going to give you my personal one."

Also, I was a new mod for his hate club. I'd applied for it earlier this week.

He didn't seem phased by my answer. "You'll meet me downstairs at four tomorrow."

"Fine," I said. "Now g— Wait, four *in the morning*?"

His little smirk was so sinister and evil, it was almost cartoonish. "You'll be joining me on my morning run. I need someone to carry my water bottle."

First of all, what kind of twisted masochist willingly started their day that early? Second of all, "I don't run."

"Oh no, I know. You spend eight light minutes on the elliptical, do a few weighted squats, then treat yourself to a coconut smoothie that weighs twice as much as the dumbbells you do your squats with. I've seen the security footage."

Jamie slapped a palm to her mouth, but the snort escaped anyway.

She and I were also officially in a fight.

"Fine," I seethed. "Anything else?"

"Yeah. Get a new email address and lose the fucking attitude."

My jaw was clenched so tight it hurt. "Your wish is my command, boss."

Adrien grinned. It wasn't nearly as warm or genuine as the one Jamie had been given. "Let's go with 'sir', shall we? I like the sound of that better."

Jamie was crying. The effort it was taking to hold back her squeaks of laughter was making her eyes leak.

I hated them both. But mostly Adrien. His face. Overly broad shoulders. The amount of space he occupied. The way he breathed. His *ridiculous* dimples.

"Great. Anything else?" I ground out.

He raised two expectant brows. I hated those, too.

His entire existence pissed me off.

I counted backward from five Mississippi. "Is there anything else you need from me, *sir*?"

I was going to vomit. Right now, right here. Right on the brown loafers he hadn't bothered to take off before entering the apartment.

"Nope. Not now," he said casually, dismissing me with a wave like he was the ruling fucking monarch.

He offered Toebeans a few more praises and kisses, told Jamie (again) how nice it was to meet her, then left without so much as another brief glance in my direction.

"Wow," Jamie said once the door was closed. "That was..."

I whipped around, my finger pointed right at her face. "*You!*" I hissed. "What the hell was *that*?"

But before she could answer, *Hoebeans* slithered between my legs, still purring. He sounded like a fucking motorboat.

"Shut up, slut!" I yelled at his stupid, fat, adorable face.

"Wow," Jamie said again.

I narrowed my eyes at her. "Have you ever seen him act like that? With anyone?"

Jamie had to press her lips together again to stop from

smiling. "Mhhmm. Yup. Lots of really surprising, unusual behavior all around."

Which reminded me. "And *you*," I hissed again, repointing my finger at her stupid, symmetrical, beautiful face. "Mark my words, Jamie Paquin, I will not be attending your and Adrien's destination wedding. I don't care how much you cry and beg. I do not approve."

She blinked at me like I'd lost my mind. Like it had literally fallen out of my skull and splattered onto the floor in front of her. "Wow."

I stepped away from Toebeans who was continuing to rub his—and Adrien's—scent all over my legs. "I cannot believe you two. I've never felt so disrespected in my life. For shame, you guys. *For shame.*"

Jamie crossed her arms, her entire face lit with amusement. "So he, like, really gets under your skin, huh?"

Where had she been the entirety of this last week? How was this news to her?

"He's Satan personified, Jamie. The man's got a stick so far up his ass that it's stabbed clean through the part of his brain that's responsible for keeping his ego in check. What do you think?"

She shrugged, lips quirking. "To be honest, he doesn't seem that bad. I got good vibes, and Toebeans obviously loves him. He's way nicer than you made him sound... kind of funny, too."

I blinked at her. "You're talking about Adrien... the arrogant gargoyle that was just in here, demanding that I refer to him as 'sir' from now on?"

What was the point of pressing her lips together like that when her smile always leaked through anyway?

"He's a lot better-looking in person, too," she said. "And taller. He also smells really nice."

I snapped my fingers at her. "No."

"I'm just saying, he smells like he'd be really good at sex."

My neck was breaking out in hives. "What the fuck does that even mean?"

"I feel like it's pretty self-explanatory. And based on the whole 'sir' thing, I bet he's into some really kinky stuff." She wiggled her brows at me. "I definitely got a vibe."

Gross. Let's fucking hope we never find out.

"I'm never going to approve. You can do a billion times better than that human mosquito bite. I will fight you every step of the way on this."

Her whole mouth was shaking now.

"Oh my god, what is so fucking funny?"

She shook her head and bit back another laugh. "I'm just saying... there's a slight chance that emotions are running high, and that you may have misjudged him. Just a little bit."

That wasn't even close to being in the realm of possibility.

"Maybe you should come on the run with us tomorrow," I offered her sweetly. "We can start talking about how nice and funny he is as soon as we wake up. It'll be such fun!"

She rolled her smiling lips. "Touché."

Toebeans placed a paw on my knee, pleading his case with soft meows.

"Find somewhere else to sleep tonight," I told him coldly before walking to my room and slamming the door.

That'll teach him.

8

DEATH. That was what I wished for when the stupid wind chimes went off at 3:47 in the morning.

I shut off the alarm with a groan, forcing myself out of bed and into the bathroom. There was no time to hit Snooze or make coffee.

How the hell did I used to enjoy this? I wondered as I splashed cold water on my face.

I used to be an early-morning person. Used to enjoy waking up before the sun and getting a head start on my day.

Now, though? I'd gone to sleep with my workout clothes on last night—socks and sports bra and all—just so I'd have an extra two minutes in bed. Except I'd been dreading the early alarm so much that I'd tossed and turned for two whole hours before finally falling asleep.

Toebeans was lounged right beside my runners, watching me curiously as I tied my shoelaces. And because we were still in a fight, I only gave him three chin scratches and one compliment before slipping out the door.

Cold, I know. But the traitor deserved it.

The lobby was empty when I got there, save for the two security guards seated behind the concierge desk, which made sense. Most people in this building were probably sane, rational humans who didn't feel the need to start their day before god herself had woken up.

Then again, most people weren't the literal devil incarnate. He was probably avoiding her on purpose.

A swift glance at my phone told me I had exactly four minutes to get my stretching in, which I desperately needed to do. I hadn't gone for a run in almost ten years, and my muscles were going to hate me for what I was about to put them through.

I only had two goals for this morning: don't stop (because Adrien would just use it as an excuse to cancel the deal), and don't throw up (because I didn't want to give him the satisfaction).

If I could manage both, I'd consider this entire day a win.

I stepped out into the chilly morning air and started to stretch. It was cold enough to warrant a pair of gloves, and probably some earmuffs, but it was too late to fetch any of that now, so I continued to stretch. And stretch.

And... stretch.

I looked at my phone. 4:09.

Maybe he's waiting in the lobby.

I pulled the door open and glanced around, but it was still empty. So I continued to wait. And wait.

And... wait.

There was still no sign of him forty minutes later, and no call, text, or email to let me know if the plan had changed. And since I still didn't have his contact information, I couldn't reach out myself. Eventually, I caved and went to the security desk.

"Excuse me. I'm sorry to bother you so early," I said, offering the two bearded men an apologetic smile as I approached. They weren't the same guys that I'd seen when I came downstairs, so the morning shift change had already happened. That was how long Adrien had made me wait. "But is there any chance you'd be able to help me get in touch with a resident in this building?"

The one on the left gave me a bit of a skeptical once-over. "Who are you trying to get in touch with?" he asked.

"His name is Adrien Cloutier. I'm not sure which floor he's on, but he was supposed to meet me down here... at..." I trailed off, confused by the way they were reacting.

They shot each other a knowing glance as soon as I said Adrien's name and one of them actually rolled his eyes at me.

"Yeah, okay," the one with the long, well-groomed brown beard said in a dismissive tone. "Miss, I'm gonna have to ask you to leave the premises before I call the cops."

Uh... "Excuse me?"

"Adrien Cloutier doesn't live here. You've got the wrong building," the one with the shorter, much lighter beard explained.

But that didn't make any sense. "Are you... are you sure? Because he—"

"Ma'am, I'm asking you to leave. *Now*." Brown Beard stood up and I instinctively backed away from the counter.

I didn't have nearly enough caffeine in my system to try and figure out what the hell his problem was, so I just nodded. "Um... okay. Sorry. I'm just gonna..." I pointed a limp finger toward the elevators. "I'm just gonna go back upstairs."

What happened next was so absurdly outrageous that I was convinced this whole thing was a dream. That my alarm had gone off at 3:45, and instead of rolling out of bed, I'd hit snooze and fallen back asleep. Because the second I started to make my hasty retreat, Brown Beard exclaimed, "We've got a runner!"

Before I could wrap my mind around what that could have meant, Blonde Beard had swung himself over the counter and was charging right at me. We went down hard and fast; me with a startled yelp, Blonde Beard with what could only be described as a barbaric battle cry.

"Gotcha," my attacker huffed smugly, securing my wrists in front of me before sitting me up. Next thing I knew, I was being cuffed.

"Dude, what the actual fuck? Let me go!"

"I don't think so," he said, cheeks pink, eyes wide. "We're sick and tired of you lot. You won't even let the man go on his morning runs in peace."

What the hell was he talking about? "I live here."

He snorted. "Okay."

Brown Beard was typing something on his phone.

"I live in this building," I repeated. "I moved in yesterday."

But he wouldn't listen. "Nice try. We've heard that one before, though."

That was when I started to get annoyed. Why did everybody and their mother think I was stalking the man? "Oh my god—here." I jutted out my hip. "Unit 1102. The key is in my pocket. Take it out."

The two guards exchanged another look, but Blonde Beard reached into my pocket anyway and took out the keys. He blinked down at them, his forehead scrunching into a harsh frown.

It was my turn to be smug. "Told you. Now let me go before I—"

"Where'd you get these?" he asked, cutting me off.

What language was I speaking? "For the last time, *I live here*."

Brown Beard shook his head. "We didn't receive a notice of a new move-in to that unit. You need to tell us where you got the keys."

I floundered, trying to come up with an explanation. The fact that I didn't have Adrien's contact information didn't bode well for me. How could I tell them he'd given me the keys when he hadn't even given me his phone number?

"Um... you can call Adrien," I tried. "And ask him yourself. My name is Ria Sanchez and I was supposed to meet him down here to go for a run at four."

Another shared look of skepticism before Blonde Beard said, "All right, ma'am, we're going to have to ask that you come with us. You'll need to wait in the back while we get things sorted."

I shuffled a few inches away from him. "Yeah... no, thank you."

They could call the cops if they wanted to, but there was no way I'd willingly follow two random men into some back room with my hands cuffed. There was just no way.

"Can you please just let me go?" I asked.

"No can do," Brown Beard responded. "We're under strict orders to take these incidents very seriously."

What *incident*? I was just doing what I'd been told!

But before I could argue with him, Brown Beard held

up his phone and looked at his coworker. "He'll be down in a bit. No cops yet, but he says to hold her 'til he comes."

And, just like that, I was being hauled to my feet and guided to the back room. I should have kicked and screamed and fought, but I knew it would have been futile. Or maybe even made things worse.

So I clamped my mouth shut and followed them, rage tearing through my veins.

"Wait here," Blonde Beard ordered before disappearing.

And, once again, I was trapped inside a locked room, forced to wait for Adrien Cloutier.

Too far. This was officially too fucking far. And we were only five hours into day one.

How the hell was I going to survive an entire month of this bullshit?

I rolled back my shoulders, my heart pounding against my skull as the realization set in. Adrien was going to do everything in his power to make the next thirty days impossible for me. The man was going to drag me through hell and back because that was what he thought I deserved. I was the villain in his story as much as he was the one in mine, and he wanted to watch me suffer. He wanted to see me react to whatever torture tactics he had planned. That was the whole point of this little stunt of his, and I fucking refused to give him the satisfaction.

So, I sat down on the blue couch, closed my eyes, and focused on my breathing.

There was nothing else. Just me and the air cycling in and out of my lungs. Inhale, exhale. Inhale, exhale.

Until, finally, the door swung open, and in came Adrien.

"Good morning, sunshine," Adrien practically purred, absolutely unable to contain his glee at the sight of me in cuffs.

He looked like a toddler discovering the joy of Christmas morning for the first time.

I kept my expression neutral, shoulders relaxed. "Good morning."

He leaned a shoulder against the doorway and crossed his generously muscled arms. He was wearing a black running tee and matching trousers. It was the first time I'd seen him in something other than a suit.

So I guess we are still going running at some point.

"Rough start to your day?" he mocked cheerfully.

I lifted a shoulder. "Just a misunderstanding, I think. The security doesn't believe I'm a resident here."

Adrien's gaze dipped to my scuffed runners. "Makes sense."

My middle finger twitched, but I kept my hands down and gave him a small smile instead. "Sure."

"And I guess I did forget to give them a heads up," he

mused lightly. "That's the type of stuff my assistant usually takes care of, but I'm short one of those right now. I'm sure you understand."

I slanted my head to the side and gave him a sympathetic little pout. "Must be so hard to have to do the little things yourself."

Adrien's attention cut to my mouth and the smug smile he was wearing faltered just slightly, the amusement fading from his eyes. He decided to try again. "You know, this wouldn't have happened if you weren't such an eager little go-getter. Why did you come down here so early?"

Ah, so the plan hadn't been to stand me up. He'd lied about the meeting time to make me wait.

I bit back a chuckle. He caught it.

"I must have misheard you last night. I thought you said to meet you down here at four."

He clicked his tongue. "Five."

"That's my mistake. I won't let it happen again... sir."

Narrower and narrower went his eyes, the arrogant smirk he'd walked in with fully gone. He studied me for a few silent seconds, and I could practically hear the stiff gears struggling to turn in his massive head. "What's with you?"

I wish. "Nothing. I just finally... understand."

He glanced down at his watch and straightened his back. And for a second, I didn't think he was going to take the bait—he looked like he *knew* it was bait, and that he didn't want to ask. But he just couldn't help himself, could he? "Understand what?"

"This." I gestured to the both of us with my bound hands. "I finally understand what this whole thing is about."

He let out a breath and leaned his head back as if he

was trying to talk himself out of further pursuing this line of questioning. He'd wasted enough time on me already this morning.

He was a busy man with a busy schedule. He had shit to do and a company to run, damn it.

But I didn't give him enough time to back away.

"You're in love with me," I revealed.

Smacking him across the face with a dead rodent would've earned me a less severe reaction. His entire face twitched.

And. It. Was. *Delicious.*

"What."

"I'm sorry I didn't see it earlier," I said, my voice laced with as much genuine-sounding sincerity as I could muster. "And clearly you're not handling it very well, so... we can talk about it if you'd like."

Adrien's gaze was darting all over my face, no doubt trying to figure out whether I was just pulling his leg or if I was actually a crazy person. The skin under his eye feathered.

"I mean... there are better ways to handle your feelings than..." I held up my cuffed wrists. "First you send your entire security team to track me down, then you lock me in your office, then you find a way to force me to spend as much time with you as possible, and now this."

His visible disgust was soup for my withered soul. I could *live* off his hatred.

So I forged on ahead. "Like... this is the *second* time you've had me locked in a room, and this time with real handcuffs. Combine that with the fact that you made me beg the other day, and this whole thing is starting to read like a generic mafia romance book. And, like, to each their own, but that's not really my genre of choice. I like fuzzy blue aliens with big horns and bigger d—hearts. And I *really* like cinnamon rolls. Both the food and the dudes, but especially the dudes that can bake the food from scratch.

"So, in conclusion, I'm gonna have to ask that you relax and take it down a notch. And if we want to stop by the bakery down the street after our run for some cinnamon buns, I wouldn't complain. Unless they had raisins in them. Then I would complain a lot."

Adrien did another one of his slow lizard blinks, trying to figure out what the fuck I was rambling about. In his defense, my expression had been kept smooth, serious, and appropriately concerned. I hadn't broken character once.

"You could have just asked me out on a date," I told him. "I mean, obviously I would have said no, but at least it would have saved us both a bunch of time. I never really understood the whole 'boy likes girl so he pulls her pigtails to get her attention' thing." I crossed my legs, smiling back at him.

I thought I'd managed to stump him. Because for a solid ten seconds, he didn't so much as blink. But then he said, "You know your left nostril flares when you bullshit?"

Um... since when?

"No, it doesn't."

"It does. And you tilt your head to the other side."

"I don't—"

He waved a hand and cut me off. "I don't care. We're running late, let's go."

The pun hadn't been intended, and he ignored me when I pointed it out.

∽

I was offered a string of embarrassed apologies by bearded Thing One and Thing Two as they fumbled to take my cuffs off.

But I wasn't feeling all that forgiving this morning.

As promised, Adrien's one-liter water bottle was handed over to me the second we stepped outside, and then we were off.

It was brutal.

I despised every painful, breathless second of the twenty-six-minute run.

But I did it.

My lungs were filled with fire, my muscles were burning and stiff and quivering, and I swear I could taste the metallic tang of blood in my mouth, but I fucking did it. I kept up with Adrien. (Mostly... save for a few meters by the end.)

I didn't know which one of us was more surprised that I actually managed to do it. Me or him.

He kept casting sideways glances at me every time I pushed my legs enough to catch up to him after falling behind, and I thought I caught a quick glimpse of genuine disbelief when we finally reached the end of the route. But by that point I was mostly trying not to hurl or pass out, so I tossed his water bottle on the grass and collapsed beside it, fighting for oxygen.

He hadn't reached for the stupid thing once. It was still full.

Fucking sadist.

Don't throw up. Don't throw up. Don't throw up.

"I thought you said you didn't run."

I don't.

Please don't throw up.

"Or did you lie about that, too?"

Why don't you measure the diameter of my nostrils and the angle my head is leaning at, jackass.

Ria, do not fucking throw up.

It felt like my blood was spinning, I was so dizzy. The worst part? Adrien barely sounded out of breath.

I really hated him. Despised him with a passion I couldn't remember feeling toward anyone or anything in my life. There was a special place in hell for someone who forced another person to run against their will. And if there wasn't, I'd carve one out for him.

But first, I needed to catch my breath.

I rolled onto my back and blinked up at the bruised purple sky. Inhale, exhale. Inhale, exhale.

"Get up."

Fuck off.

I twisted my neck to look at him, willing my legs to move. They wouldn't.

Adrien glanced down at his watch, his breathing almost entirely back to normal now. He wasn't even sweating very much. His skin was covered with a light sheen, his cheeks flushed with warm color. How could someone manage to look that good after—

No. Wait.

Sorry. Not *good*. That wasn't the right word. I meant more—

"You're staring again."

I was so depleted of energy that I couldn't muster enough to look away. "I need... to... here... for a... sec."

Another impatient glance at his watch. "Suit yourself. I'm going to the gym. You have exactly seventy-five minutes to meet me at the office."

I was going to work with him?

But before I could ask, he'd snatched his water bottle off the grass and walked away.

*Just two more minute*s, I promised myself and flopped back down.

And that was when it occurred to me that I was going to have to do this all over again tomorrow. And the next day. And the next.

I rolled over and buried my face in the frosted grass with a groan.

Alba had been right—he really was going to kill me.

And oh, what a slow, torturous death it was going to be.

10

I ALMOST DID IT. I almost picked up a small cactus off Adrien's desk and threw it at his stupid, arrogant face. My fingers twitched and my palms itched, and it didn't help that the little cactus kept begging to be picked up.

Instead, I brought my focus back to my breath and allowed it to drift me off to my happy place. I was a monk, basically. My patience was unrivaled.

"You want me to wear a bell?" My voice was pleasant, smooth, curious.

"Yes."

Pick me up, Ria, the cactus pleaded. *I'll hurt him so good if you hurl me at his idiot head.*

Adrien nudged the box on his desk closer to me. It was a digital watch with nothing but a single app installed: a butler's bell.

"It'll ring whenever I need you," Adrien explained as if I were too daft to put two and two together.

I'd be expected to drop everything and go to him whenever the stupid thing rang. And the best part? The app had a tracker running in the background, so it could (and would) inform both parties what my estimated travel time would be. *Yay for me.*

Look at all my pins and needles. I grew them all myself. Look how sharp they are. I'll stick them all in his face if you throw me.

Adrien lizard-blinked at me, looking like he was already bored of having to explain everything. "Sometimes the notification will be accompanied by a message or a request, other times it'll just provide you with my location."

Aim for his eyeballs, Ria. My pins will stick to those real good. I'm so good at stabbing into things, you don't even know. I am *violence.*

I cleared my throat. This was fine. Everything was fine. My whole brain was definitely not on screaming fire. "Will I be able to send messages back?" I asked, my tone calm and peachy.

Everything was *fine.*

"No."

"Okay... will I be provided with a different method of getting in touch with you?"

"Why would you need to be able to get in touch with me?"

My eyes hurt from the effort it was taking not to roll them. "In case I have a question about a request, for example," I explained reasonably.

"You shouldn't. They'll be specific."

Good lord. "Fine. What if something happens and I'm not able to get to you right away?"

He clicked his tongue. "You're supposed to be available to me at all times. That's the deal."

My hands were behind my back, so he couldn't see them clench. "What if I get hit by a bus while running one of your errands? Shouldn't I be able to let you know?"

Adrien waved a dismissive hand in the air. "I'll see it on the news. Plus, the app will notify me of any substantial physical impact."

I frowned. "It will? Why?"

"In case you try to smash it."

Oh. Yeah. Fair enough. That was definitely something I'd do.

Adrien leaned back in his chair, fingers intertwining in front of him. "Wear it," he ordered.

Last chance, Ria. Throw me at his freaky eyeballs.

It took every last ounce of willpower I had to swallow my pride and reach for the box. I slipped the watch on and tried my best to focus on the positives. Like, for example, at least the strap was subtle nude and not a gaudy neon orange. And at least it wasn't a collar. (Though if it had been I really would have thrown the cactus.)

"Would you like a demo?" Adrien teased, dark eyes dancing with delighted mischief.

The absolute last fucking thing I wanted was a demo. "Yes, sure. That would be great—"

I jumped out of my skin with a startled gasp when the thing went off. The vibrations were so intense they felt like mini electric shocks. And holy fuck was it loud, and *obnoxious*.

It sounded like a cowbell was having wild sex with a car alarm.

The horrific experience lasted an entirely too long five seconds, and when it was finally over, Adrien was beaming from ear to ear. "Do you love it?" he asked.

My heart was a frantic mess. "Is there a way to, um... silence it?" *So it doesn't give me and everyone else in the room a fucking heart attack every time it goes off?*

"No."

The dread that followed was so rich and overpowering, I could taste it. But then he rasped a chuckle. "You can adjust it in the settings."

Thank fuck. I released my breath.

Okay, so he did have a sense of humor. It was just a bit sadistic.

"Great," I said, ignoring the headache blooming at the base of my left eye. I very much needed this day to be over now, and it was only 8 a.m. "Do you need anything else from me?"

Adrien shook his head. "Not now. I'll ring you when I need something."

Again, the pun hadn't been intended.

∼

The "not needing anything" lasted all of nine minutes. And then the requests started to come in.

It was a drizzle at first—grab him coffee, drop off his dry-cleaning, pick up a package. The types of mundane errands I'd been expecting. But then the vibrations started coming in faster. And faster and faster and faster. Until I couldn't remember a time when I had full feeling in my wrist.

The experience might not have been as bad had my legs not been so stiff and sore from the run. Every time I had to squat or jog, or even walk at a slightly elevated pace, my muscles burned and ached in protest.

I was in so much stiff pain by the end of the day that I opted to take a cab back to the apartment. Even though it was barely a fifteen-minute walk.

"So... how was your day?" Jamie asked sarcastically when I sunk face-first into the couch with a groan.

"I'm so sore," I whined into the cushion. Toebeans hopped onto my butt and started pawing at me.

"I bet. You want some tea?"

I sighed. "Yes, please."

She was back a few minutes later with a steaming mug of mint tea, which she placed on the coffee table before sitting down beside me. "You got a watch?" she asked curiously, nudging at the camel strap.

As if on cue, the cursed thing went off again.

I whimpered a sob into the couch. "Make it stop."

He'd told me I was dismissed for the day. He'd said it with his own stupid mouth.

I turned my head just enough to peek at the screen and almost cried from relief. It was just a message. No request.

Don't forget to charge the watch. No run tomorrow.

Thank fuck.

I stuffed my face back into the cushion.

"That bad, huh?" Jamie said softly as she began running a hand through my hair.

I groaned into the couch, and as if he could feel my anguish, Toebeans started to knead my lower back.

He was such a sweet boy sometimes. Ten more minutes of the kneading and maybe I'd find it in me to forgive his slutiness.

"Your future husband is an evil sadist," I informed her.

"Every time he smiles, a pair of sleeping otters get separated. Have you seen the videos? They hold hands when they sleep. It's super cute. And he *separates* them every time he smiles, Jamie."

She hummed. "That's too bad. Adrien's got a really nice smile."

"Does not," I grumbled back. And on a completely unrelated note, "You know he claims my left nostril flares when I lie?"

She cocked her head as she started to study my nose. "It does?"

"You tell me. You're the one who's been looking at my face every day for ten years."

"I've never picked up on it," she admitted. "Then again, you never lie to me."

"What are you talking about? I lie to you all the time."

She pinched my arm.

"Ow!"

Toebeans stopped his kneading and decided to lie down on my head instead. Probably to shut me up.

But Jamie moved him to her lap before he could put me out of my misery via suffocation. I really couldn't catch a fucking break today.

"Anyways," I went on, "either he's incredibly observant and that actually is something I do, or he's bullshitting to try and throw me off and get into my head."

Not that it was working if that's what he was doing.

I was fine.

"Why don't you tell me a lie, then, and I'll let you know if your nostril flares."

I clicked my tongue. "It might not work if I'm actively aware of it."

She scooched closer. "Just try. I'll ask you a question, and you give me an untruthful answer."

It was worth a shot. I rolled to my side to give her more room. "Okay."

"All right, let's see... ummm." She looked down at her lap, thinking. And then she grinned, mischievous gaze cutting to mine. "Adrien Cloutier is a total babe, yes or no?"

"That's dumb. Pick another one."

"Nope, sorry. Adrien is a sexy hunk of a man. Yes or no."

"Literally nobody uses the word 'hunk' anymore."

"Yes or no," she pushed.

I rolled my eyes so hard I felt them hit the back of my head. "No," I said firmly.

Jamie let out a scandalized gasp. "Liar!" she accused, pointing at my nose. "It flared!"

What? "No, it didn't." I'd specifically paid extra attention to the sensations, and I definitely hadn't felt anything.

"Yes, it did. Look!" She whipped out her phone and flipped the camera so I could see myself on her screen. "Tell me Adrien has a gross face."

"Adrien has a gross f— Oh, what the hell!"

Jamie cackled as I slapped a palm over my nose. The left nostril had, in fact, twitched and widened as soon as I was halfway through the sentence.

"What the actual fuck!" I panic-complained into my palm.

Jamie's eyes were wide with excitement. "I can't believe I've never noticed it. How the heck did he manage to pick up on it so quickly?"

I didn't know—didn't care. I scrambled to my feet and went straight for my laptop.

"What are you doing?" Jamie called out after me.

"Booking an emergency rhinoplasty consultation, obviously."

I simply had no other options.

11

ADRIEN WAS HAVING me sort through his mail.

JAMIE

Well that doesn't sound too bad.

So I'd sent her a picture of the piles (plural) of the fan mail he'd dumped onto the table in front of me, accompanied by a photo of the very first letter I'd opened. Distasteful polaroids included.

JAMIE

lmfao

This is it. This is my villain origin story.

And it wasn't just an unlucky first draw, either. A solid thirty percent of the letters contained overtly sexual content, from both men and women. The rest were pages and pages of people raving about Adrien's achievements, telling him how much they admired him and what a difference he'd made in their lives, yada yada yada, and I swear if I had to read *one more* thing about how gorgeous his stupid dimples were, I was going to tie him down and fill them in.

"The next time you say that out loud, it should probably be to a therapist," Jamie had claimed when I'd told her what I planned on filling his dimples *with*.

"Joke's on you," I'd responded. "I'm gonna need therapy after all this anyway."

By the time I was "dismissed" in the evening, I wanted to scrub my eyes and brain with a medical-grade disinfectant. There wasn't enough therapy in the world that would help me forget what I'd witnessed today.

I went to bed knowing full-well I still had a small pile to sort through in the morning.

I was pretty sure that was what led to the polaroid-clad nightmares.

~

"I asked for extra hot."

I shot Adrien the sweetest, most innocent of smiles. "And that's exactly what you got."

The right corner of his mouth ticked down as he tapped the cappuccino with his index finger. He didn't believe me.

I cleared my throat. "If you twist the cup around, you'll see that the order reflects your stated temperature preference. It's written right on there... sir."

He studied me with lazy disinterest, as though simply looking at me bored him.

I wanted to rip the lid off his cup and pour the drink onto his lap. Then we could have a discussion about how hot or cold it was.

Adrien had awakened a surprisingly violent streak in me. I wasn't quite sure what to make of it yet.

"I don't care what the cup says. It was cold yesterday, too."

I jutted my lips out into a concerned pout, but only because he seemed to really hate it when I did that. Sure enough, his gaze slashed down to my mouth and hardened, his eyebrows drawing into a momentary frown.

"Would you like me to go back down and order you a new one?" I offered. "I could ask them to make it extra-*extra*-hot this time."

It would probably burn the shit out of the milk, but that wasn't my problem. And the baristas probably wouldn't have minded either. I'd been tipping them twenty dollars every time Adrien sent me down for a fresh cup of coffee. So... four times a day.

Also, it didn't matter how hot they steamed the milk. It wasn't going to offset the little ice cubes I was sneaking into his drink from my own iced coffee.

Adrien waved me off. "I have a meeting in two minutes."

That was my cue. He wanted me to go away now.

Gladly.

I made my way back to the small conference room beside his office and started working on what was left of his mail.

I didn't know how he wanted the stupid things sorted, exactly, since he'd never clarified. So, I'd kept my method as simple as possible and limited myself to three piles, because chances were good he was going to make me do it all over again anyway.

There was a pile for the gross, raunchy stuff that made me want to dip my eyes into bleach, one for the super-fans gushing over him and his achievements, and one for the thank-you letters he'd received from various nonprofits and charities for his donations and philanthropic work.

The last pile was surprisingly large, and I had to (begrudgingly) admit that some of the letters were very sweet—especially the ones that had obviously been written by kids. I'd taken special care of those, keeping them piled neatly on top of the stack with little sticky notes outlining the name and age of their sender, plus a two-sentence summary in case Adrien wasn't planning on reading them.

I really hoped he did, and I really hoped he replied. But I also knew that was just wishful thinking.

By early afternoon, I had the pile down to a short stack of a dozen unopened letters. And I was so eager to be fucking done with the task that I didn't notice the enve-lope I'd picked up was entirely bare. It had no stamp, no return address, and no destination address.

Adrien had given me exactly one instruction when I'd started the task: "If you come across a blank envelope, do not open it."

I opened it.

I didn't actually realize what I was reading at first, because the content was so bizarrely out of left field that it took me a few seconds. But then it registered, and I dropped the piece of paper, scrambling away from it like it had burst into flames.

It was a death threat. Short and clear and to the violent point.

Oh, and it included Adrien's address.

His home address. Apparently, he was in unit PH2-32.

I yanked the sleeve of my sweater down to cover my hand before carefully picking the letter back up. Though there was probably no point; my fingerprints were already all over the cursed thing.

Adrien's office door was hanging open, and my knuckles barely tapped it before I shuffled right in.

He didn't bother looking up from his monitor, his fingers continuing to move across his keyboard with uninterrupted ease.

"What?" he said when I paused in front of his desk, holding the piece of paper an arms-length away from my body. My heart was bouncing all over my chest.

"Hey. Um... do you remember when you told me not to open any suspicious-looking envelopes with no stamps?"

Adrien's fingers paused, his flat glare slowly sliding to my face. He lizard-blinked in response to my incompetence.

"It was the one instruction you were given," he said slowly.

I swear the man was convinced he could count all my brain cells on one hand. I'd never met anyone who was so relentlessly unimpressed by me.

"Mmm, it sure was," I agreed. "But that's not really important right now."

Adrien opened his mouth to argue, but I held a finger up to stop him. "Just... listen for a sec," I said, shifting on my feet. I wasn't quite sure how to deliver the news... and I kind of didn't want to show him the letter. Because it was intense and terrifying and what was *wrong* with people?

I mean, I hated the guy more than anyone, but I didn't think he deserved a literal *death threat*.

Adrien noticed how much I was struggling and stood up, rounding his desk. I took a few steps back, rotating my body so the letter remained out of his reach. But he went for it anyway.

"Wait, Adrien, just..."

He paused midreach, his head slanting to the side as something unidentifiable flicked across his features. And I realized I'd accidentally called him by his first name instead of "sir" or whatever he wanted to be called.

"It's not... it's not a nice letter," I warned.

An unrecognizable expression flitted across his face, but it hardened again before he said, "Let me see it."

He reached for it again and I hesitated, putting my palm up without thinking. It pressed against his chest when he leaned forward—his extremely broad and surprisingly hard chest.

His chin dipped, his attention cutting down to my hand as I felt his pulse kick against my palm.

I snatched it back. "Sorry."

Adrien met my gaze again and, for the very first time since I'd met him, there was no venom in his eyes when he looked at me. "Can I please see the letter?"

The surprisingly gentle politeness was a tactic, obviously—an effective one.

I slowly placed the paper in his palm, not realizing that my hand was shaking until it was in my line of sight. Adrien must have noticed it, too, because instead of snatching the letter from me, he eased it out of my grip.

"We should probably, um, tell the police," I stammered as he skimmed the note.

Except he didn't frown or look at all surprised by what he was reading. And before I could offer to call the authorities on his behalf, he'd folded the note, ripped it into an uneven half, and tossed it into the recycling bin.

As though it were just another piece of junk mail, on another uneventful afternoon. Nothing to see here, folks!

I stood unmoving in the middle of his office, utterly dumbfounded.

"It's nothing," Adrien said coolly. "Don't worry about it."

Um, I'd read that letter. And it was definitely not "nothing".

"Shouldn't you—"

"It's nothing."

"But—"

"It's *nothing*, Sanchez. Leave it alone."

A part of me wanted to argue with him... but what would I have said?

Adrien let out a breath as I continued to stand there. "It's not the first one I've received, and nothing ever comes of them. They're supposed to be filtered out along with the hate mail before they reach my desk, but sometimes one slips through."

For some reason, the fact that he'd received enough of them to be this... cavalier about it bothered me. "Okay... but shouldn't you have given it to the police instead of ripping it up?"

Adrien cocked his head and slid his hands into the pockets of his slacks. He was in a stone-grey suit today, with the top two buttons of his starched white shirt popped open. No tie.

Not that... not that I was keeping track of his outfits or anything. I was just... *how* was he so freaking nonchalant about this?

"Why do you care?"

I blinked. "What?"

Adrien shrugged. "Why do you care?"

"It's a literal death threat, Adrien. How do you *not* care? They had your address written right on there."

"That leaked a while back," he said. "Someone posted it on the hate club website you now mod for."

You could actually hear my mouth snap closed. That was how effectively he'd shut me up.

"Go home," he said, the quiet venom returning to his voice. "You're done for now. I'll call you if I need anything else today."

Heat bloomed across my cheeks, and I didn't say anything else as I turned around and walked out of Adrien's office with my chin tucked an inch lower than usual.

The very first thing I did when I got home was scour the forums on the hate club's website and start flagging posts that included any of Adrien's personal information. I didn't have the clearance to delete them, but at least this way they were hidden from view.

And then I deleted my account.

12

"What's that?"

I gave Adrien my most innocent of looks and pretended like I didn't know exactly what he was talking about. "What?"

We usually didn't converse this early in the morning, so my voice came out all dry and scratchy. I cleared my throat.

Adrien jerked his chin at me, looking pointedly at my hip as we fell into a light jog. "That," he said.

"It's nothing," I retorted, making use of my croaky morning voice to mimic him. He'd said that to me three times yesterday.

I could have sworn I saw his lips twitch from the corner of my eye. Not that I could blame him. My impression had been spot-on.

"It looks like bear mace," he pointed out.

I didn't answer him this time, keeping my eyes on the path ahead. My legs were too stiff and sore to be forced into another run. I hated this shit.

"Are you planning on running into bears out here,

Sanchez?"

I stayed quiet, but mostly because my body was already needing to hoard oxygen. A problem Adrien didn't seem to have.

"Since I know you didn't bring that thing with you to use on me or any other human. Because that would be very illegal," he went on.

You know what's more illegal? Attempted murder.

My eyes inadvertently darted around, scanning our surroundings in the dark. Rows of buildings, parked cars, shrubbery. Birds chirping in the background, an engine revving a few streets over, and—

"And even if that was your plan," Adrien said, interrupting my surveillance of the area, "you'd have at least thought to try and conceal it in some way, so the other person wouldn't see it ahead of time."

"Deterrence," I rasped. But also, I hadn't packed a small waist bag that I could put it in. I needed to go back to my apartment and grab one later.

"Yeah, I'm not sure how effective bear mace is going to be at deterring someone with a gun."

I looked up at him, already panting. "You... think... they'd have... a... gun?"

Adrien huffed a chuckle as we entered the park. "If they do, it probably won't be aimed at you."

Except I wasn't the one I was worried about.

Not that I'd ever admit that out loud. I'd barely even allowed myself to acknowledge it.

If he dies, Alba doesn't get paid, I kept telling myself. That was the only reason I was worried. I swear.

"Shouldn't... you be... bringing Frankie... or other... security... on these... runs?"

There was a long pause before he replied. "I don't

want twenty-four-hour security detail. Frankie's team is usually reserved for events and official public appearances."

That didn't make sense to me. He was worried about stalkers, received threatening letters, and didn't think he needed consistent security?

I did another scan of our surroundings, throwing a swift glance behind us just in case. And I was so caught up in trying to detect movements in between the bushes and branches and trees, that I didn't realize Adrien had stopped until he said my name.

My feet slowed and I turned around. "Why'd you stop?" I asked. Had he seen something?

He looked at me for a few moments before letting out a long breath. Then he gestured to the path behind him. "Come on. I'll take you back."

I was bent over with my hands on my knees, trying to catch a hold of my slippery breath. "What? Why?"

"Just come. Run's over."

I straightened, bringing my hands to my hips as I started to make my way to where he stood. "Why, though?"

He visibly hesitated, shifting his weight from one foot to the other. "You won't need to come on these runs anymore starting tomorrow. I'll... carry my own bottle."

That should have been the best news I'd heard all week. I should have laughed with delight and jumped with joy and kissed the first person I saw (not Adrien), like they do in movies. Because I hated everything about these stupid runs.

So why the hell did I look at him and ask, "But why? I don't get it."

Adrien huffed out a frustrated breath. "You hate doing it anyway, so stop with the million questions, and let's go."

"It's just one question," I corrected him.

"And I don't have to answer it. Let's go."

"No, thanks." I turned and fell back into a light jog.

It took him less than two breaths to catch up. "What are you doing?"

To be honest, I wasn't sure. "Running."

"I just said I'm taking you back."

"And I heard 'you're off the clock.' Which means my time is now mine, and I want to finish my run."

"*No*, you want to piss me off."

I couldn't help the smirk. "Two birds."

"Sanchez."

I stopped again, throwing my arms up in the air. "Oh my god, *what*? Just tell me what your problem is."

"I'm telling you to go home, which is what you've been wanting to hear every single morning since Monday. Why are you being so stubborn?"

Ah, yes. *I* was the stubborn one between the two of us.

"This might honestly be the stupidest fucking argument I've ever had with another person. And one time I argued with a six-year-old for over two hours about what type of peanut butter is best."

"Organic and low-fat, obviously."

I was horrified. "Literally everything about you makes me want to throw up."

Adrien's face slowly split into a grin. "That's a lie."

I huffed and started to walk away, but stopped again when I felt his fingers gently curl around my arm.

"All right, Sanchez." He dropped his hand. "If you're scared enough to bring mace with you on these runs, I'm not going to force you to come with me."

I blinked at him. "That's what you're worried about? Me being scared?"

"I'm not worried."

I smirked. "You sound worried."

He pushed a hand through his dark hair. "Let's just go. We've wasted enough time as it is."

"Okay, you go." I was going to finish the run whether he was with me or not. I was already out of bed and warmed up, it felt like a bit of a waste to stop now.

My feet were moving before he could argue with me again, but instead of going back, Adrien fell into silent step beside me.

Ten seconds later, my legs and lungs and feet were cursing me for not having gone back home. Sometimes it felt like I was my own worst enemy.

～

The small batch of unopened letters I'd left behind yesterday had disappeared, along with the sorted piles.

The table in the conference room sat empty, leaving me with absolutely nothing to do. Adrien had officially put me on standby which was arguably worse than having too much to do.

I really couldn't stand being bored. That was why I'd opened that cursed box on Adrien's desk in the first place. Boredom.

I sighed and leaned back in my chair, but just as I was about to start counting the little dots on the ceiling tiles, my wrist vibrated, sending a warring mixture of dread and relief through me.

I need your DOB.

I frowned at the screen, trying to decipher what "DOB" could stand for because I didn't think he actually wanted my date of birth. And when I couldn't piece it together, I got up and knocked on his open office door.

"Why do you need to know when my birthday is?"

As per usual, he didn't look up before answering. "I don't. I need your date of birth."

I crossed my arms and leaned against the doorway. "What's the difference?"

"Date of birth implies that I need your birth year in addition to the month and day. Which I do."

I gave him a suspicious once-over. "Why?"

"I need it to book your flight since I'm an assistant short this week."

My head jutted forward. "My what?"

"Your flight," he repeated, already starting to sound exasperated with me and my incessant line of stupid questions. How dare I continue to waste his precious time?

"Where the hell am I going?" I asked. "And when?"

"BC. Tomorrow. And we're going together."

I reeled. "I beg your pardon?"

Adrien swerved in his chair, finally giving me his full attention. "We're going to Victoria, British Columbia, tomorrow morning. The flight I'm on is at nine-thirty and I'm trying to book your seat."

Is this why I hadn't gotten any requests from him so far this morning? He'd been busy planning this shit?

I shoved a hand into my hair and tried counting backward from five.

But then he said, "I'm having a hard time understanding why this is so difficult for you to comprehend."

The little cactus on his desk started screaming again, pleading to be catapulted at Adrien's nose.

"*Why* are we going to Victoria?" I pushed through my teeth. "Is it for work?"

He shrugged. "For you it will be."

What the fuck did that mean?

"And how long will we be there for?" I tried.

Another shrug. "I'm not sure yet."

Ria, please! Please, please, please smash me into his idiot face. I'll do such a gory job of scratching him up! There'll be so much blood! I swear!

"Can you give me an estimate?"

He leaned his head back and pretended to think about his answer. "At least a week."

I tried coming up with an excuse—*any excuse*—to get myself out of being dragged to the other side of the country with him for a full week, but I could tell from the anticipatory way his head was tilted that he was just waiting for me to argue.

"I'll pack for a week, then," I said, managing to keep the irritation from seeping into my voice this time. "And just to be clear, we're flying scheduled? Like with a public airline?"

I assumed the answer was yes since he was booking a ticket, but I wanted to make extra sure. The absolute last thing I needed was for him to trick me into showing up at the wrong airport or terminal or something.

"Yes. I don't use my jet unless I have to. It's not good for the environment."

I blinked, my brain halting. "You're... worried about the environment?"

He frowned at me. "Aren't you?"

No, I was. I just... *huh.*

The cactus quieted down just a tiny bit. But only until I made the mistake of giving Adrien my date of birth.

"You look a lot older," he said, chuckling. And then I had to count backward from five again. "Oh, and you should probably head home now. You're already late."

I didn't even want to know what that meant.

∼

I had a plan.

Jamie was supposed to be at work and Toebeans usually napped until the evening, so I was going to go home, pack, and open a bottle of wine so I could seethe in drunken peace.

But then, Adrien happened.

"Excuse me, are you Ria Sanchez?"

I paused midstep, frowning at the two men standing at the apartment door. There was a crap ton of cardboard boxes and building supplies stacked neatly behind them.

"Yes... that's me."

The older man with the scraggly Einstein hair glanced down at his phone. "You're late."

"Pardon?"

"Mr. Cloutier said to expect you fifteen minutes ago. We're here to build the tree."

The what? "What tree?"

"The cat tree," he explained, squinting at his phone again. "It's a gift for a, uh—a Mr. Maguire? A Mr. Toebeans Maguire, it says here."

You have got to be kidding me. "May I see the order, please?"

It wasn't like I could text Adrien to check. "*Why would you need to be able to get in touch with me?*" he'd said.

The man shrugged and gave me his phone.

Sure enough, the order form had Adrien listed as the

buyer, and Toebeans as the gift recipient. The price had been redacted, but there was a note on there letting the men know that Toebeans was wary of strangers, and to "please respect his space if he asks for it."

The men were also instructed to cease construction if the cat started to show signs of stress in response to the activity.

I hated it. All of it.

I hated that he'd thought to do this. I hated the stupid note. I hated how deceptively considerate it made him sound. I hated how much Jamie was going to swoon over the whole thing. And I *really* fucking hated the stuttered flips my stomach was currently doing.

They were entirely uncalled for.

I let the men into the apartment, put Toebeans in my room, and went straight for the wine. Packing could wait.

The men worked for well over three hours, drilling and hammering and measuring, and I watched as the "tree" expanded until it had taken over an entire wall of the living room, floor-to-ceiling.

It was freakin' huge and... kind of incredible, actually. There were tubes, ropes, rings, and bridges, not to mention multiple hammocks (just in case one wasn't enough).

There was also a throne for Toebeans to perch himself on beside the window. He went straight for it the second I let him out of my room, meowing and chirping his approval.

He loved it.

Meanwhile, I'd (accidentally) finished the first bottle of wine while the guys worked, and was (accidentally) opening the second when Jamie got home.

"What... the..." She dropped her bag when she caught

sight of the monstrosity, her eyes flaring with what could only be fear. I mean... obsessed with her much?

"What's all this?" she asked, gaping at the wall. Could she also see how much it was spinning? Or was that just the alcohol?

"Your future husband," I explained, pouring myself another generous glass of wine. And just like that, half the new bottle had vanished. Accidentally. "A courtship offering. He's trying to seduce you by spoiling your fat cat."

"Hey!"

Toebeans meowed from his high throne, offended.

"He said it, not me." I put my hands up, momentarily forgetting about the wine. Half the glass spilled onto my sweater. "Whoops."

Jamie frowned, appropriately concerned by Adrien's weird and creepy gesture. "Are you drunk?"

"No," I said, holding up my wet glass. "More wine?"

She bit down on her bottom lip, doing a really good job of making her weirded-out grimace look like a suppressed smile. She should have been an actor. "I can't believe he did this," she sighed.

I rolled my eyes. "I know. Somebody needs to let that man know he's doing too much." And I'd happily be that person. "You jus' say the words, Jams, and I'll march right up to his apartment and tell his face how weird and creepy you think it is. I know which unit he lives in now. Long story. Short letter, but long story."

"You're super drunk, and we both know he has an exceptionally lovely face. Ruggedly handsome with the cutest dimples you've ever seen."

"I disrespectfully disagree."

"Your nose just flared."

Whatever. I took another large sip of dizzying grape

juice. Maybe with enough alcohol in my system I could staple my nostril shut and not even feel it. I technically only needed one to breathe.

"We should invite Adrien over for a thank-you dinner," Jamie said.

I cackled at her hilarious joke, grabbed the bottle of wine, and sauntered to my room to drink and pack.

13

It was a good thing I wasn't being forced to join Adrien on his morning run because, holy crap, was my head pounding.

I groaned when my wrist started to vibrate, rolling over on the bed. *What time is it?*

Bzzz bzzz bzzz.

I tried opening my eyes, but the morning light was so painfully bright that I immediately stuffed my face back into the safe darkness of the pillow.

Bzzz bzzz bzzz.

Oh my god, what did he want now? I lifted the shielding pillow just enough to peek at my stupid watch and proceeded to have an immediate heart attack.

Nineteen missed notifications.

Nineteen.

And then I saw the time.

Shit.

Shit shit shit shit shit shit.

I jumped out of bed, only to slump right back down with a whimpering moan. Oh god, the nausea.

Bzzz bzzz bzzz.

I stumbled to the bathroom and popped a couple of aspirin before shoving my toothbrush into the side of my mouth.

I was an hour late and there was a good chance I was going to miss my flight. Which would give Adrien an excuse to void the entire deal, and everything—*everything*—I'd put up with so far was going to have been for nothing.

I ran back into the room and pushed my legs into a pair of jeans, toothbrush still poking out of my mouth. My bra and T-shirt went on the same chaotic way, though thankfully I managed to get very little toothpaste on them.

Bzzz bzzz bzzz.

I bunched my tangled hair into a quick ponytail and rinsed my mouth, my body so full of adrenaline that it overwhelmed the headache and nausea as I scribbled a brief note to Jamie, grabbed my suitcase, and flew out the door.

It wasn't until I was inside the elevator that I looked at Adrien's messages. His most recent one popped up first.

I'm at the airport. If you miss the flight, our deal's off.

Fuck.

～

I'd never run so fast in my life—drunk or sober.

My legs burned, my stomach rolling as I sprinted through the airport, praying to every god documented throughout history that I hadn't missed boarding. At least one of them must have been listening because I made it to the gate just as they were getting ready to close it.

The gate agent kept calling me "lucky" as he scanned my electronic ticket. If he only fucking knew what—and who—I was currently dealing with. "Lucky" was the absolute last adjective I'd use to describe my current circumstances.

I panted my way through the loading bridge, my carryon rolling noisily behind me. And I was so nauseous and exhausted that I barely registered the fact that Adrien had booked me a first-class ticket. I simply slumped into the seat beside him as the kind flight attendant hoisted my bag into the overhead bin for me.

"You made it," Adrien noted dryly as he tapped away on his phone.

I wheeze-mumbled incoherently in response.

"With less than a minute to spare and toothpaste on your shirt," he went on, continuing to stare at his screen. How did he even know? He hadn't looked at me once so far.

"Sorry," I managed between all the huffing and puffing. And I meant it. According to his messages, he'd waited for me for an extra thirty minutes before hopping into a cab.

Adrien didn't respond to my apology. In fact, he didn't say anything at all until we were up in the air and the first round of snacks had been distributed, waiting until my mouth was full of dry crackers before he asked, "Did Toebeans like his gift?"

The crackers turned into wet lumps of sawdust in my mouth, and I had to drown half my coffee to get them down.

"He loved it," I eventually croaked. "And so did, um, Jamie," I added since that was what he was really asking.

He nodded curtly. "Good. I'm glad."

I sipped my coffee again.

My nausea had been starting to subside before this conversation, but now my head was filled with images of Jamie and Adrien getting married in the Bahamas at sunset, dancing their first dance to John Legend, and it was making my stomach twist all over again.

Our lives were going to be intertwined forever. I'd have to see him at every single Christmas and every single birthday, and I'd have to be *nice* to him the whole time.

"Sanchez?"

My attention darted back to Adrien who was watching me with his brows furrowed. And holy hell, *how* were his eyes so vibrantly green?

I wonder if their kids will inherit—oh my god, no. Please stop.

I cleared my throat. "Yeah?"

"You okay?"

I blinked at him. "What?"

"Are you... okay?" he asked again. "You look a little pale."

My mouth floundered as I tried to string together an explanation for my sickly complexion, but what came out was: "Do you have a girlfriend?"

Adrien's frown tightened, his head ticking to the side as my mouth went dry.

"Or a boyfriend?" The clarification was supposed to make things better. It didn't.

"Why?"

On the bright side, at least I had some color in my face now.

"U-um, I'm not, like, asking for *me*," I clarified eloquently. It was for Jamie. Not *for* Jamie, but for my own peace of mind *regarding* Jamie. Because if he had a romantic partner, then all my worrying was for naught. "I'm just... wondering for other people."

Adrien gave me another long, suspicious look. "No."

I sighed, slumping back in my seat. "Okay."

I guess this was really going to happen. And the only thing I could do was sit back and watch the two of them—

"Do you?"

I glanced up at him again. He was still frowning, but there was something else in his expression too. Curiosity, maybe.

"Do I what?" I asked.

"Are you seeing anybody?"

And here it was—my chance to fix this whole thing. All I had to do was cover my nose and lie. Tell him that Jamie and I were in a loving, committed relationship and I was planning to propose to her on her birthday this year. And boom, problem solved.

But even I wasn't that selfish. Because... I don't know— what if he was her lobster or something? I absolutely abhorred the idea of the two of them together, and I could voice my concerns to Jamie, but I wouldn't get in the way of her potential happiness.

I *would* figure out a way to shrink his testicles into little raisins if he hurt her though.

"No," I answered. "I'm not seeing anyone."

"Good."

Wait. "Why's that good?"

Adrien reached into his pocket and pulled something out. A dark velvet box.

"We need to talk about Victoria."

14

IT LOOKED LIKE A JEWELRY BOX. Like a ring box.

But what would Adrien be doing with an engagement ring? He just said he was single. Was he helping one of his buddies propose? Was that why we were flying down to BC? Was I supposed to be helping in some way?

And why did my chest feel so tight all of a sudden? Was I having a heart attack? Or was it a fear response?

"Is that a ring?" I whispered, keeping my voice low in case it was a secret. Adrien answered by popping the box open, and holy mother of diamonds. "It's *huge*."

"I'm gonna need you to wear it."

My hands curled away from him instinctively, clasping against my chest. "No. What? No. Why?"

"I'm going to need you to wear this while we're on the island," Adrien repeated coolly. "Give me your hand."

Was he out of his goddamn mind? "I'm not giving you my hand."

"Great. Then put it on yourself." He tossed the box.

I gasped, instinctively jumping out of my seat to catch

it... only to trip on my own foot and start to go down again. Until someone caught me.

Adrien. It was Adrien who caught me. On his lap.

"Can you just... *be* for two fucking seconds?" he growled quietly.

"You're the one who threw the box!" I hiss-whispered in his face. A hint of aftershave touched my lungs, and it was actually infuriating, how good he smelled. "What's the matter with you?"

Thankfully I'd managed to catch the ring before it rolled under someone's seat or something.

"I lightly tossed it, and it would have landed on your lap if you hadn't flailed like a freshly caught salmon lit on fucking fire."

His arm was wrapped around my waist, his other hand holding my wrist. And for some unknown reason, the proximity was... kind of slowing my brain functioning down. "Mmmkay, you should probably let me go before I start thrashing again."

Something wicked flashed across Adrien's features. "I'd get used to this if I were you, we're going to need to—"

"Ma'am, I'm very sorry, but I'm going to have to ask that you get back into your own seat." The flight attendant looked like she was having absolutely none of my bullshit as she stood above us, lips prim with disappointment. Which was kind of unfair if you asked me, since Adrien had been the one who'd practically pulled me onto his lap.

Still, I couldn't help flushing as I mumbled an apology and moved back to my own seat, a little too aware of Adrien's hard body as mine maneuvered against it. So, he worked out a lot. Who the hell cared?

Jamie, probably. She's super into muscly dudes.

Just like that, the nausea was back.

"All right, back to the topic at hand," Adrien said. He didn't look at all embarrassed over being scolded by that flight attendant. "You need to wear the ring."

I put the box in his cupholder. "No."

"I'm not asking."

I ground my teeth and crossed my arms. He was going to order me to do it, I knew he was. But I could hold out for just a little bit longer.

"Sanchez, it's part of the deal. You need to wear the ring."

I glared at him. "Tell me what we're doing first."

"I don't have to explain myself to you."

God, he was *such a dick*!

I snatched the box out of the cupholder and yanked it open, but before I could grab the ring, Adrien placed his hand on top of it, his warm fingers brushing against my skin. "Okay. All right. Just... wait. Relax for a second."

That wasn't going to happen. My blood was boiling in my veins, and I could feel the heat of anger lash at my patience as it spread through my body. How was it possible for one person to get under my skin so easily? Every time the man opened his mouth, I wanted to push my fist through a skull. Preferably his.

My chest was rising and falling with so much weight you'd think I'd just finished sprinting through another airport.

He chuckled, dimples popping. "You really can't stand me, can you?"

"Isn't the feeling mutual?"

He sucked his lips into his teeth, then said, "Yeah... we're going to need to put a short pause on this charming little dance of ours."

I met his gaze again, not at all distracted by the fact that his fingers were still wrapped around mine. Neither of us had let go of the box. "Are you going to tell me why?"

"Because my parents think we're engaged."

I laughed.

He did not.

"Wait... wait, what?"

"My family thinks you and I are engaged to be married."

Thu-thump.

My eyes kept bouncing between his, trying to figure out what the joke was. "I don't get it."

Adrien moved a touch closer and cleared his throat. "My family is under the impression that you and I are engaged to be married, and I need you to pretend like that's the case while we visit them."

I shook my head, trying to clear it. The soft smell of his cologne was making it hard to think. "Did you... did you like forget to take your medication or something this morning?"

His mouth jerked. "No."

"Are you sure?"

"Positive."

"Oh... then I still don't get it."

He sighed. It was a deep, heavy release of air that eventually morphed into a soft chuckle. "Okay. Sanchez, we are on our way to visit my family. They think you and I are engaged, and I just need you to go along with it for a few days. That's it."

Adrien paused, giving me time to process. But I had so many questions that it was hard to pick just one.

I glanced down at his hand on my lap, and the flash of

midnight velvet peeking out from in between our fingers. "But... why?"

"Long story."

"You're kidding."

"You don't need to know the reason; you just have to—"

"Then no." I made the decision right then and there. No. No way. This was officially taking it too far. And I didn't think Alba would disagree with my decision if she knew. "I'm not doing it. I'm not willing to lie to your family for you, *especially* when you won't even give me a reason. This is where I officially draw the line."

His features pinched in frustration. "We have a deal—"

"*No.*" He could call off our deal if he wanted because there was no way I was going to do this for him. It was shady as hell, and... icky. It felt icky.

Adrien huffed through his nose, his mouth pressing together. Then his eyes fell shut like he was regrouping.

"*Fine,*" he eventually ground out, "it's my mother if you must know. She's kept... *insisting* on setting me up on blind dates over the last few years, and they always go poorly. Without fail. And the amount of cleanup is usually... not worth it. Six months ago, after a particularly shitty experience, I caved and told her I was in a relationship."

I slipped my hands out from under his warm palm and crossed my arms. "*And?*"

"And I can only keep up the lie for so long. Especially since I haven't actually introduced them to the woman I'm dating... which is where you come in."

That still didn't add up. "Where the hell does the engagement piece fit? Shouldn't it be enough for you to be in a relationship? Why does a ring need to be involved?"

He was already tired of having to explain himself. I could tell.

"It's part of the long game. In a few months, I'm going to tell them that we split. A broken engagement with a person you think you're going to spend the rest of your life with tends to have more impact than a normal breakup. It'll... buy me more time before she starts insisting that I go on those awful dates again."

"It can't be that bad..." I muttered.

"The glitter bomb you found in my office was sent to me courtesy of someone I went on two dates with eight months ago. And it's not the first present she's sent me."

I quirked a brow. "Why? What did you do to her?"

"What makes you think I did something?"

And because I wasn't in the mood to answer dumb questions, I said, "Why don't you just be honest with your mom and tell her how much you hate the dates?"

"She's sensitive," he insisted. "I've tried breaking it to her gently but... let's just say this way's better for everyone involved."

I didn't believe him.

Something was off. Not... *clicking*. There were about a million better ways for him to handle this situation, and he was smart enough to know that. So, either he was lying, or he was omitting a key piece of information. There was absolutely no way this was just about not wanting to hurt his mother's feelings.

"What would this entail?" I asked him carefully. "Like... what would I need to do, exactly?"

His left cheek ticked, his jaw clenching momentarily. "We would need to act like a newly engaged couple. Happy, in love, and all that gushy bullshit. It'll need to be convincing."

Thu-thump.

"And how are we supposed to make it convincing? Just... like... hold hands in front of them?" I suddenly couldn't think of what normal couples did in public. My mind was a blank slate.

"To start. Yeah."

Thu-thump. Thu-thump. Thu-thump.

"You're out of your fucking mind if you think—"

"I'll let you out of the deal, write you a recommendation letter to provide to your future potential employer, and give Alba her old job back effective immediately after this trip."

It felt like someone had hit Pause on my brain. I blinked at him.

The look he was giving me was so intense it was poking holes in my lungs. "If you can make it believable and convince my whole family that we're happy and in love, I'll do everything I said."

Yeah... okay. There was definitely something he wasn't telling me.

"And you think *you'll* be able to make it believable?" The majority of our conversations ended with us wanting to rip each other's throats out. Just the sight of his face made my fists clench. How did he imagine we'd be able to pull this off?

Adrien nodded. With confidence. "Yeah. I don't think that part is going to be an issue."

Oh. So *I'd* be the more likely one to give us away? Was that what he was insinuating?

"Adrien, you can't even look at me without three separate veins protruding right out of your thick forehead."

His mouth did that amused twitch thing. "How about

this then: if I give us away, you'll still walk away with everything I mentioned."

I nibbled on my lower lip. Clearly, the man had all his marbles rolling loose inside that big head of his. But also... Alba would get her job back in a week, and I wouldn't have to put up with his bullshit anymore. "Can I take the watch off?" I asked him.

"Yes."

Thank fuck. "And... you said we'd be there for one week, right? Seven days?"

"It shouldn't be more than a week, but let's cap it at ten days. Just in case."

I could do that. Ten days was better than—

"Oh. Wait," I said, my spine perking into a straight line. "Rooms. I want my own room. Nonnegotiable."

Another twitch of his mouth. "We'll be staying in their guesthouse. It's a two-bedroom, and you'll have your own bath. Anything else?"

"Yeah. I want it all in writing."

He nodded, a smirk tugging at his mouth. "Deal."

"Deal."

I shook his hand and reached for the velvet box, shoving the diamond ring onto my finger with a grin. Just ten days and this whole thing would be over. I'd never have to interact with Adrien Cloutier ever again.

Let the lying games begin.

15

"Wow."

I gawked up at the mansion in awe, my fingers going slack around the straps of my bag. The place was huge. And the exterior looked a bit like one of the classic Cloutier hotels, with dark shingles and light stones. There was also a large fountain out front and a ton of flowers and shrubbery lining... well, everything.

The whole property was lovely. Enchanting and picturesque and *massive*.

"Yeah, I know," Adrien said, stepping up beside me. The car that had dropped us off made one last crunchy turn out of the property, leaving us alone with our luggage. And my ring.

I'd become hyperaware of it the second we'd stepped off the plane. It was starting to feel heavy and dense, like an anchor. There was a reason Adrien had waited until the very last minute to tell me what he was up to. The less time I had to think about it, the less time I had to realize how terrible of an idea it was.

I rolled my lips, apprehension washing over me. Was I

just overthinking things or were there a hundred different ways this could blow up in my face?

"Don't overthink it," Adrien muttered, peering down at me like he could read my mind. "Keep it simple. We're engaged, we're in love. That's it."

"How did we meet?" I asked, keeping my squinting eyes on the house. Twelve bedrooms, that was going to be my guess.

"Through your sister. At the corporate Christmas party last year."

"Where did you propose?"

"You proposed."

"No, I didn't."

Ten baths. Two half, eight full. And I bet they had a theater, a wine cellar, a library, and more than one pool.

Were ballrooms still a thing? If they were, this house would have at least one. And maybe a secret dungeon or two as well.

Adrien let out a quiet laugh. "My buddy Ethan opened an Italian restaurant a few months back. It's got a great rooftop patio. Let's say I reserved the whole place, and we had a romantic dinner, then I popped the question. You cried. A lot. The violinist shed a few tears too. Because I did such a great job."

"Isn't the whole point of this to try and make it believable?"

"I can be very romantic, Sanchez. That's a widely known fact."

It was my turn to laugh. "Anything else I should know?"

Adrien clamped his lips, thinking. "My birthday's January 9th, my favorite color is red, I hate seafood, and I'm allergic to cats."

My brows leaped at the last one. "Are you really?"

"Yeah. My throat, eyes, and nose all start to itch. It's kind of a nightmare."

That didn't make any sense. "You were nuzzling the hell out of Toebeans when you met him."

Adrien smiled again, dimples and all. "I paid the price for it, believe me. It was worth it, though. He's pretty cute."

I tucked a stray piece of hair behind my ear, looking away. My insides were doing a skipping routine. Because of the nerves and absolutely nothing else.

"Anything else I need to know?"

"Nope."

"Aren't you gonna ask me if there's anything *you* should know about me?"

"Nah." He picked up his duffle bag. "I ran a background check on you after Halloween. I know everything I need to know."

My eyes rolled. This was going to be the slowest week of my entire fucking life.

"You ready?" he asked.

"Not even a little bit."

"Perfect. Let's go."

I suppressed a groan, dragging my feet to the doorstep with my heartbeat heavy.

Adrien shot me one last look before ringing the doorbell. I held my breath.

It's going to be okay. You can do this. For Alba and Olive.

Steps echoed behind the door.

You can do anything for ten days.

The door ripped open, someone squealed, and Adrien was pulled into an embrace. "Addy! My sweet little darling! *Hellllooooo.*"

This must have been his mother. I didn't believe for

one second that anyone else would call Adrien Cloutier "sweet" or "darling" and mean it.

I released a shaky breath through my nose and forced a smile onto my lips. It felt more like a grimace than a smile, but fingers crossed it didn't look like one.

Remember, you're engaged and in love, which means you're super excited to meet his family. So act like it!

"My baby," Adrien's mother cooed in her soft, tear-stained voice. She was tall, willowy, and had the same dark hair as her son. "I missed you, honey."

Adrien chuckled softly, tightening his arms around her. "Missed you, too."

"I've raised a liar. If that were true, you wouldn't go seven whole months between visits." And when she finally released him from her embrace, her hands moved to his face, cupping it lovingly. The skin underneath her eyes was slightly wet as she sniffled, her features oozing pure love and affection as she stared at him. Then he nudged his head in my direction.

"I have someone I'd like to introduce you to."

Thu-thump.

Mrs. Cloutier's big green eyes moved to where I was standing, crinkling in their corners as her face split into another soft grin. She let Adrien go, clasping her hands in front of her like she simply couldn't contain her happiness.

"Hello," she said. "You must be Ria."

I tried to clear the ball of nerves from my throat and held out my hand. "It's so lovely to meet you, Mrs. Cloutier—"

But before I could get to the end of my rehearsed greeting, Mrs. Cloutier's arms pulled me into a big hug. I blinked, my hands frozen in the air as she squeezed me tight. "Oh, sweetheart, it's so lovely to meet *you*. And please, call me Julie."

Adrien arched a brow at me from behind his mother's back, silently asking if I knew how hugs worked. I cleared my throat again and returned Julie's embrace, patting her back awkwardly. She smelled like soft lavender and honey. It was… pleasant and comforting.

"Oh my gosh, let me look at you." Julie let me go, hands moving to my upper arms to hold me in place as she assessed the situation. I averted my gaze, heat trickling up my neck. Her grin widened, and I swear her eyes were starting to get wet all over again. "Oh. Addy, you weren't exaggerating. She's such a beauty."

I looked at Adrien, expecting his eyes to flick to the cloudy skies. But he simply pressed his lips together and dropped his chin.

It wasn't a nod. I was pretty sure he was just super interested in the ground.

"You kids must be exhausted. Come in, come in. We can catch up and talk inside. Addy, you'll get the bags, yes?"

"Oh, no, I can get those myself," I tried to insist, but Adrien waved me off.

"It's fine," he said, moving for my luggage. "I'll take these to the guesthouse while you get acquainted with everyone."

A wave of panic rushed through me. He was going to leave me alone with his family? *Already*? For how long?

"Oh, honey, no. There's work being done on the roof of the guesthouse. You can't stay there."

Adrien's entire body stuttered before hardening to stone. "What?"

"A tree branch went through the roof during the big

storm last week. It's a mess. I've got the two of you set up in a room upstairs."

Wait. Wait.

Wait.

I took a step back and shook my head at Adrien, my eyes flaring wide.

No. There was no way. I'd *told him* I wanted my own bedroom.

I wasn't the only one panicking. For the first time since I'd met him, Adrien looked at a complete loss for words. He also looked like he wasn't really breathing.

"I hope that's okay," Julie went on, turning back to me. "The room's in the west wing, so you're still secluded if privacy is a concern. I would have told you sooner, but with everything Addy was dealing with last week... Well, he had more important things to worry about."

Adrien looked from me to his mother, lizard-blinking. I swear—*I swear*—if he didn't immediately tell her we were going to a hotel or something, I was out.

I'd walk back to Toronto if I had to.

"It's okay," he said, voice strained and thick. "We're fine in the main house."

Welp, time to call a taxi.

"Um, you know what, I'm actually not feeling all that—"

"I think we're going to go straight upstairs and freshen up a bit before we say hi to everyone else," Adrien interrupted, shooting me a look.

I glowered at him.

Julie looked between her son and I, the tension making her smile waver. "Yes, sure, of course. Take your time. I'll just let the others know you're here. Dinner will be ready at seven if you're feeling up for it by then."

Adrien offered her a smile. "I'm sure we'll be down before then."

She glanced between us one more time. "Okay. All right, let's go. I'll show you which room is yours."

We grabbed our bags (I snatched mine up before *Addy dearest* could even think about reaching for them) and were led through the massive foyer of the house, up the stairs, and down a lavishly decorated hallway. I'd have been a lot more appreciative of my surroundings if I wasn't seething.

"*No*," I snapped the millisecond the door was closed.

Adrien pressed a finger to his lips, his eyes darting to the door behind me.

I didn't give a fuck if his mother was still outside.

"*No*, Adrien. We had a deal. You said—" Adrien grabbed my arm before I could finish my sentence, cutting me off. "What the hell are you doing? Let me go!"

He did no such thing, not until we were both packed inside a small linen closet. Emphasis on the word *small*. We barely fit in the thing without our bodies pressed right up against each other. I could literally feel the heat radiating off him.

He sighed. "Okay. I know this isn't what we talked about but—"

"No."

"Just listen."

"No."

"Sanchez."

"No!" How many fucking times did I need to repeat myself?

Adrien huffed a frustrated breath through his nose as he ruffled his hair. Then he stripped out of his jacket and threw it on the floor. I didn't blame him. It was blistering hot in here already.

Except the space was so tight that the movement made a whole lot of his body press against a whole lot of mine. And since he was a freaking radiator, it meant that I now felt like I was on fire.

"I'm sorry," he eventually said.

And I was so taken aback by it that my jaw went a little slack.

"I really didn't see the roof thing coming," he continued. "But I can fix it. We can probably put in an emergency patch or something within the next few days. In the meantime, you can take the bed, I'll sleep on the floor."

The proximity of our bodies was making it kind of hard to think. I really despised how good he smelled. "Not good enough," I countered.

He sighed again before closing his eyes, and then his lips were moving like he was arguing with himself.

Not that I was staring at his mouth.

His throat bobbed, and when he forced his eyes open again, they were set with stubborn determination. "I'll sleep in the bathtub and close the bathroom door. That way you have the whole room to yourself at night."

"No."

"I'll—"

Oh my god. How was he not getting this? "Adrien. Stop for a second and just *think* about what it would be like if you and I were forced to share a room for just one day. Just one."

His pupils were so dilated that I could barely see the ring of green surrounding them. They were mostly just black.

"Look at us. Right now," I said. "This isn't going to

work. Even if I agreed, there is no way in hell we're going to be able to pull this off. They'll never believe us."

All I needed to do was hold up a mirror in front of him. His eyes were dark and savage, his muscular arms flexed with tension, his cheeks flushed, his jaw strained and... shaved to smooth perfection. He smelled like, um, aftershave and soap and cedar and... a light, spicy cologne that made my fingers want to curl. With anger, probably.

His throat was bobbing now... and his lips weren't pressed together anymore. They were parted and a little red. From all the rage he probably felt and... we hated each other, so... this was...

"Sanchez."

Hmm?

"You're staring again."

I blinked a few times, pulling myself out of... whatever the fuck that was. Lack of oxygen, probably. This space was too small for one person, let alone one person and a giant fireman.

Not, like, an actual fireman. That wouldn't make any sense. I meant he was a man on fire. Because of the heat he was radiating, and—

Fuck's sake, Ria. Shhh.

God, it was so hard to think properly in here. The heat was melting my brain.

Adrien's expression had relaxed slightly, his eyes shimmering with an amused... something. I couldn't quite decipher the second emotion.

"I wasn't staring. I was *observing*," I clarified.

The corner of his mouth slanted into a smug, dimpled smile that made my stomach flip. Again, with anger. Probably.

"It's okay," he said. "It's not your fault. I've been told I have really great lips and excellent dimples."

"You've been straight up lied to. Your lips are mediocre at best, and your dimples are hella lopsided and ridiculous-looking. Now let me out so I can call a cab."

Adrien's mediocre lips continued their amused curvature. "That was a lie. And I don't think we'll have any problems convincing my family that we're a thing if you keep looking at me like that."

I could feel the color start to blot my skin, but I refused to cower. "I'm looking at you like I wanna murder you. Because I wanna murder you. All day, every day."

His lopsided dimples popped. "Sure, Sanchez. Let's pretend like that's what it is."

I held his gaze. "I'm not doing this with you, Adrien. Not if we have to share a room."

He didn't miss a single beat. "I'll double your sister's maternity compensation if you stay."

Jesus Christ. "You've lost your fucking mind."

"So you'll do it."

I meant to say no, I really did. But nothing came out when I opened my mouth. It was just... he'd double her compensation? *Double*?

I knew she could use it, that was what made me pause. With twins on the way... the mortgage, daycare when she went back to work...

"We're going to murder each other," I promised him. "I'm not kidding. It's going to be a bloodbath."

"It doesn't matter. Just as long as you can keep up the act in front of my family," he insisted. "You can draw as much blood behind closed doors as you want."

What the hell had gotten into him? Was this really just about the blind dates?

"And you're positive you can do this?" I asked him. "And be convincing?"

"It's not going to be a problem." He said it with such cocky conviction that it pissed me off a little.

"Whatever, dude. It's your funeral." Quite literally. I felt very murdery around him. But if he wanted to learn his lesson the hard way, so be it. "I want it in writing immediately. Before dinner, and before I interact with your family. Otherwise, I'm out."

Then I ducked under his arm and slipped out of the closet.

Finally. I could breathe again.

16

BY DINNER TIME, my heart was coiled into a tight, anxious mess of uncoordinated beats.

I didn't understand why I was so nervous. If shit hit the fan (which it undoubtedly would), Adrien would be the one with all the explaining to do. I'd just slip out of here and book a flight right back to Toronto. I already had it all in writing.

"Okay, we gotta go. I'm not letting you stall anymore," Adrien said, shutting his laptop. We'd spent the last two hours mostly ignoring each other while he worked. "I don't want to show up late to dinner."

I was tempted to ask him for just five more minutes, but I'd done that three times already and he was clearly running out of what minimal patience he possessed. So, I let out a resigned breath and forced myself off the recliner I'd curled up on.

The "bedroom" we'd been assigned was the size of a small studio apartment and decorated like a luxury hotel suite. There was a big four-poster bed with rich blue draperies, a large balcony, a cozy little living area with a traditional fireplace, a small bar, and a dedicated work-space Adrien had immediately monopolized.

Oh, and there were two walk-in closets (both of which were *twelve times* the size of the linen closet Adrien had stuffed us into), and two walk-in rain showers.

Under normal circumstances, I'd have been ecstatic to stay here for just one night. These were not normal circumstances.

"Fine. Let's just get this over with," I grumbled, wiping my nervous palms against my jeans. I'd spent the last hour looking up formal dinnerware settings, determined not to make a fool of myself by mixing up a salad spoon with a soup fork or whatever. (Jamie had forced me to watch *Shrek 2* multiple times. I knew how many utensils rich people used.)

"That's the spirit," he muttered dryly.

We made our way downstairs with Adrien in the lead. There was a voice in the back of my head that kept telling me to run. That it still wasn't too late to make a break for it. And I was so concentrated on trying to ignore it, that I didn't hear the soft chatter of voices until everything exploded into shouts and barks and laughter, making me jump.

"Ah, there he is!"

"Finally! What the heck took you so long?"

"*Bark bark!*"

"Lookin' sharp, kid. I like the shirt."

"Uh, he looks old as fuck. I can see the crow's feet from here."

"Thanks, Lice."

"Alice, language. Adrien, don't call your sister Lice."

"*Bark bark grrr bark.*"

"That nickname doesn't even make sense. My name's

Alice, not A*lice*. No creativity and literal rocks for brains. Zero out of ten."

"*Bark bark bark*!"

"Everybody calm down. You're going to scare her off."

"Agreed. Y'all are hella embarrassing. Especially you, Maxipad."

"Where's your girl? Did she run off already?"

"Bring her in. I need to warn her."

I'd frozen behind Adrien as soon as the commotion started, my heart hammering in my chest. We were standing in an archway leading (presumably) to a living room, and Adrien's broad back blocked the majority of my view into the space. Until he stepped aside.

"Everybody, meet my fiancée, Ria."

Four pairs of wide eyes peered at me as I took a tentative step into the room. Julie was standing beside a big stone fireplace, grinning from ear to ear. She reached out a hand, motioning for me to join her. "Come in, come in. Let's get you introduced."

I walked over with my heart in my throat. Julie placed a comforting hand on my back when I reached her, visibly unable to contain her excitement as she motioned to her husband, the former CEO of Cloutier Hotels.

"This is Anthony, my husband."

"Pleasure to meet you," I said, shaking his hand.

Anthony was an incredibly handsome man, and he looked so much like Adrien that it almost felt like I was peering into a time machine.

"The pleasure is all mine, Ria. It's so nice to finally meet you."

"And this is my daughter, Alice," Julie said, swerving me to the right.

"Hello." Alice bounced off of the couch, holding out

her hand. She was gorgeous. In her very early twenties from the looks of it, with the same raven hair and green eyes as her brother. "It's so nice to finally meet you! Adrien's been so secretive about you that I was seriously starting to suspect you weren't real. Like I definitely thought he was either dating a dude and being weird about it for some reason, or he was getting sick of all the blind dates that Mom kept insisting—"

"Okay, that's enough, Alice," Adrien cut in. Alice giggled and slumped back into her seat on the couch.

I liked her already; and not just because she'd told Adrien he had rocks for brains.

"And last, but certainly not least, this is Robert, my father," Julie said after throwing her daughter a chiding look.

The older gentleman sitting on the red recliner stood up, using his thick walking cane for support. He was wearing a lime sweater vest that matched his socks, and the lenses of his oval glasses were so thick, they made his eyes look like tiny little almonds. Oh, and he had an African grey perched on his right shoulder.

"Hello," I said. "It's nice to meet you, Robert."

"Ah, call me Gampy. Robert makes me sound like an old man."

I really didn't want to. This was already so awkward. "Gampy it is," I said.

"And this is Maxwell."

The parrot tilted his head at me curiously, then barked.

"Did he just..." Had he been the one barking this whole time? I'd thought for sure there was a dog in here.

"Some days he likes to pretend he's a dog," Alice informed me. "And he gets super sulky if you correct him, so please don't. Comforting him is a whole process and I can't do another forty-eight hours of aggressive Eminem."

"He's got good taste," Gampy claimed, his white mustache twitching with pride. "Gets it from me. Lice is just jealous."

I bit down on my cheek as Adrien laughed.

"*Bark. Rap God. Rap God.*"

"He talks?" I didn't know why I was surprised. He was a parrot, of course he talked.

"We're not playing *Rap God* at dinner," Alice told him. "It's not your music time."

"*You shut up.*"

"Manners, Maxwell," Julie chided as Anthony placed a chuckling kiss on her temple. She was starting to sound slightly exasperated. "We have a guest."

"Tell me to shut up one more time and I'll have you spit-roasted right in your cage you little shit. Bet you taste real good with garlic sauce."

"Alice!" Julie was horrified.

Maxwell's feathers fluffed up, wings spanning. "*You shut up.*"

Alice lunged, but Maxwell was quicker. He jumped with a *squawk*, flapping his wings all the way up to the small chandelier. It started to sway back and forth with the weight of his landing.

Julie had a palm pressed to her forehead, a flush rushing to her cheeks. "I am so sorry. They had a big fight just before you got here, and he's still not calm," she said to me before ordering Maxwell to get down. He wasn't supposed to be up there, and he knew it.

The bird barked at her, refusing to cooperate.

Alice called him a glorified chicken.

He lost his fucking mind.

"I'm hungry. What's for dinner?" Adrien said, leaning a shoulder against the wall with his hands stuffed into his pockets. Like this was just another regular evening with his family.

Maxwell chirped something about his mom making spaghetti, and Alice swatted at the chandelier with a throw pillow. "No quoting *Eight Mile!*"

Maxwell squawked manically, wings flapping as he swayed. There was a chance that the chandelier was going to fall right onto Gampy's head. Yet he stood there calmly, smiling.

"I actually did make spaghetti," Julie admitted, sounding entirely resigned. "There's also a variety of grilled meats and a few vegetarian options. We weren't sure if you had any dietary restrictions, Ria, but I hope there's something you like."

I shook my head, clearing my throat. "That all sounds great. Thank you."

Alice spun on her heel, throwing the weaponized pillow back onto the couch. "Yeah, I'm hungry too. Can we eat?"

Anthony rubbed his hands together. "Yup. Let's go."

Gampy looked up at Maxwell. "Come Maxy, dinner truce is on."

The bird obeyed right away, flying down to his right shoulder.

And then they all started to file out of the room, laughing and chatting. I blinked after them, slightly dumbfounded.

"C'mon." Adrien nudged my shoulder softly and we followed suit, the chandelier continuing to swing behind our backs.

≈

Dinner was turning out to be... kind of epic.

There were a normal number of utensils, the food was incredibly delicious, and the entertainment was unrivaled. It was the opposite of what I'd been expecting.

Maxwell was smarter than most humans, and he knew it too. He and Alice had a hilarious rivalry thing going on, and when they weren't butting heads, it was her and Adrien.

Or *Addrain* as Maxwell called him; also known as *Poopy Shithead*.

Alice cackled when that one came up. "I taught him that when I was six," she claimed proudly, much to her grandfather's amusement and mother's visible dismay.

Adrien started to tell the both of them to go choke on a word that started with a big fat D but was cut off by the end of his grandfather's cane poking into his ribs.

"Dinner truce," Gampy reminded him. Maxwell—who had his own place set at the table beside Gampy—continued to eat his mangoes, completely unbothered by all the ruckus.

"So, Ria, tell us a bit about yourself," Anthony said as soon as his kids had enough food in their mouths to be quiet. "And start from the beginning. Adrien has been annoyingly secretive about you so far. Wouldn't even give us your name until a few days ago."

"Wait, wait," Alice interjected before I could say anything. "Do you wanna hear our theories first? They started to get pretty wild after a while."

"Hush, Alice." Julie *tsk*ed at her daughter. "Ria, darling, ignore her. We've just been so excited to meet you. Adrien had been so secretive about your relationship... and the engagement news was so sudden. Naturally, we're all very curious."

Everyone's eyes seemed to be on me now, anxiously waiting. And I was suddenly very aware of what my left nostril was doing. Because if Adrien had been able to spot my tell, who was to say the rest of his family wouldn't pick up on it as well? I bet he hadn't thought that part through when he'd come up with this brilliant little scheme of his.

You don't have to lie, just... give them as much truth as possible and omit the rest.

I placed my fork down and took a small sip of water. "Um, well, I'm sorry to say that the real thing is probably a lot less interesting than your theories," I started, averting my gaze. They were going to be so incredibly underwhelmed. I wasn't very well-versed in Adrien's dating history (mostly because I'd never cared enough to keep up with the media coverage), but I was willing to bet he'd dated some interesting women. "I was born in Toronto— grew up there. My father was originally from Colombia, my mother from Sicily, and... uh, let's see... I have an older sister..."

And what else? There was Olive and Ben, and... why couldn't I think of anything else to say about myself other than listing off members of my family?

"Oh, come on," Gampy complained when I paused for a beat too long. "That's not it. That's just a brief, incomplete overview of your family. Tell us about *you*, kid. Where'd you go to school? What d'you do for work? Any sports or instruments you play? What're your hobbies? And how many of them include dead bodies?"

Alice snorted. "That was part of his theory."

The air around me had slowly started to thin. I knew this conversation was going to come up, and I thought I was somewhat mentally prepared for it. I wasn't. The last time I'd met a significant other's family was just over ten years ago. And I'd... had a lot more to talk about back then.

I looked down at my half-empty plate, my fingers fiddling with the cloth napkin on my lap. "I actually, uh, didn't go to college," I admitted quietly. "As for work... I'm currently in-between jobs. And as far as sports and instruments are concerned..." I dipped my head a little more in case my nostril was going to disagree with me on this next one. My words were chosen carefully. "I don't currently play anything."

A bout of silence fell over the table as they all started to undoubtedly wonder what Adrien even saw in me. What we had in common.

The answer was, of course, nothing. Adrien and I had absolutely nothing in common. We made no sense as a couple.

"She's being modest."

My fingers stilled in my lap, my blood turning cold. Adrien was going to start lying about my accomplishments to save face and make our relationship more believable. Because it was glaringly obvious that he'd never actually end up with someone like me, and his family knew it.

"She was elected as valedictorian of her class in high school and graduated with a near-perfect GPA."

My head snapped in his direction, my eyebrows leaping.

"She was student council president and has more academic awards than everyone at this table combined. She plays the saxophone, was captain of her school debate and soccer teams, and we run together every morning." He stopped, tapped the table with his index finger. "She also left out a whole lot of volunteer work."

My lips had peeled apart. What the actual hell? How comprehensive was the background check he'd run on me, exactly? Did it include my blood type, too? What shampoo I used?

"Wow," Alice said, crossing her arms as she leaned back. "You really underplayed that."

Had I? Or did I just not like to admit that my most recent and relevant successes dated all the way back to when I was a teenager.

High school was over. I wasn't that person anymore. All those awards were sitting in an unmarked box in Alba's basement, gathering cobwebs and dust. And the only reason they weren't in a garbage dump somewhere was because she'd caught me trying to throw them out and had intervened.

I didn't play soccer anymore, I wasn't a runner, and I hadn't touched a saxophone in ten years. Not to mention... I didn't miss Adrien's careful wording around the valedictorian thing. Just because I'd been *elected* as valedictorian didn't mean I'd made it to the podium.

But how the fuck would he have known that?

I plastered on a smile, but it wavered and drooped too quickly to be convincing. "It was a long time ago. I don't do most of that stuff anymore."

Anthony wiped the corner of his mouth, shaking his head. "Don't diminish your accomplishments like that, kid. It's a bad habit."

I don't have *accomplishments to diminish anymore*, I wanted to say. But I bit it back and gave him a quick nod instead. "That's good advice."

"Is there a reason you didn't go to college?" Gampy

asked as he started to slice off a second piece of mango for Maxwell. The bird barked and chirped, bopping his head excitedly. "My wife was on the admission boards of a few universities over the course of her career. You'd have easily qualified for a bunch of scholarships if it was something you were interested in pursuing."

"No kidding," Alice chimed in, saving me from having to actually answer him. She was still leaning back with her arms crossed, watching me somewhat thoughtfully. Then she glanced over to Adrien. "Hey, you know who she sort of reminds me of? This conversation just unlocked a memory I forgot I had."

Adrien shook his head. "Doesn't matter. Should we get started on dessert?"

But Alice was still watching me, her eyes starting to narrow like she was trying to recall the details of her foggy memory. "No. Seriously. What high school did you go to, Ria?"

"I don't think we would have overlapped," I said with a small smile.

She cocked her head. "How old are you?"

"Alice," Adrien said in warning.

"I don't mind," I said, shrugging. I'd never been shy about revealing my age. "I'm twenty-eight."

She blinked, the fingers wrapped around her left arm twitching like she was counting. Then her hand suddenly froze, her eyes flared, her lips popped open, and she sucked in a sharp breath.

"Alice, can I talk to you in the other room for just a sec?" Adrien was already rounding the table.

"Holy shit. No wa—"

"Excuse us." He grabbed her arm and practically

dragged her out of the room while we all watched, confused.

"I can't believe how many times I've had to apologize for my children's behavior today," Julie said with a sheepish smile.

A door banged shut somewhere in the house.

"Ah, she'll be joining the family soon enough. She might as well get used to it," Gampy said. "It's only going to get worse from here," he promised me with a wink.

I smiled back at him politely. I didn't mind this at all. It kind of reminded me of our family dinners when I was a kid, with Alba, our dad, and our abuela. I missed it.

"Speaking of which, have you decided on a date or location for the wedding?" Julie asked.

"We haven't really talked about it yet," I said, scratching at my nose. Technically not a lie. We *hadn't* talked about those things.

"We'd love to host you here," Anthony offered softly. "If that's something you'd be interested in. No pressure."

"Even if it's just the engagement party," Julie went on. "Or if you need any help with the planning at all, you just let me know."

And that was the exact moment the guilt began to set in. It was in the looks they were giving me. The way they were clutching onto each other's fingers on the table.

Like this was *it*.

Like it was finally happening.

Their son was finally getting married, and they couldn't wait.

And I was the piece of shit sitting here, lying to them about what was supposed to be one of the happiest events of their lives.

I tried to swallow back the barbed clump of shame

knotting in my throat, but it didn't seem to budge. "That's so kind of you to offer. I'll discuss it with Adrien, and we'll let you know."

They looked pleased with that answer, exchanging an excited look that pulled uncomfortably at my chest. I really hoped Adrien had a plan for delivering the breakup news to them. And I hoped he'd at least be gentle about it.

He and Alice walked back into the dining room less than a minute later with Adrien in the lead. He looked calm and collected, as though absolutely nothing out of the ordinary had happened. His sister on the other hand looked like a guilty six-year-old who had a secret she was trying her absolute best to hide.

"Sorry about that," Adrien said as he took a seat beside me.

Alice remained silent and kept her eyes down.

"What was that all about?" Gampy asked, shoving at the bridge of his thick glasses.

"Nothing," Adrien said coolly.

Maxwell chose that moment to flawlessly spit out a string of Eminem lyrics about Shady being back, and Gampy snorted, scratching the bird's neck affectionately.

Adrien used the opportunity to smoothly divert the conversation to the arrival of additional family members later this week. Apparently, we were all here to celebrate Julie and Anthony's 35th anniversary. There was a big party planned and everything, none of which he'd bothered to mention to me before we'd come downstairs.

I tried to keep up with the conversation as best I could, but I was a little too aware of all the glances Alice kept throwing my way. Though every time I caught her eyes, she immediately looked away.

She knew. About me being Waldo.

17

I HAD A PROBLEM.

It was not a small problem.

My hands were on my hips, my lips clamped as I stared down at my open suitcase in disbelief. Three unopened boxes of tampons, two crumpled T-shirts, a pair of yoga pants, a handful of hair elastics, a small pouch of tuna-flavored cat treats, an unidentified remote controller (with the batteries taken out for some reason), my passport, and an empty bottle of wine. That was what drunk Ria had packed for this trip. Cat treats and an empty bottle of wine in lieu of underwear.

Oh, and I had nothing to wear to the big party that Adrien had failed to warn me about before we arrived.

Fuck my mess of a life.

I sauntered out of my designated closet with my hands stuffed into the back pockets of my jeans. Adrien was sitting at the oak desk again, working away on his laptop.

"Hey, any chance there's a mall close by here some-where?" I asked him, trying to sound as nonchalant as possible.

He didn't look up. "There's a big one ten minutes away. Driving."

"And what are the chances you'd be cool with me slipping away for a couple of hours tomorrow?"

"Do whatever you want, just be back here in time for dinner. I'm going to be working most of the day anyway."

Huh. Well, that was easy.

"And, um, we haven't discussed sleeping arrangements yet," I said more quietly. Just in case anyone was outside.

That got his full attention. "Didn't we already agree I'd sleep in the bathtub?"

I rolled my eyes. "I'm not going to make you sleep in a bathtub for ten nights, Adrien. Unlike you, I actually have a conscience."

He snorted. "Thanks. I'll take the floor then, on the right side of the bed. You can sleep on the left. That way you won't be tempted to stomp on my face in the middle of the night and pretend like it was an accident."

I bit my bottom lip to stop the smile from forming. He'd plucked that one straight out of my revenge fantasies. "I'm good with that."

"Great."

"Cool."

It was a natural end to the conversation, but I lingered. "And what was with you and Alice at dinner? Anything I should know?"

"It's nothing," he said after a short pause.

I crossed my arms, deciding to give him one more chance to tell me the truth. "Are you sure?"

This pause was even longer.

"You're staring, Cloutier," I said.

He didn't crack a smile. "Can I ask you something?"

"That depends. What is it?"

He shut his laptop. "Why didn't you go to college?"

That had been at the bottom of the list of things I'd been expecting him to ask. It was a good thing I had my answer locked, loaded, and practiced to perfection.

I shrugged. "I didn't want to."

I'd said it so many times that it didn't even feel like a lie anymore. Almost like I'd convinced myself that it was true.

"Bullshit."

I tensed slightly, my arms pressing tighter to my chest. "Not everyone can afford a university education, Adrien."

"But you could have," he countered, standing up. "I've seen your transcripts, and I know about all the extracurriculars. Soccer, student council, jazz band, debate, prelaw programs, precollege this and that, and you *still* somehow managed a near-perfect GPA."

I wasn't breathing anymore. I just stood there, trying to look and act as casual as possible as Adrien approached. He stopped a couple feet away and crossed his corded arms, mirroring me.

"Not everyone can afford a college education, but not everyone is you," he said.

I shrugged. "I don't know how playing in a jazz band was supposed to help me pay off seventy-thousand dollars' worth of tuition fees."

The right corner of his mouth hooked up. "And you do that thing."

"What thing?"

"That thing where you pretend like you don't know what people are talking about. Like you're a hell of a lot less intelligent than you actually are."

I willed my nostrils to stay still. "I don't do that."

His mouth twitched. "You're really going to stand there

and pretend like you couldn't have gotten a full ride to half the universities in the country?"

I took a step back and calmly pressed my shoulders to the wall behind me. "And you're really going to stand there and pretend like you don't know about my record? Any half-decent background check would have flagged it, and you hinted at it in your office, remember?"

Adrien's dark gaze sharpened, and he took another step forward. I had to crane my neck to maintain eye contact. "It doesn't quite add up."

"Is there a reason you've been so intent on invading my personal space today?" I asked him, trying not to inhale too deeply.

"You don't like it?"

"No." It was automatic, I didn't even think to hide my nose.

His dimples flashed, and something in my chest skipped. "Liar."

"Do you *want* me to like it? What's with the shit-eating grin?"

He shrugged. "Makes the pretending easier if you're attracted to me."

"I'm not attracted to you."

He let out a low chuckle. "It's worse when you try to stop it from happening."

I was going to grab the stapler off his desk and staple my nose shut the second this conversation was over.

"And I'd get used to the proximity if I were you," he went on. "Engaged couples don't constantly stand four feet apart."

"Can't we just be one of those couples that respect each other's personal bubbles and don't engage in PDA?"

"No."

"You didn't even consider it."

"And I'm not going to."

I chewed on my bottom lip. "Why am I really here?"

Adrien's eyes dipped down to my mouth for a split second, his expression entirely blank as he said, "I don't know. Why didn't you go to college?"

"I already told you I didn't want to go. Didn't think it was worth it," I insisted, ignoring the tug in my chest. "And you know we've been talking for almost ten minutes without actually saying anything?"

Adrien took a step back. "You're right, this is kind of a waste of time. I'm going to take a shower. The left one in case you give into temptation and want to take a peek."

And then the fucker *winked at me*.

I flipped him off and he laughed like my middle finger was the funniest fucking thing he'd seen all day. I didn't know how or why we'd veered into this line of teasing, but I hated it with every fiber of my being.

~

I barely slept.

Adrien didn't snore, he didn't toss or turn or talk in his sleep. He was mostly silent and still, his breathing quiet and even. But it was a mental thing. Just knowing that he was sleeping in the same room made me feel... restless.

Plus, I'd been weirdly agitated since dinner last night, though I couldn't quite figure out why.

When his silent alarm went off at 4:30, I was wide awake, staring up at the dark ceiling.

I sat up. "Are you going for your run?"

He lurched back and almost tripped. "Jesus fucking Christ. I thought you were sleeping."

"Nope."

"You look like the girl from *The Ring* with your hair down like that. Scared the shit out of me."

"That might be the rudest fucking thing anyone's ever said to me this early in the morning."

"You sound like her too," he grumbled.

"That's the second rudest thing anyone's ever said to me this early in the morning."

He sighed and shoved a hand through his hair. "Yeah, I'm going for a run. Sorry, I didn't think my alarm would wake you."

It hadn't. But before I could respond to him, my attention snagged on the massive bulge tenting his sweats, and my whole brain shut down.

"Take a picture, Sanchez. It'll last longer."

Fuck. I tore my eyes away and forced them back up to the ceiling, genuinely grateful that it was too dark in here for him to see the crimson creeping up my neck. I should have just pretended like I was asleep.

Adrien chuckled and mumbled something incoherent under his breath. Three seconds later, the bathroom door clicked shut.

Well, that was... kind of humiliating.

I sat there for a few minutes with my heart hammering and my skin buzzing, until I decided that I was too wound up to sit still for another two hours. So, I pushed myself out of bed and gathered my hair into my usual ponytail. I hadn't packed a sports bra, but at least I had the yoga pants (that I'd worn to bed, because drunk me apparently didn't think pajamas were important).

"What are you doing?"

Adrien was already in his running gear when he stepped back into the bedroom—a long-sleeve running shirt and matching black trousers. It took active effort for my eyes to stay on his face and not flick down.

I placed my hands on my hips and shrugged. "I kind of feel like going on a run."

"You're wanting to join me on my run?"

My head tilted toward one shoulder. "Is that what I said?"

I could see the amusement begin to worm its way over his features. "Did you bring your mace with you?"

The question made me stop short, horror-stricken. But no. No, if I'd hidden it anywhere in my bag or suitcase, airport security would have probably arrested me or something. So it was probably at home.

I made a mental note to double-check anyway.

"What's that look?" Adrien asked, eyeing me.

"Nothing. Let's go." I turned on my heel and walked out of the room. I didn't have my running shoes with me, but my sneakers would do.

"Oh, so we *are* running together."

"What? No. I was talking to myself," I said quietly. "Go away."

"I kind of need to go this way to get to the front door."

I gave him a side eye and put four feet of distance between our bodies. There. Now we were just two random people walking in the same general direction.

It was still mostly dark when we stepped outside, but the air was warmer than I'd been expecting. And it smelled significantly better than Toronto ever did.

I lingered on the stone steps, listening to the soft chirps of small birds and crickets as I waited for Adrien to start moving.

"What are you doing now?" he asked, coming up behind me.

"Waiting for you to start running so I can go in the opposite direction," I told him, stepping away. No one was watching us. He didn't need to be inside my bubble, coating all my fresh air in soap and toothpaste and spicy cedar or whatever. I didn't understand how he managed to smell so good all the time.

I probably should have brushed my teeth first or, at the very least, used the washroom.

The tented sweatpants thing had really thrown me off.

Not that I was still thinking about it.

My skin was buzzing again, my muscles jittery. Adrien didn't move right away, so I jogged down the steps, flipped a mental coin, and turned left.

Two breaths later, his steps were pounding the gravel behind me. I veered left again, he followed. I went to the right, same thing.

"Stop following me," I demanded.

"I'm not following you. This was the direction I was going to run in."

Fuck's sake.

I stopped, turned around, and started to jog the other way. Guess what he did.

"On second thought," he said as he casually fell into step beside me, "we did tell my parents that we run together every morning so it might come across as some-what suspicious if we split up."

"*We* didn't tell them anything of the sort. It was all you."

"I was trying to help you."

"Uh, no. You were trying to help yourself," I argued. My feet were starting to move quicker. I had no idea where all this energy was coming from, but I was just so... *agitated*. The feeling had been gnawing at my insides since dinner. "How embarrassing it must be for you to bring someone home that isn't highly educated and accomplished and... I mean, I get it. You and I don't exactly make sense, and you wanted to save face."

"What? That's not what I was doing."

"Bullshit." I picked up my pace.

"Slow down."

"Fuck off."

A low, frustrated growl rumbled out of his throat. "What's the matter with you? Can't you be civil for two fucking seconds?"

I took a sharp right turn. He didn't falter.

"With you? No."

"Why? What the fuck did I do to you?"

That one made me stop right in my tracks. "Is that a serious question?"

Adrien slowed to a stop, hands going on his hips as he turned to face me. He was more out of breath than I was for once, but I didn't think it had anything to do with the physical exertion. "Yeah, Sanchez. It's a serious question. Why the hell do you hate me so much?"

"Uh, let's see. You fired my sister for something that wasn't her fault, then you made me pick a bunch of glitter out of dirt—" I cut off when he started shaking his head.

"No. I mean before all that. You weren't sorry about what happened on Halloween, or about what you did to my office. In fact, you laughed like you thought I deserved it. Why?"

I pushed a frustrated breath out of my nose and rolled my lips. "We don't need to have this conversation now."

Another shake of his head. "No. We're talking about it."

"Why does it even matter?" I asked him. "We've got

one more week of having to put up with each other, and then that's it. Not like we'll ever see each other again."

Unless him and Jamie ended up dating. Which... honestly just the thought of the two of them together made me queasy again.

"Just tell me the reason," he pressed, stepping forward.

I wasn't sure what to do with my hands, so I balled them into fists and crossed my arms. "I don't know. You just... you weren't exactly the best boss to my sister. And it was kind of frustrating for me to sit back and watch."

He studied me for a few breaths, then nodded. "Okay. Why do you think that? Why was I such a terrible boss?"

"Well, for one, she missed her daughter's sixth birthday party because of you."

His dark eyes narrowed at me. "What are you talking about?"

"Olive's birthday celebration. Alba was supposed to get off work at two to come to the theme park with us, but you pulled her into a last-minute meeting. Something about a construction mishap something-something in Quebec. Everything was on metaphorical fire, and she needed to stay."

A solid ten seconds ticked by with him silently staring at me. And then he said, "Alba has a six-year-old daughter?"

Oh my *actual* fucking god. "Dude."

"I don't think she ever told me."

"Do you hear yourself? How's that even possible?"

He frowned to himself.

I rolled my eyes and walked right past him. "That's about all the explanation you need as to why I think you're a shit boss. Not to mention the long hours, the weekends, and all the holidays you forced her to work."

"I didn't *force* her to do anything. Your sister was made fully aware of the job requirements before she was hired. She knew the hours, she knew how demanding it would be, and she was well compensated for it. I didn't sugarcoat anything."

"I never said you did." We fell into another light jog. "But making her miss her daughter's birthday isn't just demanding, it's outright cruel. I was the one that had to tell Olive that her mom wasn't coming. And I was the one that had to comfort her when she cried."

Ben had been too busy trying to reach Alba again. Probably to argue.

"I didn't know," Adrien insisted.

"Well maybe you should have," I huffed. "Alba worked for you for *four years*, Adrien. If she didn't feel like she could come to you with a request as simple as that. And how the hell could you not know about Olive? When she told you she was pregnant, didn't you think to ask if it was the first one?"

After a long pause, he said, "It's not... that simple, Ria."

Bullshit.

Neither of us said anything else as our feet fell into their usual rhythm, Adrien leading the way this time. I didn't argue or veer off, just followed him through the grounds and down to a small lake. We stopped there just as the sun was starting to come up.

My lungs still burned, my muscles still ached, and my body had protested against every step taken, but it seemed just a little bit easier this time. And it almost felt good now that it was over.

I sighed and sunk down onto the grass, watching the sky bleed soft shades of purple and pink with the impending sunrise. The view was incredible, the morning air was dewy and crisp, and the birds were still chirping sleepily.

It was so calming and perfect that it almost made all the pain worth it. Or maybe the cardio endorphins were starting to set in.

Either way, I was so engrossed in watching the water and the sky, and listening to the crickets and the birds, that I didn't notice Adrien approaching until he was about a foot away.

He sat down beside me and dusted off his hands, trying to rid them of the wet grass. It was going to be all over our damp butts when we got up.

"I'm sorry," he said after a while. "And I'll talk to Alba too. I... really, Sanchez, I didn't know. We only ever talked about work stuff."

I peeled my attention away from the soft warmth of the sunrise and met his gaze. His eyes really were an unbelievable shade of wild green, and their surrounding lashes were so thick, I wondered how he could blink without getting them all tangled up.

"You're staring again," he said quietly, a smug smile tilting the side of his mediocre mouth.

Okay, you know what? "You keep saying that like you're not staring right back."

The little smirk expanded into a full-blown dimple-fest, and it made my blood pressure spike so hard I had to look away.

"And now you're blushing," he teased.

"I'm not blushing. I'm turning red because looking at your face infuriates me."

He was sitting on my right side and couldn't see my left nostril. Not that I was lying.

He let out a dark chuckle. "Is that what it is?"

"Yes."

"Which part angers you, exactly? Is it my mediocre mouth or my lopsided dimples?"

"Both. And your eyes are weird."

He snorted.

I looked down at the damp grass my fingers were mindlessly playing with. "I'm sorry too," I said quietly. "About Halloween. And about the glitter. I didn't... mean for it all to blow up the way it did... with the investors and the media. It was a lot."

I could feel him watching me as I struggled through the insufficient apology. And I thought he was going to push for more, but instead he nudged my knee with his knuckles.

"I think we should call a temporary truce," he said. "Just for the duration of this trip."

I eyed him suspiciously. "What does that mean?"

"Do you not know what a truce is, Sanchez?"

"Bye." I started to get up.

Adrien chuckled as he grabbed my arm and pulled me back down. His sizable hand circled my upper arm with ease, which made me think of another unexpectedly large part of his anatomy. I could feel myself tinting pink all over again. With anger, obviously.

"I'm being serious. What if we started over? We don't have to be friends or anything, but I'd like for us to at least be civil."

I thought about it. "And I'd have to be nice to you? Like all the time? Not just in front of your family?"

A flash of a dimple. "That would be ideal, but I won't hold you to it. I'm just asking for us to... take the aggression and animosity down a few notches. Mostly because

I'm ninety percent sure that if we keep going down this path, you're going to kill me in my sleep on night three."

I sighed. "And then I'll have to go to court and stand trial. It'll be a whole thing. Lawyers are expensive as hell too."

"The life sentence will also be a bummer," Adrien agreed. "I bet they don't have any cinna*man-bun* or horny blue alien books in there. I bet it's all highbrow literary fiction."

He knew full well it was cinnamon rolls and blue aliens *with* horns, and I refused to acknowledge the wordplay.

"A nightmare," I said.

"They'll probably make you read it as punishment. And then you'll have to write five thousand words on all the motifs and shit you found."

I cut him another brief glance. "Can I be honest with you about something real quick? I don't fully know what a motif is. And I got an A in AP English."

Two unaligned dimples. A chuckle.

"Do you?" I asked, breaking out into my own reluctant smile.

"No fucking idea."

I wedged my bottom lip between my teeth and looked away, trying not to laugh. I felt much less agitated than I had earlier, and lighter too. I wasn't sure if it was the run, the nature, or just getting some of the Alba stuff off my chest. Either way... maybe a truce wouldn't be a bad idea. For my own sanity if nothing else.

"So, what do you think?" Adrien eventually asked. "Temporary truce?"

I inhaled deeply, tilting my head up to the sky. "I'll think about it."

18

JAMIE

Ariana Francesca Sanchez.

Are you fucking kidding me with this note?

"Brb like 666 days (rough estimation). Satan's dragging me down to hell. Sorry forgot to mention last night. xx R"

First of all, "xx R" sounds porny and you know it. Second of all, it's been 48 hours and I've received 0 calls, 0 texts, 0 explanation.

And wdym "forgot to mention?" We drunk watched 2 Bridget Jones movies together that night! LITERALLY NOTHING HAPPENS IN THEM. THEY JUST BABBLE BRITISHLY AT EACH OTHER FOR 90 MINUTES. YOU HAD PLENTY OF TIME .!!

And is that why you pulled out your suitcase in the middle of the second movie and started shoving those jumbo tampon boxes into it? Because I know you like to anger organize sometimes and I definitely thought that's what that was

We got those tampons to share, btw

HELLO???

ARE YOU DEAD

No I wish. Tied up brb

What like literally or figuratively

Both

Idk what that means. How sexy are we talking?

-100/10

Are you with Adrien?

No. I'm with his mom and sister. Currently trying on a dress with way too many straps. I'm stuck

...

?????

Same.

Can you call me?

Give me 5 mins gotta untangle and excuse myself to the washroom

～

JAMIE PICKED up on the first ring. "I'm so fucking mad at you, it's not even funny."

"In my defense, your future husband is a loose-marbled lunatic."

"Where are you right now?" she asked, lowering her voice to match my whisper.

"Victoria, BC," I answered, reaching for a small leather stool tucked under the vanity. This was hands down the nicest mall bathroom I'd ever been in. "More specifically, I'm at a private department store with Adrien's mom and sister. Did you know those were a thing? Because I didn't."

"What are you talking about? Why are you in BC?"

"Why are you whispering?"

"Why are *you* whispering?"

"Because there's a bathroom attendant outside and I don't want them to overhear," I said quietly.

"Oh. Okay." Her voice went back to normal. "Can you start from the beginning, please? I'm really confused and somewhat concerned."

I sighed, sneaking a glance at the door. "You're absolutely not going to believe any of this."

There was a rustling of thick plastic on the other end, followed by a little yowl. *Feed me, human*, Toebeans was demanding.

"Adrien didn't kidnap you or anything, did he?" Jamie asked.

"Technically, no. I got on the plane willingly. Although I probably wouldn't have if I'd known why he wanted to drag me over here."

The familiar clinks and clanks of cat food hitting metal filled my ear as I talked, and I could imagine Jamie taking a seat at the kitchen table beside Toebeans. He liked it when we watched him eat. The internet said it was a vulnerability thing. He trusted us to watch his back while he was busy munching.

I already missed the slutty little fiend.

"And what's his reason? Why are you there?" she asked.

"He wants me to pretend to be his fiancée in front of his family."

Silence.

And then, "What?"

"He wants me to pretend to be his fiancée in front of his family."

"Are you fucking with me?"

"No."

"Is he fucking with you?"

I thought about it. "Probably."

"Wait. Do you... is there a ring and everything?"

"Yes, and it's the size of Maguire's biggest toe bean. Same shape, too."

"I don't get it. Why does he need you to pretend to be his fiancée?"

I worried the inside of my cheek. "He says it's to get out of all the blind dates his mom's been setting him up on."

Jamie waited for a few seconds before nudging me forward. "You don't sound like you believe him."

"I don't," I admitted. "You know when you've got... like a gut feeling that you're being lied to?"

She hummed.

"But I'm not sure if he's actually lying or if he's just omitting information. Also, there was a little incident last night with his sister and she's... I swear she's avoiding eye contact with me today. At first, I thought she knew about the Halloween incident, but I'm starting to doubt it. She's not acting angry, just awkward. It's weird."

"And you're at a department store with her now?"

"Yeah. Drunk packing for this trip was a terrible idea.

If you're missing a remote for anything in the apartment, I have it."

Jamie chortled quietly as I double-checked the time. I'd be okay for a few more minutes but anything beyond that might prompt someone to check on me.

"Anyway. I needed to go shopping for necessities and made the mistake of mentioning it over breakfast. His mom immediately insisted on turning it into a girl's day and wouldn't take no for an answer. It's supposed to be a bonding thing. I've never been so stressed out in my life."

"This is so fucking weird," Jamie said.

"I know. And instead of going to the mall, his mom dragged me to this... it's like a private, invitation-only department store. It's suffocatingly fancy, *none* of the tags have any prices on them, the personal shopper I've been assigned keeps following me around like he's imprinted on me, and Julie's been insisting on covering the whole shopping trip because she's 'more than happy to spoil her new daughter-in-law.' I'm going to die of a guilt-induced heart attack."

"Julie's the mom?"

"Yeah, Alice is the sister. Oh, and we have spa appointments lined up after this. Massages, facials, nails, hair. And every time I try to say no, Julie acts like I've stabbed her in the heart. Is this what it's like to have a mom? My back's been sweating nonstop for two hours. I hate it here. There's too much guilt."

The most annoying part? I *still* didn't have Adrien's stupid number, so I couldn't text him about how out of hand this whole thing had gotten. Julie had already sent her driver home to drop off the first massive batch of bags we'd collected.

Because the car was already full... mostly with stuff she'd bought for me.

I felt like throwing up.

"Okay, uh, wow. Anything I can do?"

"Can you tell me how to get out of here unscathed?" I pleaded desperately.

"No... this one's tough. She obviously really wants to bond with you. I'd maybe keep the tags on all the clothes and have Adrien return them after... I don't know, I'm assuming there's an expiry date on this fake engagement thing?"

Okay. Yes. *Yes*. I'd just keep all the tags on! Problem solved! (Kind of. Not really. But it was better than nothing.)

I opened my mouth to praise Jamie's brilliance but was interrupted by a soft knock on the door.

"Ria? You've been in there for a long time. Is everything okay?"

I tensed at the sound of Julie's voice, my insides twisting. *Shit.* "Yes, sorry! Be out in just a second!" I called before lowering my voice again. "Jamie, I gotta go. I'll call you later."

"Was that her?"

"Yeah, I gotta go."

"Promise me you'll actually call me later."

"Promise."

I hung up and took three deep breaths before stepping back out to the private suite. I plastered a smile onto my face and sat down next to Alice on the couch, snatching a champagne flute off the table as Luke—my personal shopper—dragged yet another rack of dresses into the room for me to try on.

Maybe the bubbles would help drown out the guilt.

Was I drunk? Yes.

Did I regret it? Absolutely not.

But also, a little. The ground was starting to twist and slide a bit, and it was making me dizzy.

The plan had been to get just tipsy enough that it took the edge off all the shame and guilt I was feeling. I just hadn't expected said edge to be so relentlessly sharp. And it got progressively worse as the day went on.

I lost count of how many shopping bags we racked up and stopped trying to say *no* about halfway—and three champagne flutes—into the four-hour appointment. There was no point. Julie would wave her hand and tell Luke to "add it to Ria's pile. She's just being shy."

The lingerie selection was the worst part. I had to chug two full glasses to get through the digital catalog Luke had slipped onto my lap. Finally, after scrolling through sixty-four pages of silk and skimpy lace without having selected a single item, he suggested going with the *Autumn Honeymoon Collection*. I didn't know what the collection entailed, but I was more than ready for the experience to be over, so I agreed and put the tablet aside.

The spa was located one floor above the department store. It was also just as ridiculously exclusive, and just as secretive about its pricing. There wasn't a single number listed beside any of their services.

We were greeted by warm, ambient lighting, soft color palettes, subtle wafts of lavender and mint, and more champagne as soon as we walked through the glass doors. And I slowly started to lose track of... everything.

The alcohol was fizzing underneath my skin, warming and numbing me enough that I began to float through the experience instead of resisting it. There was the massage and the mud bath and the facial, the healthy lunch filled with light chatter, laughter, and (more) bubbles, and finally the hair, brow, and nail appointments.

The sky was dark by the time we finally left, Alice wasn't trying to avoid talking to me anymore, and all my limbs felt like soft goo.

The guilt was going to come back tomorrow with a vengeance, I knew it would, but I was too relaxed and drunk to care anymore. All I wanted to do was float on this fluffy, careless cloud of bliss forever.

"It sounds like the boys are out back," Julie said softly when we entered the house. I didn't know where all our shopping bags had gone, but I hadn't seen them since we left the department store. "Come on." She reached for my hand, wrapping her smooth fingers around my palm.

I liked Julie. She was kind and generous and soft, and she spoke about her kids with so much love that it made my chest squeeze in a strange, longing way. She'd gushed about Adrien over lunch. About how proud of him she was, how hard he always worked, how happy she was that we'd found each other.

"I was starting to worry about him," she'd said, tearing up. "Between the stress of his job, all the bad press, and everything that happened last year... Well, it doesn't matter now, does it? I'm just so glad you're here, and I'm so happy he's finally happy."

Tomorrow. The guilt was going to suffocate me tomorrow.

"I'm gonna shower then head to bed," Alice said, stretching her arms all the way above her head. "I'm tired from all that relaxing. Night, Mama."

"Night, sweetheart." Julie gave her daughter a warm kiss on the cheek, and my heart squeezed in that peculiar way again. The new way I wasn't familiar with.

"Night, Ria."

"Goodnight," I replied softly, offering her a small smile.

Then I was being guided through the foyer, the living room, the kitchen. All the way to the sliding doors that led to the backyard. The large, lavishly decorated patio was illuminated by a mixture of soft lighting and an outdoor fire pit. And it was just so... *warm*.

"There you are," Anthony said, standing up. He *tsk*ed playfully at his wife as she released my hand and floated straight into his arms. "Our dinner reservation was over an hour ago," he chided softly, smiling into her hair.

Another pang.

"We got carried away," Julie replied. "I'm sorry."

"Don't be. You had fun?"

She hummed. He smiled.

Pang.

And I was so busy watching their interaction that I didn't notice Adrien until he stood up. I blinked, my lazy gaze refocusing. He was wearing a pale blue shirt with the top buttons undone, his sleeves rolled up to reveal those tanned, corded forearms. A watch. Belt. slacks.

His eyes were black in this lighting. And they seemed stuck. Like time had frozen for them midblink. His mouth was parted ever so slightly, and it... they weren't mediocre. His lips. I'd lied.

Pang.

This one was different. This one didn't squeeze my chest with yearning; it kicked and swooshed with something much more unsettling.

You're staring again, Sanchez.

The musical sound of soft laughter plucked me out of my drunken daze. "It suits her, huh?" There was a smile in Julie's voice.

Hmm?

"Your hair looks very nice, Ria," Anthony agreed kindly.

Oh, right, yeah. My hair was a lot shorter now, trimmed down to my collarbones. It was also lighter—both in color and weight—fading from my natural chocolate brown to a honey blonde. I ran my fingers through the strands again and almost purred. Feathers and liquid silk.

"Addy," Julie nudged, "what do you think?"

Adrien's throat worked and he gave me a curt, professional nod. "Looks nice."

"Thanks," I muttered as his parents looked between us expectantly.

This wasn't how couples greeted each other. They

didn't stand awkwardly apart, staring at one another from ten feet away. Even my alcohol-riddled brain knew that. But I couldn't move, couldn't get my body to initiate any physical contact. Because just the thought of slipping into Adrien's arms ignited a hurricane of flutters in my stomach that I couldn't make sense of.

Was it fear of rejection? Did I think he'd push me away in front of his parents if I tried to hug him? And why did it matter? Who cared if he was disgusted by the idea of touching me?

Adrien held out an inviting hand, his brows flicking once. We were being weird. This was awkward. I needed to move.

I stepped forward and slipped my fingers into his large palm, and then he took over. His warm hand curled around mine and he gently pulled me to him. My cheek pressed to his hard chest, my arm snaking around his waist. He felt... broad. And warm. Pleasant.

"Your hair does look very... nice," he whispered. The words were too quiet for our small audience to overhear.

Swoosh.

I needed another drink. Or maybe it was the alcohol that was causing the fresh bout of swirls and unsteadiness.

"Breathe, Sanchez. It's just a hug. It won't kill you." The light chuckle in his voice was laced with something I couldn't quite pinpoint.

I released the lungful of air I'd been holding, but that turned out to be a mistake because it meant that I had to inhale again. I really hated how good he smelled.

And before my greedy lungs could defy my strict orders against another inhale, Adrien peeled himself away. He didn't let go of my hand, though, and used his grip to guide me to the couch. We sat down, arms touching, knees brushing, and when I tried to slip my hand out of his grip, he gently squeezed it. *No.*

"Did you already have dinner?" Anthony asked. "I can fire up the grill if you want."

Julie shook her head. "We were talking about ordering pizza if that works for you guys."

"Sounds good. Shall we open a bottle of Pinot while we wait?"

"We spent the whole day drinking champagne," Julie informed him happily.

Anthony kissed his wife's plump, smiling cheek. "Good. Then you're already warmed up, and we can dive into the hard stuff."

She giggled and off they went, fingers intertwined. I watched as their backs retreated into the house, a little awe-struck. I wondered what it would feel like to find your person. A best friend. Someone who loved you and cared for you in such a—

"Sanchez?"

My gaze snapped to Adrien's dark eyes and my heart kicked again.

His face spread into a slow grin, his lopsided dimples popping. Then he brought a hand to my chin and very gently pushed up, until my mouth closed. I hadn't even realized it was hanging open.

"How drunk are you right now?" he teased.

"Um... just a bit."

His chuckle was deep and dark, and it sent another swoop through my stomach. I didn't like that feeling. It wasn't supposed to happen.

"You had a good time?" he asked.

I sucked in a deep breath. "Well, there's around fifty shopping bags worth of dresses and clothes and shoes that you're going to have to return once we, uh, break up or whatever. I tried to stop her, I swear, but I'm not used to mom-guilt."

Mine had left when I was two. It wasn't something I'd ever needed to worry about.

"Relax. It's fine."

"No. You don't understand. We went to this, like, private department store, and *none* of the tags had prices on them."

"I know. It's fine."

He still wasn't understanding. "Adrien. We were in a VIP suite and our assigned private shoppers brought the clothes *to us*."

His dimples dipped deeper, amusement flittering across his features. He hummed.

"It's not funny. I feel terrible."

"Really? Because you looked very relaxed when you walked in here five minutes ago."

"Yeah, well, my masseur's hands were pure magic," I admitted. "He was also funny. Made me laugh a few times and it helped. Plus, all the champagne. I expect the guilt will hit me full force tomorrow once I'm sober and my muscles are back to a solid state."

Adrien's smile waned slightly. "What was his name?"

"Whose name?"

"Your masseur."

Oh. "His name was Lee. He gave me his card if you want." And it wasn't until I tried reaching into my pocket that I realized we were still holding hands.

I blinked down at where our fingers were leisurely

intertwined on my lap, and my brain just sort of... fizzled. But before I could get it to work again, something weird happened. Adrien's thumb moved across the back of my hand in a tender stroke, and I remained fully entranced as visible gooseflesh spread over my forearms.

Five full seconds passed, and then he did it again. A spark shot up my spine, spreading to my cheeks.

What is he doing?

What are you *doing? Pull your hand back.*

I didn't know whether it was all the alcohol or the fact that my muscles were too liquid to take orders from my brain, but instead of pulling away, my thumb moved. One stroke across the side of Adrien's large hand.

The hairs on his arm rose in response, almost in slow motion, and something subtle in his breathing changed.

But then he slid his hand out of my grip and cleared his throat. "We're good. They've stopped looking."

My mind stumbled a step before reality hit. Adrien's eyes were on the large window looking into the kitchen. His parents were there, at the bar, pouring amber liquid into crystal tumblers.

Heat crept up my chest, expanding over my neck and shoulders. Of course. Of course, that was... what that was.

I blinked, trying to clear my head. Apparently, bubbly alcohol really messed with me.

"Do you think they believe it?" I asked Adrien quietly, crossing my fists over my chest.

"Believe what? Us?"

"Yeah. Do you think they believe we're actually engaged?"

He shrugged. "We haven't given them a reason not to. Not yet, anyway. So why would they doubt it?"

I shifted an inch away from him. "Because we couldn't

be less believable as a couple if we tried. We don't make any sense."

A small pause. "And why's that, Sanchez?"

I looked up to find him watching me curiously with his head tilted. I lifted a shoulder, trying very hard to ignore the fact that my hand was still tingling where his thumb had brushed it. "We just don't. There's no way you and I would end up together in real life. And I don't think I'm the only one who realizes it."

Adrien's brows were starting to scrunch. "Why?"

"Stop asking *why*. It's just... we're too different, I think. Our lives are too different. There's no... I don't know, Adrien. It's a chemistry thing."

The scowl dug deeper. "A *chemistry* thing."

"Yeah."

He brought his arm up to rest behind me on the couch, and the movement sent another waft of his clean scent my way. "What does that mean?"

My fists were tight against my thumping chest. He was starting to lean a little too close, his narrowing eyes flicking to my nose every time I opened my mouth.

"Uh... I don't know. It's hard to explain. Some people have very obvious chemistry. You and I don't."

For the next twelve seconds (I counted), the only sounds echoing through the backyard were the soft crackles of the fire pit and the hiss of the cool night breeze weaving through leaves.

"I just mean..." I started, mostly because I was starting to vibrate against the intensity of his stare. "If you look at your dating history, for example, how many of the women you've been in serious relationships with were like me? In terms of their lifestyle and jobs and looks and personality and—"

"None."

My mouth stuttered. "Well then, there you go."

His dark gaze meandered over my features, slowly, before coming back up to my eyes. "And what about you, Sanchez? I'm really all that different from the men you've dated in the past?"

"You know, you say my name a lot more than is necessary. There's no one else here. I'm not confused about who you're talking to."

The right side of his mouth curved up. "You don't like it?"

"It's just not necessary."

"So you *do* like it."

"That's not what I said."

"And your new plan is to avoid answering my questions directly, so your nostril won't give you away?"

"Just until my consultation with the rhinoplasty specialist."

"Plastic surgery won't help. Your eyes also have a tell."

"Well, then I'll have those traitors sewn up too."

The corners of his lips continued their subtle climb upward. "Why don't you answer my question about your dating history first? Is it all just a collection of cinna*man-buns* and blue horny aliens?"

I bit the inside of my lip, punishing it for wanting to expand into a smile. "First of all, it's cinnamon *roll*. Those books are not about dudes with man-buns, that's not what that means. Second of all, it's not *horny* blue aliens, it's blue aliens *with* horns."

His throat worked as he tried to suppress a chuckle. "That's my bad."

"Although, the blue aliens are also horny a lot of the

time. Strictly for reproductive purposes, obviously. But that's neither here nor there."

He hummed. "You know what I think of every time you say blue aliens?"

"Please don't tell me."

"Do these blue aliens live in blue houses with blue windows, perchance? And do they da ba dee and da ba di?"

My teeth sank harder into my bottom lip. Alba and I had been obsessed with that song when we were kids. I still had my Eiffel 65 poster tucked away in the back of my closet somewhere.

"Have you seen the music video?" he asked, his gaze dipping down to my bite. "It's a masterpiece."

"Haven't seen it."

He nodded at my nose. "Lie. But that's how I'm imagining them in my head. Four-foot nothing, massive bald heads, scrawny bodies. But with little devil horns added."

"That's... aggressively inaccurate."

"Is that your type?"

"Are scrawny blue aliens my type?"

"Yes. Is it the idea of an extraterrestrial being with blue, hairless skin and tiny horns that turns you on? Or do they have to be holding a cinnamon roll for it to work?"

A chortle escaped that time. *Damn it.*

"I'm just trying to understand where the cinnamon roll thing comes into... *play*," he went on, leaning in a little more. "Do they feed it to you? Eat it off you? Do they unravel it and then try to tie you up with it?"

Jesus Christ. "How weirded out would you be if I said yes to all that?"

One dimple. "We all have our kinks. I'm not one to judge."

Heat licked at my stomach, thickened the air around us.

Two dimples. "You're blushing, Sanchez."

"Do you hear how much you actually say my name?"

"I can switch it up if you'd like, Ria."

Swoop, swoosh, tingle. "How about we just put a ban on names altogether?"

He clicked his tongue. "No."

"How would you like it if—"

I started at the sound of someone clearing their throat.

"Sorry," Anthony whispered quietly. "You were so engrossed in your conversation, I didn't want to interrupt. I brought drinks, and the pizza will be here in around forty minutes. I'll leave you alone until then."

There were two crystal tumblers filled with amber liquid, ice, and curved orange peels sitting on the table in front of us.

"Uh—thank you," I said quietly. My head felt a little fuzzy. "That's very sweet. You're free to join us if you'd..."

But he was shaking his head. "I'll let you have your space. I'm more than happy to catch up with my wife for now." He left with a friendly wink and knowing smile, and when the patio door slid shut, my heart bounced.

Suddenly I was very, *very* aware of how close Adrien and I were sitting. Of how his arm had curled around the backrest of the couch, his hand grazing my shoulder. Of how he hadn't taken his eyes off me once since his dad had walked out here.

I leaned forward and grabbed one of the tumblers off the table, making sure to scooch a few inches away from Adrien in the process.

He leaned over, grabbed his glass, and scooched a few inches closer to me in the process.

I took a sip, gaze glued to my lap.

He took a sip, gaze glued to my face.

"Sorry," he eventually said, amusement tilting his deep voice. "I didn't hear him come out over the deafening sound of all the chemistry we don't have."

20

"Just because we argue doesn't mean we have chemistry," I told Adrien.

It was really important to me that he understood that. I didn't know *why* it was so important, but it was.

"Were we arguing just now or was it more of a playful banter?"

"We were arguing."

"I don't think so."

"We're arguing right now," I pointed out.

He clicked his tongue. "Slight disagreement. Still banter."

He was unbearable. "We don't like each other enough to engage in playful banter, Adrien."

"You don't have to like me for us to have chemistry, Ria."

"I disrespectfully disagree."

Adrien's eyes narrowed with a bizarre mixture of annoyance and amusement. "Prove it, then."

I twisted on the couch to fully face him. "What do I get if I do?"

"The satisfaction of being the very first person to ever prove me wrong."

I rolled my eyes. "How do you not annoy yourself when you talk?"

He huffed a light chuckle. "It's called having a sense of humor, Sanchez."

That. That right there. "I know what I want if I win."

"You want me to stop saying your name so frequently."

Damn it.

That was exactly what I was going to say, but I didn't want to give him the satisfaction of being right. So, I racked my brain, trying to—

And then it hit me. It was so painfully obvious. I just hadn't thought of it right away because of the bubbly fog of champagne my brain was currently drenched in.

"No. What I really want is for you to lighten Alba's workload when you rehire her. I want her to get *every* weekend and statutory holiday off, to be able to actually use her vacation days, and I want you to put a reasonable cap on the amount of hours she has to work every week. Hire a second assistant if you need to."

A new emotion flicked over his eyes in response to my request, but it was gone before I could place it.

"Sure," he eventually said, recovering. "But if I win, you have to admit that you're attracted to me."

"I'm not attracted to you."

And then he frikkin' *booped* my nose. "Such a liar."

I swatted his hand away. "Terms, conditions, rules. Go."

"And bossy."

"I don't think you of all people have any right to call anyone bossy."

His little smirk widened into a dimpled grin.

"Touché."

It did *not* make me flustered. This was fine. I was fine. Everything was under control.

"I'm adding one more thing then: if I win, you have to stop insisting that I'm attracted to you."

"You get two things and I only get one? That doesn't seem fair."

I shrugged. "What else do you want?"

Adrien rolled his lips as he studied me. "I want you to tell me why you didn't go to college. I want the truth, the full story."

He really didn't want to let that one go, did he? "What makes you think there's a story there?"

"Like I said, it doesn't add up. I've seen your academic record."

"You've also seen my criminal record."

"It doesn't add up, Sanchez. You had an entirely spotless record for eighteen years, a near-perfect GPA, you were chosen as the class valedictorian, and less than a month before graduation you get charged with mischief of all things? For vandalism?"

"High school students do dumb shit all the time," I said, ignoring the uncomfortable tugging in my chest. "I did a dumb thing, and then I paid the price for it."

Adrien shook his head. "It doesn't make sense. Even if you did do a dumb thing... I understand losing any scholarships as a consequence, but not the opportunity to pursue a postsecondary education altogether. If I win, you have to tell me what happened."

The tugging grew stronger, making my insides curl.

Why wouldn't he just let this go? Why did it even matter to him?

"Fine," I said. But only because I really wanted him to

lighten Alba's workload, and I hadn't thought to make it a condition before agreeing to the fake engagement nonsense. "But the burden of proof lies with you. You have to prove, beyond any reasonable doubt, that you and I have chemistry. And that I'm attracted to you or whatever." Which was impossible. Chemistry wasn't something tangible you could see or touch or *prove*. It was a feeling; a connection; an obscure pull between two people.

And how the hell could you provide solid, irrefutable evidence of something so incredibly abstract? How would you go about proving that two people were attracted to each other without hooking them up to a bunch of machines and monitoring their heart rates and hormone levels?

Adrien finished off his drink with a cocky smirk, then put the empty tumbler down on the table. "Deal."

His voice held so much confidence that it made the hairs on the back of my neck stand in warning. I polished off my own cocktail and put the empty glass beside his. Then I crossed my arms, leaned back, and eyed him warily. "Okay... now what?"

"Now you pick a safeword."

I reeled, my stomach flopping upside down. "Pardon?"

"A safeword is a code word that signals—"

"I know what a safeword is," I snapped at him, already annoyed. My cheeks were starting to feel hot.

His grin widened, his dimples deepened, and my blood pressure climbed higher and higher. "So pick one."

I crossed my arms tighter. "I'm asking you *why* I need one. What the hell are you going to do?"

He shrugged. "You'll see."

My eyes narrowed. "Do you get a safeword?"

"I don't need one."

"How do you know?"

Adrien pushed a hand through his dark hair and released a sharp exhale through his nose. The smile never left his face, though. It was like he couldn't decide whether he was annoyed or entertained.

"If you don't pick a word, I'm going to pick one for you," he said.

I tilted my head. "If you pick mine, I'm picking yours."

"Fine."

"Fine."

He slighted closer. And I honestly hated, hated, *hated* how good he smelled. It was so inconveniently distracting.

"Cinnamon," he said, dark eyes swimming over my face. "That'll be your safeword. If you use it, I'll play nice like those guys in your books and stop whatever it is I'm doing."

"So you *do* know what cinnamon roll means."

"I may have done some research. Is that what you're into? Nice, wholesome guys who are sweet and supportive?"

"Yes. Obviously." Wasn't that what everyone was into?

His mouth quirked. "I see."

"Waldo is your safeword," I decided before he could expose me to whatever depravity was running through his mind. "Let's just get this over with. Tell me what we're doing."

Adrien's gaze continued its lazy swim across my features. "The game is simple. For the next half-hour, I'm going to try my best to seduce you. The timer stops when the food arrives."

I frowned. "And?"

"And all you have to do is... not melt into a puddle of lust on my lap."

I blinked at him slowly. Sarcastically. "You're joking."

"Nope."

Good lord. "You cannot seriously be this cocky. A *puddle of lust*?"

He grinned. "I give you fifteen minutes, tops. By thirty, you might be on your knees, declaring your undying love for me."

My mouth twisted into a disgusted scowl. He looked like he was mostly serious. It was concerning. I was concerned for him. "Dude."

He tried holding back his grin. He failed miserably. "I'm assuming that means we have a deal?"

"Just to be clear, you're going to try and seduce me, and all I have to do is not, like... somehow end up on your lap?"

"Yes. Exactly."

"You're fucking delusional," I told him. "And I mean that with genuine sincerity. Check my nose."

"You're really that confident?" he asked, his eyes dancing with playful amusement. He was really enjoying himself. The fool. Wait until he got a taste of bitter failure.

I couldn't wait to turn that smile upside down.

"I've never been more sure of anything in my life. Ever. The sky is blue, the grass is green, and I, Ria Sanchez, am never going to be tempted to go anywhere near your lap."

"Except the sky famously turns a mixture of orange, pink, and purple at sunrise and sunset, and gray when it's cloudy." He looked incredibly pleased with himself. "And grass withers to brown in the winter."

I blinked at him. "Don't be a smartass."

His dimples popped as he chuckled. "I don't think you of all people have any right to call anyone a smartass, Sanchez."

"Is this part of the seduction? Have we started? Because if so, you're doing terribly. I'm less seduced now than I was two minutes ago."

"Really? Because you're smiling quite a bit."

"I'm definitely not smiling," I assured him.

"You're *trying* not to smile. That's not the same thing as not smiling."

"It's also not the same thing as smiling. Do you see what I mean about the arguing thing?" I said, my arms uncrossing. "I literally can't remember a time when we weren't fighting."

It must have been nice. Peaceful. Quiet.

"That's very sweet. I can't remember a time before you either, Sanchez." His dimples flashed.

Swoosh. "That's not what I said."

Adrien leaned in, bringing his arm to rest beside my shoulder again. "You know I'm still finding glitter on my clothes? I don't know where the fuck they're coming from. I had my office deep cleaned twice, I replaced my chair, and the suit I was wearing that day is at the dry cleaners. I don't know where they're hiding."

My grin broke free. "I'm so sorry to hear that."

He nudged my chin with his knuckle. "Yeah. You look real devastated."

"In my defense, you overworked my sister. So you kind of deserved it a little bit."

"You cost me a nine-figure investment deal."

"You made me pick glitter out of dirt with tweezers."

"You signed up to be a mod for my hate club."

"You were the reason I was tackled and cuffed by the building security last week."

"You smashed my dick in with a cane."

"You're a sadist."

"You're a liar."

"For the last time, *I'm not attracted to you.* I'm not lying." I said it slowly, loudly, clearly. I annunciated every individual word, leaning in so he could properly hear me.

"Tell that to your nose." Another *boop*.

"If you boop me one more time I'm going to bite your finger."

His grin turned devilish. "Is that a promise?"

I refused to let another smile slip. "For the record, this is the worst seduction attempt I've ever had to endure. You're incredibly bad at this."

His lips wobbled with the effort it was taking to hold back his laugh. "I'm admittedly a little rusty. I normally don't have to try with women. They tend to come to me willingly, in shiny-haired hoards."

That comment earned him another slow blink. "Every single thing that comes out of your mouth annoys the ever-loving shit out of me, Adrien. Like, to the point where it's shaving years off my life. My blood pressure has never been this consistently high."

He laughed way harder than was appropriate. It was a deep, rumbling sound, accented by those boyish dimples and squinty eyes. It was annoying. And you know what else was annoying? How straight and white and perfect his teeth were.

I was annoyed. That was why things were starting to feel tight and breathless. That was why my stomach felt funny. That and the alcohol, probably.

"You're so fucking easy to rile up," he said.

I watched as his chuckles subsided, leading to a soft silence. The fire still crackled, the grass still hissed, crickets still chirped, and the whiskey worked its warming magic through my limbs. It wasn't... entirely horrible.

"You're staring again, Sanchez," Adrien eventually murmured.

"And you keep saying that like you're not staring right back, Cloutier."

His midnight gaze latched onto mine for a few quiet seconds, then he leaned in another inch. "Can I ask you something?" He reached up and brushed a gentle finger right underneath my left eye. "What is this?"

I ignored the subtle buzz his touch left on my skin. This was one hundred percent part of the seduction thing, and I wasn't going to fall for it.

"Sectoral heterochromia," I responded in an even, unaffected tone. My eyes were a chestnut brown, but the left iris had a small section of honey cut into it. It was pretty cool if I said so myself. "It's kind of like a birthmark."

"Was the hair thing on purpose?" he asked.

"What d'you mean?"

Adrien ran his fingers through the freshly chopped strands. "The new color matches your eyes. It fades into the same light gold. Was it on purpose?"

"Um... I don't know. The whole day was a bit of a blur if I'm being honest," I muttered. My voice sounded a tinge softer than I'd intended. "We had the hair appointments and there was champagne and Ricardo said a balayage would look good and I didn't really know what that meant and suddenly I was somewhat blonde."

Adrien was starting to smile again. "It was worth it." He picked up another small lock of my hair and rubbed it between his fingers. "It's crazy soft, too."

"I know. I made him secretly write down all the products he used so I could buy them when I got home."

"Why didn't you just buy them while you were there?"

"Because your mom kept refusing to let me pay, and I was drowning in guilt. And the worst part is, I *still* don't have clothes to wear this week." Or underwear. So I was going to have to sneak out at some point and go on a sleuthy shopping trip.

"Just wear what you bought today. I already said it was fine."

"Absolutely not."

"It's not a big deal, Ria. I'll call the store and quietly take care of the bill if you really want."

"That doesn't make it much better. I don't want your money either."

He lifted a shoulder. "Think of it as a clothing allowance for the job I've hired you to do. If you don't wear the clothes, she's going to get offended."

I sighed. "But you don't understand just how much she actually spent on me."

"It doesn't matter. I'm officially insisting that you wear them because I don't want to have to deal with the consequences otherwise."

I rolled my lips and glared at him.

"Stop plotting your revenge." He nudged my chin lightly.

"You're going to regret this." I didn't know how yet, but he would.

"Great. Can't wait."

And that was when I noticed he was still playing with my hair, his fingers toying with the fringes.

"I almost didn't recognize you when you came in," he said quietly. "It took a second for my brain to catch up."

I cleared my throat. "Well, you did tell me I looked like the girl from *The Ring* this morning, so I'm assuming that's a good thing."

He chuckled. "You really did scare the shit out of me."

"I don't feel bad about it."

He let out a breath. "Can't you play nice for just two minutes? I'm trying my best to seduce you here."

"You should change tactics. None of this is working."

"No?" His hand had moved up a little bit, his fingers twisting and twirling strands of my hair.

I shook my head. "Not even a little bit."

"That's a shame." His gaze dropped to my mouth. "Tell me, Sanchez, what type of men do you normally date? The sweet and caring kind we were talking about earlier?"

Technically, my only romantic experiences since high school had been a handful of short-lived flings and hookups that fizzled before they could turn into anything even remotely serious, so I didn't have a type that I "normally" dated. But that wasn't information he needed.

"I like men that don't insert my name into every other sentence," I said.

That earned me a dark chuckle. "And?"

"Men that don't make my blood pressure spike to lethal levels every time they open their mouths."

Adrien tutted. "Boring."

"Is it boring or is it healthy?"

"It's boring. What else?"

"Men that don't compare me to the girl from *The Ring*."

"Wow. I'm oh for three, huh?"

"You're oh for a thousand, Adrien."

He huffed through his nose. "If it makes you feel any better, I had a small crush on a girl in eighth grade that dressed up as *The Ring* girl for Halloween."

I suppressed a smile.

"Granted, the costume was what led to the end of my

short-lived crush, but only because she got on all fours and did the crawl. Instant unattraction. You really can't unsee something like that," he went on, not realizing what a sweet little prank idea he'd willingly handed me. "Also, she kept making the bone-cracking noises. I swear the whole thing made my teenage dick shrivel up and into itself."

I chuckled reluctantly. "Is that really the story you want to have told me just now? While trying to turn me into a lusty puddle?"

"If the mental image of my shriveled-up dick doesn't do it for you, then I honestly don't know what will."

I pressed my palms to my eyes. "Please stop. Forever stop."

"Do you even *have* a libido, Sanchez?"

Another laugh burst out of me, and I dropped my hands to find Adrien watching me with soft, warm amusement.

It was weird.

No. That wasn't correct. It *should have been* weird. But it was just... I felt a little...

Adrien brushed his knuckles over my cheekbone. "I didn't mean to hurt your feelings with the *Ring* comparison. You're very... you know how attractive you are."

I arched my brows at him, far too aware of the tingling left behind by his touch. "So you think I'm attractive."

"That's not exactly what I said."

"It's what I heard." It was my turn to tease him, and I was never going to let him live this one down.

He reached up again, this time brushing a strand of hair away from my forehead and eyes.

That should have felt weird, too. So why didn't it? It just felt... fluttery. And a little breathless.

"Fine. Yes," he said. "You are... stubborn, and exasperating, and a massive pain in my ass."

I clicked my tongue. "Worst seducer on the planet."

His lips twitched. "But you are also aggravatingly, inconveniently... maddeningly beautiful, Ariana."

My smile faltered. I blinked.

"It's very distracting," he went on, his gaze dipping to my parted lips for a single clumsy heartbeat. "Especially when you look at me like that."

I scanned his face, looking for an inconsistency—a *tell*. My brows pinched when I pulled up short, my heart crawling up to the base of my throat.

"What?" he said.

"What's your tell?" I asked him.

"My tell?"

"For when you lie. What is it?"

One confused dimple. "I'm being honest. You're incredibly attractive. It's fucking infuriating."

Nothing. No twitch or flare or dip that I could see.

Th-th-thump.Th-thump.Th-th-thump.

I scanned his face again.

"Why is that so hard for you to believe?" he asked.

"Because you have good reason to lie. For seduction purposes."

"I don't need to lie to seduce you. And believe me, I wish I was lying about this. Or even exaggerating."

I squinted at him, trying my best to detect any slight movement or change that would give him away. But, once again, I came up blank.

Maybe he didn't have a tell. There was only one way to find out.

"Let's play a game," I said.

"We don't have time for a game, I'm supposed to be

charming you into a puddle of heat."

I waved a dismissive hand. "You've already lost. We're just running out the clock at this point. I'm not even close to puddling."

"Because you keep distracting me and the conversation keeps straying."

"That's a you problem." I brought both legs up onto the couch, crossed them, and twisted my body to fully face him.

"What are you doing?" Adrien asked with curious amusement.

"I need to be able to see your face really well."

His brows pinched, though the bemused smirk remained. "What game are we playing, exactly?"

"Two truths and a lie."

He huffed a chuckle. "Fine. One round. And I get an extra five minutes of seduction time."

I rolled my eyes. "Take ten." It wouldn't make a difference. "Now go. Start. Tell me two truths and one lie, and I'll try to guess which is which."

Adrien tilted his head, thinking. "Let's see..." He trailed off, observing me almost as closely as I was observing him. "Okay. One, I knew who you were when you marched up to me in the Waldo costume on Halloween, and I recognized you almost immediately. Two, I used to have a genuine, debilitating phobia of clowns when I was a kid, and I cried when I met Loonette from The Big Comfy Couch. And three, the pizza arrived ten minutes ago, and you still haven't noticed."

I blinked. *Wait... what?*

A devilishly arrogant smirk tilted Adrien's mouth as my gaze snapped to the large kitchen window. Sure enough, two pizza boxes sat on the counter.

My forehead scrunched into a frown. "It's been thirty minutes already?"

No way.

"Forty-five. The doorbell went off, and my dad signaled at us through the window. You didn't notice."

What the hell?

"So," he said, looking far too pleased with himself, "which is the lie?"

My eyes moved back to the window. How had I not heard the doorbell? Had it really been a whole forty-five minutes already?

Adrien stroked my cheek with his knuckles again, setting off a string of sparks across my skin as his touch moved down to my jaw. He softly grabbed my chin, turning my head back to him.

"Which is the lie?" he asked again.

There was a long, dense pause as our gazes locked, and I heard my own breath hitch when his thumb brushed the skin underneath my bottom lip.

"Answer me, Ria," he demanded quietly, his eyes sliding to my lips. My fingers dug into my palms when his thumb moved again.

"Two?" I sounded a little breathless. "The clown thing is the lie?"

His mouth curved into a pleased half-smile. "Good."

The purred approval dripped straight to my core and settled there, simmering.

My throat worked as I swallowed. "How did you know who I was?"

His gaze was still fixed on my mouth. "Alba keeps framed pictures of the two of you on her desk. Your face isn't exactly easy to forget."

"And here I thought my disguise had been rock-solid."

His half-smile slowly spread. "I'd have recognized you from a mile away. And I did, every time I caught a glimpse of you in the office. You're impossible to miss."

That was... a lot of new information.

Adrien's hand moved to cup my jaw, his thumb caressing my cheek. "You're so fucking pretty it's annoying," he chided, his voice dropping to a low, molten gravel. "I hate how much I love looking at you. I *hate* it, Sanchez. And I can't tell what I'm more angry about anymore, all the bullshit you put me through, or the fact that your lips are so fucking plump and pink."

I stilled, my breath catching.

"Do you still think I'm lying?" he asked.

My mouth had slighted open, my throat drying so rapidly I thought I might choke.

"Answer me, Ria."

What the fuck was happening?

My tongue darted out to wet my lips as I tried to summon a single coherent thought. Adrien's dark gaze turned feral, though his touch remained a smooth, gentle caress.

I was so confused, holy shit.

"Um... I honestly don't know," I managed.

"No?"

"Mm-mm." I shook my head.

"I'm admitting to losing my mind over your lips, and you won't even believe me?"

Fire ants were starting to crawl underneath my skin where he was stroking it.

His mouth twitched. "Look at how pretty you are when you blush," he murmured approvingly. "I never stood a fucking chance. It really is too bad that we don't have any... chemistry."

His hand slid to the back of my head, fisting a handful of my hair. "So fucking soft," he praised. And then slowly, and with excruciating gentleness, he pulled my head back until my mouth was level with his as he peered down at me. His dark eyes were unrecognizable, they were so glazed over.

"Such a pretty girl."

I shivered when the heat of his molten whiskey breath grazed my lips. We both felt it.

A small part of me knew that I should have wanted to stop whatever the hell was currently happening.

I *should have* wanted to.

I didn't.

"The things I would do to those plush lips if you were attracted to me." He was so, *so* close. Just a few more millimeters and... "You can't even begin to imagine. I'd devour you, Sanchez."

My eyelids kept fluttering, wanting to close. I couldn't remember how to breathe.

"And then I'd properly punish you for everything you've done. The investment; the glitter; the insults. For constantly running that smart, bratty little mouth of yours." His grip on my hair tightened a touch. "I'd punish you for being so fucking pretty. For making me want you like this, against my better judgment—against my will."

I felt dizzy.

His scent, his breath, his words. They were all starting to mix and mash with the alcohol, making my head spin.

"It's too bad that we have no chemistry." His lips brushed the corner of my mouth and my breath snagged, my eyes shuttering closed. I tilted my head, feeling drunk off the sweet air we were sharing.

And then...

He let me go.

The absence of heat was what hit me first. It sent an unpleasant shiver down my body that made me want to reach for it again. My eyes popped open. I blinked.

Adrien stood and rounded the patio table, putting way too much distance between our bodies.

"All right, you win," he said casually, his voice snapping back into its normal octave, as though the last few minutes had been a very vivid figment of my imagination.

The only evidence suggesting otherwise was the very large and prominent bulge in Adrien's slacks, which he made no effort to disguise or hide.

I was very aware of how embarrassingly labored my breathing had become, and I was even more aware of how many inappropriate seconds I'd been gawking at—

"You're staring again."

My gaze darted up to his as my cheeks colored. His smile was as dimpled and arrogant as ever, though his eyes were a vividly charred black.

"Um..." I started, my tongue failing to reconnect to my brain. "What."

"You won," Adrien said. "The food arrived, and you weren't puddled on my lap so... well done. I'll reduce Alba's workload and all that other stuff."

I blinked at him slowly.

He cleared his throat and shoved his hands into his pockets. "I'm pretty beat so... I'll see you upstairs. Enjoy the pizza."

And then he turned around and left.

Just like that.

What.

The.

Hell.

21

It started as a flickering ember in the deepest, darkest edge of my core. And as I sat there, staring blankly into the fire pit, it spread. Slowly, methodically. Until my entire soul was on raging fire and fighting to tear its way out of my body.

It had been a half-hour since Adrien had left me out on the patio after... whatever the fuck *that* had been. And the more I thought about it, the more I wanted to... I needed to...

UGH.

I stomped into the house and stormed up the stairs (but only after turning off the fire pit, the lights, locking the door, and putting the pizza away—because I was a guest in this home and not a wild animal), and then I barged right into our shared bedroom.

Adrien Cloutier, the undisputed bane of my entire fucking existence, was sitting behind his desk, casually tapping away on his phone.

He'd changed into a white T-shirt and black sweats. His hair was damp, and I could smell the soap and spice all the way from the other side of the room. How many fucking showers did the man take in one day? Why was every little thing about him so relentlessly *aggravating*?

The door shut behind me.

He looked up, took in my terrifyingly livid appearance, and had the audacity—the fucking *gall*—to smile. "Enjoyed the pizza?"

Embarrassment tore through me, clashing with the anger. He didn't look like *his* soul was lit on scorching fucking fire. He didn't look like *his* insides were a tangled, wobbly mess.

He'd won. Not in the timeframe we'd specified, but he'd won.

And I hated that we both knew it—that *he* knew it. And I *really* hated how cool and unbothered he seemed by the whole thing.

The air rushed out of my nostrils with so much force that it made me sound like a taunted bull. My chest was beating like an incessant war drum, propelling blood through my veins with enough force to make it sizzle. I was on fire.

None of it had been real, obviously. He'd been fucking with me the whole time. But I'd... for a second... stupidly...

UGH.

I shoved a frustrated hand through my hair and pinned him with one last devastating glower before I stormed into my designated closet, ignoring his sticky, questioning gaze.

The small room was filled with an overwhelming number of shopping bags. And because I didn't know what else to do with myself, I snatched one off the floor, tore into it, and began anger-organizing.

Obviously, he hadn't meant any of the things he'd said. Obviously, it had all been for the sake of the bet.

But if the bulge he'd been sporting downstairs was any indication, he wasn't as unaffected by the experience as he wanted me to believe. And that little sliver was all I needed.

He wanted to play this game with me? Fine.

He wanted to push all my buttons and get me all riled up? Fine.

He wanted me to wear the clothes his mother bought? *Fine.*

Be careful who you fuck with, Lucifer.

⁓

The *Autumn Honeymoon Collection* Luke had suggested consisted of fourteen full sets of silk and lace lingerie, each of which included a bra, a thong, and matching slips. (Some of them even included a garter).

The collection was incredibly beautiful—full of elegant autumn colors and intricate designs, and the material melted against my skin like butter. Too bad I was too bloodthirsty to actually appreciate any of it.

I plucked a dark green slip off the perfectly organized shelf and slid it on. It was a flimsy, delicate little thing that barely covered my ass.

It was also the most conservative piece in the collection.

I paired it with the matching lace thong and finally sauntered out of the closet. Adrien had been smart enough to leave me alone while I took my rage out on the clothes, hangers, and shelves.

The room was darker now, the space illuminated by

the soft glow of a single bedside lamp, and Adrien was in the process of laying a blanket out on the floor like a makeshift mattress.

"Okay. Listen," he started. "Maybe I shouldn't have taken things—"

He cut himself off when he saw me, his jaw falling open. It took him ten full seconds to recover enough to ask, "What the... what is *that*?"

I glanced down at myself, feigning innocence. My nipples were poking right through the buttery silk.

"Pajamas," I answered simply. Wasn't it obvious?

"What." He was talking to my breasts. His eyes were glued to them.

"These are the pajamas the personal shopper picked out for me. Cute, no?"

I watched with fluttery satisfaction as his demeanor changed—darkened. His gaze traveled all over me, shamelessly drinking in every inch of my body.

I crossed my arms, effectively shoving my breasts together without covering my nipples.

"You're drooling, Cloutier."

His eyes snapped to mine, blazing. The tips of his ears were crimson. "What are you doing?"

"Getting ready for bed." Again, wasn't it obvious?

"This is because of the bet? Downstairs?"

I shrugged. "I don't know what you're talking about."

He shifted on his feet, tension worming through his jaw. "You need to change. Right now."

I cocked my head and pushed my lips into a little pout. "No can do. I wouldn't want to hurt your poor mother's feelings."

"I'm not fucking around, Sanchez."

"Neither am I," I said. "You're the one who insisted I

wear the clothes your mom got me, and this is what my private shopper selected for my sleepwear. I don't understand why you're complaining."

This was already so fucking gratifying.

"You really don't want to start this game with me," he promised. The muscles in his shoulders and neck were tensing, the veins in his forearms popping as his fists clenched, unclenched.

Still, a little smirk kept pulling at the corner of his lips; like he was somehow also enjoying this.

"I don't know what you're talking about," I purred sweetly.

"Last chance to call that truce," he practically growled. "Stop being a brat and go put on some fucking clothes. We'll call it even and move on."

Fuck his truce. And fuck him.

"No."

His whole face twitched.

I floated to the bed and crawled onto the covers, allowing the slip to ride up my thighs and hips as I twisted to my side, facing him.

He didn't even try to pretend like he wasn't staring.

He let his eyes roam over me slowly, head to toe. Heat licked at the trail his gaze left behind, and I squirmed, my knees inching up to my stomach.

Adrien shut his eyes with a breathy curse and scrubbed a hand over his face.

"You're blushing," I teased sweetly.

"Last chance, Sanchez. Take the truce." Tension snapped through his jaw, and the heated glare he cut me then could have melted glass.

I licked my lips. "No."

Our gazes locked, our chests rising and falling with

effort. There was no oxygen left in the room. The air felt too charged, too thick to breathe in.

Adrien's mouth twitched like he wanted to say something, but he seemed to think better of it.

"What's wrong?" I teased bitterly. "My pretty, plush lips got your tongue? Or do you just wish they did?"

Just because he hadn't meant the words didn't mean I couldn't shove them in his face.

Though that one may have pushed it a tiny bit too far, judging by the dangerous flash of... whatever evil had just crossed his eyes. Color crawled up his neck, spreading to his cheeks. And before I could see where else it would reach, he snapped off the bedside lamp with an angry jerk of his wrist.

An onslaught of rustles and thumps followed as Adrien kicked and punched his makeshift bed into place before his body practically slammed down on it.

I smiled into the darkness and closed my eyes to the sweet, soothing sounds of Satan restlessly tossing and turning in the grave he'd dug himself.

It wasn't until I was on the cusp of sleep that the little voice appeared, claiming that Adrien had lost the bet on purpose. That he'd waited until the timer ran out to pull out the big guns. But I slipped into the deep end before it could tell me why.

22

"STOP STEALING MY FRUIT, you little shit! You've already had your breakfast!"

"Alice, no swearing at the breakfast table, please."

"We're technically not at a table."

"*Want some?*"

"No, thank you, Maxi. Very sweet of you to offer, darling."

"It's not your fruit to give out!"

I smiled into my mug as I watched the small circus that was the Cloutiers preparing breakfast.

We were gathered around the large kitchen island, Alice cutting and slicing fruit for her morning smoothie bowl, Maxwell continuously stealing the fruit that Alice was cutting and slicing for her morning smoothie bowl, and Julie trying her best to keep Alice from strangling Maxwell for stealing the fruit that she was cutting and slicing for her morning smoothie bowl.

"Alice. I'm trying to do my crossword. A little less screeching, please?" Anthony said to his daughter.

"Y'all let him get away with murder. *This* is where he

gets all the audacity from. A bunch of enablers," Alice countered, glaring at Maxwell as he began his stealthy sneak toward her cutting board.

"Newsflash, kid: you spoil him more than anyone else in this house," Anthony said, a smile in his voice. "No one else has a timer on their phone to put fresh ice in his water every few hours."

"Because the spoiled brat won't drink room-temperature liquids," she argued.

"Because *you* keep putting ice in his water," Anthony said.

Alice grumbled under her breath as she returned to her aggressive chopping.

It was awesome. I hadn't been expecting to warm up to his family this much or this quickly. I really hoped my real future in-laws were this homey and warm. And entertaining.

"Ria, honey, what do you like in your pancakes?" Julie asked as she began opening cupboards and gathering ingredients.

"I'm fine with anything." Except raisins. But nobody in their right mind put raisins in pancakes (or in anything else for that matter).

"Blueberries okay?"

I smiled at her. "Blueberries are perfect. Thank you."

Gampy was out on the patio, doing his morning Tai chi, Anthony was seated beside Alice, drinking his coffee and doing his morning crossword puzzle, and Adrien was... somewhere. I'd woken up to an empty bedroom around an hour after he normally went for his runs. And he still wasn't back yet, so—

My spine perked as the front door opened just then,

and sure enough, Adrien rounded the corner a few moments later, holding two small red boxes.

He was wearing a crisp white button-down, black slacks, and did not look like someone who'd just come back from a run. A boardroom, maybe.

"Good morning, everybody." His face split into a sinister grin, his eyes scanning the room until they landed on me. Then they narrowed. "*Sweetheart*," he sneered.

I blinked.

He was walking. Advancing. Practically charging at me.

I released the handle of my mug and took an inadvertent step back. *Uh oh.*

Adrien tossed the boxes onto the counter and reached for me. He was going to strangle me. Right here, right now. I could see it in his feral eyes. He was going to wrap his fingers around my neck and squeeze until—

My breath caught, my heart jumping into my throat as his one hand slipped to my lower back, the other into my hair. And just as my life began to flash before my eyes, his mouth crashed into mine.

It took a moment for things to click. For my neck to realize it was still attached to the rest of my body. For my heart to realize it was supposed to continue beating. And then...

And then...

My eyes fluttered shut, my thoughts melting to goo against the unexpected warmth of Adrien's mouth. He tilted his head slightly, his fingers curling into a fist in my hair as he pinned my body to his, deepening the... kiss. He was kissing me.

And that was when the sparks started.

Tiny little tingles biting at my lips and fingertips, my chest, my spine, my curling toes. Until my whole body had flared to life with them. Until my hands were sliding up his chest, fisting the front of his shirt, trying to pull him closer. Until I'd forgotten who I was, where I was, what I'd been—

"Gross. Get a room."

Alice's voice tore through the dizzying trance I was in, and I jerked back with a sharp inhale, breaking the kiss.

What the hell?

Adrien didn't let me go, didn't allow me to take a step back. His eyes were hazy, his red mouth slowly slanting into an arrogantly victorious grin as he took in my expression.

"Geez, you guys," Anthony teased lightly.

Julie was beaming like we'd plucked the moon out of the sky and gifted it to her.

"New rule," Alice decided, her mouth bent with distaste. "No moaning at the breakfast table. Or the kitchen counter. Or anywhere else in the house. Just no moaning, period."

Red-hot color streaked my cheeks as I contemplated wrestling my way out of Adrien's arms and bolting for the door. Leaving the country. Changing my name. Who the fuck had *moaned*? I hadn't moaned. Had I moaned?

I released my grip on Adrien's shirt, acutely aware of the greedy little indents my fingers had left behind, and tried to subtly shove myself away.

It backfired.

Adrien sidestepped my attempt at establishing physical distance between our bodies and repositioned himself behind me. His arms snaked around my waist and pulled my back to his hard chest. "I went to the bakery bright and early this morning and picked up a box of your favorites, sweetheart."

He said *sweetheart* like it was a vulgar expletive, though I seemed to be the only one that heard it.

"I'm good, thanks," I croaked, very much tempted to elbow him in the ribs.

I was *not* tempted to melt against him like butter.

I was *not*.

"Oh, but I insist. I had them make an extra special batch just for you."

He'd definitely done something shady and vile to whatever was in the red boxes.

Fucking heathen.

"Julie's making pancakes," I informed him. "With, um, blueberries. So, I'm just gonna wait for th-those."

There should have been a law against smelling so abhorrently good that it messed with people's abilities to navigate their way through fully coherent sentences.

Adrien's arms tightened around me, and I refused— absolutely *refused*—to acknowledge the hardening ridge pressing to my lower back. I was *not* turned on by any of this. I did *not* want to turn around and ravish him against the fridge. I did *not* want him to drag me up the stairs, pin me to the wall, and punish me for what I'd pulled last night.

I was fine.

This was *fine*.

Anthony kindly poured his son a fresh, steaming cup of coffee before returning to his... sudoku? Crossword? Last will and testament?

I was losing brain cells at an alarmingly rapid rate.

"Oh, don't worry about the pancakes," Julie chirped, barely able to contain her excitement as she watched us, entirely unaware of how I was currently plotting her beloved son's gruesome demise. "Since Addy went through all that trouble to go to the bakery first thing and special-order your favorites..."

She was melting.

Her dreams for her son were coming true, and she was positively *melting* with happiness.

Adrien brushed the hair away from my ear and neck. My breath did *not* hitch when his fingers brushed against my skin. I did *not* shiver.

"Just a bite," he murmured into my ear evilly. "Since I went through all that trouble."

"Did you get *us* anything while you were there?" Alice asked him, glaring at a sneakily approaching Maxwell. The bird had balls, I'd give him that. He wasn't even remotely deterred by the jab-ready way she was holding that knife.

Or maybe I just had murder on my mind.

Adrien reached for the smaller box and placed it in front of me, then nudged his chin at the bigger one. "That one's yours."

Alice threw the lid open, visibly excited as she snatched a chocolate croissant out of the box and bit into it, her shoulders jiggling with happiness. "Yes! Thank you!"

Maxwell took this opportunity to nab a piece of mango out of her bowl and hurriedly hopped back to Anthony for protection in case Alice's distraction was short-lived. It wasn't.

"And for you, *my love*," Adrien purred hatefully, opening the smaller box. A cinnamon roll, freshly baked to golden perfection. "Just how you like it."

It looked like a cinnamon roll, it smelled like a

cinnamon roll, my mouth drooled like it was in the presence of a cinnamon roll... but something about it was off.

"Um, why is the icing pink?" I dared to ask, knowing full well I wouldn't like the answer.

"I'm so glad you asked." *Fuck me.* "Since I know how much you love raisins, I had them blend some into the icing for you."

Ew... ew, what?

Alice made a face as Adrien peeled back the outer layer of the bun to reveal... raisins.

So. Many. Raisins.

Double, maybe even triple, the amount of raisins you'd expect.

Yeah.

Fuck no.

I pushed the box away. "Thanks, *babe*, but I'm really trying to watch my sugar intake."

"Nonsense," he argued softly. "We're on vacation. You're allowed to treat yourself."

"Aren't they just the sweetest?" Julie said to her husband.

"Very cute," he agreed.

"They remind me of us."

"We're cuter." He winked at her; she giggled.

"You're all equally gross," Alice informed the four of us flatly.

And that was when Adrien made the mistake of reaching for his coffee. I acted before the idea had even fully formed, reaching for two of the ice cubes Alice had put aside for her forgotten smoothie. And then I plopped them right into his cup.

Adrien stiffened, his fingers digging into my hip.

Alice frowned at her brother. "Ew... you like your coffee lukewarm now?"

"I don't know," he answered slowly, a dangerous edge to his voice. "Do I?"

I smiled at Alice. "Cat's out of the bag, I guess. I sneak ice into his morning coffee because he insists on drinking it before it's had a chance to cool, which is not only bad for his teeth, but my medical intuitive says that's what's causing the erectile dys—"

The rest of my sentence was muffled against the massive piece of dough Adrien had torn off the cinnamon bun and stuffed into my mouth.

I almost gagged.

"What's a medical intuitive?" Anthony asked curiously.

"She's joking," Adrien said.

"She's *choking*," Alice corrected.

My eyes were watering, my fists tight as I forced the cursed piece of tainted abomination down my gullet.

I downed the rest of my coffee. It barely helped.

"A medical intuitive," I started, my voice wobbly, "is a medical practitioner and energy healer who uses their psychic abilities to talk to the dead via tarot cards, crystal balls, and elder wands to—"

Adrien ripped off another piece of dough, ready to shove it into my mouth. But I stomped on his foot before he had the chance, and he dropped it with a sharp exhale.

"Are... the two of you okay?" Julie was frowning now. As was the rest of his family.

Probably because Adrien and I were both breathing rather violently, the air around us cracking as we clenched our jaws, teeth, fingers.

"Excuse us," Adrien bit out. He grabbed my wrist and

dragged me out of the kitchen, up the stairs, into our shared room.

The door banged shut.

I glared at him, my chest heaving with hatred.

He glared at me, his jaw rigid with rage.

"You are," he started, voice grating with frustration. "Ria, you are *the most*... I can't... you just..." His teeth snapped shut, like the amount of sheer exasperation he felt toward me was beyond words.

"I told you," I seethed. "I *told you* we wouldn't be able to do this without wanting to rip each other apart."

And that was exactly what I wanted to do—rip him apart. Tear into his sanity, his patience, his shirt. I wanted to... I *needed* to...

I didn't know which one of us moved first. Whether he grabbed my waist, or I seized his shirt. Whether he pulled me to him, or I yanked him to me.

We collided like two dying stars, our mouths crashing into each other with hungry desperation as everything exploded. My body was burning from the inside out, my limbs vibrating as Adrien backed me up to the wall, his hard length pressing into my stomach.

Finally.

Finally.

I shouldn't have wanted this. I shouldn't have whimpered when he pinned me to the wall, or when his tongue shoved into my mouth. I should have pushed him away when he fisted my hair and bit my bottom lip. I should have hated the way my returned bite easily pulled a groan from the pit of his throat. I should have hated the way he felt and tasted.

But holy hell was it a good kiss.

So much so that it started to become confusing. Somewhere along the way, things... shifted. We went from overly frustrated grabbing and biting and clawing to something else entirely. Something a hell of a lot more alarming.

Our tongues stopped shoving, pushing, fighting. And gradually started to explore, nudge, caress. The rough bites turned to gentler nibbles; grabs turned to brushes and strokes; the violent boil in my blood fizzled to warm, tingling sparks, and it... it...

Wow.

I sighed against him, my arms sliding around his neck as we melted into each other, entirely helpless against whatever sorcery had taken over. Adrien let go of my hair, but only so he could cup my jaw, tilt and stroke it as he nibbled at my bottom lip, my chin, jaw, neck, and *oh...*

Wow.

He grazed his teeth across the sensitive dip between my neck and shoulder, kissing and licking my skin until I was a whimpering, trembling mess. My fingers dug into his shoulder and hair, my breathing labored as the heat pooling in my core threatened to spill over. I was sizzling, buzzing, panting, clinging onto him like my life depended on it.

It felt incredible. He was barely even doing anything, and yet it felt *incredible.*

I almost whined when he peeled his lips away from my skin, my fingers clawing at his shoulders, trying to pull him back down. But he wouldn't budge.

"No more," he panted, his voice rough and grating, almost like he was in pain. He tapped his forehead against mine as we both fought for breath. "No more of whatever... fucked up game this is. I can't... you're so deep in my head that I can't... I can't fucking *think* anymore,

Sanchez. I can't sleep... I spent all night..." He shook his head. "I'm not doing this anymore."

I barely knew what he was talking about. What game?

"I'm going to give you two options," he said. His hands were on my waist, preventing our bodies from colliding again. "I'm leaving for a meeting in ten minutes and I'll be gone until the evening. When I come back, you won't be here."

Wait. Wait... *what.*

I tried to take a step back, but his hold on my waist tightened, keeping me in place.

"That's option one," he went on. "I book you a flight, you pack, you leave, and we never see each other again. I'll keep my end of the deal with Alba. I'll rehire her, double her maternity compensation, reduce her work-load, all of it. But I never want to ever see you again."

The bitterness in his voice as he repeated the last bit was so palpable, I could almost taste it. It curdled in my ears and sent an unexpected stab through me.

The feeling's mutual, asshole, I wanted to spit back at him.

So why didn't I?

"Option number two." He paused, his eyes searching mine. "You stay. Willingly. And we continue to play." His thumb brushed my hip, his gaze dipping down to my mouth. "But with new rules. You can run your smart mouth all you want, throw your punches, pick fights, continue to torment me however you see fit... but I get to respond how *I* see fit."

The look he gave me left very little room for interpre-tation. And if it had, the way he pressed our hips together would have cleared things right up.

I opened my mouth to pick the first option—because

obviously I was going to pick the first option—but I stopped.

Why did I stop?

"Your flight details will be in your inbox within the hour, and I'll arrange for a car to pick you up at a tea shop down the road," he said quietly. "I'll be back around eight."

His fingers seemed to hesitate and linger for a moment longer than was necessary, but then he let me go.

"Think about it."

And then he left.

23

I YANKED my suitcase out of the closet, threw it open, and started stuffing shit into it.

Because I was sane.

Because I still had *some* rationality left.

Because choosing anything other than the first option *wasn't actually an option*.

I didn't care what my insides were doing. I didn't care how good that kiss had been. I didn't *care* that there were all these voices in the back of my head protesting the decision.

Frankly, no voice in my head should have been trying to stop me from leaving this nightmare. So, I either needed to book myself a CT scan when I got back home, enroll in extensive therapy, or both.

Probably both.

I was packed before the email hit my inbox. My flight was in four hours and the car would be at Black Sheepish Tea in two. But there was no point in waiting here.

I snuck down to the basement using a set of stairs I didn't know existed until I read Adrien's instructions, and left through the doors beside the theater, which, apparently, no one ever used.

I turned the corner, rushed through the gates, and I was done. I was free.

And I never had to see him again.

My feet moved quickly, my suitcase rolling noisily behind me.

I never had to see him again.

I never ever had to see him ever again.

Which was good. Great. *Fantastic*. It was exactly what I needed. It was exactly what I wanted. It was exactly what I should have wanted.

So why did I stop?

The teashop was right there. I could see its cloud-shaped sign from where I was standing.

So move.

I stood there and stared.

Move, damn it!

I shoved off the strange tangle of emotions gnawing at my gut and forced my legs to move forward. The Black Sheepish Tea was small, quaint. It had dark blue walls, light oak furnishings, and was decorated to the brim with greenery. Potted plants of all shapes and colors had been stuffed into every possible corner, peppered across every possible surface, and hung from every possible hook and curve.

I bit back a reluctant smile. There was around a half-dozen cafes on this block, and of course this was the one he'd thought of.

What a freak.

I ordered a pot of jasmine green tea and sat at a small round table tucked in the back corner, right by the window. Just so I could see the car when it arrived.

Because I was leaving.

I was going to get into the vehicle the second it pulled up to the curb, I was going to leave, and I was never going to talk to, or think about Adrien Cloutier ever again. He'd go back to being a random dude I'd see pop up on the news occasionally, and that would be it.

I'd wake up tomorrow and my life would go back exactly to the way it was.

I blinked down at the steam rising from the small ceramic teacup.

Tomorrow I'd wake up... and my life would go back... to the way it was.

I'd find another bullshit job, and I'd go back to...

Alba. Olive. Jamie. And... what else?

I frowned down at the teapot. Why couldn't I think of anything I looked forward to doing when I got home? Why couldn't I remember a single memorable experience I'd had in the last year that was just my own? Something *I'd* done, an accomplishment *I'd* made, a milestone *I'd* passed—not Jamie, not Alba, not Olive.

I came up wholly, entirely blank.

So, then I tried extending the perimeters of my internal search to two years, then to three... four. Nothing.

Not one thing.

I hadn't traveled; I hadn't expanded my minuscule social circle; I hadn't really dated or taken up any hobbies or learned anything new. I'd just...

"... I don't recognize you anymore, Ree... You've let him win. You keep letting him win. You don't care about work, you don't care about meeting new people or making new friends, you don't date. You don't have any goals or ambitions anymore. You laugh and make jokes and pretend like nothing ever bothers you, but you've given up. You've numbed yourself to

the point where you just... you don't live. You exist and that's all."

There was a soft ringing in my ear as I stared blankly out the window, watching the sky slowly turn a darker, angrier shade of gray. The glass eventually fogged in the corners, and little droplets of rain splattered against my view.

My tea had gone cold, but I couldn't bring myself to drink any of it. I couldn't bring myself to do anything other than sit there, stare, and feel... nothing.

No. Not nothing. It was more of... an emptiness. Like something fundamental was missing. Except it wasn't scary or alarming. It wasn't like The Fundamental Thing was gone forever. More like I'd maybe just misplaced it. Or hidden it away a long time ago for safekeeping and couldn't quite remember how to get it back. It was in there somewhere, I just needed to look for it now that I knew it was gone.

And I could do that at home, during my seven hundredth rewatch of Bridget Jones. Or sitting at my new desk, dying a slow death at my new bullshit job.

It was going to be fine. All I had to do was get in the car, get on the plane, and never allow myself to think about Adrien Cloutier ever again.

All I had to do was go back.
You exist and that's all.
You don't live.

∼

I accidentally missed my flight.

And by accidentally, I meant I shoved my suitcase behind my chair and pretended like I'd never heard the name Ria Sanchez in my life when the suited driver came into the teashop asking for me.

Did I then haul my suitcase back to the house and sneak up to the cursed bedroom I'd been sharing with Adrien? Yes.

Did I spend the majority of the day playing backgammon with Gampy and baking with Alice while Maxwell sang a whole bunch of D12? Yes.

Did I enjoy myself? Immensely.

But none of that mattered. Because I'd come back to do one thing, and one thing only: prove to myself that what I'd felt when Adrien kissed me had been a total and utter fluke.

Emotions had been running high, and all that murderous rage had blasted straight to my head and messed with my hormonal wiring. The increased heart rate, the trembling, the inability to breathe properly had all been part of a fight-or-flight response thing—an adrenaline kick, if you will. I was ninety-nine-point-nine-nine-nine-nine percent sure of it. I just needed to be one hundred percent sure of it so I could go back and move on with my life without that pesky little question mark poking into the back of my brain.

Which was why I was restlessly pacing the room when Adrien came back from his meeting. I halted midstep when the door handle finally twisted (seven minutes and thirty-eight seconds later than when he'd said he'd be back) ... (not that I was counting).

"It's not what it looks like," I blurted before he'd even had a chance to enter the room. "I'm obviously not staying."

Adrien's eyebrows climbed when he saw me, a cocky smirk toying at his mouth. He shut the door and leaned

against it, arms crossed. The man was arrogance personified. "It's nice to see you, too, Sanchez. How was *your*
day?"

"I'm not staying," I said again, just in case he hadn't
heard me the first time. Then I wiggled the diamond ring
off my finger and held it out to him. "Also, this is yours."

He stalked to where I stood in the middle of the room,
his midnight-green gaze bolted to mine. I had to tilt my
chin up to maintain eye contact, the man was so irritably
tall.

"You could have just left it on my desk," he pointed
out.

I arched my eyebrows at him. "Why? So you could
claim it was missing—that I stole it—and lure me into a
predatorial slave-contract to pay you back?"

Even in the dim lighting of the single bedside lamp I
could see his ears tinting red as he studied me. "You really
think that little of me?"

"No," I answered truthfully, "because even that's giving
you too much credit."

A muscle in his jaw bounced. His smirk was gone. "I
told you I didn't want to play this fucked up game with
you anymore. So just tell me why you're still here."

I shoved the ring into the pocket of his jacket since he
refused to take it. "I need to confirm something really
quick, and then I'll be on my way."

I'd called the airline and had my flight rebooked. The
earliest they could do was tomorrow afternoon, but I'd be
more than happy to spend the night at the airport or a
motel. I just really needed to get this out of the way first.

"And what's that?" he practically growled through
clenched teeth. "What do you need to confirm?"

My tongue darted out to wet my drying lips, my heart

doing its best to crawl right out of my throat as I shoved my fists into my jacket pockets. I was dressed and ready to go. The second my little experiment was over, I'd grab my suitcase and march right out.

"I need to kiss you super quick," I told him directly.

His eyebrows twitched, then slammed together. Twitched, slammed. "Pardon?"

"I need to kiss you," I repeated as evenly as possible. "I'm telling you in advance for consent purposes. I'll keep it short and PG-13, and we'll both keep our hands to ourselves. Just so we're not tempted to strangle each other at any point."

Just so I'm not tempted to rip away your clothes on the extremely off chance that this morning wasn't a fluke.

He was looking at me like I was a crazy person. Because I sounded exactly like a crazy person.

"Why?" he asked.

I cleared my throat, my gaze darting away from him momentarily. Thinking was easier when he wasn't in my direct line of sight. "I felt a lot of things this morning that I shouldn't have when you kissed me. And I just need to prove to myself that it wasn't real."

Adrien eyed me for a few moments, something entirely unreadable flashing across his face. He let out a frustrated breath, glanced up at the ceiling, then yanked at his tie like it was suffocating him.

I shifted on my feet. "You don't have to say yes, this is why I asked first—"

"Has it occurred to you *even once* over the last couple of weeks that I'm an actual human being, Ria?"

I blinked.

Huh?

"I—what?"

"Has it once occurred to you over the last two weeks that I'm a real person?" he repeated. "With real feelings and all the other bullshit that comes with it?"

It was my turn to frown. Of course he was a real person. "What are you talking about?"

His throat worked like he was trying to swallow back whatever response was bubbling up his chest. Then he scrubbed a hand over his face, his lips pressing together. The redness from his ears had crept to his cheeks and was beginning to drip down his neck.

"Fine," he eventually muttered. "Go ahead. Do what you need to do."

I hesitated. He'd completely thrown me off with the human comment. "Maybe we should—"

But he cut me off, his voice readopting its usual sharp edge. "What were the parameters? PG-13 and hands to ourselves?"

I nodded and he shoved his hands into his pockets, mirroring me. "What else?"

I studied him carefully. "You don't have to say yes. You can just tell me to fuck off and kick me out of the house."

"I don't want to tell you to fuck off, and I don't want to kick you out of the house."

"Okay... what do you want?"

There was a long stretch of silence before he answered. "I want you to be honest about the results of this little... experiment."

I didn't know why that made my gut wiggle the way it did. It was fine. I'd kiss him, feel nothing, then tell him I felt nothing. It would be like kissing a lamp. Kind of warm and solid, with a slight chance of being mildly electrocuted. And not much else.

"Deal," I said.

"Deal," he said.

And then we just stood there.

"Can you... um... like lean down a little?" I asked awkwardly. He was too tall for me to reach, and I couldn't use my hands to pull him down.

The one side of his mouth twitched with reluctant amusement, his shoulders somewhat relaxing. He lowered his head. "Better?"

"Mhmm." Whatever soap or cologne or aftershave the man used deserved a whole bunch of awards for its longevity. And scent.

"Sanchez."

"Yup?"

"This is the part where you kiss me."

"I'm getting there." I was just trying to get my insides to calm down a little first. The whole point of this was to feel nothing.

His eyes meandered lazily over my face, deliberately lingering on my lips. It didn't help. "What are you waiting for?" he asked quietly, his warm breath gently caressing my skin.

Goosebumps. Goosebumps everywhere.

"Can you just... be still for a few seconds?" I ground out.

"I'm not moving very much."

"Your eyes are. And you keep talking."

"I'm just looking at you. Am I not allowed to look at you?"

"Shut up and *shhh*."

"I like looking at you. So much so that I actually hate it. You're very pretty. It's beyond outrageous."

Swoosh.

"Stop. Talking." My heart was a tiny, frantic bird,

trying to burst out of its too-small cage.

"Can you tell me why first?"

"You're messing with my vitals—er, variables. You're messing with the variables of my experiment."

The cocky smirk was back. He seemed a lot more relaxed now, and entirely too amused at my expense. Always at my expense. "I see. Sorry."

He did not look sorry. He looked like he was the opposite of sorry.

I shut my eyes, pushed an irritated breath out of my nose, and tried to recenter myself. Then I made the mistake of opening them again.

Adrien had moved closer, his gaze boring into my freaking soul. He had so many eyelashes, and they were so rich, dark, and breathtaking. His eyes were absolutely breathtaking. Especially when they'd gone all... tender and cloudy like that. I hated them.

"You can touch me if you want," he murmured softly. "I'll keep my hands to myself from now on. Until you tell me to."

From now on, like I wasn't leaving after this. *Until you tell me to*, like it was inevitable.

I should have rolled my eyes at him, but instead, I found my right fist unfurling, hesitating, then sliding out of my pocket.

Just to hold him in place, I told myself. *Or to push him away when I inevitably want to.*

So why did the tips of my fingers reach for his face instead? Why did they trace over his sharp eyebrow, cheekbone, jaw, his parted lips? Why did my chest flutter when his breath hitched in response?

I watched as his eyelids drooped, his focus grew hazy, and his breathing picked up. He cursed under his breath when my featherlight touch moved down the line of his throat, and I could feel the frantic flutter of his pulse.

It was fucking intoxicating.

Distracting.

"Sanchez..."

"Mmm?"

"Remember your little experiment?"

"Mmm."

"You should probably conduct it now."

"This is part of it," I decided. My fingers moved back up the column of his throat and over the full length of his jaw. His muscles were taught, and his throat kept working with one rough swallow after another.

I wondered how it would feel to touch his entire body like this. How he would react if I ran my teasing fingers all the way down his naked chest, his abs, his thighs. What would he do if I lazily traced the length of his cock—

My hand froze. My eyes flared. My brain halted.

Excuse me? You wonder what *now?*

My eyes snapped to his.

What the hell just happened?

You just wondered what it would be like to tease Adrien Cloutier's cock, you kinky little perv! That's what!

"Is torturing me a part of it, too?" Adrien chided quietly.

I didn't answer him. I tried to, but the comeback stuck itself at the base of my throat and refused to come out. When was the last time I'd... I couldn't remember the last time I'd thought about...

Huh.

"Sanchez, kiss me before I—"

I didn't give him a chance to finish.

24

THREE UNSEXY MISSISSIPPIS had been the plan.

I was supposed to touch his mouth with my mouth for three boring, awkward, and unsexy Mississippis, prove to myself that this morning had been a fluke brought on by (literally) raging hormones, and peace the hell out of Adrien Cloutier's life forever.

The exact opposite of that happened, and it was all his fault.

I mean, how were his lips so unrealistically soft? Did he moisturize them twenty-four times a day? And how much electricity did his body produce, exactly? Was he a scientific marvel on top of everything else? Because there was a concerning amount of zips and zaps shuddering through my body and... how exactly...

Wow.

My knees wobbled as I slid my arms around Adrien's neck, my awareness zeroing in on three things. One, he tasted like mint, fire, and forbidden fruit. Two, he wasn't touching me. Three, I very, *very* desperately needed him to be touching me.

I stepped closer, pressing my body to his as my mind slowly shut down. I could feel how hard he was, how his muscles vibrated if my tongue caressed him the right way. Still, he continued to keep his hands to himself.

I curled my fingers around his collar and pulled him closer as I tried to deepen the kiss. *Tried* being the operative word.

"Sanchez," Adrien murmured as he peeled his lips from mine.

I didn't realize he was capable of saying my name with such soft... tenderness. It sent a tremor of warm pleasure through me, and I had to stop myself from pushing him onto the bed.

I kissed him again.

"Ria." He tugged at my bottom lip with his teeth; punishment for not listening.

Except I didn't want to stop.

Stopping meant talking. It meant coming to terms with what had just happened and admitting things I wasn't ready to acknowledge.

And, most undesirably, it meant putting distance between our bodies.

So I kissed him harder. Until I was drowning in his scent, his groans, and the overwhelming feel of his hard body against mine. Our limbs were vibrating, our movements growing heavier, harder, rougher.

But he still.

Wasn't.

Touching.

Me.

He'd broken me. He'd broken my brain, shattered my willpower to bits, and still had the audacity to maintain enough self-control to keep his stupid hands to himself.

I wanted to break him.

I wanted him to lose every ounce of composure and restraint he possessed, to be engulfed in the same irrational, all-consuming fire he'd drenched me in. I wanted him to feel as frustrated and out of control as I did... which was exactly why I broke the kiss and took a step back. Then two. Three. Four.

Because *what the hell*?

I pressed the back of my hand to my tingling lips, trying very hard not to show Adrien how much I was trembling.

"I think... I think that's enough data." I didn't know whose voice that was but it sure as hell didn't sound like mine.

Adrien's hooded eyes stared back at me for a few moments, foggy and dazed. His fists were stuffed in his pockets, his arms and shoulders rigid.

Neither of us said anything for a solid minute, until Adrien finally cleared his throat, straightened his spine, and asked, "And?"

I shifted on my feet. "Um... it wasn't... horrible."

Technically not a lie.

"Be more specific," he commanded.

"You were there, you know what it was like. Why do I need to—" I cut myself off when he scrubbed at his face in frustration, my fingers curling into my palms. "Fine. It was... good. Or, like, great or whatever. About as good as kissing can get, I imagine. Or better than what I could imagine. I don't know."

Okay. Shush. That's more than enough.

Adrien dropped his hands, the tightness in his features easing as he studied my blazing cheeks. I averted my gaze.

"You're so fucking pretty when you blush, Ria. It's unreal."

Something about that specific comment, said in that specific tone, accompanied by that specific look, caused a central wire in my brain to snap in half like a stale breadstick.

And everything went to shit.

"Welp," I practically bellowed, startling myself. "Now that that's been established, I'll be on my way."

And then I saluted him.

…

I *saluted* him.

And I didn't know which one of us was more shocked by it, me or Adrien. His lips parted as he watched me, his brows arching.

My idiot hand was frozen midair, and I gaped back at him as my entire body turned into a Flaming Hot Cheeto.

Good god. What the hell are you doing?

My palm slammed to my side, and I stiffly marched toward my suitcase, determined to make my exit as swift and uneventful as possible. But Adrien stepped right in front of me, blocking my path.

"Excuse me," I said in a strangely polite tone, attempting to step around him.

"Sanchez," the bane of my existence purred, once again blocking my path.

"That's me." Was it just in my head or did I suddenly sound like I'd inhaled a bunch of helium?

"Are you flustered?"

My heart tripped. "Crikey. I don't phink so, mate. It's just a bit hot in 'ere, innit?"

My teeth snapped together, my face prickling in complete and utter horror. What in the ever-loving fuck was *that* accent? If Steve Irwin and Moira Rose had unprotected Essex, their lovechild would pop out of the womb wailing in that accent.

It was *horrible*.

Adrien's mouth began to spread into a slow full-faced grin that made me think of the cat from Alice in Wonderland, but a lot sexier.

"Oh my god," he said, voice airy with amused disbelief.

"I'm gonna leave now." My declaration was followed by another failed attempt at making an escape. I rolled my lips and glared up at him stubbornly.

"You're so flustered," he observed inaccurately.

Did I become weirdly polite, forget how speaking worked, and turn a medically alarming shade of blotchy purple when I was extremely flustered? Yes.

But did Adrien Cloutier possess the power and ability to make me flustered? Absolutely fucking not.

"I told you, I'm not flustered," I responded coolly, threatening my tongue with ghost-pepper sauce if it even thought about rolling a single one of those words into a non-Canadian accent.

His eyes searched mine, softening. "Well, this is unexpectedly adorable."

I didn't know his voice could go all gentle and tender like that when he was talking to me. And I definitely didn't realize someone calling you *unexpectedly adorable* would be so butterfly-inducing.

I wasn't sure how to respond so I shifted on my feet and put my hands behind my back, clearing my throat.

"Sanchez," he said in that confusingly gentle way, taking a step forward, "how about that truce?"

I stepped back and leaned lightly against the wall, trying to come off as casual as possible despite the ruckus in my chest. "Why are you so dead set on this truce thing?" I managed.

"Why are you so against it?"

"I asked you first."

Adrien pinched his lips together and tilted his head. "I have a theory."

I eyed him. "Okay. What is it?"

"I think you and I are a lot more..." He paused, presumably trying to think of the right way to phrase it. "I think we might be more compatible than we realize."

I blinked at him. Did he know what the word *compatible* meant?

"In what way?" I asked dubiously.

"In every way."

My lips jerked, my faculties returning to me one by one as the ridiculousness of his words set in. "You're joking." Surely, he was joking.

"Nope."

"Adrien, we despise each other," I reminded him.

"Right." He paused again, this time to wet his lips and clear his throat. "Except for the part where I don't actually despise you."

A solid ten seconds passed before I asked, "What?"

He shrugged. "Despise is a strong word. I'm not even sure I hate you."

Had a shooting star crashed through the roof and boinked me on the head I'd have been less flabbergasted. Was he serious?

"And I'm not convinced you hate me, either," he went on.

Uh, wrong. I opened my mouth to tell him just that, except what came out was, "What? Why?"

"A hunch."

A *hunch*? In what distorted version of reality had I given him any indication whatsoever that I felt anything toward him other than pure contempt? Other than the whole kissing thing, but that was new and didn't count.

Also, you could hate someone and still want to kiss them. Case-in-point, me and Adrien. Right here, right now.

Did my eyes keep flicking to his not-so-mediocre mouth against my direct orders? Yes.

Were my fingers twitching with the desire to grab his collar and yank his body to mine again? Sure.

Did I still want to strangle him? Abso-fucking-lutely I did.

Or wait... no. Strangulation was maybe a bit too violent. A kick to the shin would probably yield more appropriate results, as long as it wasn't hard enough to break a bone, since he'd probably use it as an excuse to pull me into another absurd agreement as payback.

What would be next? He'd force me to actually marry him? I'd have to plan a whole wedding and walk down the aisle in a white dress? What then? I'd accidentally moan during the "you may now kiss the bride" part without realizing it? In a *church*? In front of a *priest*?

Wait. Why was I thinking about marrying Adrien? How did I get—

Real-life Adrien said my name, yanking me back to reality.

"Huh?" I inquired eloquently.

"You went all quiet."

"I…" *I swear to Mother Gaia herself, if you blurt anything about marrying him out loud, I'll hurl you out the window.* "I do."

No.

Wait.

I shook my head as Adrien quirked a brow.

"I do. Hate you, I mean. I do hate you," I clarified quickly, trying not to pay too much attention to any flaring sensations around my nose.

He wasn't deterred. "You know, people who hate each other generally don't enjoy making out."

"You can hate someone and still be physically attracted to them," I argued. "Unfortunately, those two things aren't mutually exclusive."

"So you admit you're attracted to me."

"Believe me, no one is as disappointed in me as I am," I said gravely.

"I'm not disappointed. And what do you propose we do with the immense amount of physical attraction you feel toward me?"

"First of all, no one said anything about an *immense* amount of anything."

"It was heavily implied."

"Second of all," I went on, ignoring him, "just because we're attracted to each other doesn't mean we have to act on it."

"Do I get a say in this?"

"If I say no, will you listen?"

"Unlikely. And I think we should act on it."

I mimicked his signature lizard-blink, regarding him with vague disinterest. "Hands down one of your worst ideas. And that's saying something."

"Would it help change your mind if I grew a man-bun and painted my skin blue?"

"For the last time, it's cinnamon roll, not cinna*man-bun*. And you literally couldn't be farther away from the archetype if you tried—wait," I interrupted myself, my brain stumbling back a step. "If I said yes, would you do it?"

He didn't answer right away.

...

He didn't answer right away.

"Shut up. Would you actually do it?" An unexpected bout of excitement rushed my bloodstream, my imagination running wild with image after image of a blue-skinned Adrien sporting an atrocious man-bun.

He lifted a shoulder. "Maybe."

Holy shit. "Would I be able to take pictures?"

"Would you post them anywhere?"

"On the internet? No. On my walls in the form of life-size posters? Yes. I'm extremely cultured and have always been really big on art. It's *so* important."

His mouth twitched. "I don't think that counts as art, Ria."

"That's because you obviously don't get art, Adrien."

He laughed, his eyes doing that new thing again where they went all soft and gooey. So weird. "Guess not."

And because the molten gooeyness was doing more funny things to my insides, I diverted. "Also, quick reminder, the aliens have horns and tails and fangs. So make sure you include all those things."

Adrien shook his head in amused exasperation, his eyes crinkling in their corners, dimples fully popping.

And he said *I* was annoyingly attractive.

He stepped forward, chin tilting down as mine tilted up. "You're staring again, Sanchez."

I swallowed, and his gaze dropped, tracing the movement.

"And, as usual, you're staring right back, Cloutier."

"Can't help it," he claimed, smile waning slightly. "Believe me, I tried. Especially at the beginning."

"The only thing you did at the beginning was glare at me," I told him.

"There was a lot of that, too," he admitted.

"There still is."

"Less of it."

"Barely."

His head tilted. "Do you always have to argue with everything I say?"

"Yes."

"Brat," he said softly. Almost affectionately. Like this was just our thing; what we did.

Seriously. What the hell had gotten into him all of a sudden? And what the hell had gotten into *me*? Why was I enjoying this so much?

My blood was thrumming, my heart galloping. And my gaze kept gravitating down to his mouth, no matter how many times I tried to stop.

"Ria. You have to stop looking at me like that."

"Why?"

"Because I promised I wouldn't touch you until you asked."

I licked my lips, my stomach flipping. "I'm never going to ask, but I give you my consent. You have it, so... you can touch me if you want."

There. Ball was in his court.

His brows furrowed, his dark eyes bouncing between mine. "But is it what *you* want?"

"Would I still be here if it wasn't?"

"I'd still like to hear you say it," he insisted.

I folded my arms across my chest. "And you have the nerve to suggest we're compatible."

"We are compatible."

"I honestly can't tell if you're fucking with me or if you're actually that deluded."

"And I honestly can't tell if you really don't see it or if you're in active denial because you don't want to see it."

"Do you remember this morning? At breakfast? With the raisins and the foot stomping?"

More amusement. "I do."

"Newsflash, Adrien: people who are compatible—*people who don't despise each other*—don't do shit like that."

"Anger isn't the same thing as hatred. Neither is pent-up frustration."

"I never said it was."

"So you don't think things between us would be different if we'd met under normal circumstances?"

"Do you?"

"Hell yeah, Sanchez. Look at us. Right now."

"Yeah. We're bickering. We bicker about everything, Adrien. Every single thing."

He grinned. "We're quite good at bantering, I agree."

"That's not what I said."

"It's what I heard," he countered. "But that's only part of what I was referring to."

"What's the rest?"

"The fact that you find me immensely attractive, and I find you aggravatingly beautiful. The part where I think you're smart, funny, and charming when you're not actively trying to pick fights with me." His gaze turned molten. "I can show you the rest when you finally cave and beg me to touch you."

I pressed my lips together, pushing a lungful of air out of my nose. "I've given you my consent. It's enough. I'm not going to beg you to touch me," I said adamantly. I had far too much pride for that.

His mouth curved into a cocky little smirk. "That's too bad. I really think you'd enjoy all the unspeakable things I've been wanting to do to you."

Don't ask, don't ask, don't ask. Please don't ask.

"Like what, exactly?" I asked, my crossed arms tightening. "The last time the topic came up, you said you planned on punishing me for everything that's happened."

"I did."

"And which of the depraved punishments in your twisted, evil mind do you think I'd enjoy?"

"All of them. Every single one."

For whatever reason, the way he said that made my heart want to beat itself into cardiac arrest.

I swallowed, my thighs clenching. "Give me an example. Just so I can tell you how much I'd hate it, and we can put this whole thing to rest."

He braced a palm on the wall, right beside my head. Then he leaned in, stripping the air around us of oxygen. "They're called *unspeakable things* for a reason. But I'm happy to discuss our likes, dislikes, and hard limits. Those are important."

My chest was whirling, my skin felt flushed and overly sensitive. He was so close now that I could feel the kiss of his warm breath on my skin. God, he smelled amazing.

His smile widened. Dimples, dimples, dimples. "You're

so fucking pretty when you blush like that, Sanchez. I can't handle it."

My heart skipped. My breath shuddered. And I really needed him to touch me now.

When the hell had this happened? When had he gone from Man I'd Like To Choke, to Man Whose Dick I'd Like To Choke On?

Great. Now I was thinking about choking on Adrien's dick. And I didn't hate the idea. Not even a little bit.

What happened to you? To me. To us. We used to be so mentally stable.

My brain pointed a metaphorical finger at Adrien's asymmetrical dimples. It was *their* fault.

He was smirking like he knew exactly what I was thinking. Like he knew exactly what he'd done to me, how he'd ruined me.

What I'd give to ruin him right back.

"Sanchez."

If I had a dollar for every time Adrien said my name, I'd be the richest person in this room. Probably. I couldn't really wrap my head around how much a billion dollars was, and according to the internet, he had a whole bunch of those, so.

"Tell me what you like," he murmured.

My throat was starting to go dry. I tried to think of the sexiest possible way to answer him, but my brain had melted into lusty goo.

He tutted when I took too long to answer, like he was getting impatient with my rebellious little pauses. "Tell me how you like to be fucked, pretty girl."

My heart stopped, my mouth slighting open.

Pretty girl.

The nickname fluttered through me, feeding the fiery

ache between my thighs. I very much wanted him to call me that again. And again, and again, and again.

Before or after he makes you choke on his dick?

During. Definitely during.

What have you become?

"I'll tell you after you touch me," I managed.

"I'll touch you after you ask nicely."

I was so turned on it was starting to become uncomfortable. My hips and thighs squirmed, and his gaze dropped down to the motion, his jaw flexing.

I couldn't take it anymore. I really couldn't. The air had turned electric, my body was on fire, the planet was depleted of oxygen, and I was going to detonate.

And that was exactly what happened—I detonated.

I erupted in a way that stripped me of all rational thought and reason. In a way that could only end up backfiring. But I didn't care.

He wanted to play this game? *Fine.*

In one fluid—and incredibly frustrated—movement, I yanked off my jacket and tossed it onto the floor. Then I went for my shirt.

"What the hell are you doing?"

"What you won't do." I threw my shirt on top of my jacket.

I was wearing a burgundy lace bra and matching thong, courtesy of the honeymoon lingerie collection Luke had so kindly picked out for me.

Adrien's eyes went black.

Lighting. Thunder. Somewhere in the distance, sirens.

The hand he'd braced on the wall dropped to his side.

"Ria."

It was in the look he gave me. The tone of his voice.

"You can run your smart mouth all you want, throw your

punches, pick fights, continue to torment me however you see fit... but I get to respond how I see fit."

And how exactly did he plan to retaliate if he wouldn't even touch me? Hadn't thought this one through very well, had he?

His demeanor began to shift; his earlier arrogance overtaken by blistering tension.

I unbuttoned my jeans and pulled the zipper down, slowly, slowly, slowly. He watched my every movement, jaw working, molars clenched tight.

I waited, allowing the tension to simmer, allowing him to look as much as he wanted. His fingers twitched toward my hips before he curled them into fists.

That was my cue.

I hooked my fingers underneath the waistband of my jeans, peeled them down my thighs, and kicked them off. Then I stood in front of him, half-naked, wearing nothing but two dainty strips of wine-colored lace.

He wasn't breathing or moving anymore. A bunch of veins in his neck and forearms were protruding, his muscles bulged, like he couldn't decide whether he wanted to fight me or fuck me. To be fair, I wasn't sure which one I wanted either.

I toyed with the delicate hem of my panties, flicking it once. Twice. Three separate muscles in his jaw spasmed as he watched my fingers hungrily. His fists were white.

"I know," I said. "I look *great* naked."

His glare was lethal.

The silence even more so.

We were locked in a staring contest now, neither of us willing to back down.

And then he said, "Get on the bed."

It was an order. There was no question about it, no room for argument.

Excitement shot up my torso. I leaned forward, my lips brushing his as I whispered my defiance. "Make. Me."

Time stood still for exactly one heartbeat.

And then his hands were on me, and the world went up in flames.

25

It was fire on blistering fire.

Our bodies crashed into each other as Adrien's muscled arms wrapped around me, his hungry mouth crushing mine.

The kiss wasn't soft. It wasn't pretty or nice or romantic. It was weeks of anger and frustration and pent-up tension boiling over. It was all the hatred he claimed we didn't feel for one another. It was pure hunger and need.

Neither of us wanted to want this, and we were hell-bent on punishing each other for it. To me, it was all his fault. To him, it was all mine.

So, we fought.

I clawed at his back, and he dug his fingers into my hips. I pulled at a fistful of his hair, and he crushed me against the wall. Our tongues pushed and shoved at each other, our teeth biting too hard. It was feral, hungry, savage.

Maybe this was what we needed. Maybe we just had to fuck each other once, get it out of our systems, and move on. Maybe we weren't physically compatible, and this whole thing would be a dud anyway. We were being too combative, too aggressive, too ferocious. It felt like a competition, like we were fighting for dominance, neither of us willing to submit to the other. It was—

Adrien broke the kiss.

"Stop fighting me," he demanded, body pressed flush against mine. I could feel every hard edge of muscle and arousal on him.

"You're fighting *me*," I panted back.

"Because you're trying to take control."

"Well it's not like I'm going to let you have it."

"We're going to draw blood if we keep going like this," he said.

"Why do you sound surprised?" What had he been expecting?

"Ria, you're being—"

"No more talking, we've done too much of that already. We just need to get this thing over with, and we'll both feel better after. Or worse. Either way, we'll know."

I reached for his belt.

His brows were pinched together, and before my fingers could so much as graze the leather of his belt, he'd grabbed my wrists and secured them firmly behind my back with one large hand.

Good lord. "What now?"

"No," he said.

The word rammed into my lungs like I'd jumped headfirst into an ice bath.

No, as in he didn't want this.

No, as in I'd misread the situation, or he'd changed his mind.

No, as in *stop*.

"Okay." I didn't even think, just tried to take a step back and give him some room.

But he wouldn't let me budge.

"Wait. I just... need a second to think," he said.

I stood unmoving as he took in a breath, two, three. Then he pressed his forehead to mine. Seconds passed, then minutes. Slowly, we breathed. Slowly, the too-tight tension in our muscles began to ease, his grip around my wrists softened, and his thumb began stroking my skin. My body started melting against the heat of his until I was fully molded against him.

It was way more pleasant than it had any right to be. For all the fighting we did, our bodies fit quite perfectly together.

When he finally lifted his head, his eyes were softer—more lucid.

"Tell me this is what you want," he said. "Ask me to touch you."

"Oh my god. It's like we're stuck in a timeloop." I was surprised at how much less aggressive my tone sounded. That little breather had done wonders.

"Say it." His thumb caressed my wrist bone again, and my breath hitched.

"Hate to break it to you, but you're already touching me."

"If you don't say it, we stop."

"I gave you my consent, my tongue was in your mouth less than five minutes ago, and I'm standing in front of you half-naked. How could that possibly not be enough?"

"I need to hear the words."

"Why?"

"I just do."

"*Why?*"

"Because I'm not going to willingly give you another reason to resent me."

My brain stuttered. "What?"

His nose brushed against mine tenderly, a soft breath escaping his lungs. "You're in my head, you're under my skin, you're fucking everywhere, Ria. I can't think properly when you're around, and I can't trust that I'm not misreading the signs."

Something in my chest compressed, causing my mouth to flap uselessly as I struggled to string together a response. I hadn't expected that to be his reasoning.

"I need to make sure," he reiterated. "I need to know this isn't just teasing, or anger, or you trying to get back at me. Tell me this isn't an elaborate revenge scheme. *Tell me* you want me to touch you."

What kind of sociopath would have sex with another person for revenge? But before I could voice that thought out loud, Adrien brought his other hand to my neck, running his palm up the column of my throat. He used his grip to tilt my jaw up until my lips were level with his. His other hand remained firm over my wrists.

And *oh*kay. According to the way my nether regions reacted, my body *really* enjoyed it.

"You only have to say it once," he promised, his fingers squeezing my throat lightly. "Admit you want it, stop waging war, and I'll fuck you until you're nothing short of incoherent, Ria. I'll bend you over my desk and eat you out for as many hours as I've spent torturing myself fantasizing about it, and then I'll punish you for making me want to taste you so fucking bad."

...

Wow.

His lips brushed mine as he spoke, his thumb stroking the spot my pulse was trying to beat out of my neck.

"What else would you do?"

I hadn't instructed my mouth to ask that, but I wasn't complaining. Because, again, *wow*.

His lips quirked. "I'm not sure you wanna know. My imagination's started to get a bit out of hand."

"More unspeakable things?"

"And they're growing increasingly unspeakable by the second. It might scare you off."

"That would be the best-case scenario. Then we'd avoid all the mistakes we're about to make."

"And this feels like a mistake to you, does it?"

It wasn't until I'd opened my mouth to say yes that I realized it might not be entirely accurate. It was a mistake, yes, it just didn't *feel* like one. Not with the way our bodies were melted against each other, his thumbs caressing my skin.

"Just tell me what you'll do," I insisted.

One more hesitant heartbeat, almost like he was debating how honest he was going to be, and then, "I'll make you wear that little green slip, take you over my knee, and spank you for what you put me through last night. I'll tie you up and edge you once for every lie you've told me." He paused to run the tip of his tongue across my bottom lip as his fingers squeezed my throat again. "And as punishment for being so fucking pretty, for making me want you like this, I'll keep you tied up while I force you to come for me. Over and over again. Until you're well beyond begging and pleading for me to stop; until the only word you remember how to say is my name."

Holy shit.

"And that's just to start," he promised.

He waited for me to respond, but my brain was buffering and the only thing I could do was gawk up at him.

"You wanna know more?" he teased, evidently amused by the silence he'd stunned me into.

When my faculties finally decided to return, I said, "I —you're talking as if this isn't just a one-time thing."

"Do you think this is going to be just a one-time thing?"

"I know it is."

"I see." He didn't even attempt to hide the fact that he didn't believe me. "So you don't want to know the rest. We should just... move on to the main event?"

The fact that his thumbs continued to caress my skin in that mind-melting way wasn't helping my rational thinking abilities.

"You should just, um, tell me anyway. Just so I know what bullets I'm dodging," I said.

He let out a low rumbling laugh, as if I'd made a joke. "When you're good, I'll want to reward you. I'll buy you toys and play with you. I'll bind your wrists and feed you my cock. I'll praise you, lick you, and fuck you the way you need." He bit my bottom lip, then licked it soothingly. "I'd spoil you absolutely rotten if you let me, Ria."

Good fucking lord.

"How does that sound?" he murmured.

"You have quite the filthy mouth on you, Mr. Cloutier."

"You don't seem to mind it one bit, Miss Sanchez."

I didn't. Quite the opposite, actually.

"Answer my question. How does that sound?"

"I shouldn't want any of that."

"But you do." It wasn't a question.

I swallowed. "Yeah."

"Which part?"

"All of it."

"Say it."

The resistance eased, my desire to rebel overwhelmed by the much more urgent and rabid need for Adrien to make good on every one of his threats and promises. Arousal was one hell of a drug; especially when it had been repressed for so long.

"I want it."

His breath hitched, his grip on my neck tightening slightly. "Be specific."

"I want you to touch me. I want to be punished, praised, and everything else you just said." And then, because he'd promised to reward me for being good, I swallowed a small chunk of my pride and said, "Please."

A pleased rumble rolled from the depth of his throat. "What's your safeword?"

"Cinnamon."

"When I kiss you, are you going to wage war again?"

I shook my head.

"Good girl."

His mouth lowered to mine again. This time it wasn't a battle. This time our teeth weren't out to draw blood, and our tongues weren't trying to take each other down. We withdrew our fangs and our claws, I let him take over, and holy shit, it was so much better. My toes curled, my heart leaped, fireflies swarmed my stomach, and it felt like I was burning from the inside out, but in the best possible way.

Adrien didn't release my neck or wrists, using his grip on them to keep me exactly where he wanted me, and didn't give me much choice in the matter. It was shocking (concerning?) how much my body enjoyed that once I stopped resisting it.

I was just about to pass out from the lack of oxygen when he finally pulled his lips away. I almost whined.

"Take my belt off," he said in a low command.

He let go of my wrists but kept his other hand where it was, his thumb stroking the side of my neck. My head remained tilted up so he could watch my face while I fumbled with his belt.

"You are aggravatingly, inconveniently... maddeningly beautiful, Ria."

My heart tripped all over itself as the words replayed in my head, and his smirk told me he'd felt it. I peeled off his belt, and he took it from my hand.

"Get on the bed and spread your legs for me—"

Obviously, I wasn't going to keep obeying him so easily. I still had most of my pride, my dignity.

"—pretty girl."

The air rushed out of my lungs so fast it made my head spin. My lashes fluttered, my heart slammed into my ribs, and, fuck me, I couldn't believe how much I *loved* it when he called me that.

His mouth expanded into a slow grin as he watched my reaction, his dimples popping in delight.

"God, you're beautiful," he murmured, leaning down to suckle on my bottom lip. "How is it fair? How was I supposed to stand a chance?"

I didn't know, but he definitely needed to make me pay for it. For sure.

"Get on the bed for me," he said again.

"I thought you wanted me to change into the green slip first."

He nipped at my chin. "That's for tomorrow night. I've got a different score to settle with you right now. If you keep making me wait, there might be consequences," he said in a playfully devilish tone.

I considered it. "Like the fun kind of consequences, or no?"

He chuckled. "The reward will be much better. I'd choose to listen if I were you."

I didn't argue with him this time. Didn't feel the need to insist—once again—that there wasn't going to be a tomorrow night. I got on my back, holding his gaze as my thighs spread for him.

He stepped up to the edge of the bed, searing gaze trailing fire down my body.

"Sanchez." He *purred* my name before running a single finger down my stomach. A whole bunch of muscles south of my bellybutton quivered. "You've soaked through these panties. They're ruined. Is this all for me?"

I wasn't going to dignify that with a response.

"Yes," my slutty mouth tattled immediately.

"You like it when I talk about all the depraved things I want to do to you?"

"I'll like it more when you actually do them. But yes, apparently dirty talk is a big thing for me." Who knew.

He hummed. "Put your wrists together."

I listened, watching as he expertly looped his leather belt over and under my wrists, securing them. Another unknown kink of mine unlocked. It was like a video game.

"How's that? Too tight?"

I shook my head.

Then he walked away from the bed.

I was tempted to bang my head against the mattress. I knew he was doing it on purpose. The waiting was part of my punishment. But at this rate I was going to die from horniness before he even touched me.

And then I heard the strange *clink*s. I frowned, twisting my head to look at Adrien as he approached the bed again. He was holding a crystal tumbler filled with... oh god.

"Tell me, Sanchez. Did you really sneak ice into my coffee last week? Is that why they were always lukewarm when you brought them to me?"

Okay, well, I could say with absolute certainty that I hadn't seen this one coming.

"Maybe."

Where the hell had he gotten the ice from? There was a mini fridge in the room, but he'd walked in the opposite direction.

"And you lied to me about it."

"I did."

"You thought it was funny."

"Hilarious," I confirmed.

"Would you do it again?"

"In a heartbeat. You were being a huge dick that first week."

His mouth quirked as he set the glass down on the bedside table. "I see."

He leaned over me then, bracing a palm beside my head on the mattress as he lowered his lips to mine. The kiss was deceptively tender and sweet. It pulled an eager little whimper out of me, making my toes dig into the duvet.

"And have you ever had your clit teased with ice, Miss Sanchez?" he murmured against my lips.

I could feel my cheeks flush as arousal boiled in my core. "Can't say I have, no."

He kissed me again, soft and torturously sweet. "Any theories as to what it might feel like?"

"Cold," I deadpanned.

He chuckled, and before I could make a smart comment about stupid questions, he pressed the small cube of ice into the crook of my neck, and *oh*kay, wow. There was cold, and then there was being touched by frigid ice when your body had spent the last twenty minutes burning from the inside out.

Adrien swallowed my gasp with a deep kiss, his tongue caressing mine as my back arched off the bed. I shivered and whined when he began to move the already-melting cube of torture down my neck, chest, cleavage. My hips squirmed, my wrists jerking against their restraints. I wanted to wrap my arms around him and pull his body down to mine.

"How's that?" he teased, slowly sliding the frozen cube down my ribs.

"*Cold.*"

Another small laugh. I couldn't pinpoint when he'd started to find my humor amusing exactly, but it sparked an oddly pleasant sense of satisfaction in my chest every time he smiled or laughed at one of my jokes. Especially when they weren't particularly funny.

"Have we started to learn our lesson yet?" he asked as he continued to run the piece of ice over my ribs.

"I don't know, should we check? Go grab some coffee and see if I dump any—*oh*."

Apparently, my lower stomach was incredibly sensitive to extreme temperatures. Especially when it was caught off-guard by them.

"Don't move," Adrien ordered as he guided the ice up to my bellybutton. He left it there. "If you let it fall, you won't get to come tonight."

"What? That's so mean," I argued. It would take one

inadvertent jerk of a muscle or limb for the slippery little fucker to slide right off my skin, and my abs were already starting to quiver.

"But if you manage to keep it there while I strip you naked, I'll let you come on my tongue before I fuck you."

Oh.

Oh, okay.

Cool. Cool cool cool.

"I mean, sure, if that's what *you* want."

He flashed me another mischievous grin as his fingers began trailing down my hips, thighs. "Think you can do it?"

"I think the ice will be fully melted before this conversation is over. Do you normally talk this much during sex?"

"No," he answered. "Not even close."

"Ah, another torture method, then." Well, the joke was on him since I was quite enjoying this.

He didn't answer, his attention glued to my skin as his hands roamed up to my chest. Then he peeled the lacey bra down my rib cage, until my breasts were on full display for him.

"Jesus. Look at how fucking perfect you are."

Objectively, this wasn't true. *Objectively*, I wasn't anywhere close to being perfect. However, that knowledge did absolutely nothing to temper my body's response to the compliment. I practically melted into the mattress.

And I was so wrapped up in the warm burn of his words, and in trying to remain as still as possible under the freezing pinch of ice against my stomach, that I hadn't noticed he'd reached for another cube until I felt him drag it over my left nipple.

Goosebumps spread across every available inch of my

skin as I gasped, but I managed to stop my body just before it squirmed and flailed. A miracle.

"Good girl," Adrien praised lowly, circling my pink bud with the fresh cube. That felt... so much more intense than I'd been anticipating. Maybe because of the surprise element.

I breathed out a small curse and made the mistake of closing my eyes. Adrien chose that exact moment to take my teased nipple into his scorching mouth, and, "Oh!"

The sudden contrast between the ice and the heat of his mouth was *everything*. He suckled and nipped and licked, and I moaned, my neck arching as a string of involuntary tremors ran down my limbs. Beads of melted ice trickled down the side of my stomach, and I had to keep my wrists from fighting against their restraints again. I wanted to shove him down onto the bed and have my wicked way with him. *Now*.

I'd had enough teasing.

"Adrien," I pleaded.

"You're doing so good, pretty girl," he praised, rewarding me with another tantalizing flick of his tongue.

Oh god.

I bit back the *please* that had formed on the tip of my tongue and tried to remain still as Adrien's hand moved down to my hips, nudging and playing with the dainty lace covering my aching center. Just an inch lower, I just needed his fingers to move one inch lower.

Then he pressed the ice against my inner thighs, and I almost lost it.

I shivered, gasped, moaned. "Adrien," I pleaded.

"Do you have any fucking idea how good it feels to hear you moan my name like that?"

A dry, breathless laugh scraped out of my throat. "You should reward me for it."

He hummed, and just as the concentrated pinch of frozen ice on my belly was becoming a little too much to bear, my panties were peeled down my legs and discarded. *Finally*.

"Can I move now?" I asked breathlessly.

"Have you learned your lesson yet?" he asked, edging the wet ice closer to my labia.

"No. This is kind of amazing." I'd have drowned his coffee in ice if I'd known this was how he'd get back at me for it. "If this is how you intend to punish me for—"

I choked on the rest of my sentence when he slid the melting ice to my center. Any control I had left over my body evaporated. My limbs seized, my torso curved, the ice slipped off my skin, and all the air whooshed out of my lungs.

"Oh my god," I breathed. And then I repeated it four more times, because *oh my god*.

"What about now? Have you learned your lesson?" He circled my clit twice, adding just enough pressure to make my hips buckle. And I couldn't decide whether I wanted to scramble away from the biting cold, or to press closer and chase the friction I desperately needed.

"Adrien. I need—ah."

"Look at how fast the ice is melting against your pussy. Does that feel good, pretty girl?"

"Yes." I wasn't crying, but it sounded like I was crying.

"How do you think it'll feel when I replace it with my mouth and lick you fucking senseless?" He was sliding it over my center, around my clit, teasing, teasing, teasing. Little droplets of water were dripping through my folds, driving me insane.

"Show me," I rasped, grinding my hips into his hand.

"Is that what you want?" He pressed the ice firmly against my clit. "My mouth on your cunt?"

So desperately it hurt. "Yes."

And just when it felt like I was going to burst from desperation, he sunk down to his knees in front of the bed, pulled my hips toward his face, and *ruined my fucking life*.

The stark contrast between the cool ice and the searing heat of his mouth set my oversensitive nerves on blazing fire, making me scream. The ice was discarded, and he splayed my thighs wide open as his mouth started working me with a relentless hunger that made me shudder and moan. Over and over and over again.

"Look at what you've done to me, pretty girl," he murmured into my center before spoiling it with another string of agonizingly slow and thorough licks. "I should punish you for tasting so fucking sweet."

I whimpered his name, my fingers digging into his hair as my hips began to grind against his mouth with shameless need. I was getting close, the tension in my stomach coiling unbearably tight. And the more I said his name, the more feverish his hunger became.

Then he nipped at my labia with his teeth.

The shock of pleasure zapped me so hard I gasped, my upper body jolting off the mattress. And before I could even think about recovering, he bit me again, then sucked my clit into his scorching mouth, flicking it with the tip of his tongue. Over. And over. And over again.

I saw stars.

My mouth was wide open, but no air went in, and no sound came out.

My grip on his hair tightened as the pleasure of

release slammed into my body, my legs wrapping around his head. My muscles twitched and spasmed, my ears rang, and my speckled vision blurred around the edges. I was falling, gasping, and panting as Adrien continued to lick and suck me eagerly—*enthusiastically*—keeping his mouth buried between my legs well beyond the crash of my orgasm.

His tongue dipped into my soaked entrance, and he let out a growl of pleasure, shuddering against me.

Too much.

Too much too much too much.

I couldn't.

But I'd lost my voice.

I nudged weakly at his forehead with my palm, trying to get him to relent. His defiant groan vibrated against my oversensitive clit, and I swear I almost cried. My thighs were quivering against his ears, my seizing lungs desperate for oxygen. I needed to breathe, but every time he licked me it sent another zap of electricity through my body.

I choked out a whimper, my liquid knuckles prodding his forehead with desperation.

Please, please, please.

Finally, I managed to get him to lift his head. He looked up at me with a dazed and drunken expression, his cheeks flushed, eyes unfocused, his mouth wet and shiny with the evidence of my moans.

I puddled. My bound hands collapsed onto my wet stomach, my bones lost all structural integrity, and I melted right into the mattress.

It took a minute or two, but little by little, my senses started to return. Little by little, I became aware of the physical sensations coursing blissfully through my body.

Of Adrien placing soft kisses along my skin, and of his tongue tracing the wetness of my folds and inner thighs like he wanted to keep my taste in his mouth for a little while longer.

Eventually his kisses began to trail up my stomach, my chest, and neck, until he was leaning over me again. He gazed a little too deeply into my eyes, kissed my lips a little too sweetly.

"How was that?" he murmured.

I half-blinked up at his dark emerald eyes. They were so unbelievably stunning.

I lifted my head and kissed him as softly as he'd kissed me, my hands reaching for the front of his shirt. I pulled him closer, my legs snaking around his waist.

"Ria."

I kissed him again, my fingers working to unbutton his shirt. It was his turn. I wanted to make him feel just as good as he'd made me feel. *Better*, even.

The desire to break him came back with a vengeance. This time, though, it didn't carry the same sharp edge as last time. This time I wanted him to crumble from pure pleasure. To make him fall apart *for* me—*because* of me. We fell into a tangle of desperate and breathless kisses, the needy heat returning to my core with impossible speed. I shouldn't have been turned on again this quickly. Then again, Adrien shouldn't have been able to make me come that hard.

Nothing made sense.

He rasped a curse against my lips when I ground my hips against his, chasing further friction. Then he was throwing off his shirt, unbuttoning his slacks. Our mouths separated for exactly four seconds so he could fish a condom out of his wallet and get rid of his pants (I knew because I counted), and then we were back, making out like our lives depended on it.

I ran my fingers down his chest and abs while our tongues were tangled, swallowing the broken groan I pulled out of him when my fingers reached the his briefs. He stopped me before I could go farther down south, though, gripping the belt he had snaked around my wrists, and using it to pin my hands above my head.

I fucking loved it. My insides purred, my throat sang, and my thighs widened an extra inch.

"You still haven't told me how you like to be fucked, Ria," Adrien murmured against my skin. His lips were on my neck, kissing and biting and nibbling.

I wanted him to fuck me just like this, holding my wrists above my head. I wanted to see him lose control because of me. I wanted him to come so hard he saw stars and heard ringing in his ears and lost the ability to speak coherently.

"However you want," my mouth said. Half the major circuits in my brain had melted, and the remaining half were highly compromised. "Use me."

If we were only going to do this once, we might as well get carried away and go all out. Get it out of our systems.

I'd never see him again after this, so who cared?

A curse rumbled out of Adrien in response, and then his mouth was on mine again, kissing me with feverish desperation.

When we were forced to come up for air, he pushed himself off the bed, pulled off his briefs, and ripped the square foil he was holding. But I paid absolutely no attention to any of that.

Because of course.

Of course, he was packing the most beautiful cock I'd

ever seen in real life. It snapped against his hard stomach the second it was freed. Thick, long, perfectly curved, and leaking at the angry tip. If cock museums were a thing, his would be the biggest (literally) featured exhibition. The building would be named, shaped, and modeled after his dick. I wanted to lick it.

God, I hated him.

"How dare you, on top of everything else?" I asked him quite seriously. "Where the hell do you get off, Adrien?"

He smirked, taking his gorgeous member in his fist. He knew exactly what I was talking about. "Inside you, Sanchez. That's where I get off."

Ooooh.

I grinned. "Good one."

His eyes flickered down to my smiling lips, his smirk fading as his fist began to move up and down. After a few strokes, he rolled on the condom and leaned down again, placing a palm beside my right ear.

"Do you have any idea how many times I've fucked my fist over the last week, thinking about that smart mouth of yours wrapped around my cock?" he murmured darkly as he cupped my left breast, rolling my nipple between his fingers.

"Mmm" was my response.

"Keep your hands up," he ordered when I instinctively reached for him. I obeyed, placing my bound wrists back above my head. "Now, answer my question."

"Thousands, probably," I said cheekily. "I've got it on good authority that my lips are plump and pink, and that certain egotistical men with weird eyes and mediocre mouths tend to lose their itty-bitty minds over them."

He flashed me two amused dimples. "Oh, yeah?"

"Yeah. I'm also very pretty when I blush. It's no

wonder the aforementioned men never stood a chance. Poor suckers."

He chuckled. "And how fair do you think that is? What gives you the right to be so pretty and distracting?"

"Clearly I'm the wrong type of distracting, because we keep talking instead of fucking."

I couldn't even make it sound like I was complaining anymore. I'd never talked so much during sex; didn't realize it was something I'd be so into.

"Did it occur to you that maybe I'm buying myself a bit of cooldown time?" He kissed me once. "That I enjoyed eating you out so much that I almost came in my pants like a fucking teenager?"

The words slithered straight to my core, making it clench.

"You have no idea," he murmured. I felt it then, the tip of his large member aligning with my entrance. "You have no fucking idea how distracting you've been. How much space in my *itty-bitty* mind your smart mouth has been occupying."

My teeth sank into my bottom lip, a shudder rippling through me. I wanted him to thrust into me so bad my core kept pulsing, trying to suck him in. He stroked the tip of his shaft along my slit, his heat-doused eyes locked on mine. Up, down.

I whimpered, wrapping my legs around him again, trying to pull him in. I'd had enough foreplay and teasing for a lifetime.

And right before I was about to break down and start begging, he thrust into me at *just* the right angle.

Oh.

My head rolled, my clit fluttering as a moan tore from my throat in response to the pleasure of being filled. That felt... way too incredible, way too quickly. Even the pinch of pain felt good.

"Fuck. Ria." His lips were on my neck, the crook of my shoulder, kissing, licking, biting as his hips rolled, working him deeper.

My ankles pressed into his lower back, pleading for more.

"Deeper?" he rasped.

My nod was frantic. "Yeah."

He began to thrust harder, a growl rippling from the depths of his chest. Until he was buried all the way inside me. Until the world around us melted away. Until all the talking and banter was replaced with desperate curses and shallow breaths, and, "Oh god, Adrien."

He trembled when I said his name, a shuddering hiss escaping his lips.

Fuck it felt good.

It felt so, so, so good. Unreasonably, illogically, indis-putably amazing. Like I'd been misusing my body my whole life, and *this* was what it'd been made for.

"Sanchez."

It was a warning, a plea, a groan, all rolled into one. My muscles clenched possessively around him, and I felt him shudder again in response.

"Harder," I pleaded. I could tell he was holding back, and it wasn't because he wanted to. "I can take it."

"Fuck. Fuck." His fingers dug into my hips, his groans raw and feral as his movements became increasingly punishing. And the more I cried out, the more he let go. It was heaven.

He was thrusting into me like he was mad at me. Like he hated how much he loved it, and it was all my fault.

"Is this what you wanted, pretty girl? You need to be fucked hard like this?"

"Yes," I gasped. Holy shit. I was close again. So, so close. My fingers tightened around a fistful of the duvet above my head, my toes curling as a familiar, all-consuming tingle sprouted in my core.

The pressure built so fast I couldn't keep up—couldn't grasp the reins and pull it back, make this whole thing last a little longer. And I really wanted it to last longer.

"God. *Fuck*. Ria." Each rough word was punctuated by a deep, bruising thrust. On the last one I unraveled, clenching hard around him as another orgasm ripped through me.

He growled, fingers digging into my flesh as he sped up, chasing his own climax. It didn't take long. I felt every jerk and spasm as he came, memorized every sound he made. Until he finally collapsed beside me, spent and exhausted.

We were both heaving and gasping for breath, our bodies covered in a light sheet of sweat. I stared up at the ceiling, unsuccessfully trying to parse out the range of emotions tangled in my stomach. When I finally managed to turn my head to look at him, I found him watching me with the same expression I was wearing.

Because holy fuck.

There was good sex, and then there was *that*.

26

I woke up to the soft pitter patter of rain hitting the window, and it took me a few sleepy seconds to register why I was so warm, or why my lips were automatically curling into a satisfied little smile, even though I was dead tired and my body felt like it'd been hit by an actual bus. Every single one of my muscles were sore, yet I'd never felt so... satiated.

Adrien was pressed to my back, an arm draped over my bare stomach, a muscled leg tangled between my knees. He was fast asleep, according to the gentle way he was snoring into my neck. It tickled.

I swallowed the small giggle bubbling up my chest and tried to slip out from under his arm so I could grab my phone from the bedside table. But the second I moved, he stirred against me, his limbs tightening around my body instinctively.

"No," he growled into my neck, barely awake.

I sighed. "I need to check the time. My flight's at noon."

"*Fuck* no." He snaked both arms around me, trapping

me against his chest. The giggle that escaped my throat when he bit my shoulder was nothing short of unhinged.

I'd lost it.

"Adrien." I writhed against him, but he wouldn't budge.

"No."

"I need to call a cab."

"You can't. This is officially a hostage situation."

"That's extremely not legal," I pointed out. "But also kind of kinky."

He chuckled into the crook of my neck. "Are you into it?"

I considered the scenario. "Depends. Any hardcore weapons involved? Like, could I be 'accidentally' murdered midorgasm?"

He nipped my earlobe with his teeth. "Absolutely not."

"Then no." I wiggled my hips, trying to escape.

He rasped another laugh, bulky arms tightening around my chest and stomach as he pressed his hard length into the small of my back.

Knowing that the only things separating us were two pieces of easily discarded underwear made my core quiver like the slutty little fiend it was.

My libido and I were in a fight after last night.

"You shouldn't be allowed to be funny on top of everything else," Adrien grumbled into my hair.

"And your dimples shouldn't be allowed to hang lopsided, but alas, I'm perfect, and life isn't fair."

His nose brushed the shell of my ear. "Is that your way of admitting you like my dimples, Sanchez?"

I could feel him smile against my skin, and the mere image of his dimples flashing in my mind made my heart flutter like an overexcited songbird.

My heart and I were also in a fight. This was not appropriate behavior.

"I just said they're lopsided. And they dip so frikkin' deep, I'm pretty sure they're direct portals to the second circle of hell." That was the lusty one if my memory served.

He placed a kiss just underneath my earlobe and my whole backside puddled against him.

"You're avoiding the question," he said.

"I honestly can't even remember what it was."

"Do you like them?"

"Does it count if it's against my will?"

"Yes."

"Then the answer's still no," I lied.

He continued to place soft, smooth kisses along my neck, and my eyes fluttered shut for a moment, my nipples hardening.

"Adrien, I have to..." I cut off when he palmed my breast, the flutter in my chest spreading down to my clit.

"What, pretty girl? What do you have to do?"

"Shower. Flight," I breathed. My brain was already turning to putty. "And we... It was just supposed to be once."

"I fucked you more than once last night," he purred into my skin.

My cheeks colored at the reminder, and I swallowed, trying to get my thoughts in order. Because yes, okay, *fine*. I'd kind of lost my mind last night.

We both had.

Something in me had snapped after our first tumble. It unlocked this deep, impossibly starved craving, and suddenly we couldn't keep our hands off each other. No matter how many times he made me moan and scream, or what angle he took me from, it hadn't been enough. We'd be satiated for a short stretch of time, and then one of us would reach for the other again.

We kept going until our bodies gave out. I couldn't even remember falling asleep. I think I was just so exhausted at one point that I blinked and that was it. I was out.

"Speaking of," he murmured, "how are you feeling?"

"Sore," I rasped. My muscles were about as solid as jelly, my pelvic area felt like it'd lost a boxing match with a jackhammer, and my throat was charred from chanting his name all night. But in the good way. "You?"

He inhaled deeply, his embrace softening just a tad. "I'm processing."

And here I was, doing my best to avoid that exact thing.

"I need to shower and get ready," I muttered. This time, though, I made no effort to move away from him.

"Or you could stay," he said.

"That's a horrible idea. One of your worst."

"Why?"

"Oh, I don't know. Maybe because I don't want to keep lying to your family about this whole engagement nonsense?" Especially since I was almost certain he hadn't been entirely honest about his reasoning. "Or maybe because absolutely no good could come out of this?"

"Out of what, Sanchez? You and me?"

"Yeah."

"Why?"

"You ask a lot of questions."

"And you rarely ever actually answer them."

I sighed, realizing only then that at some point during the conversation, my fingers had started playing with his.

"What would be the endgame? I stay, we have more sex, and then what? We just... keep going until this thing fizzles?"

I frowned to myself as soon as the words were out because that wasn't a half-bad idea. I mean, eventually, it had to burn out. We'd fuck each other out of our systems, shake hands, and be on our way.

It would only take a week. Two, max.

But then he said, "What if it doesn't?"

"If it doesn't what?"

"What if it doesn't fizzle out? What if the opposite happens? What if you actually start to like me?"

I laughed. "That's never going to happen."

Had our fingers not been tangled just then, I may not have picked up on the subtle way he stilled for just a moment. And it was either in my head or he shifted slightly away from me.

"Why? Because of Alba?" he asked. "Because I wasn't a good boss?"

I could feel the drift begin. If I pushed just a little more, the frail little tether holding us together would snap, and he'd let me go.

So I shoved.

"Among other things," I said.

"Like what?"

"You've got a reputation for being an asshole, Adrien."

"Do you believe everything you read on the internet?"

"When something's that prominent and widespread, there's usually some truth to it," I retorted. "Plus the fact that I've experienced it firsthand, and that I've had to watch my sister suffer through your bullshit for years."

"She never... I'm not a mind reader, Ria."

"No. You're just selfish, arrogant, and a shitty human being to boot."

I braced myself. *Here we go.*

He was going to pull away, storm out of the room, and leave me to pack my shit and make my escape in peace.

"Bullshit."

I blinked at the rain-splattered window I'd been staring at. "What?"

"Bullshit, Sanchez."

"On what?"

"On all of it. On whatever you're trying to do right now. Bullshit. It's all an excuse."

I shot a glance back at him. He was smirking, looking down at me like my skin was see-through.

A sensation akin to panic sprouted in my stomach as I slithered out of his embrace, taking the flat sheet with me so I could wrap it around my body before I stood up. Then I gathered my clothes from the floor and slipped into the bathroom without a word.

Adrien didn't say anything, nor did he make any move to stop me. Which was fine.

Great.

Exactly what I'd wanted.

I stepped into the scalding hot shower, turned off my brain, and gave myself five minutes to scrub down. I really needed to catch that flight.

≈

"What's that supposed to mean?"

Adrien was still on the bed, but he'd put on a pair of gray sweats and was scrolling through his phone.

He glanced up at me, brows ticking with an unspoken

question. Either because he didn't know what I was talking about, or because I was dripping all over the carpet.

"Do you have something against drying off after a shower, Sanchez?"

"Don't be annoying," I said, clutching the towel wrapped around my torso like my life depended on it.

The rest of me was still soaked, and there was a small chance I still had shampoo suds lurking in my hair, mascara smudged under my eyes.

"I don't understand what you meant by the bullshit comment," I said.

"And it couldn't wait until you washed all the shampoo out of your hair?"

Okay, well, that answered that question.

"Seriously, what did you mean by it?" I pressed.

"Seriously, you have makeup smeared all over your face."

"Adrien!" I meant for it to be snappy, but somehow it came out as amused and bubbly.

He chuckled. "Go rinse off first, then I'll tell you."

"No. Tell me first."

"Did you look in the mirror before you stormed out here?"

"Bold of you to assume I care what I look like in front of you."

"You don't?"

"No."

He smirked, probably because my nostril flared. And then, to my complete and utter horror, he raised his phone *and snapped a picture of me*.

"My new wallpaper," he said.

Oh, *hell no*.

"Your corpse is going to be mine if you don't delete that picture right now."

"That's *dark*, Sanchez. Even for you."

I practically lunged for his phone, but he quickly hid it behind his back and pressed a palm to my towel-covered chest, keeping me at arm's length.

"I told you I have a fake fear of clowns. This is incredibly triggering for me," he said.

I tried not to laugh. Really, I did. "That's rude as hell! Give me your phone!"

"No."

"Adrien!"

"Ria!" he exclaimed, mimicking my voice.

And before I knew what was happening, I was on top of him, trying to wrestle his phone from behind his back with my one free arm. I really should have dried off and changed before storming out here.

"Sanchez, if you get a single drop of shampoo on me—"

I rubbed my wet head against his cheek. "You'll what?"

My warning came in the form of a single dimple, and then his arms were hooked around my waist, and I was being lifted.

I squealed with what could only be described as unhinged delight as Adrien picked me up, threw me over his shoulder, and stormed us into the bathroom.

I still had my towel on when it started to rain hot water, though he'd managed to throw off his sweats and briefs before stepping into the walk-in shower.

I was laughing so hard tears streaked my cheeks. "Put me down, you hooligan!"

He smacked my butt over the wet towel, then obliged. The second my feet were planted on the firm tiles, my cheeks were cupped in his hands, and his smiling lips were pressed to mine.

I should have stopped it. I knew I should have. So why did I drop my towel and sling my arms around his neck instead? Why did I giggle when he nibbled on my lip, and melt right into his warm embrace?

And why were we laughing so much? What was so funny?

I'd have contemplated the ever-loving, overthinking hell out of these questions just two days ago. Right now, though? All I could think about was how nice it felt when Adrien's fingers sunk into my hair. I purred against his mouth, my knees almost caving when he started to massage my scalp.

God, that felt good.

He chuckled at my reaction, pulling away so he could peer down at me.

"What did you do? Dump a bunch of shampoo on your hair and immediately step out of the shower?"

"Mmnmunm," I answered, crossing my eyes euphorically.

"Don't be cute."

"Don't be wet!" I demanded of the water raining down on us.

It wasn't funny. I was delirious and high on a plethora of sex hormones. But he laughed anyway, like he found my malfunctioning brain delightfully amusing.

I couldn't make sense of when, how, or why the switch had flipped for him. A small voice in the corner of my head kept trying to flag the abruptness as a warning, but Adrien's fingers massaged it into blubbery incoherence. I was a giddy pile of putty, barely able to keep my body upright without clinging to him for support.

We giggled and played, splashing each other with water and soap, unable to keep our mouths separate for longer than a few laughing seconds. And once we'd managed to stumble out of the shower, he carried me right back to bed.

"What time is it?" I breathed as his hot mouth moved down to my neck. I felt drunk.

He answered by slipping his fingers down to my center, teasing my opening. I whimpered, my thighs widening under his weight.

"Adrien, my flight."

He pulled away just enough to glare down at me, right before he rolled my swollen clit between his index and middle fingers. I had to turn my face into the duvet to muffle the cry that escaped.

"What about it?" he demanded to know, rolling, rolling, rolling.

"I don't wanna miss it," I muttered, my hips grinding against his touch.

He chuckled darkly. "What part of hostage situation are you not understanding, Sanchez?"

My breathy laugh quickly turned into another moan as he inserted a finger, then two. His palm moved to knead my button as his fingers fell into a maddeningly perfect rhythm. I was already tingling.

"God, that feels so good." After this, I was going to get on my knees and lick him all the way to the high heavens. I'd blow his mind through his dick, then run off into the sunset, never to be seen again.

That sounded like a great plan.

"Should I keep going?" he murmured.

"Yes," I pleaded.

Which was precisely when he stopped.

"What the hell?" I breathed, frowning up at him.

He brought his glistening fingers to his mouth and proceeded to suck them clean. "You taste like a fucking wet dream, Sanchez."

"Again, *what the hell*?"

"Again, what part of *hostage situation* are you not understanding?" he imitated lightheartedly.

My jaw fell slack. "You're holding my *orgasm* hostage?"

That evil dimpled grin told me everything I needed to know. "Here's the deal. The last direct flight from Victoria to Toronto is at 9 p.m. If you're still here by then, we'll finish the game."

"You're joking."

"Not even a little bit."

I sighed, my head sinking into the mattress. "This is so dumb."

He leaned down to kiss me. "9 p.m. Wear the green slip. You and I have another score to settle."

"I can just use my own hands, you know."

But he was already pushing himself off the bed. I fumed silently as I watched him slip into a pair of jeans and a fresh white shirt. He was, without an iota of doubt, the most infuriating man in existence.

"Breakfast is ready when you are," he said cheerfully on his way out.

He shot down the pillow I hurled at his idiot head and winked at me before shutting the door.

I hated him.

So, so, so much.

Then why are you smiling?

...

Shut up.

27

I WASN'T proud of my decision to stay. Nor could I justify it.

All I knew was that by the time I managed to put on a sweater and jeans, the idea of going to the airport was even more unappealing than it had been yesterday. I kept staring at my bags, trying to convince myself to pick them up and leave. But I couldn't do it.

No, that wasn't true. I *could* do it, I just didn't want to.

What I wanted to do was join Adrien's family for breakfast.

I was halfway down the stairs when I first heard the muffled laughter and teasing happening in the kitchen, and I found myself pausing just to listen. I'd always loved the idea of a big, loud, and lively family. My mom left when I was two, Dad worked night shifts for the majority of my childhood—right up until he got the gig at Abehill when I was fifteen—and our abuela was a big fan of naps.

But on Sundays when Dad was home and we had our big family dinners, the house felt alive. Like it was finally breathing after six long days of stillness. There was laughter and mayhem as Alba and I excitedly fought to tell our father about everything that had happened over the last week. We'd be chided by our abuela for bouncing in our seats, letting our food go cold, and signing over each other. All the while Dad encouraged our restless shenanigans, keeping us riled up and squealing. He'd make us laugh, feel heard, appreciated, and loved.

I used to think to myself, *this is what I want when I grow up. I want it to be like this every night.*

I loved it. I missed it. And I really missed them.

I swallowed the small lump forming in the back of my throat, blinked the memories from my mind, and trotted into the kitchen.

Adrien was the first to spot me. His eyebrows rose slowly as the corner of his mouth curved into the cockiest smirk I'd ever seen. He stood a little straighter, his chest puffing victoriously as he crossed his arms.

I did a poor job of concealing my smile as I glared at him.

"There she is," Julie said, her voice light and teasing.

"Good morning," I said.

"You must be *exhausted*," Alice chimed in. She was in the middle of decorating her smoothie bowl with coconut shavings and blueberries.

Um... "What?"

"They heard us last night," Adrien claimed, leaning a casual shoulder against the fridge. "Apparently the west wing isn't as secluded as we were led to believe."

Oh god.

"Not when you're *that* loud," his sister said. I could hear the eye roll in her voice.

My cheeks flamed, my body temperature spiking as my ears began to itch.

"Sorry. I'm a screamer," Adrien said smoothly, offering me a comforting wink.

Anthony and Julie laughed, and Alice made a face.

I stood frozen and embarrassed, my hands tucked awkwardly at my sides. I should have left. This was karma biting me in the ass.

"At least Gampy had the option of turning his hearing aid off," Alice went on, entirely unaware of how badly I wanted the ground to fall open and chew me whole.

"Alice, that's enough," Julie chided. She was still smiling.

"FYI, Mom spent over an hour this morning brainstorming nursery themes."

"Alice." Anthony this time. He was also smiling.

"Dad helped pick out a crib. It's *pine*." She stuck out her tongue and gagged.

Her father flicked her arm, and she snickered, plopping a blueberry into her mouth.

I didn't know what to do with myself. I wasn't sure what to say or where to look. And just as it felt like I might burst into flames, Adrien walked over to where I was standing, threaded his fingers through mine, and leaned down to whisper in my ear. "They're just teasing, it's not a big d—"

He cut off when the rubber end of a wooden cane shoved itself between our stomachs. Gampy—who'd appeared straight out of thin air—started to maneuver his walking cane back and forth, separating our bodies until a very confused Adrien and I were standing approximately three feet apart.

"Now, Lice," he said.

And then, grinning evilly as though she'd been waiting her entire life for this exact moment, Alice whipped out a spray bottle and aimed it directly at Adrien's frowning face.

"Don't you dare," he threatened, releasing my hand.

She dared. Four sprays of ice-cold water hit her brother's tanned, shielding arm while I stood there with my mouth hanging open.

Maxwell hopped off Gampy's shoulder, squawking gleefully as he flew right into the line of fire.

"New house rule," Alice declared loudly, continuing to hold the bottle up as a weapon. She didn't seem at all scared, even though Adrien looked like he was going to punt her right into the afterlife. "The two of you are to maintain four feet of distance at all times. You've lost all PDA privileges as a direct consequence of being disgusting and gross."

"No," Adrien responded easily, catching the small towel Anthony tossed him from across the kitchen. Maxwell had landed on his head and was eyeing the spray bottle like he was waiting for it to go off again. "And you barely even heard anything."

"I heard enough!" More sprays.

Adrien squeezed his eyes shut, a laugh bursting out of him as Maxwell once again dove gleefully for the water.

"Stop blocking my aim, you little twat! It's not your bath time!" Alice complained, trying to maneuver around his flapping wings.

I found my embarrassment slowly thawing until I was smiling and laughing along with them. Adrien kept trying to grab a hold of my hand again—probably to pull me into battle and use my body as a shield—but kept getting intercepted and blocked by swats of Gampy's cane, excited flaps of Maxwell's wings in his face, and sprays of Alice's water.

Chaos.

"All right. Enough, enough, enough," Julie interjected at one point, snatching the bottle from her daughter's hands. "Mop this up. Now, please. Before someone slips and breaks something."

"Worth it." Alice smirked, smacking her grandfather's raised palm on her way to grab the mop. Up high, down low, and in perfect sync. Maxwell flew after her.

"You need to stop encouraging her behavior," Julie told her father pointedly.

"I can hear you!" Alice called from the other room.

"Why? She's hilarious," Gampy argued.

"Thanks, bestie!"

"Alice, stop yelling," Julie yelled. "Dad, you only think that because she's turning into *you*. Addy, go change before you catch a cold. And Ria, honey, take a seat. I'll pour you some coffee."

Instead of leaving the room to change, Adrien stripped out of his shirt right then and there, wiping his face and hair with what little dry fabric was left.

Muscles. So many corded muscles. His arms and shoulders bulged, his abs impossibly—

"Take a picture, Sanchez." He winked at me, dimples popping.

"Lice!" Gampy called.

"On it!"

This time she flew at him with a wet mop.

～

"Where's your ring?"

I stopped chewing, my eyes darting down to my naked ring finger in response to Alice's question. "Um..."

"We're getting it resized," Adrien cut in before I could stumble over a much less reasonable excuse. "It's too big. Keeps falling off."

We were sitting at the kitchen table. He had one hand draped over the back of my chair, the other cradling a fresh cup of coffee. Half his body was turned in my direction, and his knee kept brushing my thigh.

The weird part? My body language wasn't all that different. My torso was twisted toward him, my foot hooked behind his ankle. And every time I looked at him, it felt like either he'd moved closer, or I had.

I also felt a little on edge. My gaze kept cutting to the clock every few minutes, as if that would somehow make the handles move faster toward 9 p.m.

"Have you started looking for dresses yet?" Julie asked.

I stiffened slightly, swearing internally that if she even *hinted* at taking me dress shopping, I'd run. Hostage situations be damned. "No, I—um, haven't really had a chance yet."

"Okay, because if you're interested, I can start to make some calls and set up appointments," she offered kindly.

Uh oh. Divert, divert.

I could tell Adrien was struggling with this one, too. His knee jolted against mine in silent apology, and his mouth opened like he wanted to say something, but he shut it again.

"You'll probably want to skip Kilarni, but if you've got any other designers in mind, I'm happy to make the arrangements."

My palms were starting to clam, my heart pounding roughly against my eardrums. I was not—*I was not*—going to go wedding dress shopping with Adrien's mother and sister. That was a firm, sacred line I wasn't willing to cross.

"Wait, why would we skip Kilarni? Their bridal collection is amazing," Alice said, buying me a few seconds to figure out how the fuck I was going to talk my way out of this. "That's the first designer I thought of."

Julie cleared her throat, her shoulders inching back. "Well, because it sounds like Mandy has her eyes set on a few of their pieces. And I thought we might not want a potential run-in or overlap. But it's, of course, up to Ria."

Alice made a face, as though her mother had said something vile.

"Who's Mandy?" I asked, taking advantage of the small opening. *Let's talk about her instead.*

The question was meant to distract them, turn the attention away from me and the nonexistent wedding, but the only thing it did was suck all the air out of the room.

All eyes turned in my direction, wide and unblinking. Beside me, Adrien had stiffened to absolute stone.

Uh oh. I'd fucked up. I didn't know how yet, but I'd fucked up.

Alice was the first to move. Her slimming gaze slipped to Adrien, and she quirked a brow.

"She's joking, right?" Gampy said. He shoved at his glasses, as if that would help him see the humor in what I'd said.

Okay. See? *This* was what I'd meant when I'd asked Adrien if there was anything important I needed to know before we started this whole mess. To avoid situations like this one.

I licked at my lips, daring a glance in his direction. I half-expected him to look pissed or exasperated with my carelessness. What I didn't expect was for him to look... shellshocked? Panicked?

"I..." he started, his voice thick and unsure. "It's not like I talk about her a ton."

The words were meant for his family, but his eyes were bolted to mine like he was trying to communicate a silent message I wasn't getting.

"Your new fiancée doesn't know about your ex-fiancée?" Alice asked, the judgment clear in her tone.

Wait. *What*?

Adrien rolled his lips, his knee brushing my leg underneath the table. "She knows," he said.

"Yes, sorry," I said, playing catchup. "I knew. I just didn't... I've never been great with names, and he's only mentioned hers once or twice."

It was the best I could come up with. Especially since half my brain was preoccupied with dissecting the little bomb that had just been dropped. Adrien had been engaged? For real? Since when? Had she broken it off? Or had he? Was he still in love with her? Was that the real reason he'd brought me here?

I wiped my palms against my jeans. It was suddenly so hot in here. Like hot enough to make my stomach twist.

Or maybe it was the eggs. Did bad eggs make your heart palpitate? If so, then it was definitely the eggs.

"Okay." Alice sounded more than a little skeptical. She turned her attention back to her brother. "And you're *both* aware that MJ's coming to the party, right? Like both her and—"

"They can do whatever the fuck they want. We don't have to talk about it."

The anger was apparent in his voice, and the glare he shot his sister made it obvious she was overstepping. But

Alice didn't seem to want to back down. Her arms were crossed defiantly over her chest, and she was tapping a finger on her elbow, her jaw visibly set on edge.

"He's right, that's enough of that," Anthony said calmly before Alice could go on the offensive again. He offered me a small smile. "What do you kids have planned for today? Anything exciting?"

"Ria and I are going sightseeing," Adrien answered.

We were?

"Can I come?" Alice asked. Her tone was so dry it sounded almost sarcastic.

"No. But we'll be taking your car, so it'll be like you're with us in spirit."

"Why can't I come?" She cocked a single brow, stretching out her sentence like it was synonymous with *are you scared*?

"Because I'd like to spend some quality alone time with my fiancée while we're on vacation."

She rolled her eyes. "It sounded like you got plenty of that last—"

He chucked a bread roll at her face. She laughed, then chucked it right back at him. This caught Maxwell's excited attention. He hopped across the table, bouncing on his little legs, his wings expanding as he danced, waiting for the bread roll to be tossed again.

I'd have found it adorable had my stomach not been twisting into knots. I took another sip of my plain black coffee, hoping it would help.

It didn't.

"Now, if you'll excuse us." Adrien stood up, and I quickly followed suit. We grabbed our empty plates, thanked his parents for the breakfast, and just as we were about to make our exit, he turned to his dad again.

Anthony waved his hand dismissively before Adrien could speak. "Yeah, yeah. I said I'll take care of it. It'll be done by the evening."

"Thank god," Gampy and Alice said in perfect unison.

I had no idea what they were on about. And, to be honest, I didn't have the mental capacity to care.

He'd been *engaged*?

28

"You were engaged?"

The question hurled out of me before the passenger door of the black SUV had slammed shut. I hadn't meant to pull it that hard.

Adrien sighed as he clipped his seatbelt into place. "For a very short period of time, yes."

"And that's not something you thought I should know going into this?"

He pursed his lips. "It's not a big deal."

"In what world?"

The car turned out of the property, the ornate iron gates closing behind us. "It lasted less than a week. It's not a big deal."

He was lying. I could hear it in the forcefulness of his tone, see it in the tension he held in his shoulders and jaw. But why?

"Wear your seatbelt, please," he said, eyes glued to the empty street ahead.

"Is that the real reason I'm here?" I had one hand on

the dashboard, my torso twisted in the seat to face him. "She's going to be at the party, so... you didn't want to go alone?"

His jaw worked. "Seatbelt."

"She's getting married?"

"Sanchez..."

"Your mom mentioned something about Mandy shopping for wedding dresses, and Alice said *they'd* be at the party. So... her and her new partner?" No wonder he didn't want to go solo.

He didn't respond.

My fingers were fiddling with the dashboard as I studied him. Something slimy and hot was tangling unpleasantly in my gut.

"How long ago was it?" I asked. My heart was thumping restlessly, and I couldn't figure out why. Who cared if he'd been engaged? Or if he was still in love with her, and had brought me here to make her jealous? It wasn't like that changed anything. It wasn't like I had actual *feelings* for him. He was hot and the sex was mind-blowing. That was it.

The silence stretched long enough that I assumed he wasn't going to answer. But then he said, "A little over a year ago. Fourteen months to be exact."

Oh.

A part of me had been hoping that it might have been a long time ago. That they were young, and stupid, and realized a week into the engagement that they were making a huge mistake.

"Sanchez. Seatbelt."

Fourteen months was kind of fresh for a relationship you thought would last a lifetime... right? And how was she already engaged to someone else? Didn't that seem too soon? Dating, sure. Getting married? Too soon. Maybe.

I wondered which one of them had broken it off.

I wondered if that was where he'd gotten the ring from. Had it been hers at one point? Was he trying to rub salt in her wound by making his new "fiancée" wear it? Because that would be a terrible idea, and not just because it made me want to vomit.

And I was so deep inside my own head that I didn't realize the car had pulled over until Adrien looked at me, brows ticking expectantly. And when I didn't move, he sighed and leaned forward, reaching for something behind my back. Except I didn't see his arm move, which was what led to my miscalculation of why he'd leaned in. It was the only reason I cupped his face and pressed my lips to his. I swear.

He inhaled sharply, freezing momentarily as if taken aback. And then he thawed right into me, his palm coming up to cradle the back of my head while his other hand slipped underneath my thigh, pulling me closer.

And that hot, slick tangle in my stomach? It eased the moment my tongue caressed his, teasing a low, guttural sound out of his chest.

One caress led to another, and before I knew it, he'd unclasped his seatbelt and we were full-on making out like a couple of teenagers with pent-up hormones on prom night. Hands roamed, grips tightened, we touched and pulled until—

HONK.

I startled back, my head hitting the roof hard enough that I should have felt it. But my body was buzzing with too much static tension and heat to notice.

"Shit. Sorry. Elbow," Adrien said, each word punctuated by a heavy exhale. He leaned back into his seat and raked a hand through his dark hair. After a few long breaths, his head turned in my direction, and he grinned. "Just can't keep your hands off me, can you?"

"You're the one that leaned in," I protested, willing my chest to calm the fuck down. "I just closed the gap."

And either I was seeing things, or his dimples and eyes were twinkling. "I was trying to put your seatbelt on."

"I'm supposed to believe that?"

"It's cool. I'm flattered."

I wasn't smiling. My mouth was allowed to curve upward without being accused of smiling.

He chuckled. "You know that one Jessica Simpson song?"

"Don't you dare bring 90's pop into this," I demanded. Again, I was absolutely *not* smiling.

"Am I *irresistible* to you, Sanchez?"

I glowered at him.

He laughed, then leaned toward me again. "Sit properly for me."

I sunk into the seat and glared at this dimple as he reached for my seatbelt, clasping it into place. My gaze did *not* immediately dip down to his mouth; my thighs did *not* clench when I caught a whiff of his intoxicating cologne; and my chest absolutely did *not* stutter when he pecked my cheek and shot me a wink.

"Where are we going anyway?" I asked, crossing my arms. My knees came up to the dashboard, and I decided right then and there that the only place I'd be looking for the remainder of the car ride was out the window.

"The weather's kind of nice. We can start with a walk by the harbor, then go from there."

That actually sounded really appealing until he instructed the car to blare Jessica Simpson, then proceeded to bellow the lyrics at the top of his lungs. I rolled my eyes so hard, it was a miracle they didn't pop right out of their sockets.

I did *not* have to press the back of my hand against my mouth to muffle my laugh. It was *not* funny.

~

There was a teeny tiny chance that I was going to die, and it was all—of course—Adrien's fault.

By the time we managed to crawl back to his car, the sun had started to set, and I'd forgotten what it felt like to properly breathe. My eyes were swollen from the tears, my cheeks felt bruised and sore, and my stomach muscles hurt so much I couldn't stand straight. Every time I so much as glanced in Adrien's general direction, I burst into a torturously fresh bout of hysterical laughter and inched closer to the sweet release of death.

He looked so fucking stupid.

We'd spent the majority of the late morning and after-noon walking along the harbor, drinking hot chocolate, eating, and banter-bickering about everything we could possibly banter-bicker about. I made fun of him every time someone came up to ask for a picture, he poked fun at me every time I choked on something trying not to laugh at his jokes. And then, it happened. We walked past one of those face-painting stands for kids.

He didn't even hesitate.

One second, he was walking next to me, our laughter overlapping, steps swaying, hands brushing. The next, I was holding his bagel while he plopped himself onto the too-small plastic stool, pointed at a large tube of blue body paint on the table, and instructed the makeup artist to, and I quote, "Go crazy."

The lady seemed confused (and maybe a little concerned), and triple-checked with him to make sure that he did indeed want to be painted a bright, eye-catching cobalt blue. He took off his jacket and watch, then said, "Yup. Arms, neck, face. Let's do this."

And that wasn't even the best part. I didn't know how he did it, exactly, but within minutes, he'd somehow recruited a small army of tiny hands to help spread the paint over his tanned skin. There were squeals, and giggles, and parents taking pictures of their little monsters wreaking blue havoc on Adrien Cloutier.

And once he was sufficiently coated in a sloppy, uneven paint job (that had inevitably also stained his white T-shirt), he stood up, bumped a whole bunch of small blue fists in celebration, paid for all the kids to get their own faces painted, and asked the lady if there were any costume shops around.

She'd said yes, and our slow descent into madness had stopped being slow. He'd slipped his fingers through mine, and I'd giggled all the way down the street to the store she'd recommended.

Yes, they did have large bull horns. And yes, they did have a blue tail. It was short, fluffy, and looked like a fox's tail on acid, but, according to Adrien, it was "perfect and exactly accurate."

Unfortunately for us, though, Stevie (the owner) had *just* run out of fake fangs, but, "I do have a full set of raptor teeth lined with black gums if you'd like."

They were thin, sharp, fangless, had a greyish-yellow

tint, and were too big for Adrien's mouth. But, once again, they were deemed "perfect and exactly accurate." As was the black samurai wig he put on in lieu of a man-bun.

I tried to stop him when he went for the loincloths, but I was cry-laughing by that point, and my arms were too weak to wrestle the leather out of his hands. Thankfully, I was able to at least convince him to put the slutty strip of fabric *over* his pants.

The horns and tail were also attached to his person, and he puffed out his chest proudly when he came out of the changing room.

He looked like he'd walked straight out of my childhood nightmares; or a 90's grunge album cover.

"How turned on are you right now, Ssanchesz?" he lisped through his large fangs as soon as we left the store, his spit spraying everywhere.

It sent me into hysterics. I crumpled to the ground, tears streaming down my face as my forehead hit my knees. And from that point on, every time I looked at him or he spoke, it became funnier. Until I was convinced this was the end. That *this* was how Adrien had decided he'd end my life as payback for what I'd done on Halloween.

By the time we made it back to Alice's borrowed SUV, I was clutching my sides, gasping for breath, and begging him to stop talking. I climbed into the car and sunk against the seat, my arm draped over my liquid stomach.

Adrien took off the horns and tail before getting in.

"Sseatbelt, Ssanchesz."

I huffed a weak laugh, my head rolling against the seat. My hand flailed for the seatbelt, but my muscles were too weak to pull it all the way across my torso. So I just gave up, letting it spring back to my shoulder.

Adrien chuckled before clipping it in place for me.

"Sspoiled brat," he murmured affectionately. Or maybe it wasn't affectionate, and I was just punch-drunk.

"These pictures are going to be all over the internet by the end of the week," I predicted.

"I don't fink anyone recogniszed me after I put the teef in. Didn't ssee any phones."

That was because said *teef* bulged out of his mouth and pushed his lips back. And he was right. Between that, the blue skin, and the rest of his ridiculous costume, he was almost entirely unrecognizable.

"I took lots of pictures. I'll be more than happy to share," I said. The ones we'd taken in the photobooth were gold, and they'd been *his* idea. He'd practically thrown me over his shoulder and carried me inside. The man's survival instincts were about as sharp as safety-scissors.

He shot me a look as the car pulled out of the parking lot. "You promissed."

I had. And I fully intended to keep my promise. But that didn't mean I couldn't tease him about it.

"At the very least, it'll be my wallpaper for the foreseeable future. I'll order a life-size cut-out when I get home, put it beside Jamie's bed while she's sleeping."

Speaking of giving my best friend a heart-attack, I needed to call her at some point and let her know I'd slept with her future husband.

"This was fun," I muttered at the window, watching the lights and the trees blur by. The sun was starting to set.

"Yeah?"

"Mmm. Good exercise, too. Feels like I did a thousand sit-ups."

Adrien pulled the monster teeth out and chucked them into a plastic bag, then wiped his palm against his thigh. Once, twice. "Would you want to do it again?"

"What? The costume thing?" Because yes. Yes, I would.

"No, I mean... would you want to hang out like this again?"

And for the first time in the last two hours, I didn't feel the urge to laugh when I looked at him. Was he asking what I thought he was asking? Or was my brain doing that thing where it made shit up and lied to me?

"I dunno," I said carefully. "It depends."

He seemed very adamant on keeping his eyes strictly on the road ahead. "On?"

"Well, what would we do?" I began fiddling with a loose thread on my sleeve, my heart skipping a beat. Then two, then three. A tickle ran up my spine as the atmosphere shifted to something lighter, more fluttery. Like a basketful of butterflies had been let loose in the car.

I mirrored him, fixing my gaze onto the red taillights in front of us.

"Whatever you want," he answered. "Something casual like today. Or we could go to dinner. Drinks."

I paused to think before answering. "I'm going to leave tomorrow."

"And we can't see each other when we're both back in Toronto?"

The butterflies had infiltrated my stomach. "I'm not sure if..." But I stopped. I wasn't sure why I stopped, but I did. "Can I think about it?" I asked instead.

"Okay," he said.

"Okay," I said.

I brought my knees up to the dashboard and turned toward my window.

And, no, I did *not* spend the rest of the comfortably silent car ride fighting a smile. My reflection was a damn liar.

29

"Ew, what the hell?"

I choked on a laugh in response to the palpable disgust on Alice's face when we walked into the house. She was sitting on the floor in the living room, an open textbook laid out on the table in front of her.

"Why are you dressed up as the blue Koolaid Man wearing a suede diaper?" she asked Adrien judgmentally.

I laughed harder. She should have seen him with the raptor teeth, bull horns, samurai wig, and fox tail still on. Her reaction would have been priceless.

"It's a loincloth, Lice. Not a diaper."

"That's worse, not better. You look like an idiot," she said, and then, as though suddenly struck by a realization, her eyes flared in horror. "You did *not* get into my car like that."

"I'll take it to get detailed tomorrow" was Adrien's response.

"Adrien! My seats are beige!"

"They're also leather. It probably won't stain."

"Your blood will when I gut you!" She hurled a highlighter at his head, but he snatched it out of the air with ease.

"What's with all the—Addy! What did you do!" Julie stopped in her tracks, her hands flying to her mouth. Anthony, who'd walked in behind her, burst into laughter.

"It was Ria's idea," Adrien accused without hesitation, pointing the highlighter at my head.

"Wait," Alice said, her narrowing eyes gliding suspiciously between her brother and me. "This isn't like a weird sex thing, is it?"

"No!" I exclaimed at the same time as Adrien said, "Absolutely it is."

I smacked his arm. He laughed. Alice threw her whole pencil case at him, slammed her textbook shut, and declared that she'd be in dire need of extensive therapy after our visit.

Adrien winked at me, Anthony started snapping pictures with his phone, and Julie pinched the bridge of her nose, quietly chuckling to herself.

I'd have been a lot more mortified if this whole thing wasn't so ridiculously *ridiculous*. And if I wasn't so charmed by it.

Once the ruckus had somewhat died down, Julie insisted that Adrien go upstairs and shower before he got body paint on her beloved hand-picked furniture.

"Dinner will be ready in thirty," Anthony called after us as we made our exit. He also said something about a patch being installed somewhere, but I was too busy trying to fight off Adrien's hands to put two and two together.

"You're gonna smudge blue all over my clothes!" I giggled as he tried to grab my hips.

"It'll wash out."

The struggle quickly escalated, turning into a foot chase. I squealed and laughed as I booked it up the stairs, swatting at Adrien's fingers every time they got too close. My foot caught the edge of a carpet when I took the last turn to our room, but I made a quick recovery and managed to beat him to the door. My heart was pounding, my blood rushing as I scrambled to shut the door in his blue face, but he was too quick and strong.

To make matters worse, he'd managed to pop his fake teeth back in during the chase.

"Noo!" I cried out dramatically as his arms wrapped around my torso. "Gross, you smell like plastic and paint!"

He puckered his lips over his grey-yellow needle teeth and I scream-laughed, twisting my face away from him.

"I*ss* thi*ss* what you wanted, S*s*anche*sz*? Are you hot for me?"

I couldn't breathe. Tears streamed down my cheeks as I tried to wiggle out of his arms.

"*Sch*ould I put the manbun wig on again?"

"You're spitting on me, you hooligan!"

"I*ss* it turning you on? Do you *f*ink I'm ire*ssisss*table?"

"I can't—Adrien!"

He licked my cheek, pointed teeth tracing the long stroke of his tongue, and I was half-convinced I was going to pass out from laughter.

"Ki*ssth* me."

"No!" I pressed my palm against his mouth and pushed his head back. "Go shower!"

"Wamn cmne wimme?" he muffled into my hand.

"Absolutely not."

His tongue squirmed against my palm, and I yelped, my hand recoiling. And the second he was free he attacked my neck. Burrowed his face and mouth and teeth right in its crook and refused to be nudged away.

"You ssmell like jassmine and fabric ssoftener," he said. "And Ssanchezs."

I didn't know what a Ssanchezs smelled like, but judging by the gentle way he inhaled and pulled me closer, it must have been a compliment.

"What time is it?" I asked for no particular reason whatsoever.

"Five forty-five," he muttered into my neck. "Give or take a couple minutess."

"How do you know that off the top of your head?" I'd have checked myself, but my arms seemed adamant on returning Adrien's hug, even though he was getting blue body paint all over my clothes.

"I've been counting."

"Mmmm" was what I responded with instead of a smart quip or tease, my cheek laying against his head.

And then we just... stood there. Hugging.

Seconds turned to minutes, and neither one of us moved to separate. Because maybe I opted to close my eyes instead of backing away; and maybe I started to gently stroke the back of his head instead of pushing him off me; and maybe it made me smile when he rumbled something incoherent out of pleasure and held me tighter.

"Ssanchezs, how about that trucce?"

He really didn't want to let that one go, did he? "I'm still thinking about it."

He sighed into my neck. "You're sso sstubborn," he grumbled, as if I couldn't feel his mouth spread into a smile against my skin.

Eventually, we managed to peel away from each other

so he could go shower. I unzipped my bag and reached for the travel-sized pack of makeup wipes I'd picked up during our walk, unable to keep the smile off my face.

Okay, so *maybe* Jamie had been a teeny tiny bit right. Maybe emotions had been running high at the beginning, there were a few misunderstandings, and Adrien wasn't *as bad* as I'd originally thought. Maybe there was a bit of chemistry between us, and maybe it wasn't all just physical.

Not that I'd consider pursuing anything long-term or serious with him. Fooling around like this was one thing, getting emotions involved and our lives entangled was another. It would be too complicated with him, and not just because we'd been lying to his parents about... *Wait, why is this...*

My previous train of thought derailed when I realized I'd been scrubbing the same spot on my forearm with a makeup wipe for what must have been a full minute now, but the color still hadn't fully come off.

I rubbed harder, checking every few strokes to see if my skin was back to its normal olive. It wasn't.

Oh, shit.

My palm slammed against my mouth, muffling the shocked giggle bubbling up my chest. If the blue couldn't be erased with a makeup wipe, chances were high that a bar of soap wasn't going to do the trick, either. Adrien was going to lose his fucking mind.

Sure enough, a few minutes later the glass shower door slammed open, panicked wet footsteps pounded against stone tiles, and Adrien stormed back into the bedroom with a grey towel wrapped haphazardly around his waist. His eyes were wide with genuine terror. "Fuck my life. *Look!*"

I looked. His arms, neck, and face were all still covered in sloppily applied cobalt. You could tell where he'd tried to scrub the paint off his left arm, because the top, most vivid layer had been subdued. But a noticeable tint remained.

I lost it. My knees caved, and I hit the floor laughing so hard my body rolled.

"Sanchez!"

I knew I'd said this before, but this was it. *This* was how I was going to die. I was one hundred percent sure of it this time.

I was fighting for air, my stomach muscles spasming in protest against the uncontrollable laughter. I was in genuine pain, but I couldn't stop. He looked so fucking *goofy*.

"Help!" I wailed theatrically, clutching to my sides. "Make it stooop."

"I can't believe they put this shit on kids. Every single one of the parents from today is going to send me hate mail."

I couldn't believe he hadn't thought to double-check to make sure it didn't stain. I was crying into the carpet, dying.

"This is all your fault," he said.

I'd gladly take credit for this. I hadn't earned it, but I'd take it.

It took almost ten minutes for me to calm down enough to sit up and look at him without my lungs seizing. He was seated on the edge of the bed, facing me. His elbows were on his knees, his hands clasped loosely in front of him, and his head hung in defeat. He'd fucked up. He *knew* he'd fucked up. But even so, his cheeks were tight like he was trying to hold back his smile.

And... all right, fine. Yes. I really, *really* liked that he had a sense of humor. When I sat up and we looked at each other, my stomach did a weak little flip when he grinned at me, and I found myself returning his smile easily.

"Are you done?" he asked.

"For a lifetime," I decided. I was never going to laugh again. But on the bright side, "I'm gonna wake up with abs. Guaranteed they'll be even nicer than yours."

His smile twitched. "Sanchez."

"Cloutier."

"I'm fucked."

"It's not a big deal."

"I've got two video conference calls I've got to be on tomorrow morning."

"Aren't you supposed to be on vacation?"

"They're important."

I sighed. "We'll fix it."

His right eyebrow quirked. "*We*?"

"Don't get too excited," I said, pushing up to my feet. "I'm only helping because I was promised an orgasm and I refuse to have sex with you like this."

"I'm more than just a piece of meat, Sanchez." His dimples were trying their best to stay hidden, bless their dark little souls.

"Mmmkay."

I plopped down beside him on the bed, fished out my phone, and typed *Gargomel's guide to turning Smurfs into gold* into the search bar, but the phone was snatched out of my hand before I could hit Enter. And thus began the wrestling match.

"You're the one that said you're more than just a piece of meat!" I exclaimed when my wrists were pinned to the mattress. "I'm just trying to help you reach your full poten — Don't you dare kiss me right now, Adrien Cloutier. *Don't you dare.* You're going to get your stupid blue all over my mou*phnmnm.*"

We made our way downstairs fifteen minutes later, Adrien with his proud shoulders pushed back and a cocky smirk toying at his mouth, while I rubbed at my kiss-swollen lips with a makeup wipe.

Alice rolled her eyes when she saw us, then proceeded to haul herself off the couch to go find her spray bottle.

30

ONCE AGAIN, coconut oil had proven to be the magical cure-all for literally everything.

It took three hours, six full sets of cotton pads, and half a jar of the organic coconut oil we'd found in the pantry, but we were almost done. His arms, hands, neck, and the lower half of his face were all back to their normal color, and I was slowly working my way up his face while he simply watched. Because he'd decided halfway through the process that he enjoyed being pampered way too much to continue helping.

There were a few other things that had slowed us down. Number one, you had to really work the oil into the skin for it to be effective. Two, there was a lot of paint, so you had to go over each little section multiple times, with multiple fresh pads. And three, Adrien and I could not stop talking and giggling about the dumbest shit.

Had we just shut up and focused, we'd have been able to get it all done in less than two hours, and moved on to the only reason I was still here: the hostage situation. But we couldn't seem to shut up. Even though it was slowing us down, and my cheeks were sore, and my butt was hurting from sitting on the floor for way too long.

And we were so caught up in invading each other's personal bubbles, with our legs tangled and our laughter mingling, that we accidentally lost track of time. Those initial three hours turned to four, then five, and half his face was still blue.

Every time I instructed him to close his damn eyes so I could clean them, he'd shut them for a few seconds before slighting one open to peek at me. And then we'd fall into another banter-giggle trap.

It also didn't help that he had an index finger hooked through one of my belt loops, or that his other hand was curved around the side of my thigh. And it really didn't help that he kept caressing me, his soft gaze constantly traveling from my eyes down to my mouth like he couldn't decide which one he liked looking at better.

"Adrien, if you don't close your eyes, we're going to be here all night," I told him once I was (finally) done with his forehead.

"Okay," he said, keeping them wide open. That playful little smirk of his was going to be the absolute end of me.

"That wasn't an invitation."

"I'm taking it as one."

It took another fifteen minutes of bickering, but he finally complied, and I managed to wipe away the remaining paint. It also gave me an opportunity to look at his annoyingly attractive face without being teased about it.

Or so I thought.

"You're staring again, Sanchez," he said, his gorgeous lips curving into an infuriating smirk. His eyes were still closed.

I tossed the last dirty cotton pad into the trash. "All right, you're done. Go shower."

We had a hostage situation to take care of and I was running out of patience.

He chuckled, rubbing his palms against his eyes as he stood up. "Yes, ma'am."

I bit down on my own grin and began cleaning up the mess we'd created. Once I was done, I looked to see if there were any flights heading to Toronto in the morning.

I needed to go back at some point, and preferably before the big anniversary party. Because I wasn't all that keen on being used as a tool to make Adrien's ex jealous. And I really didn't want to be there when they made up, after she inevitably realized how big of a mistake she was making marrying that other chump.

There was a flight at ten-thirty tomorrow, which was perfect. My thumb hovered over the booking button as my eyes scanned the information one last time, just to make sure it was all correct.

It was.

So... you should probably go ahead and book it now.

I didn't have to book it right this second, though. It was probably a good idea to wait until tomorrow morning, just in case.

In case of what?

I don't know, just... in case.

The hiss of the shower cut off before I could start a full internal argument with myself. And I didn't miss the way my heart leaped with nervous anticipation for what was to come (pun intended).

Adrien walked back into the bedroom wearing his sweatpants, no shirt, and my mind did an immediate nose-dive into the gutter. There was no point in denying it anymore. I wanted to lick every inch of those abs before getting on my knees for him.

But only after he tied my wrists behind my back and ordered me to do it.

"It's eleven-thirty," I said, just in case he'd lost track.

He tossed the towel he'd been using to dry his hair onto the red ottoman, crossed his arms and leaned a shoulder against the wall. "And?"

My mouth twitched as I plopped down on the bed. "And I'm super tired. So, if you could please stop being so disruptive, I'd like to wind down and go to sl*mphnmnmh*."

He practically pounced on me, caging me between his arms as his smiling mouth smashed into mine. I returned the kiss with ferocious enthusiasm, my thighs spreading to accommodate the press of his body.

"You taste like candy, Sanchez." His lips trailed lava from my mouth to my throat before he growled his complaint. "But you didn't follow my instructions. You were supposed to be waiting for me in the green slip."

That hadn't been an accident. "I've never been good at listening to authority."

I yelped when he flipped me onto my stomach, my hands fisting the duvet as my body began to purr. *Yes. Punish me.* I deserved it.

His palm flattened across the small of my back, pressing me down. "What's your safeword, pretty girl?"

"Cinnamon," I sighed.

His other hand went to cup my ass cheek. He squeezed it once before giving it a little smack over my jeans. I held back my moan, stuffing my face into the duvet I was clutching.

I wasn't going to make a peep tonight. I'd learned that lesson the hard way.

"Can I trust you to use it when you need to?" he asked. "If it becomes too much? If I get too carried away?"

"Yes."

Another light smack that sent a shock of pleasure right to my clit, making it hiss. I'd have lifted my hips to give him better access, but he was still holding me down.

"I want to be a little rough with you tonight, Ria." His voice had dipped into a rugged, hot gravel. He squeezed me again, harder this time. I needed to grab a pillow to stuff my face into, muffle any noise that escaped my throat without permission. "I've been looking forward to fucking you all day, and I'm not in the mood to practice any more self-control. Not when it comes to you and that smart little mouth of yours."

"Then don't."

He didn't miss the way that came out as a plea. I might as well have sunk to my knees and begged him to use my body however he wanted. My filter was gone. If I was only going to get one more night of this, I was going to take full advantage of it.

"You sure about that?" he teased dangerously. But before I could answer, his fingers had hooked under the waistband of my jeans and the cotton panties underneath, making my breath stutter. He yanked them down to my upper thighs, leaving my ass exposed to him.

I was vibrating.

"Fuck, Sanchez. Look at you." His tone was a mixture of praise and awe as he nudged the hem of my shirt up to my waist. "One day I'm going to fuck you just like this," he promised, trailing his palm back down to my ass. "I'll bend you over, pull your pants down, and take. And you'll love it, won't you, pretty girl?"

That shouldn't have sounded nearly as tempting as it

did. I shouldn't have imagined him bending me over his desk back in his office, yanking my jeans down, and fucking me raw. And it shouldn't have made me nearly as wet as it did.

Smack.

The sting of skin-on-skin contact made my hips buckle. I choked back a delicious whimper.

"But tonight, you and I have another score to settle," he rumbled, soothingly rubbing the cheek he'd just smacked. "So, here's what's going to happen. You're going to change into the green slip, and immediately come back to bed. Any questions?"

"What if I don't listen?"

His fingers dug into my flesh. "Then your sweet little pussy doesn't get fucked, and you don't get to come."

"Are you sure?" I challenged, a thrill spinning up my chest. "You're willing to punish both of us for my mistake?"

He flipped me again, like I was as light as a pancake. "I said your pussy wouldn't get filled, Sanchez. I have no problem tying your hands to the bedpost and fucking your tits."

Good lord. "Such a dirty mouth on you," I chided.

He cupped my bare sex, a devilish smirk pulling at the corner of his sinful mouth as his middle finger teased its way through my soaked folds. "Again, you *really* don't seem to mind."

My lips parted to let out a sigh of pure pleasure. "My body and brain aren't exactly on the same page when it comes to you," I admitted.

He quirked a brow, the thick pad of his finger circling my entrance. "What's your brain telling you?"

"That I shouldn't want this with you."

"And your body?"

"My body has lost its mind."

"That's not what I asked."

I licked my bottom lip. "My body is currently telling me to rebel. It's wondering what it would feel like to be tied up, watching you fuck my tits. And whether you'd come in my mouth if I asked nicely enough."

His finger stopped moving, his hooded gaze taking on a new level of intensity.

I smirked. "What? You think you're the only one with a filthy imagination?"

Without warning, his middle finger slid into me, curling at just the right angle. My hips arched, and I gasped as his palm pressed against my swollen clit.

"Do you have any idea how fucking perfect you are?" he growled, sounding utterly pissed off about it.

"Yes," I responded cheekily.

Then his fingers and palm moved, working me in the most maddeningly perfect way. I squeezed my eyes and lips shut, gripping his forearm.

"Look at me when I'm fucking you, Ria."

I released a shaky breath, opening my eyes. The problem was, he was looking at me with such heated concentration and intensity, and my body was so fucking attracted to him, that I wasn't going to last very long if I watched him. And I didn't want him to know how fast he could push me over the edge. His ego was inflated enough as it was.

"Don't you want me to go get changed?" I asked quietly, trying to mask the quiver in my voice.

He retreated his hand, making a rather lewd show of sucking my arousal off his fingers. Then he gently pulled my pants back up, my shirt back down, and kissed the corner of my mouth. "I'll give you one minute."

Another thrill rushed through me as I sprang off the bed with a light giggle and ran into the closet. I stripped out of my clothes, my underwear, and slipped into the green silk with twenty seconds to spare. Then I reached for the door handle... and proceeded to lock it.

This was going to be so much fun.

31

HE HAD a key to the closet. It took him less than a minute to find it.

I was halfway through a fit of laughter when the door ripped open, and Adrien barreled inside. His eyes were blistering, his lips spread into a wicked grin that matched my excitement. I was in his arms in a second, my feet lifted from the carpet. He had a fist in my hair, an arm wrapped tightly around my waist, and I was sandwiched between him and the wall when his lips met mine. He left me no room to breathe.

It was perfect.

"Brat," he grumbled against my lip before biting it punishingly.

I wrapped my legs around his torso and grabbed a fistful of his hair as I kissed him back. "You like it," I told him.

"I fucking love it."

This shouldn't have been nearly as much fun as it was. I'd never had this much play incorporated into sex before, and I was only now realizing how much I'd been missing out.

Although, if I were being completely honest with myself, I couldn't imagine having this much fun with any of the other guys I'd hooked up with.

Adrien used his grip on my hair to pull my head back, then his lips, teeth, and tongue were on my neck. I came utterly undone. My filter caught fire, logic and reason left the building, and I was completely lost in Adrien's touch, his scent, and the overwhelming amount of sensations coursing through my body.

I moaned his name, and it pushed everything over the edge. The fire became an all-encompassing inferno. His grip on me tightened, his hips pushing forward, working his steel length against my oversensitive clit. I trembled, panting like I'd been forced to hold my breath for the last hour.

I wanted to yank his sweatpants down and have him thrust into me right here, just like this.

"I want you inside me," I pleaded softly against his ear. And then, because I'd really lost it, I said, "I'm on the pill. Tested recently. Haven't been with anyone since. If... you want."

He was shaking, his fingers digging into my flesh hard enough to hurt. He nipped at my jaw, my cheek, my ear. "Same. Tested. You're sure?"

"Yes."

He ground his hips into mine, and I stuffed my face into his shoulder when the whimper escaped. I could feel his heartbeat slamming into my chest and it was fucking intoxicating.

"Do you still hate me?" he rasped.

"What?" Where had that come from?

"Do you hate me?"

I frowned. "Is now really the time to talk about this?"

"Ria." He pulled his head back to look at me, releasing my hair so he could tilt my chin to meet his gaze. "Do you hate me?"

I should have veered. But instead, I whispered, "Yes."

His face split into a devastatingly handsome grin when my nose inevitably flared. I wanted to kiss his dimples but that seemed just a little too affectionate for my brand, so I resisted the temptation.

"Do you have feelings for me, Sanchez?"

My own smile was forming, even though I kept telling it not to. "Absolutely not, Cloutier."

"Do I give you butterflies?"

"No," I breathed, unable to summon my full voice because of the overwhelming amount of non-butterflies fluttering through my stomach, chest, soul.

His grin widened. "We really need to do something about all this lying."

"No, what we need to do is stop talking. It's—"

I cut off with a gasp when he hoisted me over his shoulder in one smooth move, like I was a massive sack of feathers.

"Adrien!" It was embarrassing, how much giggling I'd been doing around him lately.

My back bounced off the mattress when he dropped me, and before I could yank his body down on top of mine, he... rolled me? Three times.

"What the hell?" I asked, looking down at the microfleece blanket my body was now trapped in. And then it clicked. The fucker had wrapped me in a blanket fucking burrito!

"Adrien!" I exclaimed, positively appalled by his unacceptable behavior.

His grin was a wicked, evil thing as he reached for the two other items on the bed. A necktie, and a belt. The tie was wrapped around my upper arms, the belt around my calves. The burrito had been secured.

"I'm going to strangle you the second I'm free," I told him after he—once again—flung me over his shoulder. "And that'll only be the beginning. Mark my words, Adrien Cloutier."

He carried me out of the bedroom.

"I'm going to put soap on every toothbrush you ever own, cilantro in every single thing you ever eat. It's all you'll taste for the rest of your life."

Down the stairs.

"I'm going to glue Legos inside all your shoes. You'll never eat an unlicked Oreo ever again. Do you hear me!"

Through the hallway, and into the kitchen. The lights were on.

"I'm going to glitter-bomb your whole world, Adrien. You'll be shitting the stuff by the time I'm done with you. I'll be a permanent papercut in your life."

We passed by two pairs of feet.

"Oh god, you two." Julie laughed in sing-songy delight, as if her son and I were just a couple of rowdy kids in love.

"The wedding is off!" I snarled at her perfectly manicured toes. "I will not be marrying your hooligan son!"

She laughed harder. Anthony also chuckled.

And then we were outside, on the patio.

"What the—" Alice's voice said. "Fuck's sake, you guys. You're traumatizing the rest of us! I'm basically still a child!"

"It's not a sex thing!" I insisted.

"It absolutely is," Adrien retorted.

Alice threw something soft and round at Adrien's back, just as I tried to knee him in the chest. She met her target, but I just ended up failing uselessly like an idiot mackerel. Adrien gripped me tighter.

"Do not fall," he ordered. "We're almost there."

"Almost where?" I demanded to know. We were walking over dark grass now. "Adrien, I am not into outdoor sex. I don't do bugs, dirt, or fresh air. So don't even think about it!"

But then we reached a stone pathway and a new set of porch stairs. A door creaked open, and we were inside another house from the looks of the hardwood floor. When he finally put me down, it was on another bed, in another extremely expensive-looking bedroom.

I glared savage daggers at him.

"There," he said with a smug grin. "Now nobody will hear you when you scream."

"That's so murdery, you freak!" I hissed angrily. "Untie me this instant!"

He chuckled but complied. I lunged for him the moment I was free. But instead of strangling him like I'd planned, I accidentally wrapped my arms around his neck and crashed into his mouth with my mouth. And instead of murdering him dead, I giggled against his luscious lips and tried to pull him down to the mattress.

But he—of course—had other plans. I was put over his lap before I could even think about protesting, the flimsy bottom of my slip was flipped up, and my bare ass was exposed to him. And I... loved it. I fucking loved this.

It was so much fun with him, unexpected and exciting. I loved the way he touched me, I loved the dirty talk, the punishments, the praises, the unending foreplay. All of it.

"You didn't follow my instructions," he chided, his warm hand cupping my cheek. "Was that on purpose, pretty girl? Did you want to be punished?"

I chewed on my lip, my heart slamming into my ribs.

"Answer me, Ria. Do you like being a brat?"

"Sometimes," I breathed. *Only when I play with you.*

I couldn't imagine doing this with anyone else. Nor did I want to, I realized grimly.

"Have you ever been spanked?"

"You did it upstairs, like ten minutes ago," I pointed out.

He squeezed my cheek. "Before that. Has this perfect little ass been properly taught a lesson?"

"No. I—um, things have been kept fifty shades of vanilla for me up until now," I admitted.

"Really?"

"Yeah. I didn't even realize I'd..." I trailed off, recognizing that non-horny Ria would probably want me to shut up now.

"Tell me," he coaxed, his palm moving in smooth massaging circles. "Finish your sentence."

"A lot of this is new for me."

His touch moved down, slipping between my thighs. "Had you ever been tied up before?"

"No."

"Did you like it?"

So much. So, so much. "It was cool, I guess."

His chuckle dripped over my skin like sizzling honey. And then, without warning, *smack!*

My body arched, my mouth falling all the way open as my fingers fisted the blanket.

"Did you like it?" he asked again.

"I loved it," I said, my stomach trembling. The impact had shot right to my clit again.

"Good girl."

Oh god.

His hand was soothing the spot he'd just smacked, rubbing delicate circles over the residual tingle. "What else do you like?"

"This," I breathed.

"And?"

"The playing. The talking."

"You like hearing all the depraved things I want to do to you?"

"Mmm."

His hand ran up and down the curve of my cheek, his fingers teasing the seam. I shivered on his lap.

"Adrien, please."

"Please, what?"

I didn't know. "Just... more."

Smack! Smack!

Holy mother of— *How* did that feel so good? The mixture of pain, pleasure, and pure vulnerability was unreal. I couldn't believe I'd gone my entire adult life without experiencing sex like this.

"You wanna know a little secret?" His voice was grating, rough and filled with crackling lust. He was panting almost as hard as I was. "I've never spanked anyone before."

Wait... what?

I heard him swallow, his hand back to soothing my tingling skin. "I've never even been tempted to. But then you stormed into my life like a fucking hurricane, wreaked absolute havoc on it, and I haven't been able to see straight since. Is that enough for you? Or do you still want more?"

My forehead was pressed to my fists, my breathing labored. "More."

Smack!

I whimpered, my eyes squeezing shut. The sting was growing more intense, electrifying my senses. I could feel his body shaking, feel how much this was turning him on.

"I can't think clearly anymore," he said. "Every single thought that runs through my head seems to loop back to you. I can't get it to fucking stop, Ria. And the worst part is, I don't want to. Is that enough?"

Not nearly. "More."

Smack!

I choked on the whimper this time, my stomach tightening.

"You drive me fucking crazy. Everything about you makes me wild. Your personality, your sense of humor, your smart mouth. And you're so fucking pretty, baby. I'm so attracted to you, it... I don't know how to handle it. Is that enough?"

Baby.

"More," I begged, my voice quivering.

Smack!

I cried out this time, tears springing to my eyes.

"I want you. And the more I deny it, the worse it gets. I want to spoil you fucking rotten, Ria. I've become obsessed with the idea. I want to buy you pretty things, fuck you, praise you, play with you. I want to take you out on dates, I want to tell people you're mine for real. And you know what's fucked up? I've started to fucking fantasize about cuddling you. Literally just holding you in my arms all night. No fighting, no bickering. Is that enough for you, Sanchez? Or do you still need more of me?"

I couldn't breathe. "More."

Smack!

My thighs quivered, my core clenching. My skin had become incredibly sensitive, and the ache of need was bordering on unbearable.

"This is incredible. You're so fucking beautiful. I'm tempted to make you get on your knees and suck my cock like a good girl while I tell you how pretty you are," he murmured. His fingers traced my seam again, this time making their way all the way down to tease the center of my embarrassingly wet core. "You're making a mess, baby. Dripping all over my leg."

I was beyond words at this point. The only thing I could do was spread my thighs a few inches, giving him better access. I didn't know whether I wanted him to spank me again or just thrust his fingers into me and put me out of my misery.

What I *did* know was that I'd never been this turned on in my life. Also, I really, really wanted to get on my knees and suck him off like a good girl while he told me how pretty I was. Very badly.

I shivered with a moan when the pad of his finger slid down to my clit. He pressed down on it once, twice... and then he pinched it. I choked on a cry, my entire body clenching. He kept a hold of my swollen, incredibly sensitive clit, and began rolling it between his thumb and index finger with enough pressure to make me moan his name.

I yanked the duvet, my vision speckling with stars.

"I want to fuck you so bad." His voice was taking on a desperate, pained edge, like he was barely keeping it together. "But we've got a score to settle first. I need to punish this pretty little pussy for all the lying you've been doing."

I wasn't really listening. How could I? The tension built and built, making my hips buck and squirm. I was practically humping his thigh, and I couldn't bring myself to care. I was so close, just a little more, and—he let me go.

Damn it.

I collapsed with a frustrated sigh, turning my face so he couldn't see my smile.

"How many times do you think you've lied to me since we met?" He gripped the inner part of my left thigh and pulled my leg farther onto the bed, leaving me more open and exposed.

I bit my cheek and remained silent, and he let me get away with it for exactly five seconds. And then he spanked my pussy.

It wasn't hard or rough, just a light tap. But it shot through my body like a flaming arrow and brought me right back to the edge.

"Holy shit," I breathed.

"Answer me, Ria. How many times?"

"I don't know. Ten?"

"Not even close." He went back to rolling my clit, making my hips squirm and spasm. And just as I was about to spill over the edge, he stopped.

I tapped my forehead against my fists in frustration.

"I can't wait to do this to you with toys," he murmured, slipping a finger inside me. "I wonder how many times I can force you to come for me before you cry and beg for mercy."

"Sadist," I laughed weakly.

He chuckled, and before I could make another smart remark, he inserted a second finger.

"Oh god, Adrien," I whimpered. "This is amazing."

"I know, baby. I'm right there with you."

"I can't believe... ah." My hips lifted off his lap, my left thigh shaking uncontrollably as his fingers scratched just the right spot. But then he stopped, and my body cried.

He released an unsteady breath. "I'm losing my goddamn mind over here. I've never... fuck, just look at you." He squeezed my cheek, gave it a punishing slap, then went right back to fucking me with his fingers. "You need to be taught a lesson for making me feel like this."

I released a guttural moan, my toes curling as the pleasure became too much to bear. I needed release.

"I'm going to buy you a house full of lingerie when we go back," he promised. "You're too pretty to be left unspoiled, baby. Too pretty to be left unpunished."

It was all a bunch of nonsense, but that didn't stop the ancient lizard part of my brain from hissing in pleasure.

"We also need to do something about this mess you're making," he chided, pulling his hand away.

He lifted me from his lap, placed me facedown on the mattress, then slid a pillow under my stomach, angling my hips up for better access. I felt like a boneless ragdoll, succumbing to his every whim. And I loved it.

"I'm going to lick and suck your pretty pink pussy clean, but I'm not going to let you come. Not yet."

"Adrien," I whined.

"You shouldn't have lied to me so much."

"This is so not a proportionate response," I sighed, my core already starting to clench as he positioned himself behind me, spreading my lips wide open with his thumbs. "There is such a thing as too much foreplay, you know."

"You keep telling yourself that." The heat of his breath tickled my center, and I clenched. "I'm really going to enjoy this."

He licked me. It was a firm, thorough lick, the thick pad of his tongue sliding from my clit all the way up to my entrance. And once he started, he didn't stop. He licked, kissed, sucked, and praised, but never gave me enough to push me over the edge. At one point he nipped a trail down my labia with his teeth, and I reached behind me and gripped his hair, begging for him to please, please, please keep going. He didn't.

I stopped counting how many times he edged me at around eight, mostly because I didn't have the mental capacity to keep going. By the end, I was so wound up and sensitive, that he was getting me there with just a couple of licks, or a small suckle of my clit.

"I need... how many..." I tried.

He was trailing the tip of his tongue along the crease between the inner part of my thigh and my sex, placing little kisses on my skin. I was going to die.

"Well, we were done with the lying count about three edges ago, but I'm a greedy man," he murmured. "It's your fault for tasting so sweet. I could spend all night with my face stuffed between your legs, pretty girl, listening to you whimper and moan like that."

No. Really. I was going to die.

"I hate you," I breathed.

"Still haven't learned our lesson, I see."

"Adrien." I was going to cry. The mixture of pure pain and pleasure was becoming agonizing. Or amazing. I didn't know anymore.

"What, pretty girl? What do you need?"

"You. I need... please?" If I still had bones, I'd have reached for him again. But my arms were deadweight.

The mattress dipped as he moved. There was some shuffling, and then I had an entirely naked Adrien leaning over me, hard cock pressed to the cheek he'd spanked.

He brushed my hair away from my face and neck, then trailed soft kisses from my shoulder to my ear. "Use your words. Tell me exactly what you need."

"I need you inside me."

"Beg, Miss Sanchez," he murmured into my ear, nibbling gently on the shell. He aligned himself with my entrance, taking a moment to breathe before making his full command. "Ask me to fuck you nicely."

He used the same dark tone he had that day in his office when he'd instructed me to beg for the opportunity to earn Alba's job back. But this time it made my stomach quiver in an entirely different way.

"Please fuck me nicely." The words were so full of blubber, they barely sounded English.

He huffed a low chuckle. "There's nothing nice about the way I plan on fucking you, pretty girl, but close enough."

Then he pushed the tip of his cock inside me, and we both moaned in agony. Or ecstasy. I really, really couldn't tell anymore. Couldn't think or breathe as he worked himself deeper and deeper, until he was buried all the way to the hilt.

"Fuck. You feel..." He stopped to take a breath, then circled a hand around my throat and used his grip to lift my head.

I turned my face slightly, just far enough for him to nibble on my lip as he began to roll his hips.

"Adrien." The moan was barely audible, but it was

enough. Whatever sense of control he still had snapped, and he slammed into me.

I was done. Between the hour-long edging and the added friction of having him inside me with no barrier, I was done. It only took a handful of hard thrusts for the orgasm to hit. And it hit with a fucking vengeance.

I choked out a cry, clenching around his punishing thrusts as an uncontrollable quake ripped through my leg. My breath was stolen, my vision speckled with tiny white stars, and I felt the tingles all the way in my toes, the tips of my ears.

It was *incredible*. Like all the orgasms I'd been denied rolled into one.

Adrien growled a string of dirty praises in my ear, his thrusts growing increasingly erratic. His hand switched from my throat to my clit, and I saw ten different versions of The Light.

"Fuck, baby. You take it so fucking well. Keep coming for me. Just like that."

I would have begged for mercy, but I was too far gone to form the words. He kept going, kept rubbing my over-sensitive ball of nerves to prolong my orgasm and keep me clenching and spasming around him. The second wave of ecstasy hit so impossibly hard and quick that I felt it seize muscles I didn't know I had.

"Fuck. Fuckfuckfuckfuck."

Adrien came with a guttural groan, his cock pulsing as he buried himself deep inside with one final thrust. Our bodies quivered and trembled against each other for what felt like blissful eternity, our breathing ragged, desperate, and sharp. From the feel and sounds of it, his orgasm had hit just as hard as mine.

Eventually, he collapsed beside me, his heaving

chest glistening in the moonlight. His head lolled to the side, his heavy, drunk gaze latching onto mine. We stared at each other in... awe? Mind-blown confusion?

I had a cheek pressed to the bed, a thin curtain of hair covering my face, and absolutely zero strength to move. There was a possibility that I'd never move again. Just stay like this in my new liquid form, entirely satiated for the rest of my life.

Adrien's lips twitched as he took in my state. He reached over and brushed back the hair covering my vision, then he grazed a knuckle over my cheekbone and said, "You good?"

"I might be dead," I whispered back, still panting.

His dimples flashed, his throat working with a huffed chuckle. Then he rolled over to his side, cradled the back of my neck in his palm, and leaned forward to kiss me. It was deep, gentle, and sweet, and made my heart flutter with alarming intensity. I almost reached for him again when he pulled away.

"Stay here," he whispered, placing one last kiss on the tip of my nose before pushing himself out of bed. As if I had a choice.

There was some rustling in the ensuite bathroom— cupboards and drawers being opened, the tap running— and when Adrien reappeared, he was cradling an armful of stuff. He climbed back into bed, positioning himself behind me again.

"Does this hurt?" The tips of his fingers grazed the cheek he'd spanked, gentle and soothing.

I swallowed, a shiver tickling at the base of my spine in response to the little touch. What the hell had this man done to me?

"Not really," I mumbled. "Why? Did you leave a mark?"

"Kind of. It's a little red," his voice was back to a charred, almost pained tone. His fingers moved down, sliding to my center again. "And I'm spilling out of your pussy. It's the hottest fucking thing I've ever seen, Sanchez."

I shuddered, a sigh escaping as my stomach began to quiver all over again. But before I could do something stupid, like curl my ass up toward him like a feline in heat, he began caressing my inner thighs with a warm wet towel.

"What are you doing?" I asked, trying to twist my head to look at him.

"Just relax."

I frowned skeptically but lay my head back down as he delicately swiped away my skin's slickness. He took his time, treating my body with the slow gentleness you'd use to handle a newborn kitten. Once he was done, he picked up a small jar of something that smelled like lavender and began to work it into the cheek he'd spanked.

"What's that?" I mumbled, eyes half-mast. This was so nice and relaxing.

"Skin soothing cream."

"You don't have to—"

"I want to," he interrupted quietly.

I sighed with pleasure, closing my eyes. After a few silent minutes, I smirked into the dark and muttered, "Hey, remember when you said you wouldn't touch me with a level A hazmat suit on?"

And that was what got us back onto the uncontrollable laughing track.

32

I WOKE UP IN HEAVEN. Sore and satiated, with a naked Adrien pressed to my back, trailing soft kisses along my shoulder and neck.

A hum rolled out of my throat when his teeth got involved, my back curling against him. He was hard and ready, and the moment I felt it, my body melted into a puddle of needy lust. Again.

I was broken. We'd had sex two more times last night, and I was still hungry for more. After he'd cleaned me up, I'd sat on his lap, kissed and thanked him for being sweet and taking care of me. One compliment led to another, and the next thing I knew, my wrists were tied behind my back as he sunk me down on his cock, murmuring filthy, brutishly possessive things in my ear as I rode him. He'd said the types of things that appealed strictly to my lizard brain, and that I'd only allow in bed. The types of things I'd replay in my head over and over again every time I reached for the purple vibrator in my bedside drawer at home.

I'd told him so afterward, which was what had led to the third round.

"Show me, baby. Show me how you'll touch yourself, thinking about me," he'd demanded.

Four minutes later, he'd had my slick-covered fingers pinned to the mattress, one of my knees hooked over his shoulder, and was growling angrily about "losing his mind" over me as he pounded into my "perfect little pussy," punishing it for being so "tempting and pretty." The declaration had been followed by more brutish and possessive dirty talk.

Three times in one night should have been more than enough. I shouldn't have wanted more so soon.

"Good morning," he hummed, arms tightening around me. "How did you sleep?"

"It's only been four hours," I complained, stuffing my face into the fluffy white pillow.

He was already lifting the hem of my slip. "You want me to stop?"

"Mmm," I responded, grinding my ass against his steel length.

He hissed, fingers digging into my hips. "Use your words, Ria."

"Don't stop," I sighed, already feeling the ache and dampness building between my thighs. "But go slow, please. I'm sore."

He got me off with his fingers first, making me arch and gasp and shudder against him before he slowly entered me from behind, whispering a smooth string of desperate praises in my ear while he fucked me.

I latched on to them, memorizing every last word.

We managed to crawl out of bed a half hour later and get into the shower. He washed every inch of my body, shampooed my hair, ran conditioner through it with gentle fingers, and kept spoiling my skin with soft, affectionate kisses, despite my halfhearted protests.

And that wasn't even the best part. The best part was how much we laughed, how much genuine *fun* we seemed to have when we weren't fighting.

It didn't hurt that my anger had thawed, and that I didn't see him as the inherently selfish, unredeemable asshole I used to.

After calling Jamie and filling her in on all the non-sexy stuff (because it was going to be so much more fun to see her freak out in person over a bottle of wine), I spent the morning with Adrien's family while he took his work calls.

We went through a whole stack of photo albums, laughing at stories of a rowdy young Adrien wreaking havoc on the world around him. It was fucking adorable and provided me with endless teasing ammunition, so I decided to stay for just one more day and use it.

Except the one extra day turned into two. Then three. And by the fourth morning, I couldn't remember the last time we'd bickered or fought. Bantered, yes. We did that constantly. But there was no venom or bitter animosity behind our jabs anymore. It was just... I don't know. When we weren't fighting, we just... *fit*.

There was never a dull or awkward moment. Not when his parents took us out to dinner, not when spent an entire day hiking, kayaking, and enjoying the seven hours of blissful sunshine bestowed upon the island before the clouds took over again, and not when we cooped ourselves up in the guesthouse the next day, "resting."

And then there was that. The sex. We were insatiable;

and the more we did it, the more our bodies seemed to want.

Yesterday afternoon, as he'd been wrapping up another conference call, I'd changed into a cream-colored babydoll and crawled under his desk, nuzzling and kissing his hardening bulge over his slacks until he caved, hung up before the speaker had gotten through his last presentation slide, and grabbed a hold of me before I could make my escape.

I was on my knees again less than a minute later, my hands bound behind my back as Adrien unzipped himself and ordered me to "suck him off properly. Like a good girl."

Like *his* good girl.

His pretty girl.

It was new. And instead of panicking or rebelling against his claim on me, I reveled in it, aching for him every time he said it. And he kept saying it until he was gripping my hair and shooting down my throat. Then he'd lifted me onto the desk, one hand fisting my ponytail as he fucked me with the other, demanding I repeat his words.

"Say it," he kept insisting as I moaned, my wrists pulling against the leather belt wrapped around them. What was it about being restrained that made everything so much hotter? "Tell me you're mine, Ria."

I'd resisted until the ache in my core became unbearable, until Adrien's eyes were half-feral again, swimming over my blushing face like it was the most awe-inspiring thing they'd ever witnessed. And just as I hit the brink of shattering, my lips moved out of their own violation. "I'm yours."

His mouth had swallowed every whimper and moan

that accompanied my orgasm, and then I was freed, my hands unbound so they could hug Adrien back as his kisses slowed, softened, became... tender. He'd carried me to bed and that had been it. We hadn't climbed back out again until well past dinner time.

And even though I still didn't think it was a great idea, I was starting to... at least consider it. Turning this little affair into something without an impending expiration date. Conducting a new experiment of sorts.

Adrien had brought it up again last night, asking if I was open to the idea. "It's okay if you need to think about it," he'd said when I hadn't answered him right away.

So I was. Thinking about it. And other than the mess with his family and the engagement we'd lied about, there was one other sore spot I couldn't get over: Alba.

"Tell me something," I said, plucking a small strawberry out of the fresh bowl of fruit that had been hand-delivered to us by Julie this morning while I was still sleeping. She'd brought pancakes as well, and fresh whipped cream. I adored her. Truly. I could only hope that my future mother-in-law would be half as kind and nurturing as her.

Adrien and I were in the kitchen of the guesthouse, right under the temporary patch that had been installed on the roof to accommodate us. I was sitting on the granite kitchen counter with Adrien standing between my knees, his palms resting on my bare thighs.

I de-stemmed the strawberry, dipped it into the whipped cream, and brought it up to his mouth. He flashed me a devilish dimple before accepting the gift, making sure to lick and suck all the juice and cream from my fingers.

Aaaaand I was turned on again.

Focus, I chided myself.

"How is it possible that you didn't know Alba had a child when she worked for you for four years? That doesn't make any sense to me."

His eyebrows twitched upward, before tightening slightly. He shoved a hand through his damp hair. "To be honest, that's all on me. I had a really shitty experience with my assistant before her, and I was still... recovering from that when she was hired. I thought it would be better if our relationship was kept strictly professional, so I made it clear to her that the less we knew about each other's personal lives, the better. But looking back now... I obviously took it a little too far."

He grimaced when he said the last part, his regret clear. "I've said this before, but I *am* sorry, Ria. She never told me the workload was too much. She never complained about anything or gave any indication that she wasn't happy. She just... she never said no, so I never questioned it. A better boss might have, but I—I'll talk to her when I'm back. I promise."

"What happened with your last assistant?" I asked. My hand had moved to his hip, my thumb stroking his sweater. It happened instinctively, the moment his voice dipped into the apologetic range.

He cleared his throat, briefly averting his gaze. "Long story short, I found out he was leaking my information online. Flight schedules, home address, phone number, vacation spots, meeting locations, you name it." His tongue darted out to wet his lips, his gaze hardening. "You know that website for people who hate me? The information eventually made its way there, and all over a bunch of fan sites. But the original place it was posted was a lightly moderated forum for... I mean, there are fans, and then there are people who get obsessive, and delusional."

A sense of unease tugged at my gut. "What do you mean?" I asked carefully. *Please tell me this isn't leading where I think it is.*

He shifted his weight from one foot to the other. "Well, to start, he had a lock of my hair wrapped around a green lollipop that he kept in the top drawer of his desk at work. It was wet when we found it."

I gaped. "*What*?"

"Tip of the iceberg."

My stomach churned. "What the fuck."

"He'd taken hundreds of photos of me without my consent or knowledge, kept prints of them in the dashboard of his company-issued car. We found stolen pocket squares, drawings of me, handwritten letters that were incredibly uncomfortable to read, and he'd.... he'd very clearly made a habit of going through my trash. In my apartment. That I'd never given him the keys to. Think used condoms, floss, tissues."

I was speechless. Creeped the fuck out, and utterly speechless.

"I'd never suspected anything," Adrien went on. "He seemed like a normal guy, and he was good at his job. I trusted him. But then my phone started to blow up, and the same people were showing up everywhere I went. Airports, restaurants, my apartment building, my running route. A leaked phone number is one thing, but I didn't understand how they were getting their hands on my schedule. Turned out, Keaton had been sharing my information with a small group of people on that forum for well over a year. But it had remained contained to their private chat until one of them decided to leak it. It happened after they'd had an argument."

My mouth was still hanging open. "That's... insane. I'm so sorry."

"I was still dealing with the aftermath of it when I hired Alba, both logistically and emotionally. And since we were trying to keep the story out of the media, the information was distributed on a need-to-know basis only. So, your sister doesn't know what happened. Just that I had her sign a bunch of NDAs and made sure she knew how much I valued my privacy. She had limited access to my schedule and personal information, and she wasn't allowed to ask questions about my personal life. In return, I wouldn't ask about hers."

Bit by bit, his behavior started to make sense. No wonder he wouldn't give me his phone number. I picked up another strawberry and bit into it, thinking. "I can't imagine working with someone for four years and never breaking that seal. But, I mean, I get it. That's a really traumatizing experience."

"It broke once," he said, eyes darting down to my lips as I popped the rest of the strawberry into my mouth. "Alba was the one that caught Mandy cheating."

My chewing slowed, my fingers going still around the grape I'd reached for. She'd cheated on him?

His eyes met mine, searching. "Alba really never did tell you, did she?"

I shook my head. My sister was excellent at keeping secrets, so that part wasn't surprising. "She said you owed her a favor, was that it?" I asked. She'd informed him of the affair, and kept quiet about it afterward, so he'd owed her one?

A nod.

"And the guy that Mandy's marrying... it's not the same person she cheated on you with, is it?"

He rolled his lips. "My cousin. It started shortly after the whole Keaton thing happened—that's actually how they met. She was on our PR team; he was the lawyer taking care of my sealed restraining order. It was happening right under my nose for a little over three years, and once again, I'd had no idea. I proposed, thinking—" He cut off, color sprinting to the tips of his ears, his temples.

What the fuck?

My head had jutted forward, my mouth hanging open again. "She cheated on you with your cousin and they're both coming to your parents' anniversary party? They were *invited* to your parents' anniversary party?"

"It was a long time ago," he responded gruffly, his jaw tight. "And they've apologized."

"*So?*" There was some shit people didn't deserve to be forgiven for. This was pretty high on that list. "Please tell me you have some elaborate revenge scheme planned. If you've brought me here because you think it'll piss her off, I'm officially in. Let's do it. Give me the ring, and I'll—"

"They announced it on Halloween."

My heart hurled itself against my ribs, a shot of adrenaline spiking through my bloodstream.

"Their engagement," he clarified before I could ask. "Alice texted me fifteen minutes before I greeted the investors in our hotel lobby."

"This Halloween?" My voice cracked. "Right before I..." Right before I'd assaulted him, cost him a shit ton of investment dollars, and ran away? "Shit. Adrien, I'm so sorry, I—"

"Why did you do it?"

I almost didn't want to say it, because it didn't excuse my actions the way I'd originally allowed myself to justify. Suddenly, picking glitter out of dirt didn't seem to be enough of a punishment for how I'd acted.

"I told you, this guy in a blue suit grabbed me, and I thought it was—"

He shook his head, leaning closer. "No. Why did you smash his car window?"

I reeled. "What?"

His eyes were searching mine like he was trying to peer into my soul. "The vandalism charge on your record is for damage to a sports car. What happened?"

The sudden change in topic was so jarring, I had to take a moment to mentally re-align myself. "Where did that come from?"

"It's been bugging me since I saw it. Like an itch in my brain I can't scratch," he said. "You were set on an incredibly clear life trajectory, then derailed at the very last second. I don't get it."

"Why are you so weirdly stuck on this?" I asked, frowning at him. "For the last time, I did a stupid thing, I got caught, I paid the consequences. End of story."

"No, Sanchez. You spent your entire academic career working toward utter perfection, then picked up a brick, and shattered it all to bits just three weeks before graduation. I'm willing to bet my right arm that you hadn't so much as stolen a stick of gum before then, so what happened?"

"You didn't know me back then. How are you so... sure..."

...

Oh my god.

"What's his name?" I asked. My heart was starting to

palpitate, pumping every drop of blood in my body up to my head. "The guy that Mandy cheated on you with. You said he's a lawyer? What's his name?"

When Alice had said "MJ" was coming to the party, I'd assumed the "J" stood for Mandy's middle name. *Like an idiot.*

Adrien flinched, taking a step back.

"*Josh* is your *cousin*?" I shoved myself off the countertop. "*Josh* is the person she's engaged to? *Joshua Motherfucking Goldman*?"

"I was going to tell you."

"When?" I yelled. Sparks tingled under my skin, cooking my flesh.

"Right now." He raked a hand through his dark hair, the tips of his ears bruising. "I was getting there, I swear."

"Adrien, *what the fuck*?"

"I can explain."

"Let me guess. You wanted to get back at Josh for sleeping with your fiancée, so you orchestrated this whole thing to fuck with him. By fucking *me*." It didn't take a rocket scientist to figure it out.

Holy shit. I'd been so stupid.

I *knew* things weren't adding up. He'd claimed he knew who I was because Alba kept framed pictures of me on her desk, but that couldn't have been true. Because for every picture of me on her desk, there would have been three of Olive, and he didn't know who she was.

But I'd had just enough alcohol in my system that night not to question it.

"Okay, Ria, you have every right to be angry with me, but I really need you to hear me out on one thing: I did *not* sleep with you to get back at Josh, okay? None of that—*us* —was fake. I swear."

I swatted his hand away when he reached for me, a hot mixture of anger, hurt, and betrayal thrashing in my chest.

I didn't need to know what his tell was to know he was lying. Of course that was why he'd slept with me, called me pretty, told me the things he had.

What? Did I *really* think that Adrien Cloutier wanted to take me out on dates? Did I *really* think he'd meant it when he said he wanted to tell people I was his for real? That he'd fantasized about us cuddling?

Was I really that naïve?

The thrashing in my chest began to boil up to my throat, cheeks, eyes. I blinked it back, refusing to shed a single tear in front of him—*over* him.

"What exactly was your plan when you brought me here? What were you thinking?" My heart squeezed out a string of fluttery pulses that pulled at my gut. I felt sick. "Were you really going to tell me? Or was it supposed to be a horrible little surprise when he showed up to the party?"

His expression said it all. "You have to understand how angry I was," he tried, holding a palm up. It was clear how much effort he was putting into keeping his tone even and calm. "After the breakup, I threw myself into work. It all happened around the time my dad retired, and... no one thought I could do it. The media, the board. I was too young, too arrogant, too inexperienced. And I decided to prove them wrong. I put everything I had into the East Asian expansion, Ria. It was—*is*—my baby. I'd been planting seeds and working on the plan before I even became CEO. That investment wasn't just about the money and resources the Japanese firm was going to provide. It was about building confidence with my board of directors. Proving that I could do this job, and I could do it well."

I'd crossed my arms while I listened, trying to reel my emotions back in check. I remembered how the media had reacted when Anthony decided to retire early to spend more time with his family. Everything Adrien was saying lined up with what I recalled being reported, as well as what little Alba had mentioned about the internal pushback when Adrien had been promoted.

It lined up, but it didn't excuse any of it.

"Ria, I spent six months pouring my soul into securing that deal. I lived and breathed it for half a year. They were already a little flighty because of my age, and the lack of confidence surrounding my promotion, but I managed to get them on board anyway. And the Halloween incident—right after Alice texted me... it all... threw me off. I fumbled through dinner that evening, the signing got pushed until the morning because they suddenly needed more time to think, and by then the video had gone viral, and the public reaction was... I think maybe that's what did it. I don't know, I'm not sure anymore. But I was just so frustrated that..." He trailed off, shoving a rough hand through his hair for the fifth time that minute. "It's been a really shitty few years, and this one just pushed me over the edge. I'd done nothing to instigate that attack. And it seemed really fucking unfair that—not only did everybody and their mother seem to think I deserved it—but just as it felt like things were finally starting to go my way, it... I'm sorry, I'm not trying to make excuses, but I really need you to understand where I was operating from."

My throat felt too tight to speak, so I kept my mouth shut and let him get it all out.

"I knew who you were because of how much Josh

talked about you when you dated. He showed us pictures, told us about your plans to go to the same law school, and gloated about your accomplishments like they were linked directly to his own résumé. You couldn't pay the guy to shut up about your relationship. Even Alice managed to put two and two together, and she was eleven —maybe twelve—back then. I'd seen you around the building at work, so I knew… Honestly, I didn't need the security cameras to tell me it was you on Halloween. I recognized you right away."

My muscles tightened when Adrien looped back to Josh. My molars pressed harder together, my nails digging into my palms.

"I wasn't thinking clearly," Adrien went on. "In my head, this plan was killing three birds with one stone. I'd finally get my mom to stop trying to set me up with all her friends' daughters, Josh would absolutely loathe seeing you and I together, and I couldn't think of a better way to get under your skin than to make you pretend to be in love with me. And I assumed that being blindsided when you ran into Josh at the party wouldn't be fun for you, either. From how he acted after the breakup, I think it's safe to assume you didn't part ways on friendly terms." The tail end of his statement curled like it wanted to be a question, but when I made no indication of entertaining it, he let out a heavy breath and said, "That's it. That's all my cards on the table. Now you know pretty much everything."

A long stretch of silence followed while I processed, half fuming. If Alba had been the one to catch Mandy and Josh, had she recognized him? Would she have warned me if I'd let her know I was coming here with Adrien?

"Why are you telling me all this now?" I finally asked

him. He could have convinced me to stay for the party instead. It was less than thirty-five hours away. He could have continued to play the part until then, and I'd have been just as blindsided as he'd hoped.

"To be honest it took less than two days of us being here for me to yank my head out of my ass. It was like reality slapped me across the face when I saw my family." Tension squirmed under his skin like he was frustrated with himself. "And then you... I don't know, it was a clarity thing. I started to realize just how deep you'd managed to get under my skin, and curiosity set in. I wanted to call a truce, but you wouldn't bite. And one argument led to another... I was going to tell you before the party, whether you stayed long enough to attend it or not. I made that decision on the second day. It occurred to me that I didn't have the full story of what happened between you two, and knowing him... Like I said, it was a clarity thing. I realized what an asshole move it would be to blindside you with it."

I chewed the inside of my cheek, observing him as my arms tightened against my chest. "Adrien, your poor mother thinks you're *engaged*. She's fucking beside herself with happiness because of it. How did you imagine this would all end?"

He winced. "I know."

"You made me think—" I had to cut myself off when my voice broke. After a shaky inhale, I tried again. "We've been sleeping together."

His gaze snapped to mine, sharp and intense. "That has nothing to do with him."

"Adrien—"

"It has *nothing* to do with him, Ria. I swear it. If you

don't believe anything else I've told you, I need you to believe that."

I didn't. Not for a second.

Suddenly all the dirty talk felt less sexy, more ugly and degrading. None of it had come from a place of desire for him. I felt... used. Hurt. Humiliated. Betrayed.

And the worst part? I kind of understood where he was coming from, which made it significantly more difficult to be angry with him. So I had to stand there and process the hurt and humiliation without being able to hide behind the anger.

"Ria, I—"

I stepped back, turning my cheek away when he tried to touch it. I genuinely couldn't believe I'd been so stupid.

"Don't you have another meeting this morning you need to get to?" I took another three steps back, putting more distance between our bodies.

He hesitated. "We're not done talking. I need you to believe—I wasn't expecting this with you. I didn't plan for us to fit like—" He kept cutting himself off, trying to get his thoughts in order. He stopped to shove two hands through his hair and release a breath. "It's not just physical. Sanchez, I—"

"Adrien, enough." Did I say I was finding it difficult to be angry with him? The fucking *audacity* of this man.

"I'll prove it. You just have to give me the chance."

"No," I said firmly, "I'm done with this. Here's what's going to happen. You're going to go to your meeting, and by the time you're done, I'll be gone. You and I—whatever fucked up thing this was—are done. We're even. I don't owe you shit anymore, and vice versa."

Two hands through his hair again. They ruffled. "Shit, okay. Here's the thing. There's a pretty big storm out East right now. Flights have been getting redirected and delayed all morning."

"I don't care. I'll sleep at a hotel for a night or two." Big deal. "I just need to get changed and grab my suitcase from the main house. I'll sneak out the side again."

Adrien had changed into jeans and a burgundy pullover, but I was still in my silk slip from last night.

His eyes pinched as he winced again. "That's the other thing. A few of the guests coming in from Toronto rescheduled their flights to get ahead of the storm."

I narrowed my eyes at him. May every god in recorded history have mercy on his soul if he was saying what I thought he was saying. "What?"

Adrien looked like he was in physical pain. "Alice texted me before you woke up. He's here."

My heart hurled itself into my ribs, trying to get a go at him. "Are you fucking with me right now?"

He shook his head. "There's only one route back to the house and it's in full view of the main patio where they're all having brunch. We were invited. I said we weren't in the mood, so my mom brought us fruit instead. And... she took our laundry with her. Your clothes are with the household staff."

I was pretty sure I was having an out-of-body experience. My pulse was thrashing against my eardrums, the ringing in my right ear growing louder and louder.

"My stuff is in there. The main house," I whispered. If she'd taken our laundry that meant *all* my stuff was now at the main house, except for my phone, purse, and... maybe that's all I needed. Who the hell cared about my suitcase and a few clothes—

My passport.

My passport was in my suitcase. My drunk brain had

packed it even though my flight had been domestic. I couldn't just leave my passport here, could I?

"I know," Adrien said, even though I'd been talking to myself. "I can bring it all to you, but you'll still have to follow the same path to leave the property and go to the airport."

My eyes refocused. "*You* brought me here! *You* said I could leave all my stuff in the other room and just bring a handful of clothes!" I accused with a pointed finger. And I'd *listened*.

He rolled his lips, nodded grimly.

I was beyond livid.

"Adrien, *I'm going to fucking kill you*." I barely managed to pry my jaw open enough to hiss the threat. My skin was bruising purple. I could feel it.

He released a resigned breath. "At this point, I don't think I'll stop you."

33

I NEEDED AN ESCAPE PLAN. One that didn't include me having to interact with the man who'd ruined my life at eighteen.

According to the most recent update from Alice, the main house was currently a frenzy of hired staff setting up for the big party tomorrow. And since the weather was so "uncharacteristically nice for this time of year," it didn't sound like their group was too keen on moving indoors anytime soon.

These updates from Alice were the only reason I'd let Adrien live this long. It really wasn't easy. He kept offering to have me airlifted out of the front yard.

"I've got a helicopter on standby," he said at one point, tapping away at his phone. "Never mind. Pilot says there's enough room to land, so you can just get in."

I'd always had my suspicions that too much money made people crazy. This confirmed it.

I ignored him as my frustration and impatience boiled over, and stormed back into the bedroom we'd been using

so I could change into the single pair of jeans and crumpled long-sleeved tee that hadn't been in the laundry bag
Adrien had handed over to his mother this morning. I
shut the door in his face when he tried to follow me.

"I can fix this. Can you please just talk to me?"

I threw on the clothes, bunched my hair into a messy
ponytail, swiped on some deodorant, and stormed back
out with my heart hammering in my throat.

Adrien was still standing outside the room when I tore
out of it. "Give me ten minutes. I just need you to listen."

Right. Except he could spend an entire lifetime
inventing a myriad of elaborate excuses for why he'd done
what he'd done, and it wouldn't make a difference. I
wouldn't believe a word that came out of his lying mouth.

I shoved past him, heading straight for the front door.
It opened exactly one inch before his hand pressed it shut.
It was official. The man had a death wish.

"Talk to me."

I whipped around, glowering up at him with my fists
heavy at my sides. "I don't *want* to talk to you anymore,
Adrien. We've been talking nonstop for a week and everything you've said up to this point has apparently been
total bullshit!"

"That's not true. If you'd just let me explain—"

"Adrien, listen to me carefully," I ground out through
my rising anxiety and frustration. "I. Don't. Care. I don't
care if you have more excuses or sob stories. It's not going
to change a damn thing. So do us both a favor and fuck
the fuck off!"

He didn't stop me this time when I ripped the door
open, but ten seconds into my sneakers pounding against
the stone pathway, his shadow began to trail behind me like

an imprinted duckling, following my every turn and swivel. I marched on, ignoring him, until I could hear the faint chatter of his family enjoying their brunch out on the patio.

My pulse thundered as I slowed down. I couldn't see them yet, which meant they couldn't see me. Adrien and I were hidden behind a large, perfectly groomed hedge. Three more steps and we'd reach the corner, in full view of the table and its occupants.

I stopped walking.

Sweat trickled down my back, my fingers beginning to tremble as the nausea kicked in. This was the most anxiety-inducing and uncomfortable situation he could have possibly put me in. As far as the revenge thing was concerned, he'd really outdone himself with this one.

I pressed the base of my palms to my eyes and let out a shaky breath, trying to think. I only had three options at this point.

One, march up to the house and come face-to-face with the people that had ruined my life.

Two, march up to the house with my head down, ignore the whole table, go inside, and leave Adrien behind to do the explaining.

Three, stay here and wait them out. Eventually they'd go inside, and I'd sneak upstairs through the side entrance.

"Ria."

I jerked away when I felt Adrien's fingers graze my wrist.

"Don't touch me," I hissed.

The fact that he was starting to look utterly miserable did nothing to cool my rage. In fact, as far as I was concerned, he had no right to be upset. This was his own doing. He was the one who'd gotten us into this fucking mess.

"I'm sorry," he whispered.

"I don't give a fuck."

Unless his apology could teleport me out of this nightmare, I didn't want to hear it.

"I can fix this if you just— What are you doing?"

But I'd already turned the corner.

I was going to bolt into the house. It was the best option out of the three. Not only did it get me out of here faster, but having to explain my behavior to his family would keep Adrien preoccupied while I grabbed my stuff.

My lungs grew too big for my ribs as the carefree chatter and laughter became more prominent, Adrien hot on my tail.

Just don't look up. Whatever you do, do not make eye contact.

Julie spotted us first, seconds after I turned the corner.

"Ria! Addy!" she called out. I could see her begin to wave in my peripherals.

Keep your head down. Do not engage.

"I'm so happy you guys decided to join us. Come, come."

Stay strong. You're less than twenty feet away.

The door was right there. I just needed to—

"*Ariana?*"

His voice spider-crawled up my spine, making my shoulders hunch instinctively. My feet stuttered.

Don't look up. Please, please don't look up.

"Ariana Sanchez?"

I looked up.

Eight pairs of eyes gazed up at me from the long,

extravagantly adorned table, but my attention immediately cut to him. Joshua Motherfucking Goldman.

"You two know each other?" Julie asked.

Beside her, Alice sipped her tea, brows arching.

"What the hell are you doing here?" Josh asked, his tone on the rude side of accusatory.

He was dressed exactly how I would have expected. Fitted silver suit. Six-figure watch. Blonde waves tousled away from his sharp, handsome features. He screamed money, privilege, success, stolen dreams.

I'd known what to expect, but it still ripped open the wound in the deepest, darkest pit of my soul, poured salt on it, and set it ablaze.

Life really wasn't fucking fair, was it?

Josh's steel gaze flicked to a movement behind me. Adrien, I assumed.

"What's going on? What's she doing here?" The question came from the middle-aged man sitting across the table from Josh. His father—Kenny Goldman.

"I don't understand. How do you all know each other?" Julie asked, her smile flickering. The conversation was already starting to go in circles.

I recognized the shift in him before Josh even opened his maw, and managed to steel myself for the bite. "Ariana's father used to clean the toilets at our high school." His eyes gleamed, his vicious mouth curling into an all-too-familiar condescending sneer.

Heads twisted in his direction, shoulders tensed. Gampy visibly bristled, his white brows ramming together with disapproval.

"Watch your fucking tone, Goldman." Adrien stepped closer, his presence behind me growing broader.

Josh didn't pay him any attention. He'd already locked in on his prey, there was no letting it go now.

"I heard the news," he said. "Car crash, right? After a night shift?"

There was a ringing in my head. Somewhere near my left ear. The outskirts of my vision were beginning to blur, the air growing too thick to breathe.

"It's too bad," he went on. "Nice guy. Makes you think, eh?"

"Josh, enough," Kenny cut in. "Can someone explain what the hell she's doing here? Did you hire her as part of the staff?"

I was rooted in place, my throat constricted. I knew I had to move, knew that I was less than ten steps away from the door. But I couldn't seem to get my body to follow the orders it was receiving from my brain.

Suddenly I was too aware of myself—my disheveled appearance, the deer-in-headlights expression, my lack of spine.

I was, in a word, pathetic.

There was a woman sitting to Josh's left, the impressive diamond on her left hand winking at me.

Mandy was unsurprisingly lovely. Ethereal and elegant. Unlike me, her hair was not bunched into a haphazard ponytail that spilled out in all the wrong places. She was not in jeans, nor was she wearing a some-what-crumpled shirt with growing sweat stains.

No. Mandy was wearing an off-shoulder summer dress with frills and flowers galore, dark hair spilling down her back in a silky waterfall that had never even heard of the word frizz.

She looked exactly like the type of woman you'd

expect to see on Josh's arm—the type of woman you'd expect to see on Adrien's.

"They're engaged."

Anthony's voice jerked me out of the depths of my own head. My lashes fluttered, cheeks bruising.

"We were going to wait until they joined us to share the news," Julie said politely. "It's their announcement to make, and we— Ria, honey, are you all right? Do you need to sit?"

"Who's engaged?" Josh.

Warm fingers grazed the small of my back, a gentle nudge toward the door. My feet remained cemented to the spot.

"Adrien and Ria." Anthony.

You could hear a pin drop. For what felt like three full karmic lifetimes, no one said a word.

Josh's disbelieving gaze slid an inch to my left. "You're joking."

He was ignored.

Adrien's full hand was now splayed across the dip of my back. He leaned down to my ear, whispered, "You're okay. Come on."

I didn't know how his voice managed to reconnect the wiring between my brain and my legs, but it did. I took one stiff step forward, then another.

Adrien said something to the table, but I was already inside the house, and the door had already clattered closed behind me.

My muscles loosened, built momentum. I ran up the stairs.

Fuck the clothes. Just grab the suitcase and get the fuck out of here.

But my blood was roaring too loudly in my ears by the

time I reached the bedroom, and I had to squat down, put my head between my knees. It felt like I'd been sucker-punched in the gut.

"Makes you think, eh?"

Acid boiled in my stomach, pain stabbed at my throat, behind my eyes. I was going to throw up.

"Hey."

I bolted upright. Bad idea. My head spun, my vision darkened, stars spotted Adrien's pinched features, and gravity tilted. I stumbled back a few steps and almost tumbled to the floor when my foot snagged the edge of my suitcase.

He caught me before I could crash, one arm linked around my waist, the other braced on the wall to steady us.

"Jesus," he breathed. An indent of feigned concern etched itself between his dark brows as he studied me.

Like he actually fucking cared.

Like this wasn't *exactly* what he'd wanted.

"Let me go," I ordered.

"Sanchez, you're white as—"

"Let me go!" I shoved at his hard chest with my fore-arms, my back slumping against the wall when he reluctantly released me.

I gripped my knees as a bead of sweat slipped down the nape of my neck. I'd had nightmares sweeter than this. My subconscious's imagination had nothing on Adrien Cloutier's scheming capabilities. He should have been proud.

He stood two feet away, his fingers twitching in and out of fists like they weren't sure what to do with themselves.

I straightened. Looked him in the eyes.

"Does this feel good to you?" I asked through the hot coals churning in my throat. I didn't try to hide it. He deserved to see exactly how much damage he'd done. "You wanted to break me, right? Does it feel good?"

He had the audacity to stand there and look miserable instead of owning up to it.

My breathing slowed, my muscles regaining some of their strength as the hollowness in my chest spread, a familiar numbness taking over.

The back of my head hit the wall.

"You still wanna know why I didn't go to college?" I asked him. At this point, he deserved to hear the story. Just so he could sleep better at night, knowing how deep he'd cut me with this one. The man had earned it. "Based on the questions you've been asking, I'm assuming Josh's version of our breakup had a few major holes in it, so let me enlighten you."

He looked like he might say something, but I shook my head, silencing him. It was my turn.

"We dated for six months. I broke it off four weeks before graduation." I swiped at the corner of my mouth with the back of my shaky wrist as the memories rushed back. "Private school. I was a scholarship student, and my dad worked there as a janitor—that's how we learned about the scholarship program in the first place."

Abehill was the best school in the province. It popped out Ivy Leaguers like a gumball machine.

It also had an annual price tag of sixty thousand dollars, but I'd had my greedy sights set on the most competitive law school in the continent, and Abehill was my first step to reaching my goal. It wasn't just about the education, it was about the connections.

The school was filled with kids from the country's

wealthiest, most influential families. Plus me and the two other scholarship kids, neither of whom were in my year.

"I was a fish out of water there. Spent the first two months eating alone in the library."

My dad had offered to eat with me every single one of those days, even though I'd set a very strict "pretend like you don't know me while at school" rule. Because I was a spoiled teenager who cared way too much about what her peers thought of her.

The offer's always open if you change your mind, he'd Sign back.

I swiped at my wet cheek with a hard fist. What I wouldn't give to share just one meal with him now.

"Anyways," I went on, "Josh was my first... friend, I guess. Had two classes together, and one day he asked me to go to the movies with him after school. We started to date, and it was... fine, for the most part. But he was pretty outwardly ashamed of my family's socio-economic background and grew increasingly disrespectful about it over the course of the relationship. Eventually, I got sick of it, grew a backbone, and broke things off."

And then everything went to shit.

"He tried to get back together. I refused. He tried some more. I still refused. Then he became mean, belligerent, vindictive. Started messing with my stuff, spreading rumors about me. I had to stop using my locker because he kept putting shit in it."

Literally. Dog poop, shaving cream, and hair. Every single day for a full week. I kept staying late after school to clean it all out because if I didn't, my dad would have to. And he didn't deserve to be caught in the crossfire.

"The administration was aware of what was going on, but Josh's dad was one of the school's biggest donors at the time, so no one batted an eye." They would have let the guy get away with murder if it meant the money would keep flowing in. "I ignored him as best I could. At that point, I had less than three weeks left before graduation, and I told myself that I could stand anything for three weeks. The finish line was so close... everything I'd worked for was *right there*. Hell would've had to freeze over before I'd risk losing even an inch of it."

I lifted a shoulder, let it fall. "And then it did. Hell froze over."

Adrien hadn't broken eye contact with me once since I'd started talking. And except for the subtle rising and falling of his chest, he stood motionless, listening intently with his brows furrowed.

"Josh wanted a reaction out of me, and when I wouldn't give him one, he switched tactics." My throat was beginning to constrict in that tell-tale, painful way, but I ignored it and pushed through. "I was working on my independent research project in AP Bio when I got the video. Josh and a handful of his buddies had broken into the janitor's closet and pissed in the mop bucket. The video showed..."

I paused, a breath rattling out of my chest. Ten years later and it still burned.

"My dad was born deaf," I explained. "He couldn't hear anything. The video showed the guys mocking and taunting him about their stupid prank. But Dad didn't know what they were saying, he just saw that they were laughing and smiling, so he... smiled back, and waved at the camera, and..."

My breaths were rushing out of me in short, quick bursts now. I took a fisted sleeve to my face, gave it a punishing swipe.

"I don't remember it," I said. "Making the decision. Exams were coming up, I was already stressed and pulling all-nighters, and my dad was... When I was six and he couldn't afford to buy me the limited-edition lawyer doll I wanted, he hand-sewed the outfit for one of my existing ones. And that's all I remember thinking about when I ran out of class. The outfit wasn't perfect, it didn't fit my doll properly, and even at that age, I could tell he was sad about not being able to af-fford the real thing. But he always tried so h-hard. And I didn't deserve him. He was the best dad you could... I was just so fucking *angry*."

The tears were falling so hard and fast that my hand couldn't keep up. The world was a smudged and blurred oil painting, and I couldn't parse out Adrien's individual features anymore.

I paused long enough for my lungs to settle back down. I thought maybe retelling the story would have gotten easier with time. Apparently not.

"I found the mop bucket before my dad could see what they'd done," I eventually went on. "Then I dragged it to the school parking lot, smashed Josh's car window with a brick, and dumped the contents of the bucket onto the driver's seat."

And in return, Josh and his dad had ruined my fucking life.

"Your uncle owns one of the biggest law firms in the country. I didn't stand a chance. Whatever lies Josh fed to his dad about me worked. Kenny promised to bury me for 'everything I'd done to his son,' and he did. Charges were pressed, my university admissions were revoked, and I was expelled from school, which rendered my scholarship for the year void. Sixty thousand dollars."

I patted my eyes dry with my sleeve, sniffling.

Adrien's expression had tightened with a mixture of disgust and rage, his pulse jutting out of his neck as his breathing grew heavier. And I knew when he put two and two together, because his eyes flared.

For a moment, he was utterly frozen by it. Then his lips peeled apart, and a lungful of air pushed out of him.

"I heard the news. Car crash, right? After a late-night shift?"

"Makes you think, eh?"

Horror. Adrien was horrified.

"Sanchez." His voice split right down the middle. I had to give it to him, the guy was a great actor.

"It was my fault," I admitted. Dad was dead because of me. Alba would never admit it out loud, but I knew deep down she blamed me for it too. I knew she'd never forgiven me for it; probably never would. "He took that second job to help pay for the tuition I now owed the school. He was exhausted. Hit a tree. They think he fell asleep for a second behind the wheel, and that was all it took."

Silence.

I peeled my back from the wall, took a wobbly step forward. "You must be so happy with yourself, huh? Managed to get me right where it hurt."

His eyes were hard and glassy, his blinks incomplete. "You know that's not true. I had no idea. Josh—" He cut himself off, swallowing hard. "I swear I didn't know."

I didn't give a fuck.

"We're even," I whispered, my throat thickening all over again. "You did it, you got me back. I can't think of anything else you could do at this point to make me feel any more stupid than I already do. Not to mention humiliated, pathetic, naïve... *dirty*."

His mouth stuttered, but nothing came out.

"We're even, so please just... leave me the fuck alone now."

I didn't allow myself to dissect his reaction before I brushed past him, quietly gathered my things, and left him standing there, staring down at the carpet.

34

THE AIRPORT HAD DESCENDED into chaos.

The storm had more-or-less shut down all air travel to and from Southern Ontario, New York, and all surrounding areas, which meant that the airlines were slammed and scrambling, trying to accommodate their panicking passengers, all of whom had A Very Important Reason for needing to be on the very first available flight out east. And since I didn't already have a ticket booked, I was their lowest priority.

But Finn, the extremely impatient customer service agent who'd looked like he'd already had enough of my bullshit before I'd even opened my mouth, was going to "see what he could do. Next, please!"

To top off my already crappy day, ticket prices had skyrocketed due to demand, and since I didn't have a job anymore, splurging on a hotel room in addition to what would likely end up being a two-thousand-dollar flight was now out of the question.

I really should have gone home when I'd still had the chance. What the hell had possessed me to stay? How had

I anticipated this whole thing would end if not in utter disaster?

I tried not to think too hard about it though—tried my best not to feel.

The absolute last fucking thing I needed was to have a breakdown in the middle of the airport, so I nabbed the first seat that opened up in the public zone and concentrated on suppressing the hell out of my emotions.

The text came twenty minutes later.

UNKNOWN NUMBER
I'm sorry.

I blocked the number and slipped my phone back into my jacket pocket. It went off again almost immediately.

From: Adhir King <AdhirKing@CloutierHotels.com>

Miss Sanchez,
I hope this email finds you well. It has been brought to our attention by our CEO, Adrien Cloutier, that you may be experiencing travel disruptions brought on by extreme weather conditions impacting your destination and are likely stuck at the airport.
We understand how frustrating this must be and would like to offer you the use of our Presidential Suite for as many nights as you need.
A car is on its way to pick you up from the airport, and all other necessary arrangements have already been made to ensure—

I stopped reading, turned off all notifications from the sender, and got up to treat myself to a small white hot chocolate from Timmies.

Approximately forty-five minutes after *that*, Finn found me, looking significantly more chastised than he had during our first interaction. He was accompanied by a woman in a crisp black pantsuit who shook my hand and introduced herself as the airport general manager.

The introduction was followed by a rapid string of apologies about the weather in Toronto—as though she was directly responsible for its bad behavior—and the insistence that I take advantage of one of their VIP lounges while a private suite on the third floor was being prepared for my overnight use. Free of charge, of course.

She'd become increasingly flustered (and almost pleading) as I continued to refuse her offer.

An airline manager came next.

More apologies about the weather. More insistence that they were doing the absolute best they could under the circumstances. More VIP lounge access offers.

I had a headache by the time I'd finally gotten them off my back and made my escape to the second floor. I found a quiet spot to rest while I waited for the available flight notification to hit my inbox, which Finn and the airline manager were now insisting would likely be "no later than noon tomorrow."

I slept across the length of a hard two-seater with my knees curled up to my chest and woke up with a sore neck and a stiff everything else. But none of my valuables were stolen, so that was something.

By the time I'd splashed some water on my face and grabbed a cup of coffee, I'd received a notification to head to the nearest information desk as soon as possible.

I practically ran there.

"Miss Sanchez! Hello!" The young woman shot to her

feet when she saw me, beaming like we were long-lost pals.

"Hey, yeah, I just got a notification telling me to come down here. I've been trying to get back to Toronto. Is there—"

I stopped talking when she waved her hand. "We're well aware of your situation. Your seat on the next flight out has been secured, but it's in a different terminal. I'll be more than happy to escort you there if you're ready?"

I didn't even question it. At this point, I'd row back to Toronto in a fucking canoe if it meant I'd get to sleep in my own bed tonight, with Toebeans trying his best to suffocate me.

And that was the exact moment I remembered that Adrien had forced me to move into his stupid building when this whole nightmare first started. I groaned internally, so preoccupied with trying to figure out the logistics of having to explain everything to Jamie, pack up all our stuff, and move back to our apartment as soon as humanly possible, that I didn't notice how much quieter my surroundings had become until the echoing of our steps grew so prominent and loud that it finally snatched my attention.

I blinked, glancing around. The long hallway I was being led down was surprisingly empty, save for the two people walking a few meters ahead of us and a handful of suited employees standing behind desks belonging to airlines I'd never heard of.

"Um, question for you..."

"Anna," she said, noting the not-so-subtle way I was trying to catch a glimpse of her name tag.

"It's nice to meet you, Anna," I said politely, only now realizing how suspiciously quiet she'd been during our walk so far. "Can you tell me what airline I'm flying with, exactly?"

In lieu of an answer, Anna slipped her employee card out of her breast pocket and flashed it to the two uniformed men standing outside a pair of ebony doors.

"After you." She gestured to the door as one of the men held it open for us.

I stepped inside and... a lounge. She'd led me straight to a fucking lounge.

My molars crammed together as my frustration peaked. I tried to keep my voice calm and centered. I really did. "Listen, I'm not trying to be rude or anything because I know you're just trying to do your job, but I've had a really rough twenty-four hours and I just need to get home. So, if you could please just give me my flight information—"

"That will be all, Miss Ross, thank you very much."

My brain tripped over itself when the voice registered. I turned to the source, my brows leaping when I saw him.

"*Gampy*?" Or was I supposed to call him Robert now? I wasn't sure what Adrien had told his family about us since I'd left yesterday—if anything.

"Good morning, Ria." He smiled.

He was decked out in a pale pink sweater vest, a checkered bowtie, and matching socks. I'd have spotted him from ten miles away had my brain not been so mushy.

"Wh-uh... what are you doing here?" I asked.

"Impromptu visit to Toronto," he answered swiftly. "Long overdue. My college buddies live out there."

I fiddled with the handle of my carry-on, twisting my fist around it. "You decided to spontaneously fly to Ontario on the tail-end of the biggest storm of the year?"

He simply shrugged in response.

"On the day of Julie and Anthony's anniversary party?" I pushed. Wasn't it supposed to be kind of a big deal?

"Oh, they were quite understanding. In fact, Julie insisted I go. Tea?"

He meandered over to the stacked bar where the bartender was already pouring two steaming cups of freshly brewed... peppermint tea from the smell of it, and began filling a large plate with a colorful variety of pastries and scones.

My stomach twisted and growled as I eyed him. I'd skipped two meals yesterday and it was starting to catch up with me.

"Did Adrien put you up to this?" I asked when he moved to sit at a small walnut table. The bartender followed with the teas.

Robert's mustache twitched. He thanked the bartender before returning his attention to me. "No, my dear. That boy isn't putting anyone up to anything today. Not in his state."

I wasn't going to ask.

He wanted me to ask, but I wasn't going to ask.

My lips rolled as I shifted on my feet. I needed to leave, find Anna, and beg her to at least give me a hint about when I could expect to get my hands on some flight information. But also, I didn't want to be rude, because Adrien's family had been nothing but sweet, kind, and welcoming from the moment I'd lied my way into their home.

"We've got just under an hour to go before boarding," Robert noted as he spread a thin layer of red jam onto a small scone. "You're welcome to stand there and stare at me the whole time, but I'd really love it if you'd join me here."

I chewed the inside of my bottom lip, eyeing the doors. "When you say *not in his state*... is he... what does that mean?"

Not that I cared whether Adrien was okay or not, because I definitely didn't. It wasn't even curiosity. It was just small talk while I decided whether I should sit down and have a pastry before leaving.

Robert's lower lip pushed at his mustache as he considered my question. "On one hand, he's doing significantly better than Joshua. A fractured ring finger and a split brow will heal much more quickly than a broken nose, fractured cheekbone, and dislocated jaw. I reckon it's a lot less painful too. Could have been much worse, though. It took five people, including three members of our staff, but they managed to pry Adrien away before any permanent injuries were sustained."

My mouth popped open.

"On the other hand, however, I've never seen my grandson quite so... distraught, for lack of a better word. What happened yesterday morning really did a number on him. He's inconsolable. Wouldn't seek treatment for his hand until his mother put her foot down and dragged him to the hospital."

Maybe this should have been good news—like justice being served or karma doing its thing—but it just felt awful. I was nauseated all over again.

"Ria, I would really love it if you'd sit down with me, please."

I hesitated. It wasn't a good idea for me to talk to him about anything Adrien-related. And I'd spend the entire week partaking in one bad idea after another.

"Thank you, but I really think I should... go..."

His phone went off as soon as I started talking. Five

little dings in quick succession, and a sixth when I trailed off. But he simply kept smiling up at me.

"You should maybe get that," I said.

Robert waved me off. "It's likely just Alice with more Adrien updates."

A seventh ding, an eighth.

"What if it's important?" There was a good chance my carry-on handle was going to be permanently mangled by the time this conversation was over.

"It probably is."

Nine notifications. *Nine!*

Fuck. Okay. I'd sit down with him for five minutes, but only because my stomach was turning inside out with hunger. And if, in the meantime, Robert decided to check his messages and confirm that his idiot grandson hadn't done any more idiotic things or sustained any more idiotic injuries, then so be it. That was his prerogative.

I sat down, very much pretending like I didn't notice the way Robert's mouth twitched in amusement as he watched me, his eyes glinting. As soon as I reached for a scone, he reached for his phone. I sipped my tea, he checked his messages. I scooped up a small spoonful of honey, he... frowned.

And in what could only be described as a gross overreaction, my heart leaped up to my head and immediately filled it with a plethora of highly improbable worse-case-scenarios as I watched him tap away at his screen, his face scrunching farther into itself with every passing second.

"Is everything okay?" I eventually asked.

"Hmm?"

"Is Adrien okay?" The panic cut clear through any effort I may have put toward keeping my tone casual and calm.

"Oh," Robert said, not taking his eyes off the screen. Then, "No."

Instead of elaborating, he simply put his phone away again and bit into a cucumber sandwich.

I grit my teeth, squirmed in my seat, told myself it was fine. After all, Adrien deserved to suffer a little over what he'd put me through. What he didn't deserve was to have me sit here and care about what happened to him; or to have my insides lurch with worry over him.

"Oh, and before I forget, I think it's important for you to know that Joshua is no longer welcome in our family home."

My scattered attention zoomed back in on Robert. "Pardon?"

"That boy has been on thin ice with us for a while now," he said with a new firmness. "I never really did forgive him for what happened with Mandy, but Addy insisted we let it go because he didn't want it leaking to the media. They have a bad habit of twisting stories about him to get clicks so we... Anyway, the point is, you won't have to worry about running into Joshua should you decide to come back here and visit us again. Which, by the way, we really hope you would."

That was never going to happen. If Robert knew—

"Adrien told us everything."

I doubted he actually meant *everything*—

"And I do mean everything. Addy spilled the beans once Joshua, Mandy, and Kenny were removed from the property."

Okay. But there was no way he'd told them about the relationship—

"Including the true nature of your relationship. We're aware the engagement wasn't real."

I felt my shoulders deflate as my gaze dipped to the untouched scone resting on my plate. Things were about to become very awkward.

"Addy was also very adamant that we all understood none of this was your idea or your fault," he said firmly. "So please don't think anyone is angry or upset with you, because that simply isn't true, and it's also not what this conversation is about."

I risked a glance up at him. "What's it about then?"

He considered my question before committing to an answer. "In light of all the recent... dishonesty, I think it's important for me to share a few truths with you. Just so you have a better understanding of how things look from where Alice, Julie, Anthony, and I stand."

I sipped my cooling tea as the realization crept in. He was about to hit me with one of those "we're not angry, we're just disappointed" talks, wasn't he? In his defense, I deserved it. In my defense... I still deserved it. My justifications and excuses weren't his problem, so I just kept my head ducked and listened.

"I understand that your engagement wasn't real, but the changes I've seen in my grandson over the course of this trip certainly are. And I believe—as does the rest of my family—that these changes have everything to do with you."

I sunk a little lower in my seat, preparing myself for the worst. But then he said, "I've never seen him laugh with anyone the way he does with you."

And it was so unexpected that it snagged my full, undivided attention. His smile was faint but kind, and his eyes carried none of the judgment I was expecting.

"That's a truth," he said softly. "We were all very surprised by it. It was a rather hot topic of discussion among us just yesterday morning, shortly before the guests arrived. We've also never seen him quite as enthralled with anyone as he is with you. Look at anyone the way he looks at you. And don't get me started on the fact that you somehow managed to convince the boy to turn himself into a human blueberry."

My neck warmed. "I didn't convince him to do it," I defended. I hadn't needed to. He'd all but dove into the makeup stool headfirst.

Robert nodded, looking suspiciously like he was suppressing a quiet laugh. "Fair enough. The point is, I also haven't seen my grandson engage in that level of play since he was two feet shorter than he is now. It was refreshing, to say the least."

Okay, well, you know what wasn't refreshing? Being lied to and straight-up manipulated.

...

But I guess Robert would already know that.

Still.

"Here's one more truth for you to consider," he went on. "I was there the day Adrien found out about Joshua and Mandy's affair. I saw his reaction in real-time. He may have held on to some feelings of resentment toward Joshua that ended up festering, but with Mandy... it was night and day compared to what he's been like the last twenty-four hours. Josh was lucky the confrontation happened while others were around to mediate the situation. And Addy will be lucky if charges aren't pressed, but I digress."

"To be clear, I didn't encourage—or expect—there to be any physical retaliation when I told Adrien about what happened between Josh and myself." I just thought he'd...

I don't know, maybe feel shitty about what he'd done for a bit, then move the hell on.

Robert shook off my concern. "Adrien's a grown man, and he's very capable of making his own decisions. I'm not here to blame you for his actions."

I sucked on my cheek, wondering how I could ask this next question without being rude.

"You're wondering what my angle is," Robert cut in before I could string the question together. "What I'm trying to achieve by telling you all this."

"Kind of," I admitted.

He made a point of checking his wristwatch. "All right, I'll cut to the chase, then. I'm trying to stall."

Huh? "Stall for what?"

"Well, I could sit here all afternoon and talk your ear off about more truths we've all witnessed, but I really don't think I have the words to accurately describe what Adrien's currently... well, you'll see."

Uh... the fuck I would.

"Please tell me he's not on his way here," I pleaded as the panic set in.

"Okay. He's not on his way here," Robert deadpanned.

My eyes narrowed. "Are you lying?"

"Doesn't feel so good, does it?" he chided with a pointed look.

Fuck.

"You said Adrien didn't put you up to this!" I exclaimed, positively appalled by the level of treachery. It was always the innocent-looking ones you had to watch out for.

"Oh, that part was true. This was all Alice and me. Mostly me, though I'm sure she'll try to claim otherwise if all goes according to plan." He took a long sip of his tea.

"But if it backfires, she'll say she had nothing to do with it. Just watch."

"Is this more stalling?"

"No. The next stalling item I had on the agenda was to ask for your input on a very serious disagreement Alice and I are currently having about the physical location of the matching tattoos she wants us to get for her birthday. She is being extremely impolite about the ordeal, and we're both convinced that you're the exact right person to settle the argument. But don't worry, it should only take a minute or two of your time.

"You see, I've suggested a lower back placement for the tattoos, because then I can inform people who didn't ask that I have a gramp stamp. But Alice claims that I'm not, and I quote, 'a basic enough bitch' to get away with a lower back tattoo. And even though I've repeatedly pointed out to her that you can't get more basic *or* fragile than an overprivileged elderly white man, she simply refuses to see things my way. What do you think, Ria? Am I basic enough to pull off a gramp stamp? Or is my judgmental granddaughter correct?"

He nodded at his phone. "It's actually what she was texting me about before you sat down."

I rolled my lips, my palms hitting the table as I pushed up to my feet. "Well, I wish I could say this was nice, but I've very recently been taught a hard lesson about lying, so I'll just say this: Alice is wrong, gramp stamp is hilarious, and I'm really sorry about lying to you all, but I'm going to leave now, and hopefully we never have a reason to—"

I cut off when I heard his gruff voice echoing outside, the rushed and unhappy pounding of his feet. My heart thrashed in my chest, adrenaline spiking through me.

Robert leaned back in his chair, his hands folding in

front of him like a man who'd gotten exactly what he
wanted.

I muttered a curse, twisting around just in time to
watch the doors open, and for Adrien Cloutier to strut
into the room in all his... glory?

Oh.

Oh, my god.

35

ROBERT MAY HAVE SLIGHTLY DOWNPLAYED Adrien's... *state,* as he'd called it. Though, to be fair, I wasn't sure I'd have believed him had he been able to find the words to accurately describe what I was currently looking at.

Adrien's T-shirt was inside out... and backward.

That was the first thing that caught my attention. My brain glossed over the angrily askew hair, the red-rimmed eyes, the bruised cheek and stitched-up brow, and snagged on the inside label sticking out of the front of his shirt.

"Dude, what the hell?"

He didn't even notice I was in the room until I spoke. And I didn't notice he was on the phone until his shoulder went rigid and his head snapped in my direction, dark eyes pinning my soul in place.

Adrien stood still and unblinking for a few thundering heartbeats, almost like he thought any sudden movements or loud noises would make me disappear into thin air. The pause gave me enough time to really absorb and process what I was seeing.

The guy looked like he'd walked straight through the eye of a whole tornado to get here. That was the only way I could describe it. Oh, and there was a bit of blood smeared over his silver watch.

"Hey... Sunny? I'm going to call you back in a bit."

He slowly hung up, refusing to release his hold on my gaze. His feet were still frozen midstep.

"You're here," he said quietly. The question was clear in his tone. He really hadn't been expecting—

"Tea?"

We both jolted.

Robert—whose entire existence I'd momentarily forgotten about—had pulled up a third chair to the table we'd been sitting at. He patted the velvet cushion, smiling at Adrien. "You look like you could use some tea."

Adrien straightened an inch, his questioning gaze sliding carefully between me and his grandfather.

"Come sit," Robert insisted. "You're just in time. Ria was just validating my basic bitch status, and I need a witness in the very likely case that Lice decides she doesn't believe me when I rub it in her face."

Adrien's mouth quirked, the hard lines etched into his forehead softening just a touch. But he didn't move for the chair.

"I didn't realize you were traveling back together." He sounded genuinely surprised by it, but not in a displeased way. "I can wait until the jet comes back. Or see if I can fly commercial in time for—"

"Nonsense. You're the one that's always going on and on about us not using the jet unless we absolutely have to." Robert's attention turned back to me. "The boy loves his trees. You should see his apartment. It's practically a greenhouse, complete with a full-time gardener and everything."

Color crept up Adrien's neck. He tried to ruffle a hand through his hair, only to remember at the last second that his finger and knuckles were bandaged up.

Robert sat down, looking like he was tired of waiting for us to do so first. "Plus," he said, "the jet seats twelve. Even with your ego on board we should still have enough room. Until it recovers, at least."

I bit my cheeks and ducked my head, wanting to hide my growing amusement. This wasn't the time to be smiling. I was very, very, *very* pissed off at Adrien.

"Thanks, Gamps," Adrien grumbled, though I could hear the humor tilt his voice. "I'll leave it up to Ria. If she's okay with me joining you, I will."

"Oh, I'm not... I was brought here under false pretenses," I said, shooting Robert a pointed look. He smiled back and motioned for the bartender to bring fresh tea to the table. "I'll just wait until a seat's available on a commercial plane."

Adrien's facial muscles tightened in the way I'd come to learn meant he was getting ready to argue, but Robert cut in before he could open his mouth. "Addy, why don't you come sit down and tell us what you've been up to over the last twenty-four hours. Lice says the doctors couldn't even pry your phone away from you long enough to treat your hand properly. I'd like to know what was so important."

Adrien glared at his grandfather like a kid who'd just had their biggest, most important secret revealed by an embarrassing guardian, the knuckles of his non-injured hand going white over the handle of his leather duffle bag.

"Sorry. Too obvious?" Robert asked sarcastically. To me, he said, "I think he's trying to keep more secrets. The boy's always been too stubborn to learn his lessons the first time around. Though I will say, his work ethic is positively unrivaled. His shirt is wrinkled, and he's looking slightly unhinged at the moment, but you should see how much he's managed to accomplish in one day. I really don't know where he gets it from. The rest of us are all quite lazy in comparison."

Adrien's lips were now pressed into a tight line, his ears beet red. "And *Gamps* has spent the last eighty-two years refusing to mind his own business. It's where Alice gets it from."

"Come sit."

It occurred to me then that I should have nabbed my suitcase and bolted out of the room the moment Adrien walked in, but I'd been so distracted—and frankly shocked—by his chaotically disheveled appearance that I'd remained rooted on the spot, trying to process it.

"I think I'm going to head out," I said, moving for my luggage. Nothing good was going to come from me lingering back here.

But then Robert said, "Don't be an idiot."

He wasn't talking to me, I realized. His knowing gaze was locked on his grandson, his thick eyebrows pushing past the rim of his glasses.

Adrien sighed. "Okay, Ria, I know you said for me to leave you alone, but just hear me out for a few minutes."

"No."

"Fine. Thirty seconds. I've been talking to—"

"Adrien, *no*." I didn't want to hear it. I turned back to Robert. "Look, I appreciate whatever it is you're trying to do here because I think your heart's in the right place, but I really just want to be left alone. And, again, I'm very sorry about all the lying, but I really hope that I never have any reason to run into you or your grandson again."

That was about as polite as I could put it with the amount of exhausted frustration weighing on me.

I averted my gaze as my hand curled around the handle of my carry-on, and I kept it down as I made my silent exit from Adrien's life. Permanently this time.

The words "you're being an idiot" were the last thing I heard before the doors closed behind me. Though this time, I wasn't entirely confident Robert wasn't talking directly to me.

～

The apartment door tore open the second my suitcase stopped rolling against the marble tiles, before I'd even had a chance to fish my keys out of my purse.

"Hello, Ariana," a very unimpressed Jamie greeted me, looking like a cartoon villain with the way she was holding a glaring, purring Toebeans against her chest. "Fancy seeing you here, alive and not dead."

My shoulder slumped against the wall. I hadn't responded to her messages over the last two days. Not since the Josh thing happened.

"I'm sorry," I said.

"Alba thinks you've been kidnapped because you haven't been responding to her. I haven't corrected her."

That sounded about right. "In my defense, there was a lot going on."

Her left brow rose as Toebeans thrashed his tail

against her arm. I couldn't tell which one of them looked angrier with me. For my own sake, I really hoped it was Jamie.

My lips pushed against each other. She didn't know about me and Adrien, either. I'd been waiting to tell her when I got home, over a bottle of wine. Back when I thought it was going to be a fun conversation.

"I slept with your future husband," I said.

Her eyes widened, a slow grin spreading across her face as all signs of anger vanished. "You slut! Tell. Me. Everything!"

"Josh is his cousin."

Her grin died. "Wait, what?"

"We have to, um, go," I said. My vision was suddenly very blurry, my throat tight. "Now, please. We have to pack up and go now."

"It's almost midnight on a weeknight—"

"Please? Can we just go now?" I needed to be in my own home. In my own bed.

There was a beat of silence, and then she nodded, pulling me inside by my arm. "Okay. All right. Let's go now."

We packed quickly, quietly. I tried my best to ignore the worried glances Jamie kept throwing my way, and she did her best to pretend like she didn't hear my sniffling, didn't see the unsubtle ways I kept having to wipe my vision clear. And I couldn't have appreciated her more for it.

The Uber dropped us off at our crummy old walk-up two hours later. We hauled our bags up the stairs, released a yelling Toebeans into the pitch-black apartment, and before Jamie could start asking questions, I said, "I'm exhausted. Can we please talk about it tomorrow?"

She squeezed my hand. "Okay."

Then I went straight to my room, curled on top of the covers with my jacket still on, and bawled.

36

ELEVEN DAYS **later**

"All right, that's it. You're getting up."

Bright sunlight smacked me in the eyes as my weighted blanket was ripped away. I shriveled into a ball against the sudden bout of freezing air.

"What the hell!" I rasped, squinting up at my attacker. The complaint grated against the sandpaper coating my throat. "Close the window! It's like minus ten out!"

"Get in the bath," Jamie ordered with a bossy snap of her fingers. She pointed at the door. "Now."

"Why haven't you left for work yet?" I grumbled, pulling the tip of my fleece hood down to shield my eyes.

"Ria, it's almost six p.m. Work started ten hours ago. I just got back."

"Oh," I said. "Almost bedtime, then. I'll see you tomorrow."

I grabbed the edge of my blanket again and rolled it on top of me. Then I curled my knees back up to my chest, shut my eyes, and let the fuzzy darkness consume—

Something gripped my ankle and yanked.

I kicked, trying to get her to let go. "Stop that," I demanded.

"Absolutely fucking not. I've given you ten days to mope. It's more than enough." She was using both her arms now.

"Why are you doing this?" I whined, scrambling for purchase against the bed sheets as my body was slowly pulled from the mattress. I managed to hook my fingers around the edge of the bed frame but didn't have the strength to hold on for longer than a few seconds.

"Because you'd do the same for me," Jamie responded as I belly flopped onto the carpet with a dull groan. "Though you wouldn't be nearly as nice about it."

And then my—officially *former*—best friend dumped an entire fucking pitcher of ice water right on top of my head.

I gasped as the shock of the cold pierced my skin, my spine bolting upright as my mouth hung entirely open.

"You did *not* just do that to—Jamie! Holy shit—*stop!*"

She was holding the second pitcher above me like a madwoman, the spout tilted just enough to be a threat.

"Have you eaten anything today?" she asked, frowning down at me like I was a misbehaving school child.

I peeled my soaked hood away from my hair as the gears in my brain groaned to stiff motion, trying to figure out what the hell had gotten into her. "I just woke up," I said.

Her eyes thinned. "When was the last time you drank water? Or took a shower?"

Was she fucking serious?

"Literally right now. You just—okayokayokayokay!" I held up my hands, surrendering as the spout tipped far enough for a thin stream of water to escape. "God, relax. I'll drink some fucking water."

What the hell was wrong with her? My whole carpet was soaked.

I hauled to my feet, vaguely aware of how much genuine effort it took. My muscles were weirdly sore, my knees more unsteady than I remembered them being.

I dragged my feet all the way to the kitchen, poured myself a small glass of water, and forced it down even though it tasted like bitter, liquid sand.

"Happy?" I snapped. The glass cup hit the bottom of the sink with a much more dramatic *clank* than I'd intended, but I wasn't sorry about it.

Jamie ignored my small tantrum as she ripped a large plastic garbage bag from its roll and proceeded to march right back to my room.

"What do you think you're doing?" I demanded to know.

I felt a little out of breath as I trailed after her. I swiped a bunch of wet hair away from my eyes and forehead as Jamie got to work, grabbing empty cans, bottles, and clothing off the floor.

"Seriously, what are you doing?" I asked again.

"What does it look like?"

"It looks like you're cleaning my room," I said as she shoved an empty peanut butter jar into the bag.

"Then that's what I'm doing." She put the bag down, moving to strip my pillows of their cases. "You should get in the bath before it gets cold. I got that honey-lavender stuff you like, and there's already a fresh set of clothes for you in there too."

"I can clean this up myself." I just hadn't felt like it this week. Or last.

"I know," she said easily. "I'm not saying you can't. I'm just... What's this?"

My sluggish brain was exactly one beat too slow to comprehend what she was looking at.

The photobooth strips we'd taken that day at the harbor.

"Is that..." She squinted down at the pictures. "Is that Adrien? Why is he blue?"

I snatched the photos out of her hand and clutched them against my stomach.

"It's not him," I said.

Her gaze flicked to my nose, then thawed, understanding. "You keep pictures of you and Adrien in your pillowcase?"

My heart was hurling itself around my ribcage as my entire body burned scarlet. I wish I'd never told her about the nostril flare thing.

"Ria..."

"I'm gonna go take that bath now," I decided. Then I walked to the small garbage bin and forced my hand to release the strips.

I'd been meaning to get rid of them anyway. I just... eventually.

Jamie was doing that thing where she was looking at me like I was a wounded kitten, so I averted my gaze and trudged out of the room, promising myself that I wouldn't do a dumpster dive to retrieve the photos when she inevitably took the garbage out.

∾

The two voices murmuring in hushed tones stopped abruptly as soon as I walked into the kitchen, a towel wrapped around my wet hair. A very pregnant Alba tried to flash me her most convincing smile from her spot at the table, but it flickered before it could touch her eyes.

"Hey," I said as my feet shuffled noisily toward the fridge. I opened it and scanned the shelves mindlessly, even though I didn't really have an appetite.

"You're awake," Alba said too brightly.

I hummed, my attention lingering on a carton of eggs. I knew I needed to eat at some point, but was an omelet worth the energy? I'd have to gather the ingredients, prep the veggies, heat the pan, cook, wait, eat, clean up...

I shut the fridge. Eating was officially a tomorrow problem.

Alba cleared her throat, trying to draw my attention. I turned to her.

"What?" I asked, even though it wasn't necessary.

The day after I'd gotten back from Victoria, she'd blown up my phone, asking me to explain to her exactly what I'd done to prompt Adrien to request an in-person meeting with her and apologize for "literally everything," as she'd put it. She'd also wanted to know why he'd rehired her and tripled her maternity compensation. "He even gave me three extra months of leave! *And* when I go back, my weekly hours are capped at a strict forty, I'm not allowed to work on holidays, and using my vacation days is officially mandatory. Seriously, what the hell did you do?"

I'd promised to explain it all later, and it was officially later.

But instead of hounding me for all the answers she was owed, she motioned to a stack of takeout containers in front of her. "I brought Indian from that place you like. Chicken tikka masala, extra spicy. With garlic naan."

Oh. Well, that was nice.

"Thanks," I said.

"You're welcome."

"I'll grab the plates. You can just sit down, Ria," Jamie offered, springing right into action.

They were being weird. Their voices, actions, vibes were way off. I realized this but found that I didn't care enough to ask. So I just did as I was told.

There was an awkward bit of silence as Jamie set the table, and Alba struggled to say whatever she needed to say. Even Toebeans was uncharacteristically quiet, curled up on one of the chairs, bushy tail flicking.

"So," my sister finally said, and I could tell by the way her voice dipped that she was gearing up for A Conversation. "Interesting to see that this whole misery train runs both ways."

Jamie set a massive glass of water beside my bare plate. One of the football-sized ones that came with the apartment, and that we kept at the very back of the cupboards, because no one ever needed to drink almost a liter of any liquid in one sitting. Unless it came directly from a bottle of wine.

Speaking of which, "Do we have any wine?"

"No," they both said at the same time.

Bummer.

Alba cleared her throat for what must have been the fourth time in two minutes.

"Do you need a lozenge?" My voice came out sharp enough that both her and Jamie raised their eyebrows at me. *Shit.* "Sorry. Didn't mean to snap."

"What's going on with you?" she asked.

"Nothing."

She cocked her head. "Really? Because Adrien told me at least some of what happened in Victoria, and it didn't sound like nothing."

"Well, it was."

I snatched a slice of naan out of the open foil, ripped a piece off, and shoved it into my mouth. They both kept staring.

"If it makes you feel any better," Alba eventually said in a soft tone, "he's not doing great, either."

The naan turned to a clump of clay in my mouth. I forced it down with a big gulp of water.

"I don't care," I muttered, keeping my eyes down.

"Ria, you should know—"

"Okay, you know what, new rule," I decided. "We're officially adding Adrien to the banned list of conversation topics, right under Josh."

"No," Alba said.

"I'm not asking."

"And I'm not going to sit back and let you fall into this pit again," she retorted.

"What pit? I'm telling you I don't want to talk about your asshole boss—"

"*No*, Ria. No more conversation bans. You don't want to talk about Adrien, you don't want to talk about Josh, you don't want to talk about school, you *never* want to talk about Dad. You just... you keep internalizing everything, punishing yourself, and it's... so difficult for me to watch. If you need therapy, we can—"

"Alba, I *don't* want to talk about this with you," I told her as calmly as one could through clenched teeth.

"Fine, then just listen," Alba said. "We're having this conversation one way or another, because I'm not—I *can't* just sit back and do nothing anymore. Not in good conscience. So please just let me say my piece, because I think... sometimes with the things you say and how you act, it feels like you think what happened with Dad was your fault, and—"

"Alba, *stop!*"

Her eyes were welling up, her chin wobbling a little as she began to rub her stomach. "Am I right? Is that what you think?"

I couldn't pry my jaw open enough to answer her, though. Maybe because I didn't really know what to say.

Jamie was looking between us with a sad frown, her fingers fumbling with the dainty chain around her neck.

"Ria, I can't just sit back and watch you go down this self-destructive path anymore. I physically can't do it. I've given you time, I've given you space, but it's not getting better, and it feels like you keep... *punishing* yourself because you think you deserve it. And if you don't want to talk about it with me, then fine. But please at least talk to a professional about it."

Jamie reached for my hand then, squeezing it once.

"And what makes you think I'm punishing myself?" I asked her stubbornly.

"Well, for one, you've spent an entire decade holding yourself back, not pursuing a single one of your interests, and squandering every last ounce of your own potential," she said. "You've given up on your dreams, ambitions. Things you've been passionate about since as far back as I can remember."

A sudden flash of anger snaked through me like a livewire, hot and heavy. I didn't have nearly enough patience or energy to pull it back. "Newsflash, Albs: I'm not the first person in history to have peaked in high school. I don't understand why everyone is so *obsessed* with a bunch of potential I may or may not have had when I was a fucking teenager! Get over it!"

Both her and Jamie raised their eyebrows at me, but Alba recovered quickly, leaning back as her eyes narrowed with a warning glint. Her lips weren't wobbling anymore. Instead, her demeanor and expression started to take on a more... challenging tone. Like she was gearing up for a battle.

Or maybe I was projecting.

I rose to my feet, fists clenching at my sides. "You think I held myself back on purpose?" I asked her. "You think I chose this path? Alba, every single one of those universities revoked their offers. That wasn't *my* choice."

If I thought for one second that there was still a chance that I could—nevermind. It didn't fucking matter anymore.

Alba shrugged.

She *shrugged*. As if what I'd said was completely irrelevant to the argument.

"So?" she said.

My head jutted forward. "Is that a serious question? Or a pregnancy brain thing?"

"Did you ever try applying again?"

Jamie threw a piece of naan into her mouth like it was popcorn, her wide eyes sliding from my end of the table to Alba's. She looked...

Something was happening. The two of them were up to something.

"Why would I pay a bunch of money just to go through another round of rejections?" I asked.

"How do you know they'll reject you?"

"Because they will."

"But how do you know that if you've never even tried?"

"I just do!" I snarled.

"Mhmm. Sure."

Jamie peeled open the tops of two different curry containers as she watched our exchange—the extra spicy tikka masala, and a yellow curry with cubes of paneer.

My stomach growled, sending hunger pangs through me for the first time in almost two weeks. But I kept my focus on my sister. "I have a criminal record, remember?"

Her gaze dipped to her cuticles. "I'm not interested in your excuses, Ria."

My fingers dug into the table. She was goading me. I didn't know why she was doing it, but she was, and it was fucking working.

"It's not an *excuse*," I argued.

Her eyes snapped back to my face. They were fucking *glittering*. "Prove it," she said.

"What? How?"

Before I'd even asked, she'd thrust a hand into her large tote bag.

"Like this." She held out a blue folder, an oddly familiar smirk toying with the tips of her mouth. She wiggled it tauntingly when I didn't immediately reach for it. "Come on. You asked."

I snatched it out of her outstretched hand and threw it open on the table.

Time stopped.

"What—uh... what's this?" I asked stupidly. Even though the answer was written right there, clear as day.

Five separate university application forms, all of which were already filled out. With my information.

"You just have to sign 'em," Alba said, evidently

pleased with this small victory of hers. "I couldn't do that part for you. Because of the law."

"I... can't," I stammered as the rush of nerves hit my bloodstream. My mind was reeling, trying to climb out of the thick fog it'd been stuck in for the last ten days. *Come up with an excuse. Any excuse!* "Just sending these in would cost like six hundred and twenty-five dollars. Even if I had a job right now, I wouldn't spend that much money just to prove a point."

Jamie poured a bunch of food onto my plate, smiling to herself.

"Interesting that you know the current going rate for university applications in the country," Alba mused. "Almost like you've checked them recently. Or even regularly. Like maybe that dream isn't quite as dead as you want everyone to believe."

I was *this* close to developing an ulcer. But before I could try to convince her that it was just a lucky guess, she reached into her bag again.

"Five checks. One for each school. Any other excuses?"

Panic sprouted in the pit of my stomach. "I'm not taking six hundred dollars from you just to send in a bunch of joke applications to universities that are going to take one look at my record and reject them."

She blinked slowly, waiting for a beat before she said, "Except for the fact that your record wasn't the full reason your offers and scholarships were revoked. Josh's dad pulled a bunch of strings to make it happen, and you know that because he told you so. Right before he made you believe you'd never have a shot at pursuing a post-secondary education again, as payback for 'what you did to his son.'" Her fingers bent in the air when she said that last part, anger ticking in her cheek.

My jaw hit the floor. "How do you know that?"

She swallowed thickly, her gaze softening. "Why didn't you tell me that he threatened you? I could have tried to help."

My forehead hurt from the strain of my frown. "Seriously. How did you find out? And when?"

"Yesterday." She very pointedly did not answer my first question.

"What an asshole," Jamie said midchew. "Can you imagine being a grown-ass man and threatening an eighteen-year-old girl like that? Fucking loser."

Alba nodded. "Point is, Ria, if you really, truly, in your deepest of hearts don't want to go, then that's okay. But if there's even a part of you that's held on to the dream... you should send in those applications. Trust me."

"Mmm." Jamie nodded, mouth full.

I watched the two of them carefully, my eyes thinning into slits. "And how are we so sure Josh's dad won't pull his strings again?" I asked slowly.

Alba looked me dead in the eyes, smirked, and said, "He's been taken care of. As have the admission board members that accepted his bribes."

Click.

"But wait, there's more!" Jamie interjected as I continued to hold my sister's gaze. She was wiggling with excitement. "Ria, tell her you don't think you could afford the tuition even if you did get in."

I was going to have at least one cracked molar by the time this conversation was over.

Alba's little smirk twitched. "That's a very valid concern to have, *Ria*," she said, pointedly ignoring the eight separate veins protruding out of my face and neck. "Did you know that certain law firms will actually pay to put *exceptionally talented* individuals through school if said *exceptionally talented* individuals agree to work for them for a certain period of time after graduation?"

"A law firm scholarship program!" Jamie exclaimed. "They even pay for your living expenses if they want you badly enough. Who'd have thunk it?"

Who indeed.

"Now, I know what you're thinking," Alba went on. The two of them were having way too much fun with this sloppy little performance of theirs. "You're thinking, 'Alba, those sponsorship programs are for law students. I don't even have my bachelor's degree yet. Why would they ever consider *me* for such an amazing opportunity that I would be incredibly silly not to at least consider?'"

That wasn't what I was thinking.

"Well, Ria, I'm glad you asked," Alba went on.

"She really is," Jamie said to me. "You can tell."

"What if I told you that if—and only *if*—you're *exceptionally talented* enough, that one very well-known law firm in particular would also be willing to cover the costs of your undergraduate degree?"

Alba reached into her bag again as my pulse continued to thunder, pulled out a sleek business card, and slid it to me across the table.

Sunny Kanun.
Senior Partner.
Kanun, Barr, & Lee.

"Your interview's tomorrow afternoon. Details are on the back," Alba said. "Don't be late. Or do. I honestly don't think it'll matter."

Silence settled between the three of us as Alba and Jamie waited for my reaction. Finally, I picked up the card, stripped the towel from my damp hair, and declared, "I'm going to kill Adrien Cloutier. For real this time."

"Yes!" Jamie jumped out of her seat. "But do it with mascara on, yeah?"

"He's still at the office," Alba said easily. She placed her all-access pass on the table as Jamie dragged me back into the bathroom, demanding to know where I'd put my hairbrush.

I didn't even try to put up a fight.

37

FOR THE SECOND time in the span of two months, I managed to sneak up to Adrien Cloutier's office without a single person trying to stop me. Even though I'd stomped into the building looking more than a little unhinged.

Adrien started when I barged in, his head snapping away from his monitor when his door hit the wall. His eyes flared when they landed on me, and he shot to his feet. "Ria? You're here. Hey. Wh—uh're you here?"

Was he having a stroke?

"I've been trying to reach you about your jet's extended warranty," I responded sweetly before slamming the blue folder onto his desk. "*Why do you think*?"

He cleared his throat, hands fumbling with the waist of his pants before settling awkwardly on his hips. "Funny."

He had the audacity to sound like he meant it, too.

"What the fuck is this?" I pointed an accusatory finger at the folder.

He shrugged. "You're the one that stormed in here with it."

"I told you to leave me alone."

Something unpleasant—almost regretful—flitted across his face. "Which is exactly what I did."

"*This* is you leaving me alone? Recruiting my sister to trick and goad me into this Kanun firm nonsense is you leaving me alone, Adrien?"

His lips pressed into a thin line. "In my defense, she wasn't supposed to tell you I was behind it. The school and job stuff was all supposed to be presented as her own idea."

Like I'd have ever believed that. Like this whole thing didn't *reek* of him.

His gaze flicked down my body as I stood there and glared daggers at him, seething.

"You look nice," he said. Soft color was starting to bloom over the tips of his ears, his cheeks.

That was Jamie's fault, not mine. The coat of mascara had turned into winged liner, then blush and concealer and lip tint. And don't even get me started on the clothes. She'd practically wrestled me into the pushup bra.

She and I needed to re-establish some of our boundaries.

"I thought I'd at least try to look nice for when they take my mugshot later," I replied dryly.

The corners of his mouth tipped. "Mission accomplished, then. I like the dark thing you did with your eyes."

I snapped my fingers before pointing one at him. "None of that," I said.

"I'm just saying, they're mesmerizing." His shoulders relaxed a touch as he slipped his hands into the pockets of his slacks. "More so than usual, I mean."

I'd never forgive my heart for the way it reacted to his

words. To the way it hummed and hammered and sent a rush of warmth to my face as Adrien gazed into my soul.

"It's really nice to see you," he said.

I'd never forgive my brain for immediately thinking, *Same. It's really nice to see you, too.*

I steeled my spine. Retightened my fists.

"I'm not a charity case, Adrien. You had no right to do all this behind my back." But even as I said the words, I knew I was grasping at straws. Which was probably why they didn't hold any of the venom I wanted them to.

"Is that a joke? You think this is *charity*?" He paused for a few seconds, dark eyes bouncing between mine. "It's not charity, Sanchez. It's fucking karma. Two members of my family stole something important from you, and all I'm trying to do now is give a sliver of it back. But you're so stubborn and I've... been such an asshole over the last few weeks that I knew you'd never accept it if it came directly from me. Hence the elaborate scheme. I know I've been terrible to you, I just... wanted to make things right."

He stopped again to study me and give me a chance to speak. When I remained silent, he said, "If it's not something you still want, then that's okay. You don't *need* a college education or a law degree, Ria. You're fucking perfect and worthy just the way you are, and I really need you to know that. But it's yours if it's something that *you* still want. And if you decide to give it a try but change your mind halfway through, it won't matter. I already talked to Sunny. If you don't finish, he'll send me the bill."

And I'd *never* forgive myself for getting emotional over what he was saying. For my chest squeezing the painful way it did.

I tried to resummon my anger; demanded that it come back.

"I didn't ask you to make things right. I asked you to leave me alone," I said. "You're not my friend, you're not my boyfriend, you're just some guy I fucked. You have no *right* to meddle in my personal life like this."

I regretted it as soon as the words sniped out of my mouth, but by then it was too late. I was looking right into his eyes when I said it. I saw how deep they cut.

He nodded, the corners of his mouth tipping down as his blinking slowed and became incomplete. He averted his gaze. "Just some guy you fucked," he repeated. "That's..."

He stopped, chin dipping in another nod, like he was finally coming to terms with something he'd been in deep denial about.

"Has it occurred to you even once *over the last couple of weeks that I'm an actual human being, Ria? With real feelings and all the other bullshit that comes with it?"*

My throat swelled so thick that even if I did have anything else to say, I wasn't sure I'd be able to get the words out.

After what felt like an eternity, Adrien fingered the edge of the blue folder and pushed it to the side. "Okay," he said. "Point taken. I won't interfere anymore. Sorry."

He could have left if there. Told me to get the fuck out of his office, the building, his life. Called security.

Instead, he decided to return the blow.

"You weren't," he said, his glassy gaze finding mine again. "Just so we're also clear as to where I stand, you weren't just some girl I fucked. I may not be your friend, and I may not be your boyfriend, but that's only because you don't want those things with me. Not because I don't want them with you. It wasn't just sex for me. I have... very real feelings for you, Ria. If it were up to me, we... things would be very different between us. But at least now there's no confusion as to where we both stand."

My breathing had grown increasingly shallow, and no matter how hard I tried, I couldn't come up with a single thing to say back. So, I just stood there and stared.

Adrien observed me for a few moments, gaze swimming over my features like he was trying to memorize them. Or maybe I was projecting.

His throat worked, and the right corner of his extremely un-mediocre mouth tilted, revealing a single dimple. But his eyes were filled with so much regret that it just made him look more sad.

"You're staring again, Sanchez," he whispered.

It was the crack in his stupid, thick voice that did it. I was holding it together just fine until then. But the moment he said those words, in that tone, at that volume, my soul cracked in half, and my lower lip wobbled.

Adrien's sad little smirk died on the spot, his whole upper body tightening.

Shit. Shitshitshitshitshitshit. Get it the fuck together.

"Sanchez."

"I'm gonna, um..." *Go.* The word I was trying to say was *go.* But then I realized that once I turned around and walked out of here, I'd never see him again, and holy shit. It hit me hard enough to steal my breath.

I'd never hear his voice again.

We'd never have another chance to bicker and banter with each other ever again. *Ever.*

This was it.

Adrien stood frozen on the spot, looking shellshocked. "What did I say?" he asked somewhat helplessly as my lip continued to wiggle uncontrollably.

I must have looked ridiculous to him. I *felt* ridiculous.

I tried to swallow back the frog lodged in the back of my throat, but it didn't want to go anywhere. Not when my brain kept reminding it that this was the last time Adrien Cloutier would frustrate the ever-loving shit out of me.

The *one time* I'd needed him to know I was lying, and to call me out on it, he'd believed me instead.

I bit down punishingly on my stupid, ridiculous bottom lip as I glared at him, my deepening frown pushing out the tears welling up in my eyes.

He rounded his desk, looking increasingly distraught with every passing second. The *nerve* of this man.

His hands jutted forward like he was reaching for me, but then he seemed to think better of it. "I know it's my fault, but can you just tell me what I did? Because I honestly have no idea this time," he said.

I swiped at my cheeks, expecting my hand to come back with messy evidence of my streaking mascara, but there was none. Freaking Jamie. She'd *known*.

"Ria, just tell me wh—"

"Just some guy?" I asked, glaring right into his infuriatingly gorgeous eyes. "*Just some guy*, Adrien? Out of all the lies I've told you, *that's* the one you decide not to catch? *That's* the one you let me get away with? I'm pretty sure you could see my nostril flare from the fucking moon when I said it!"

I pointed a livid finger at said moon, which was fully visible through his floor-to-ceiling windows.

Adrien's lips peeled apart slowly, his eyes bouncing between mine.

"You are, without an iota of doubt, the most infuriating human being on the fucking planet, Adrien. You've driven me absolutely insane, you know that? Like really, truly batshit. All the signs are there."

The tightness in his features began to ease as realization set in, a knowing smile tugging at his willing mouth. Two dimples. Uneven and lopsided as all hell.

"Oh, it's funny to you, is it?" I asked, squaring my shoulders as he stepped closer, closer, closer. I didn't even realize I'd moved until my back hit the wall, the tips of our shoes kissing. "You've got me all irritable and agitated. I'm a mess of mood swings. I can't think clearly or about anything that isn't directly related to you. I can't even close my eyes for five fucking minutes without hallucinating images of your dimples. And no, they're not dreams. I've had dreams, and those guys aren't nearly as vivid."

Adrien brushed a strand of hair away from my face with a delicate swipe of his fingers.

"That sounds... inconvenient," he mused, sounding positively delighted by my suffering.

"It's *horrible*," I corrected him. "And the hallucinations don't stop there, either."

"Oh?"

"Colors, Adrien. All of them," I tried explaining. "Like their vividness, you know?"

To my genuine surprise, he said, "I do."

"And food tastes different. But it's not the actual food, it's me. I mean it's your fault, but it's me."

He cupped my cheek, tilting my face up as he scanned my features. "But you've been eating though, right?" he asked as his thumb traced the dip under my cheekbone.

It wasn't a relevant question, so I moved on. "Those are all signs of losing one's mind, according to the internet. All of them."

Adrien's brows furrowed, the amusement leaving his face. His cheek was healed completely, but that mark on his left brow was probably going to scar.

I hoped Josh's whole face would scar.

"Have you not been eating, Ria?"

I shifted on my feet. "Define *eating*."

"What did you have for dinner?" he asked.

"Alba brought Indian takeout with her when she came to spill the beans."

He cocked his head. "Did you actually have any before storming out?"

"I had some naan."

"Breakfast? Lunch?"

"I woke up late," I said.

His jaw ticked. "And I drive *you* insane. *I'm* the infuriating one."

"Yes," I agreed. Finally! We were on the same page about something.

His hair tickled my forehead when he hung his head, sighing like I'd put the weight of the world on his chest. "All right, let's go."

"Where?" I asked as he threaded our fingers together and began guiding me out of his office. "I'm not done yelling at you about your involvement in my deteriorating levels of sanity."

"You can yell at me in the car while I force-feed you fries."

"Oh," I said. And then, "All right."

It wasn't the worst idea he'd ever had.

∼

I yelled at Adrien in his car as he force-fed me the fries I'd been promised, with a side of steak tartare, and the most incredible roasted scallops I'd ever had. I yelled at him some more when we got to the top of that one hill with the breathtaking view of the city, where he wouldn't let go of my hand no matter how much I didn't complain.

Until, eventually, I didn't have anything more to yell at him about. No matter how hard I tried to think up new excuses.

Which meant the night was over, and I needed to get out of his car. Now.

We'd been sitting in front of my apartment building for sixteen silent minutes, watching the dashboard clock tick its way past midnight. Adrien was still holding my hand, his thumb still brushing gentle strokes over my skin. But his grip was kept just loose enough for me to slide out of it without resistance. He made no indication that he wanted me out of his car, but he'd unlocked the doors as soon as we'd parked.

The ball was in my court, but I was too scared to do what I wanted with it.

"I should go now," I eventually muttered, making zero moves to follow through with the declaration.

"If that's what you want," Adrien responded.

I chewed my bottom lip. "What do you want?" I tried.

He caught my gaze. "To spend more time with you. A chance to make things right, earn your forgiveness, your trust."

Just like that. He said it so easily, no hesitation, no fear. He just... told me exactly what he wanted.

I glanced down at our joint hands. "Are you going to leave me alone after this?"

Translation: *If I walk away, is this the last time I'm ever going to see you?*

He considered me for a long moment. Then he said, "You've told me that's what you want. I have to start respecting boundaries at some point."

My heart sank.

Tell him that's not what you really want. Say it! He just needs to hear it once.

"Okay," I muttered instead.

Silence.

He let go of my hand.

Remember how Robert said to not be an idiot? Because you're being an idiot.

"I'll be here if you change your mind," Adrien said, eyes moving back to the road in front of him.

I slipped out of his car without another word, hurried into the building, and ran up the stairs with my fists swinging stiffly at my sides, refusing to turn back around.

This was fine. In fact, it was for the best.

Is it? You keep thinking it's for the best, but why? What's the reason?

I ignored the voice of doubt and focused on keeping as quiet as possible when I entered the dark apartment. It was a worknight, so Jamie was already asleep, and I didn't want to—

No. Answer me, Ria. Why is not being with him for the best?

My lips rolled as I tore my clothes off and fumbled into a baggy sleep tee and sweat shorts.

Is it because you know he'll make you happy? And you don't think you deserve it?

I scrunched my hair into a floppy bun on my way to the bathroom.

Is it because everything Alba said is true?

Cold water splashed against my face and neck. I scrubbed.

You think you deserve to suffer for the rest of your life

because of what happened to Dad, so you're just going to keep punishing yourself for it?

You don't pursue your passions because you don't think you deserve happiness.

You hold yourself back because you don't think you deserve success.

You don't date because you don't think you're worthy of love.

I shoved a toothbrush into my mouth, squeezing my eyes shut as I willed the voice in my head to shut up.

And how do you think Dad would feel if he knew? That you blamed yourself. That you didn't think you deserved love or happiness?

I spat.

You'd be breaking his heart. He'd be devastated, Ria.

I crawled into bed, shut my stinging eyes as tightly as I possibly could... and immediately reopened them, frowning. Something crinkled when my cheek hit the pillow, and again when I lifted my head.

I sat up, brought the pillow to my lap, and carefully reached under the freshly laundered case to pull out... the photobooth strips. Picture after picture of Adrien in his ridiculous blue alien getup, arms snaked around me as I playfought against his incoming kisses.

There was a folded sticky note attached to the back of one of the strips, and my gut tugged when I snapped the bedside lamp on and peeled it open.

I wish you could see these pictures through my eyes.
It's so obvious.
Please don't be an idiot.

My heart squeezed with starved pangs as I stared

down at the two strips, running my fingers along their edges the same way I had a thousand times over the last ten days. I had every detail of every frame memorized down to each tiny blue smudge on Adrien's white shirt. So how was it that my pulse kept skipping like I was looking at them for the first time? As if there was something new in them that I was experiencing?

It's so obvious.

Please don't be an idiot.

Robert had said the same thing at the airport, and I was starting to think that maybe it wasn't a coincidence. Maybe they were able to see something with an outsider's clarity that I wasn't privy to.

I reached for my phone, navigated to my blocked numbers list with unsteady fingers, and removed the most recent number. It took another fourteen minutes for me to gather the courage to take a picture of the strips, and another three to press Send. But I finally did it.

My stomach flipped when the outgoing message status switched from Delivered to Read almost right away, and I held my breath, counting each excruciatingly long second until a blue heart emoji popped up on the screen. I exhaled, a rush of giddy relief making my heart tremble as I smiled down at the blue heart.

Then came the picture. Adrien's copies of the photo-booth prints, bent at their white middle break to accommodate the fold of his wallet.

My grin widened as I tried to come up with something witty to type back. But then I noticed the gear stick in the corner, right beside his leg.

I blinked, checking the time. He'd dropped me off like forty minutes ago, which meant he should have been home by now. Unless he was stuck in some sort of weird midnight traffic jam? It wasn't likely, but why else would he still be in his car—

"I'll be here if you change your mind."

My mouth popped open.

No way...

I scrambled to my window, hurled it open, but couldn't bend out far enough to see around the corner without risking a three-story fall to a broken neck.

There was no way he was still here, and it was very on-brand for my recent descent into madness to read that much into what he'd said. But still... it wouldn't hurt to check. Just to make extra *extra* sure that he wasn't waiting out on the street for me like one of those cheesy (but amazing) 90's romcom dudes.

I quietly snuck back downstairs, threw the building door open, and sure enough, just as I'd predicted—

...

Holy shit, Adrien Cloutier was waiting out on the street for me like one of those cheesy (but amazing) 90's romcom dudes. But so much better. Because it was *Adrien*.

He was standing outside his car now, leaned against the passenger side door, staring expectantly at his phone as his other hand fumbled nervously with his belt.

Until he heard me burst out of the building.

I couldn't tell which one of us was more surprised to see the other, but the initial shock lasted for about two clumsy heartbeats, and then we were both moving, mouths grinning, hands reaching.

"Knew it," he breathed a second before my arms looped around his neck, my lips crushed against his, and I stopped being an idiot.

Finally.

Finally.

38

WE STUMBLED into the backseat of Adrien's car, our limbs and mouths tangled with clumsy desperation.

I'd missed him. Really, I'd missed him.

"I'm sorry," I kept breathing every chance I got. "I was an asshole. I'm sorry."

"I'm sorry," he kept murmuring every chance he got. "For everything. I'm sorry."

Until it inevitably reached the point where we were arguing about who was *more* sorry, and who was *more* in the wrong.

"Stop. Apologizing," I demanded at one point, biting his lip with a scowl.

He gripped my straddling hips tighter, pressing me closer. "No. I'll be apologizing for a long fucking time. Get used to it."

How was it possible for one person to be this exasperating? He was so damn stubborn.

I kissed him harder, fisting the collar of his shirt as I fought him with my lips, teeth, and tongue.

"Fuck, I've missed you," he murmured when I moved

my attention to his jaw, my heart hammering against his heaving chest. "It's been torture, Sanchez."

"I'm sorry," I said again.

"Stop it," he insisted again.

"No," I mimicked, deepening my voice. "Get used to it."

He chuckled. "Stubborn little brat."

I pulled back and gave him my brattiest smile as my hips rocked against his hard length.

He inhaled sharply, head falling back against the leather seat as his fingers dug into my thighs.

"What's your safeword, Mr. Cloutier?" I teased, pulling a dark chuckle out of him.

"Not here. Not after all that torture and wait."

"We can go upstairs," I suggested. "But Jamie's asleep, so we'll have to be really quiet."

His hazy gaze swam across my face, tracing every little line and dip and curve. His expression had sobered by the time he reached my eyes again.

"What?" I asked. Too soon? Was I moving too quickly?

After a long, dense pause, he asked, "Do you still hate me?"

What? He already knew I didn't. He'd been telling me so since Victoria, even though I kept insisting—oh. I see.

My fingers trailed across his kiss-swollen bottom lip as I shook my head. "No," I said.

His breath caught, his throat moving with a soft swallow. "Do you have feelings for me, Sanchez?"

Th-thump th-thump th-thump.

"Absolutely yes, Cloutier," I whispered.

A single dimple. "Do I give you butterflies?"

"Yes."

Two dimples. And the man was full-on blushing now.

Adorable. Infuriatingly adorable.

"Now can we go upstairs?" I said.

He kissed the corner of my smile. "I don't put out before the third date," he muttered, then leaned back again, looking all smug and pleased with himself.

I bit back my laugh. "And which number is this?"

He made an O with his fist.

"That's bullshit," I argued. "Tonight has to count, and so does the blue alien day. So, we're at minimum two now. Three if we count the hiking day."

"No," he said.

"You're being annoying."

"Yes."

"Adrien!"

"Ria!"

It was very difficult to scowl at him when my facial muscles were fighting a grin.

"I'm not asking you out," I told him seriously.

"Your nostril just flared."

He chuckled when I went for the door handle, pulling me back to his lap. "Sanchez, go on a date with me."

I considered him with cool, unbothered nonchalance. "I shall think about it when the mood strikes," I said breezily, then I reached for the handle again.

His fingers circled my wrist and pulled it back. "Friday night. I'll pick you up at six. Dinner and drinks."

I kissed him deeply, waiting for him to melt into it before I pulled back with another bratty smirk. "Beg, Mr. Cloutier," I demanded. "Ask me to go out with you nicely."

His dark eyes shimmered with unfiltered amusement, like that was exactly the type of unexpected response he'd hoped I'd give him.

"Ariana Sanchez, please, please, *please* go out with me," he teased, mimicking my voice.

I stifled my giggle, mimicking him right back when I retorted, "You're really bad at this."

"All right. Fine," he said with a grin, right before he gently removed me from his lap, stepped out of the car, and dropped to his knees in front of the open door.

My jaw hit the seat.

"Ariana Sanchez, would you please go on a date with me this Friday night?"

My heart leaped in my chest as I glanced around, trying to make sure no one else was around.

"What are you doing!" I hissed. "Get up!"

"Will you go on a date with me?"

I was barreling toward a cardiac episode. I could feel it.

"Adrien! Get. Up." I grabbed his arm, tried pulling him back inside.

"Answer me first."

"Yes!" I whisper-yelled at his stupid, beautiful dimples. "Obviously yes! Now get up!"

He huffed another chuckle, then stood and held out his hand for me. "Come on," he said, "I'll walk you to your door."

I released a heavy breath and slipped my fingers into his large palm.

"I'm gonna make you pay for that," I grumbled with unconvincing disapproval when we reached the third floor. My pulse was still pounding.

"Can't wait." He kissed my temple, still smiling. "Night, pretty girl."

~

Adrien didn't ask or push me about the Kanun interview. When I woke up the next morning and saw his name pop up on my phone, I thought maybe he'd at least hint at it, but it was just a very sweet *good morning* text that I stared at for way too long, gushing internally.

Jamie, on the other hand, had never heard the word boundary in her life. I was in the middle of typing out my carefully crafted response to Adrien when the honey-haired Tasmanian devil kicked down my door. Next thing I knew, I was staring down a barrel of doom.

"Where'd you get a water gun?" I asked, tucking my phone under the protection of my blanket.

"Get up," she demanded coldly. "You have an interview in five hours."

"I don't even know if I'm—*pfthshh Jamie!*" I hurled my pillow at her.

"Up!" she commanded again. "I've got coffee and breakfast ready, and five outfits laid out for you to choose from."

"Do you really?"

"Yeah. And interview prep questions. I've taken the morning off so we can go over them."

"That's really nice, Jamie. You're such a good friend."

She grinned boastfully, shoulders pushing back. Like a *fool*. "I know. Some people might say I'm babying you. But to them, I say, fuck—"

I lunged the second she lowered her defenses, grappling the water gun out of her grip.

"Well, well, well," I said as she raised her hands. "If it isn't the consequences of your own actions."

Toebeans chose that exact moment to waddle gracefully into my room, meowing for attention like his tail was on fire.

"Morning, cutie," I cooed as he snaked between Jamie's legs.

"All right, actual truce," she said. "He'll throw a literal hissy fit if you get a drop on him. Also, the interview. You're going. I don't care if I have to drag you down there kicking and screaming, you're going."

I lowered my gun, pouting in thought.

Normally this would be a mistake. She'd jump for the gun the second I stopped gripping it with both hands. Today, though, she just watched as I tossed it onto my bed.

I wrapped my arms around her waist, hugging my Jamie tight. "I don't deserve you," I told her honestly.

She returned my embrace, sighing dramatically. "No one does. I'm amazing."

I hummed my sincere agreement. "And Jams?"

"Yeah?"

"Thank you."

"You're welcome," she said. "And Ree?"

"Yeah?"

"You're going."

I released her and took a step back. There was only one right answer, and we both knew it. "I'm going," I confirmed.

She smiled.

I smiled.

Three, two—we dove for the water gun at the same time.

∽

For the *third* time in the span of two months, I managed to sneak up to Adrien Cloutier's office without a single person trying to stop me. Even though I tore into the building like a tornado, looking ten million shades of unhinged.

He grinned when he saw me, rising to his feet as I ran into the room and hurled myself into his open arms.

"You crushed it," he murmured into my hair. "Fucking crushed it."

I was beyond words. I'd used all the ones I knew in the three-hour interview, and I didn't have any left. So, I just clung to him, savoring this moment, this day, the million things I was feeling.

"I'm so fucking proud of you," he said as I stuffed my tear-stained cheeks into the crook of his neck. "He called. They're obsessed with you, Ria. You crushed it."

I choked out a cry into his neck.

It was amazing. The interview, the opportunities, *Sunny*. It was everything eighteen-year-old me would have wanted, and so much more. I didn't even realize how badly I'd still been clinging on to the dream until I was there, talking to Sunny about what the next decade of my life would look like.

For the first time in ten years, I was looking forward to tomorrow.

"Baby." I was swept off my feet and carried to the couch. Adrien held me to his chest while I wept tears of sadness, joy, hope, relief, gratitude. So much fucking gratitude.

The firm was going to pay for everything—undergrad, law school, living expenses—so long as I agreed to a five-year employment term with them after graduation. Just five. It was beyond generous for what they were offering, and it was all because of Adrien.

Sunny told me all the things Adrien had said about me. All the overly generous, kind, lovely things Adrien had said to convince Sunny to take me under his wing. I'd never forget it for as long as I lived.

It had taken every ounce of willpower I had not to get emotional during the interview, which meant that it all began to spill out the second I left the building.

"Thank you," I choked out.

He kissed my temple, running soothing fingers through my hair.

Then he told me he didn't want to hear it. That I'd earned every bit of the opportunity and more. And he held me until I calmed down enough to peel my face away from the crook of his neck.

I cupped his jaw, tilting it so I could kiss him.

"Thank you," I said again, putting a stop to his incoming protests with a brush of my thumb across his lips. "Really, Adrien. Thank you. This is everything."

And one day I'd figure out a way to show him just how much I appreciated it.

He turned his face into my palm, placing a long kiss on it. "This is only the beginning, Ria. Just wait and see."

EPILOGUE

6 YEARS later

"Say cheese!"

"Cheeeeeeese!"

The twins screamed the loudest, Olena's little hands bursting through the air like she was throwing invisible confetti, while Ozie had the hem of my graduation gown slung over her shoulders like a cape.

Olive—who'd turned thirteen just last week—squeezed my waist tight, her head resting lovingly against my shoulder when the flash went off.

"Oooh, that was a really good one," Alba said. "Ozie had one eye shut, but we can just pretend like she's winking. Huge improvement over the last ten. Great job, team."

The kids celebrated the colossal achievement of taking a half-decent photo by jetting off to collect their promised ice cream reward with their dad, while Alba stayed back to snap the next round of pictures with my in-laws.

"So proud of you, sweets," Julie said once my sister

was satisfied with both the quantity and quality of the photos taken. "A whole lawyer. You've worked so hard."

She brushed my hair back from my shoulders, her voice wavering all over again. She'd cried more during the ceremony than the rest of the auditorium combined, probably. I'd never felt more loved than I had walking across that stage, hearing how loud they all cheered for me.

My heart swelled and I squeezed Julie's hand, unable to speak. Seeing her emotional made me emotional, which, in turn, made *her* emotional.

This whole day had been a mess. A teary, snotty, perfect mess. I'd loved every second of it.

Julie turned blubbery the moment I blinked one too many times, trying to fight back the tears. Adrien palmed the back of my neck, thumb caressing my skin as he placed a comforting kiss to my temple. It only made things worse.

"Oh god, here we go again," Alice said, engagement ring gleaming in the sunlight as she adjusted the strap of her purse. "Honestly. You'd think someone died."

"Be nice, Lice." Gampy poked her calf with the end of his walking cane. "We were all there when you watched *Up* for the first time."

"Addy cried more at that than I did."

"And I don't regret it," Adrien said. "Second greatest love story of all time."

Alice folded her arms. "Who's first? Jamie and Jack? Or me and Dominic?"

"You and Dominic are dead last on every list," Adrien retorted rudely. "I still have a fucking headache from that whole ordeal. And Ria and I are first, obviously."

"It's not a competition," Gampy interjected as Alice

shifted into her fighting stance. "Even if it was, my Lucy and I would have you all beat. You kids don't even know what pining *means*."

Three hours. We argued over who had the greatest love story for over three hours, making our individual cases and sharing our stories long after we'd arrived at Jamie and Jack's house for the after-graduation barbeque.

Adrien held my hand when it was our turn to share, toying with my wedding ring as we laughed through the retelling of our first meeting. The whole thing was much more amusing to look back on now, knowing what we did.

"I knew halfway through our first real date that I was going to marry her within a year," Adrien claimed, pressing a brief kiss on the back of my hand. "What I didn't know was how I was going to convince her to say yes."

"Which is what he'd told me halfway through our *second* date," I continued. My mouth twitched when Adrien chuckled at my tone, pulling me closer to him on the couch.

"I stand by my decision," he said.

"And I stand by my reaction." Which had been to tell him he was insane, share my live location with Jamie, and ask the waiter for the bill.

He'd proposed six months later. I hadn't even let him get through the question before pouncing on him and screaming *yes!*

Best decision I'd ever made. The man made me stupidly, deliriously happy.

The type of wholehearted happiness that you can't know exists until "it hits you right in the balls with a wooden cane, calls you a braindead goblin, and flips your whole life upside down" as Adrien always put it.

He caught my lingering gaze after the story baton was passed on to Julie and Anthony, and I knew he was thinking the same thing. He lifted my hand again, kissed it three times.

I love you I love you I love you.

"Forever and always," he murmured quietly.

"Forever and always," I whispered back, squeezing his hand three times.

I love you I love you I love you.

The End.

Afterword

Yay, you made it! Thank you so much for reading *A Deal With The Bossy Devil*. I had an absolute blast writing this book, and I sincerely hope you enjoyed reading it!

Good news: Jamie and Jackson's story is now available on KU!

Here are some extra goodies, depending on your mood. If you want...

- Bonus STEAMY epilogue from Adrien's POV (exclusive to newsletter subscribers)

- Free steamy novella (exclusive to newsletter subscribers)

I'd also be incredibly grateful if you would take a minute and leave a quick review of this story on Amazon, Goodreads, Bookbub or wherever else you like. Every single one goes a long way to helping other readers discover the book.

Wishing you the happiest of ever afters!

Printed by Amazon Italia Logistica S.r.l.
Torrazza Piemonte (TO), Italy

68936758R00247

Until next time,
Kyra

Also By Kyra Parsi

Failure to Match (Jamie and Jackson)

> Enemies to lovers

> Billionaire matchmaker

> Forced proximity

Fool Them Once

> Fake relationship

> Friend's older brother

> Accidental roommates

In Love And War

> Enemies to lovers

> Office romance

> Forbidden love